ON EDGE

Also by Albert Ashforth

The Rendition

ON EDGE

A NOVEL

ALBERT ASHFORTH

Oceanview Publishing
Longboat Key, Florida

ISBN 978-1-60809-200-0

Published in the United States of America by Oceanview Publishing
Longboat Key, Florida

www.oceanviewpub.com

10 9 8 7 6 5 4 3 2 1

PRINTED IN THE UNITED STATES OF AMERICA

To M.A., C.A., and the three E.A.s

ACKNOWLEDGMENTS

In thanking the people who helped me with this book, I must begin with Patricia and Robert Gussin. I was the beneficiary of Pat and Bob's professionalism and encouragement at every stage of writing. I would like also to extend my thanks to the entire Oceanview team—Emily Baar, Lee Randall, Kirsten Barger and Lisa Daily for their assistance in answering my many questions and providing whatever help I needed.

I owe a tremendous debt of gratitude to David Linzee, who provided help with an early version of this manuscript and always did so in an engaging and humorous manner. By keeping me up-to-date on the news, Maggie Emmons aided me enormously, particularly with my research into financial matters and the Kabul Bank. Patricia Allen through her detective work provided me with some invaluable information regarding life in Washington, D.C. At two critical points in the story, Bernard Whalen gave me the benefit of his professional expertise concerning police procedures. By assigning me to Kabul in Afghanistan, my boss, Paul Lovello, made it possible for me to write with authority about the particular topics covered in this book. Claudia Ashforth and I burned the midnight oil on a number of occasions, working on the manuscript and often on the chronology of events in the story.

A number of people provided helpful suggestions regarding particular events or insights into the book's characters. Thank you, Ruth Horn, Shelly Reuben, Chris Stothard and Elisabeth Ashforth.

AUTHOR'S NOTE

Green on Blue

THERE IS NOTHING guaranteed to strike terror and fear in the heart of a soldier stationed in Afghanistan like the threat of a green-on-blue killing. Or as they are sometimes called, "insider attacks."

A green-on-blue occurs when an Afghan soldier or policeman—in other words, someone who has gained the trust of the American military—turns his weapon on a NATO soldier.

Over a period of three years, from 2011 to 2014, there were over a hundred green-on-blues in Afghanistan. In one instance, two American advisers were shot in Afghanistan's Ministry of the Interior, one of Kabul's most heavily guarded buildings. In an especially unsettling instance, a killer got close enough to an American general visiting Kabul to kill the officer. The Taliban jubilantly took credit for this cowardly murder.

The difficulty in green-on-blue situations is that, short of reading the killer's mind, there is no way to anticipate a green-on-blue. The perpetrators are usually Afghans who have worked closely with their victims, and there is no way to know in advance what they have in mind.

GLOSSARY

The following explanations might help to clarify situations and expressions in common use by military and civilian personnel stationed overseas.

ANA: Afghan National Army. The Army is divided into six combat corps, which are deployed throughout the country. The President of Afghanistan functions as Commander in Chief. The Army is subordinate to the Ministry of Defense.

ANP: Afghan National Police. The country's police force, which is subordinate to the Ministry of the Interior.

Ariana Hotel: in 2002, the CIA took over the Ariana, which is close to ISAF Headquarters and the presidential palace, and has since had various uses as a hotel for transient personnel, a military command post, and the CIA station in Kabul.

Askar: in Afghanistan, any Afghan, usually a soldier or policeman, who carries a weapon.

Billets: lodging designated for members of the military.

Bird Colonel or Full Bird: the insignia worn by a colonel is a silver eagle with a shield on its chest.

Burqa: a loose enveloping garment worn by many Muslim women in public. It covers the face and the body.

CID: the United States Army Criminal Investigation Command. The Command, which has investigative autonomy, investigates violations of military law within the U.S. Army.

Class A's: as of 2014, the Army's blue class A uniform replaced the traditional dress green.

CO: Commanding Officer.

COP: Combat Outpost. Small military installations established throughout Afghanistan as part of a campaign of counterinsurgency. COPs are often effective in dealing personally with the local population.

DI: a drill instructor.

FOB: Forward Operating Base. A military installation used to support tactical operations and usually secured by high walls, barbed wire, and towers. Most FOBs have airfields; some have dispensaries and other facilities.

Gator Alley: the main street of Camp Eggers, running north from the main gate, passing the PX and terminating at the Warrior Gym.

Green on Blue: insider attacks by Afghans, usually armed members of the Afghan military or the police, against coalition members. In many cases, the victims regarded their killers as friends and colleagues, and the attacks have often been carried out against people the killers have worked with. These attacks have led NATO to boost security measures by dismissing hundreds of ANA soldiers and ANP policemen and appointing so-called "guardian angels" to deter further attacks.

Haqqani Network: a terrorist group with close ties to the Taliban and headquartered in North Waziristan, from which it launches attacks on neighboring Afghanistan.

Hooch: in Vietnam a hooch was a hut with a thatched roof. In time, GIs began referring to their own quarters as "hooches." The term continues to be used, often to describe a soldier's billet.

Humvee: High Mobility Multipurpose Wheeled Vehicle. A vehicle designed originally to carry personnel and cargo behind the lines. After Somalia, enough armor was added to withstand small-arms fire. In Afghanistan, Humvees were effective for transportation, but after the insurgents began planting IEDs on roads, the vehicle was shown to be vulnerable to rollovers, sometimes leaving occupants upside down and trapped inside the vehicle.

IED: an Improvised Explosive Device. These highly effective bombs are often made with easily available components such as fertilizer and diesel fuel. When vehicles pass over pressure plates, they close a circuit that triggers the explosion. Others can be set off remotely by a cell phone, which is connected to the power source, often a battery.

ISAF: the International Security Assistance Force was established by NATO with the aim of training Afghan security forces and assisting Afghanistan in rebuilding key government institutions.

Jarhead: a member of the United States Marine Corps. The term is based on the short haircuts worn by many Marines.

Kabul Bank: the bank, which was founded in 2004 to help pay government salaries, collapsed in 2010 with debts of 935 million dollars. About one-third of the lost money has been recovered. Twenty-two of the bank's officials have been found guilty of taking part in the fraud.

Leatherman: a versatile multi-tool favored by the military.

Leatherneck: a member of the United States Marine Corps. Until 1872, the Marine uniform had a high leather collar that distinguished Marines from the other service branches.

Light Colonel: lieutenant colonel. The term distinguishes a lieutenant colonel from a full colonel.

MI: commonly used phrase meaning Military Intelligence.

MP: Military Police.

MRE: Meal Ready to Eat. Rations for service members in combat or in other field conditions where food is unavailable. Each meal is contained in foil packaging and has roughly 1200 calories.

MRAP: Mine Resistant Ambush Protected vehicle. MRAPs were rushed to Iraq and Afghanistan to replace Humvees, which were vulnerable to IEDs with heavy payloads. In 2007, Secretary of Defense Gates announced that acquisition of MRAPs was the Department of Defense's highest priority. By 2012, the Pentagon had deployed 12,000 MRAPs for the two wars.

NCO: a noncommissioned officer, e.g., a sergeant.

NSC: National Security Council.

NVGs: Night Vision Goggles. Goggles that improve vision in the dark by using thermal imaging and other technology.

O Club: Officers' Club.

OCS: Officer Candidate School. Military academy in which college graduates are given the opportunity to become officers for Active or Army Reserve Duty.

One Star: a brigadier general. General officers are often referred to informally by the number of stars indicating their rank.

O-3: the numerical pay grade of an Army captain.

Predator: an unmanned aerial vehicle initially developed for reconnaissance. After 9/11, Predators were upgraded to carry two Hellfire missiles and have been used as offensive weapons, often against insurgent groups in North Waziristan.

Rendition: the practice of covertly sending a foreign terrorist suspect to be interrogated in a country with less rigorous regulations for the humane treatment of prisoners.

SAD: Special Activities Division. The division of the CIA responsible for covert operations.

SE: Soviet East European Division. Until 1989, the intelligence and counterintelligence division that operated against Russia and the East Bloc nations.

SOG: Special Operations Group. When the government does not wish to be publicly involved with a foreign operation, the "op" will often be assigned to one of the department's Special Officers, usually a former

Green Beret, Ranger, or SEAL who has had experience in the country in question.

Special Activities: a euphemism for a covert operation.

201 File: personal and military documents maintained by the U.S. government for members of the armed forces.

UCMJ: Uniform Code of Military Justice. The laws to which members of the military are subordinate.

VBIED: Vehicle Borne Improvised Explosive Device. Car bombs that are either set off from a remote location or when a vehicle hits a bump and closes a circuit, which triggers the explosion. These bombs can do tremendous damage when pieces of the vehicle's metal fly through the air like shrapnel. Sometimes the vehicle's fuel causes further incendiary damage.

ON EDGE

PROLOGUE

AM I DOING the right thing? He'd asked himself the same question twenty times within the past half hour. Ever since he'd returned the telephone to its cradle, slipped on his jacket, retrieved the Sig Sauer automatic from the night table drawer, and left his Georgetown apartment.

Or was he on some goddamned fool's errand?

No, he was experienced enough to know he'd be a fool to ignore what the woman had told him on the telephone—and what it was she wanted him to do.

Who was she? From her voice he guessed that she was American. She spoke unaccented English. Not southern, not Midwestern. Her sentences were precise, her tone unemotional. She hadn't wasted words.

But what had snapped him to attention and caused him to sit up with serious concern was her immediate mention of the weekly code—the five-digit number provided to a handful of administration insiders and changed each week by a special assistant to the president. She'd followed that with the name of a government functionary, someone so highly placed and so powerful, you only had to whisper the name for people to go silent. Just the fact that she knew that name meant she knew how things now functioned inside the Beltway and that she had connections at the highest levels of the American government. The individual, whose name had never appeared in a newspaper, had a reputation for being able to fix any situation or solve any problem and, with a phone call, to make or break the career of absolutely anyone in Washington, D.C. This was an individual in whom the president reposed complete trust and whom the president never second-guessed.

And like everyone else in the nation's capital, with the exception of the president, he now felt himself to be just a shade fearful. In his job, it was up or out, and he felt vulnerable now that he was being eyed for a promotion. He actually shuddered when he recalled his chance encounter last summer with a former congressional staffer stacking shelves at a Winn-Dixie in Tampa, a onetime hotshot whose career crashed and burned when he failed to show proper deference to the right people. Or was it that he showed proper deference to the wrong people?

Who could say?

"Peirce Mill," she'd said. "There are picnic tables in a wooded area just upstream from the mill. We'll talk there. This evening, ten o'clock."

Peirce Mill was in Rock Creek Park. He supposed it was as good a place to talk as any. It was certainly out of the way. But as far as he was concerned, any park bench would have served just as well. Surveillance these days was everywhere.

So here he was, nine thirty on a chilly Sunday evening in January, on his way to meet someone who had called him from out of the blue and said she "wanted to talk." She hadn't said about what. At least Tilden Street, the street leading into the park, had street lights. Now he was peering ahead into the darkness on a stretch of road over which hung a blanket of tree branches dense enough to shut out the moonlight. He also found it interesting that she had his name and private telephone number and knew the kind of work he did—or to be more accurate—the kind of work he occasionally did.

He'd jammed a magazine into the handle of the Sig Sauer he carried in a shoulder holster beneath his jacket, just in case. He doubted he'd be needing it. He didn't have the kind of high-profile job that would lead anyone to want to kill him, although these days you could never be sure about anything.

He made a left turn off the road and drove into the empty parking area. Patches of snow from last week's storm were scattered about. He was twenty minutes early. He sat in the car for maybe three minutes, then decided to get out and walk back across the highway and to the area upstream from the building. When he got there, sure enough, just as she'd said, there was a picnic table with benches on either side. He walked over, sat down, crossed his legs—and waited.

In moments like this, coffin nails used to come in handy. They were good for calming jangled nerves—and made you appear relaxed and in control even when your heart was pounding double-time. But like everyone else, he'd quit smoking years ago.

Two minutes later, at precisely thirteen minutes before ten o'clock, a woman dressed in a windbreaker and slacks came walking through the woods. She wore a ski cap pulled down over her ears, preventing him from getting a look at her hair. As she approached, he stood. He'd zippered his jacket down halfway and could have the weapon in his hand within two seconds, but he quickly decided that this wouldn't be necessary.

Without saying a word, she nodded, but didn't make any polite effort to put him at ease. He thought she might say "Good evening" or shake his hand. She did neither. Naturally, she didn't give her name.

She pointed at the bench on the opposite side of the table from her, and they both seated themselves. He was aware of a chilly gust of wind, which chose that moment to blow through the park. He felt himself shiver. The Weather Channel had predicted more snow. Back in North Dakota, in his hometown, they already had over two feet.

In a soft whisper she said, "Thank you for coming." They both knew, of course, he had very little choice. He needed to see if this woman was for real—and if so, just how real. To do that he needed to meet her and find out what it was she wanted.

She was carrying a slim briefcase, which she laid on the table and from which she removed a three-day-old copy of the *Washington Post*.

"You're aware of this news story?" The sentence could have been a statement of fact or a question. She removed a small flashlight from her jacket pocket.

Sure, he'd read the story, which had run on an inside page. A story about the incident had run in the *New York Times* as well.

The headline read AMERICAN OFFICER SHOT IN KABUL; ISAF HEADQUARTERS SCENE OF DEADLY ATTACK.

"I've read it, yes." He didn't mention that he'd met the officer on a couple of occasions many years ago. At a Pentagon Christmas party he'd also met the officer's wife, a damned good-looking woman.

She said, "What I need is someone to investigate what happened there." Her voice was cold, and again he noticed her fluent, unaccented English. He couldn't put his finger on it precisely, but for some reason she didn't sound exactly the way most Americans sound. "He has to be good, very good."

"Good at what?"

"At handling himself, for one thing. He should be former military. He is either now a case officer or former case officer. That doesn't matter. It wouldn't hurt if he'd already spent some time here." She pointed at the newspaper. "In Afghanistan."

He could have told her that most of the case officers who'd spent time in Afghanistan had one thing in common: They didn't want to go back. Even those who worked out of the Ariana in Kabul, which was the best duty over there, weren't keen on repeat tours. It was the same with SAD—Special Activities Division—officers down in Chapman. Tours there did something to people. If you weren't already nuts when you went to Afghanistan, you were definitely a little crazy when you got back.

"And something else. He should have some knowledge of . . . financial matters, banking, and so on."

You're not asking for much, he thought, but didn't say.

She said, "It's my understanding that you've been doing this job for a while. Which is why I'm approaching you rather than someone else. I also understand that you, in your duties, are permitted a certain amount of discretion." She paused. "And that your superiors have confidence in you."

He nodded. That all was true enough. He had gained the confidence of his superiors over the years. People knew they could rely on his judgment. Although the job, by its nature, tended to attract cowboy types, he wasn't a cowboy. Far from it. People liked that.

"What do you mean by *discretion*?"

"That you might be able to handle this in a highly confidential manner—that is, you could assign a person without making a big fuss, without having to ask anyone else's permission, or call unnecessary attention to the operation."

She was talking about a "black op." She wanted him to set it in motion. He knew people in the Special Ops Group, so it wouldn't be a problem. This was something that he'd done before, on a few occasions, not many.

He was getting tired of nodding his head. What she'd said was all true enough. He did have a lot of discretion in planning ops. He also knew most of the country's special operators, the guys and gals who knew their way around foreign countries and who knew how to carry out sensitive and dangerous assignments, always kept a low profile, and never made a fuss. He knew which ones were burned out—and which were still good to go. Unfortunately, these days the former far exceeded the latter. The last ten years had put a strain on the country's human resources, not to mention its material and financial resources.

"Now, my question is, can you find someone to handle this kind of assignment?"

He thought for a minute. "What will he be doing? Or she."

"At the start he will want to familiarize himself with exactly what it is that happened. In other words, with the murder. If this was in fact a green-on-blue killing."

Interesting, he thought. She seemed to be suggesting that maybe this murder wasn't a green-on-blue. How would she know that?

"Do you mean become familiar with the investigation?"

"Yes. But there will probably be more to it than that. Bribery, fraud, I'm not sure. No one can say exactly where things will lead."

"Danger?"

She shrugged as if to indicate it was a silly question. "Dangerous? Yes, of course." Afghanistan was a dangerous place. They both knew that.

He remained silent, trying to understand just what she was getting at and running the names of various agents through his mind.

"No," he said finally.

When a "black op" goes off the rails, it's the agent who's left holding the bag, not the government, whose spokesmen invariably shrug their shoulders and fall back on "plausible denial." All the people he might call would know that, and for that reason would be unavailable—and not eager to leave for a murky assignment in Afghanistan on such short notice. He almost had to laugh. Who could blame them? It would be beyond foolish to take a job and not know who you were working for.

When he shook his head, she said, "There has to be someone."

"No," he said. "I don't know anyone."

He shone his own flashlight on the report in the *Washington Post*. As he reread the story, he asked himself about the officer who'd been gunned down. A bird colonel named Hansen.

Then he had a thought. Maybe there was someone he could ask.

He said the name out loud. "Alex Klear."

"Is that his name? Would this person be good for this assignment?"

He remained silent. Whether Klear would be good or not, he couldn't say. "He's adaptable."

"That's all? You don't sound enthusiastic. Isn't there anyone else?"

After a second, he said, "I can't think of anyone, not anyone good, not offhand."

She was silent, obviously thinking things over. Finally, she said, "You say this man is competent? Would he understand financial matters? Banking? And so on?"

"I'm not sure about the financial stuff. But he's definitely competent enough." Also unpredictable, a loose cannon—a guy with an off-the-wall way of doing things. Also a guy who could drive you batty at times.

"I detect a note of reservation in your tone. He doesn't sound like the kind of person I'm interested in. Are you sure there's no one else?"

"Let me think." Finally, he said, "No one I can call on short notice. Klear may not want to take it."

"Why not?"

"I heard he's getting married."

After another period of silence, she said, "We need someone quickly. If there's no one else, I want you to send this man."

Then she started giving him orders as though he were some kind of wet-behind-the-ears second lieutenant. Her tone and manner left no doubt that she expected him to do what she said. Also that she was used to being in charge, and she was so goddamned self-confident she didn't care what he thought of her.

The first thing she said for him to do was to call the individual whose name she had mentioned on the telephone.

"Call within the hour. Here is her private line."

My God! Not only did she know her name, she had her private number! A number no more than half-a-dozen people in the entire world would know! Unbelievable!

Who was this woman?

"She'll expect your call," the woman said matter-of-factly.

He took the paper on which she'd scrawled a number but not a name.

"Next, I want you to get in touch with the officer, this Klear. I want you to present this assignment to him in a manner that leaves him no recourse but to accept it. You can do that, I'm sure."

He wasn't sure, but he mumbled acquiescence to this command anyway.

"Tell him he is to investigate this murder to determine who committed it." She paused. "I want him on his way by Tuesday, two days from now. And something else." She removed an envelope from her briefcase. "Here. Give him this. They're newspaper stories. I had to put this information together quickly, but it'll be helpful. He should familiarize himself with what's happened."

She stood up, fixing him with a hard stare that caused him again to shudder involuntarily.

As she walked toward her vehicle, he had two questions: Who the hell did she think she was?—and who in hell was she anyway?

CHAPTER 1

MONDAY, JANUARY 28, 2013

THERE'S ONE SMALL detail they leave out when you make the decision to sign on for a career as an intelligence officer. They don't tell you it's a job from which you can never retire.

Ever!

It was a cloudy afternoon, and the point regarding no retirement for former case officers was about to be made yet again, for my benefit, by my sometime boss over the years, Jerry Shenlee. Jerry, who is now a National Security Council staffer, and I were seated opposite one another at the big dining room table in my home in Saranac, a quiet town in upstate New York. Although it was only a few minutes after three in the afternoon, outside it was already dark, and I'd just switched on a lamp. We were drinking tea, which Jerry prefers to coffee, and which I had brewed while he'd been spreading papers out all over the table.

As usual, Jerry had arrived unexpectedly, flying up from D.C. without any advance notice beyond a phone call saying he was on his way to Saranac. I knew why he was here. I also knew I was going to have to disappoint him.

Until now, we'd spent twenty minutes with small talk—local traffic, the weather, new car models, Jerry's golf game. Any topic was fine so long as we didn't touch on the real reason for his visit: He wanted to send me somewhere.

"Good tea," Jerry said as he took another sip, and maybe because we hadn't seen one another in a while, he gazed at me searchingly over the rim of his cup. Before I could begin describing the blend and the spices I'd added to get the taste, Jerry was talking again—about how his putting had improved with his new set of clubs and how he couldn't wait for the warm weather to get back on the golf course.

Jerry Shenlee and I first got to know each other in Berlin back in the eighties, three years before the big Wall came tumbling down. At that time Jerry was a recent Annapolis graduate, a spiffy young guy with a windowless basement office in our intelligence section at Tempelhof. Although Jerry's come a long way since then, I couldn't help thinking that his appearance hadn't changed much over the years. Round face, ruddy complexion, reddish-blond hair cut short, in the military style. Jerry looks so good that I assume he's one of those people who thrives on the careerism and political infighting that's so much a part of life in our nation's capital. Something else about Jerry: He almost never smiles. On the plains of North Dakota, where he grew up, there maybe wasn't too much to smile about.

As he thumbed through his papers, I shook my head. I didn't need to be told that any minute he'd be shoving a contract in my direction and holding a pen.

I was ready with all my reasons to decline any and all assignments. This time I wasn't going anywhere.

"If you're thinking of me, Jerry, I have to disappoint you. I can't leave."

"Why the hell not?"

"I have a business to run. That's why. It's our busy season." I was referring to the ice business I own with my partner, Gary Lawson. We supply ice for restaurants and clubs in and around Saranac Lake. Gary is never happy when I leave, but, fortunately, we have a reliable worker we can call to fill in, a retired New York City cop named Ross.

What Jerry intended was for me to sign on to work for a construction firm, which would be some kind of a government front.

It's a ritual I've been through before—and one that, since 9/11, a lot of other men and women have gone through as well.

"You're saying your business is more important than our nation's security? Is that it?"

"Nothing like that, Jerry, but I have responsibilities. People depend on us."

I had an idea Jerry wasn't overly impressed by either my ice business or by the social situation in Saranac. From the grapevine I know that when Jerry turns up at a Kennedy Center black-tie opening or the occasional high-profile cocktail party, he's always with snazzy female company. His most recent partner, I'm told, is a statuesque African-American opera singer who's a frequent performer at Lincoln Center.

"You also have responsibilities as a citizen, you know. One reason I decided on you, Alex, you've been to Afghanistan." Before I could interrupt to say so have a few hundred thousand other people, Jerry said quietly, "I'll be honest. There's no one else I can ask on short notice."

"I'm surprised you're asking me to go back to Afghanistan." When Jerry frowned, I said, "I told you how the last time in Helmand an IED went off sixty feet from where we were working. I still have nightmares about that. The other time I was in a vehicle and—"

"Okay, okay. But this time you'll be in Kabul."

"IEDs are going off in Kabul all the time."

"You'll have a chance to get together with your colleagues at the Ariana." Jerry was referring to the former Ariana Hotel, which is CIA headquarters, and is just down the road from ISAF, where the NATO nations are headquartered. "And I figure this job shouldn't last longer than a couple of weeks."

Still hoping to come up with a reason for not going anywhere, I said, "There's something else, Jerry." When he mumbled, "What's that?" I said, "I'm getting married."

Jerry continued to go through his papers. "Congratulations. Is it that German babe?" Before I could answer, he said, "Postpone it. You can do that." He pushed a couple of news stories at me. "This should tell you what you need to know. How it happened."

Trying to demonstrate my lack of interest, I ignored what he was trying to show me. "No, Jerry. Like I say, this time I—"

My eyes dropped inadvertently to one of the news stories.

The headline read: AMERICAN OFFICER SHOT IN KABUL; ISAF HEADQUARTERS SCENE OF DEADLY ATTACK. The dateline read Kabul, Afghanistan. The date on the story was four days before.

When I recognized the name of the murdered officer, I felt like I'd been jolted with a couple of hundred volts of electricity.

Without comment, I slid the story closer. Maybe because the *Post* had buried the story on page 5, or because I hadn't watched the TV news for a couple of days, I hadn't known what happened. When Jerry saw me reading, he silently placed another story down for my inspection, this one from the *New York Times*.

Both stories were accounts of a so-called green-on-blue killing. An Afghan National Army soldier had calmly walked across the office in which he worked and placed his weapon against the head of an American officer and fired. And then he'd calmly walked out of ISAF headquarters and disappeared.

The officer was described as working in the Oversight and Accountability section of ISAF Headquarters in Kabul, Afghanistan. He was identified as Colonel Peter Hansen.

Pete Hansen was an old friend. Pete and I had been stationed together at Fort Bragg some fifteen years before. I leafed through the pile of papers. There was an ongoing CID investigation.

When I'd finished reading, I remained silent.

I felt a sickening feeling beginning at the pit of my stomach. One thing I knew. This wasn't the way Pete should have died.

"Did you know Hansen, Alex?" When I nodded, Jerry said, "And his wife, Wanda. You knew her, too?"

"I knew both Pete and Wanda, Jerry. Fifteen years ago. As I recall, I introduced Pete and Wanda. Before I knew it, they were an item. We were all stationed at Bragg. My girlfriend, Kathy Ross, was an army nurse. The four of us never missed a Friday evening at the O Club."

"These green-on-blues have people shitting bricks. Everyone's worried they're going to be next. Hansen's killer's name is Nolda. Baram Nolda. An Askar. Sergeant in the ANA. Worked right in the same office. We're still looking for him."

The fact that I knew Pete Hansen changed everything. "They still haven't caught the guy?"

"Not yet. As one of Hansen's buddies, I'd think you'd want the opportunity to find the bastard. That's what this assignment is all about." Jerry's tone hardened. "Maybe pay him off personally. Take care of him yourself, just to make sure he doesn't get away with murder. You can't trust the Afghan courts to convict these guys, no matter what they do."

Having done a couple of tours in the country, I knew about the Afghan courts. In Afghanistan, bribery is a way of life, and everyone, from the president on down, is on the take. The thought of Pete's murderer buying his way out of a conviction set my teeth on edge.

"What do you say, Alex?"

Even at that, I hesitated. For a long moment, I thought about Pete, about his understated sense of humor, his sense of loyalty, his generosity, the great times we'd had. I felt the sick feeling moving from my stomach up to my chest. When I finally nodded, Jerry handed me the contract and pen, then an envelope. "Here's your plane ticket, your orders, an ID card. Some other stuff you'll need. Homeland Security has your prints on file. I'll handle that end for you. Your passport is valid for two more years." When I seemed surprised, he said, "I checked. You leave tomorrow evening from JFK. A car will be waiting in Frankfurt and will take you over to Ramstein." I knew the drill. Ramstein is Air Force headquarters in Europe. From there I'd fly direct to Afghanistan.

All of a sudden, I couldn't wait. Couldn't wait until I had a chokehold on Sergeant Baram Nolda's traitorous neck. What kind of lowlife would do something like that? My heart was pounding double-time. I'd find this miserable creature, no question. And when I found him, I'd make him regret what it was he did to Pete.

After I'd signed and gazed through the papers, I said, "Aren't we forgetting something, Jerry?"

"What?"

"How do I contact you?"

"You don't contact me. Someone will contact you."

"Who's the 'someone'?"

"You'll know when you need to know." Jerry pulled out a large envelope filled with newspaper clippings, stuff that looked as if it had been put together quickly. "Oh, by the way. What do you know about banking, financial fraud, that kind of thing?"

"What's to know, Jerry? I have a bank account. Does that surprise you?"

"Ha ha. I'm asking for a reason." He handed me the envelope. "Read this stuff. It's important." He tapped a pencil on the table. "Oh, yeah. Something else you should know. Colonel Hansen's wife, Wanda, is flying over. She's already left. Help her out. She's never been to Afghanistan."

"I haven't seen Wanda Hansen in fifteen years." I was thinking these would be difficult circumstances under which to renew our friendship.

Jerry got to his feet, took a last sip of tea. "You know the guy who's running the investigation. Stan Jones. He'll be glad to see you."

"Stan won't be happy if I'm mainly there to look over people's shoulders." Actually, I knew Stan quite well. We'd served together in Bosnia, on a base out of which our government ran a couple of renditions, back in the days when an "extraordinary rendition" was still a song sung by Barbra Streisand.

"Put your wedding on hold." Jerry took a quick glance at his watch, grabbed his windbreaker. "I'm serious about the financial stuff I gave you. Do a little reading." After zipping up, he stuck out his hand. "They're waiting for me back at the airport." He smirked. "Buck up. It ain't the end of the world."

I resisted an urge to say, "No, but it's probably the end of my engagement." I'd made a firm promise to my fiancée that I wouldn't be accepting any more assignments from the American government.

Before leaving, Jerry made some comment about the frigid weather in Saranac. I could have told him that's what you get in the Adirondacks in January, but decided to let him have the last word.

Because of the time difference between the United States and Germany, I stayed up and made the call at a few minutes after midnight. Irmie answered on the second ring.

"Alex, darling! I'm so glad you called. We have so many things to talk about."

Irmie is a police detective in Munich, and on occasion works irregular hours. I didn't know how to break the news that I wouldn't be coming over in two weeks so we could make our wedding plans.

"I hope I didn't call at a bad moment."

"You never call at a bad moment." She giggled. "You won't believe what I'm doing."

"Putting on lipstick." When she laughed, I said, "Putting on mascara."

"I'm drinking coffee and thinking of you."

"Which machine did you use to make the coffee?" I asked because when her old machine burned out, I gave her a new one for her birthday.

"Guess."

"Does the new machine fit the color scheme of your kitchen?"

"It does, but more important, it makes great coffee." Before I could comment, Irmie said, "I have *Bride* magazine and I found—"

"I called for a reason, Irmie."

"I still haven't picked out a dress." When I again tried to interrupt, she said, "I'm leaning toward hand-beaded crystals—"

"Irmie, I have to tell you something. It's important."

"Something else I've been thinking about. You know Monopteros in the English Garden?"

"Yes, of course. The white building on the hill."

"In the morning, before the actual wedding, I was thinking we could have a champagne breakfast there. The guests will all be dressed and—"

"Irmie, I have to tell you something—"

"Alex, what's wrong?" When Irmie became silent, I knew she'd picked up the seriousness in my tone.

"We're going to have to postpone my trip."

"Alex, you're supposed to arrive in two weeks. We have so many things to do. What's so important?"

"I just had a visit from my old boss."

Irmie remained silent.

"Jerry Shenlee. I may have mentioned him. He wants me to go to Afghanistan."

"But, Alex, you promised . . ." Irmie was referring to the promise I'd made to stay retired from my job as case officer.

"I know. But this is . . . well, important." After blurting it all out, I realized I should have handled this differently. Now it was too late.

"How important can it be? They can get someone else." She paused. "Afghanistan? No, Alex, no. You can't."

"This is an . . . unusual situation, Irmie."

"You should have spoken to me first. I don't care how unusual it is. What's so special about it?"

"It's something . . . only I can handle. Someone was murdered. I knew him." I was about to add that his wife was an old friend, but then thought better of it. "I think it's best that I—"

"We've been engaged for nearly a year, and with you there and me here, we hardly ever see one another. This hasn't been exactly an easy time for me. I want you to know that. And now that we have plans to see each other, spend time together, you're telling me you can't come."

"When the assignment's over, I'll be there, first thing."

"When will that be?" Before I could say I didn't know, Irmie said, "I was so looking forward to us being together again, finally, after all this time apart. We have so many decisions to make. Just yesterday, I spoke with the manager of Käfer and . . ."

Irmie and I had been at Käfer a number of times. It was Munich's best restaurant. We'd already spoken about holding our reception there.

"I can't talk about this right now, Alex. I have to leave for work." Her words just hung in the air.

"I'll call."

"Good-bye, Alex." Before I could say my own good-bye, Irmie had hung up.

I remained sitting in the darkened room for a long time. With an awful suddenness, I realized I'd not only upset our wedding plans, but I'd upset Irmie's entire life. As a police detective in Munich, she was holding down a job that often required her to juggle half-a-dozen cases simultaneously. As I thought about it, I found it easy to understand her disappointment and her irritated response to my news. She'd been counting on me, and I'd let her down.

Although I would like to have been able to tell Jerry Shenlee that I couldn't go after all, I knew that was no longer possible. Irmie was the most important person in my life, and I now realized that no amount of excuses or explanations could set things right. I'd gone back on my promise.

She had no choice but to think that she wasn't as important as a military assignment to some distant place on the other side of the world.

When she'd said, "Afghanistan," I could hear her tone of disbelief.

I spent most of the night tossing and turning and was up before the alarm. Since Gary, my business partner, is an uncomplicated guy, we completed arrangements over breakfast at the Lakeview restaurant. I arranged for a neighbor to take care of my house and threw what I figured I'd need into my carry-on. When I checked my passport, I saw that Jerry was correct, that it was valid for two more years—just another reminder that the government knows as much about me as I know myself. I grabbed the Tuesday afternoon flight down to JFK.

As I waited for my flight to Frankfurt in the airport lounge, I recalled Jerry mentioning bribery and fraud. I know Jerry well enough to know that he made the comment for a reason. And then I remembered the envelope full of newspaper clippings he'd given me.

KABUL BANK SCANDAL was the first headline I read. FRAUD SCHEME CAUSES BANK TO GO BANKRUPT was the second. The newspaper accounts all dealt with the Kabul Bank and how hundreds of millions of dollars had disappeared. Another story reported that twenty-two bank officials were on trial in Kabul for having embezzled the money.

When I wondered how Pete's murder connected with a bank scandal, I got an uncomfortable feeling that I might be involved in something far bigger and far messier than an uncomplicated green-on-blue killing.

CHAPTER 2

THE AFGHANISTAN SUN was weak, and the air was chilly. After an hour of standing in front of the Kabul International Airport military terminal, I decided I was in the mood for something to drink. I drifted over to a long, gray brick building where the cafeteria was located. Although a beer would have tasted good, it was only three in the afternoon. I settled for a Sprite, for which I paid with a couple of euros and began drinking while sitting at a long wooden table.

I gazed at a week-old copy of the *International New York Times,* which someone had thoughtfully left on the bench and from which I learned that the recent arrival in Pakistan of what the paper called "a fiery preacher" had shaken up the nation's politics. I closed the paper, maybe because I'm from a nation with no shortage of "fiery preachers," and the story sounded exaggerated.

Back outside with my cardboard cup, I watched a bunch of GIs, young men and women loaded down with backpacks and weapons, clamber on to an armor-plated military bus. A female sergeant was standing by and checking names on a clipboard. The wind was just piercing enough to make standing around uncomfortable.

Fifteen minutes passed, and the civilian crowd, a mixed bag of foreign nationals, military contractors, and special ops people, grew smaller as their rides showed up. I felt myself becoming impatient.

Just as I was tossing my cup into a trash container, I saw a dust-covered Humvee roll into the parking area, halt, and a soldier wearing fatigues climb out. Hands on his hips, he stood, looked around, and I wondered whether this was my ride. With my carry-on over my shoulder, I began walking in his direction.

"Mr. Klear?" His name tag said "Maxson."

I told him I was Alex Klear and stuck out my hand. I tossed my gear in the back of the Humvee as I shouted a hello to the gunner on the roof.

After climbing in, I pushed aside some empty plastic MRE packages, noticed a haphazard pile of military equipment and clothing on the rear seat. On top of the pile were two assault weapons and a bunch of .30-caliber ammunition magazines.

"AR-10s, sir. I tossed them in. Just in case. You've fired them, right?"

I nodded. "At Grafenwoehr, Sergeant. Not that long ago." Grafenwoehr is the military installation in Germany where the Army provides readiness training for soldiers and civilians headed to Afghanistan—and where, some time back, I spent six days qualifying with every weapon I could get my hands on, from the MP5 automatic pistol to the M9 Beretta automatic, with the M16 and AR-10 thrown in. I took a pass on the .50-caliber machine gun.

Sergeant Maxson waited while I clicked on my seat belt. He began talking as we drove slowly across the parking area toward the airport exit. "You've been here before, sir. Am I correct?"

I smiled. "Who told you, Sergeant?"

Maxson shrugged. "People here for the first time ... Well, they're a little nervous. You can tell."

"I guess I was nervous the first time I was here. Weren't you?"

"It was a while ago, sir. I'm on my third deployment."

As we drove out of the parking area, Maxson said, "I'm sorry, sir, about the delay. We would have come out in an MRAP, but they're all in the repair shop or in mission mode. I hope you don't mind the Humvee."

"Nothing to apologize for, Sergeant."

"I know you've been waiting for over—"

"I just got here, Sergeant."

"Thank you, sir."

Although my flight had arrived an hour and a half before, you can't be too fussy in Afghanistan, where all kinds of things can delay you or even permanently prevent you from going to wherever it is you're headed. I'd flown into Afghanistan from Ramstein, Germany, an uneventful eight-and-a-half-hour flight on a C-17 loaded down with cases of ammunition on which I was the only passenger. I'd been able to grab some shut-eye on the plane and wasn't particularly tired.

To our left as we drove out of the parking area was the big terminal building where I'd just been. The parking lot was half-filled, with most of the vehicles belonging to the American military. A few sported insignia and military plates from other nations. Some were civilian, the numbers and letters written in Arabic.

As we proceeded, I continued to check out the Kabul International Airport, which hadn't changed much since my last visit a year before. KIA is divided in two. On one side the civilian flights land. On the other the military flights land. There were maybe fifty or sixty people still milling around. Some were flying out and some, like me, were flying in—and waiting for a ride to take them wherever in Kabul they'd be staying.

"It's not a long ride, sir, only five miles."

I nodded. We were headed for Camp Eggers, where I could keep a low profile and where I'd arranged for a billet and a Toyota van. I had an appointment the following morning with Major Stanley Jones. Camp Eggers and nearby Camp Phoenix are two of half-a-dozen military installations the United States maintains on the outskirts of Kabul. They're both close to the complex of buildings in which ISAF Headquarters is situated.

Stan Jones was an officer in the Criminal Investigation Command, or CID, in Kabul, and he told me on the phone he'd gotten the job of investigating green-on-blues tossed in his lap. He'd also mentioned the withdrawal of NATO from Afghanistan, which was scheduled for the end of 2014 and was affecting his ability to get his job done.

I couldn't shake the thought that Pete shouldn't have died in the way he did—an Afghan soldier with whom he worked walking over to his desk and calmly placing an M9 Beretta against his head and pulling the trigger. Nor could I shake the thought that this rash of premeditated killings may be the vilest and most upsetting development to emerge from a long and frustrating war.

Beyond the airport exit we drove around a bend before hitting a two-lane road surrounded on both sides by fields overgrown with weeds. On our right I could see what looked like a 767 taxiing on one of the airport's distant runways. We passed a heavily armored military bus headed toward the airport.

After a couple of miles we turned right onto Airport Road, a four-lane highway that I remembered from my two earlier visits. This street had traffic, mostly ancient cars and battered trucks. In the inside lane there were a few wagons being pulled by donkeys. Horns honked and clouds of exhaust from badly tuned engines hung over the pothole-scarred road. On both sides were rickety buildings, some mud and cement and some wood. Most housed shops advertising their wares with beat-up signs hand-painted in Arabic. A gentle breeze blew curtains out from windows without window panes. Some of the stores had stands in front, most containing food, others holding every kind of junk imaginable.

There was a wide dirt path, a kind of sidewalk, lining the highway. Except for a few veiled women carrying bags, the pedestrians were all males, many of them guys talking and standing around with their hands in their pockets.

"I figure this is about the way things must have looked five hundred years ago," Sergeant Maxson said.

"They didn't have cars back then," I said. "Or concrete."

"Well, sir, except for the highway and the cars, that's what I figure." As we slowed to allow a couple of guys to amble across, Maxson called up to our gunner, whose name was Rackley.

"I'm good," the gunner called down.

"Over here," Maxson said, "the guys stand around. The women do most of the work. But you hardly ever see them."

I didn't reply, but it was a good insight. In Afghanistan you notice things like that. Seeing these depressing sights again, I felt a sick feeling and couldn't help thinking I never should have said yes to this mission. Whenever I recalled my telephone call with Irmie, I remembered how upset she'd been. I should have anticipated her reaction, but I hadn't. Although she never complained, I knew Irmie's job was not only demanding, it was dangerous. It was early afternoon now in Munich, and as we drove, I couldn't help wondering what she was doing.

Two minutes later, we were bouncing along in the outside lane going about 30 mph when, without warning, a small truck coming from the opposite direction veered out of its lane and across the center line, its horn blasting, and headed straight toward us.

"Goddamn—"

Maxson had no choice. Reacting quickly, he spun the steering wheel, causing us to swerve toward the right. We rolled across the inside lane and onto the dirt path alongside the road and narrowly avoided going into a wide drainage ditch. Trying not to hit a couple of startled pedestrians, Maxson was able to get the vehicle back onto the road.

But that was exactly where someone wanted us to be.

Suddenly, there was a deafening roar, and we weren't on the ground anymore. The Humvee went briefly into the air, hit the ground with a terrible crunching, hard thud, then pitched back onto the road. As it rolled over, I held on for dear life.

Thank God for seat belts!

The vehicle came to rest upside down. Rackley, the gunner who'd been perched over us, was now beneath us. I could hear cursing, so at least he was still alive.

I saw Maxson, who, like me, was strapped in but was also upside down. "You okay?"

Before he could answer, I heard the rat-a-tat of an automatic weapon. Someone was firing at us. Probably the guys who'd been in the truck who, when they saw the IED hadn't done its job, decided they were going to finish us off themselves. Fortunately, the armor on a Humvee is plenty thick, and except for a couple of rounds smashing the windshield, the first burst didn't do any damage. Whoever was shooting would need to get closer to hit us.

Then there was a second burst from outside, this one from a different direction, and it sounded closer.

Upside down in the Humvee we were sitting ducks.

I needed to get my door open. For what seemed like an eternity and while slugs slammed against the side of the vehicle, I pushed and pulled on the goddamned handle, trying to remember which direction I should be pushing it toward. But for some reason when you're upside down, right is no longer right, up is no longer up, and it's very much like being in a different world.

"Up, and out, sir," Maxson said. He kept saying it. "Up, sir. Now back. That's it. Now out."

After another fifteen seconds of fiddling and following Maxson's shouted directions, I had the door unlocked. Reaching into the back, I found the AR-10s, lying on the roof. I grabbed a couple of ammo magazines and tossed a weapon to Maxson, who was unclicking his own seat belt.

There was another burst from one of the shooters outside. I figured the other shooter would be closing in on the far side, Maxson's side. He had his door open.

With my door partially ajar, I'd be able to shoot back, but that meant the shooter would also be able to shoot in.

I waited for maybe half a minute before an individual with a white rag around his head stepped out from behind one of the huts on the near side of the road. He was 150 feet away, in a crouch, had his weapon at his shoulder, and he was close to getting me in his sights. I let go with a random burst in his direction, not expecting to hit him, only shake him up. I figured it worked because I couldn't see him anymore and for the next twenty seconds, he remained out of sight . . .

"For God's sakes!"

I couldn't believe what I was seeing. A youngster, maybe seven or eight years old and holding an apple, came wandering out from the dark inside of one of the shops. Curiosity was written all over his face. With all the other pedestrians having taken cover, he was now alone on the dirt sidewalk with no parent around and obviously curious about the noise and shouting in the street.

He was sixty or seventy feet from the Humvee and wandering directly into the line of fire.

When I waved and shouted "Beat it!" a broad grin lit up his face. "Beat it, dammit! Get away!"

He waved back and continued to walk toward me.

How do you say "Beat it!" in Pashto?

And then the shooter reappeared and sent another burst in my direction. Slugs kicked up dirt and ricocheted against the Humvee. When I sent back an answering burst, he fired again. He was getting closer now. Slugs chewed up the ground five feet in front of me. The bastard knew how to shoot. But aware I'd be firing back, he ducked again.

I heard bursts from somewhere, and I figured that was this guy's partner. I hoped Maxson could take care of that end of things.

Then a burst kicked up dust ten feet from the kid.

"Goddamn!"

Without thinking, I pushed open the vehicle door, jumped out. The youngster was closer, in real danger of being hit. As I took off in his direction, I heard voices and someone shooting, but my only thought was the boy. Still thinking he was in some sort of game, he shouted something and tried to scoot away. He didn't get far. Within a couple of seconds I was able to tackle him, and we hit the ground together. Immediately climbing to my feet, I scooped the kid up and ran like hell across the path and hit the dirt behind a stand piled high with fruit, a maneuver that brought us closer to the shooter behind the building. But when I bumped against one of its legs, the stand immediately toppled over, sending oranges and a dozen watermelons in every direction.

And then the shooter, not that far away now, was out in plain sight and firing in our direction, a couple of the slugs squishing into a watermelon two feet to my left. Although the boy was kicking and had begun crying, I continued to hold him down while trying to get my weapon sighted. Then I saw the guy again. Moving in a crouch, he'd been able to find cover behind a wagon adjacent to the road, and close enough for me to see the curl of his lips. I fired a short burst, then ducked.

He stood up and fired two long bursts. Prone and with the boy beneath me, I fired back, emptying the magazine. I was feeling through my jacket pocket for another magazine when I saw the truck.

The shooter emerged from behind the wagon and, staying low, ran for a fruit stand that wasn't more than thirty feet away. He fired a long burst, but by this time I'd jammed the magazine into my own weapon and fired back.

The truck that had forced us off the road was now pulling up. The gunman took off at top speed for the road. A second later he was joined by his friend coming from the other direction. After they'd hopped aboard, they waved their weapons at us, and one saluted. The other was grinning. As I mumbled some profanity, the truck made a U-turn on the road and, brakes squealing, headed off toward downtown Kabul.

Good-bye and good riddance!

The child alongside me was crying. His blouse was ripped, his arm was smeared with blood, and I saw that he had an abrasion on his cheek, the result of hitting the ground hard. If that was all he had, he'd been very, very lucky.

As I climbed to my feet, a wild-eyed veiled woman came rushing at me shouting and waving her hands. She shook her fists at me, threw her arms around the boy, whispered something in his ear, then shoved him behind her. Almost immediately, she was joined by a bearded individual who could have been the owner of the fruit stand. He started shouting and pointing to the melons and oranges, which lay all over the ground.

And then he was in my face, waving and no doubt shouting Pashto curses, probably telling me I had to pay for his ruined produce. A few more people who may have been his friends joined the melee, gesticulating and shouting. I was breathing hard and had run out of patience. The loudmouth owner of the fruit stand followed me as I tried to move away, still yelling and waving his fist.

"Hey, buddy! Where were you when I needed you?"

Resisting the urge to belt this character, I turned, pushed my way past a couple more loudmouths, and headed back to the Humvee. Maxson had been able to drag Rackley out from beneath the vehicle and was now talking to someone on his cell phone.

"Ambulance'll be here in a second, sir."

People were all over now, pointing and shouting. I had the feeling that a bunch of them were talking about me. I definitely didn't have the feeling we were among friends.

We only had to wait for a couple of minutes. An ambulance arrived, and then a van full of GIs, and within minutes I was talking to an African-American infantry captain named Johnson, telling him what had just happened.

"They all seem to be pointing at you for some reason, sir," Johnson said. "They seem mad about something. What'd you do?"

I shrugged. "I shoved a kid out of the way. And knocked down the fruit stand."

"Some of them are probably Taliban sympathizers. As I'm sure you know, Americans ain't the most popular people in Kabul these days. Whatever you do for them, it ain't right and ain't never enough."

When I told him how the truck suddenly came at us, he nodded. "That's one of the Taliban's tricks. They forced you over to the side of the road because that's where they had the IED planted. They might have put it down within the last hour. When you were over it, someone touched the wires and closed the circuit. Half the people out here would have known it was there. The guys with the truck were waiting for an American vehicle."

I said, "Sergeant Maxson did one helluva job steering us back onto the road. I have a feeling we didn't go squarely over the bomb."

The captain nodded. "If you had, sir, it would have been curtains."

By this time, we were surrounded by vehicles and soldiers. I could see Sergeant Rackley being carried on a stretcher toward a waiting ambulance. As he went by, he gave me a thumbs-up and a grim smile. A tough kid. I had a feeling he'd be all right.

I waved back.

On the far side of the road was a massive crater, with clouds of smoke still billowing out. I wandered over and stared into it. The IED had contained enough explosives to destroy a couple of tanks.

A half-dozen vehicles were already on the scene, some of them belonging to ANP guys, the Afghan police, others to blue-uniformed Afghan soldiers. A van with "UN" printed on the side arrived and disgorged two men and two women. When I was approached by a pair of MPs, I began telling them my story. Captain Johnson, still carrying his clipboard, walked over and asked a few more questions.

After I'd given him information enough for his report, I asked if I could get a ride to Camp Eggers.

"No problem, Mr. Klear. And by the way"—he grinned broadly—"welcome to Afghanistan."

CHAPTER 3

FRIDAY, FEBRUARY 1, 2013

"IT'S BEEN A while," Major Stanley Jones said, stepping out from behind the cluttered steel desk in his Camp Phoenix office. It was a few minutes before 1000 hours the following day, a damp and chilly Friday. After introducing myself to his admin, I'd pushed open Stan's office door.

"Welcome to the Criminal Investigation Command and to Operation Enduring Freedom!" Stan's voice is deep and still retains some traces of a South Carolina accent.

Stan had thinning brown hair, wide blue eyes, and a fleshy face. He's a burly 210, ten pounds heavier than when I last saw him, and has a strong handshake. Because he was a CID officer, he wore no insignia on his fatigue uniform. On the phone Stan said he was running the investigation into Colonel Pete Hansen's death.

"All the comforts of home," I said, looking around and nodding my approval. "It took me a while to find you."

"They're running out of space at Headquarters, so they moved us over here." Stan pointed to a pile of folders. "I'm handling all the green-on-blues. Would you believe, there were over sixty last year?" He shook his head.

Stan's office, which was situated toward the far end of Camp Phoenix, was away from the hustle and bustle at the main gate and fifty yards from the chow hall. It was spacious, with a couple of desks, some folding chairs, two computers, a printer, and a lot of electrical cables. Against one wall stood a row of steel filing cabinets and a small fridge. The walls were plywood and obviously built with the thought that the U.S. Army wasn't going to be in Afghanistan forever. The window overlooked a row of wooden buildings across a narrow street. Upward was a patch of blue sky.

Walking to the coffee machine situated on a table next to the filing cabinet, Stan said, "You like it black, as I recall. And no sugar." Standing at the machine and glancing over his shoulder, he said, "I don't know exactly the reason, but all of a sudden things are real busy around here."

"What do you mean?"

"Well, you're here and Wanda, of course. But you won't believe who else was here in the office yesterday." Before I could ask, Stan said, "Douglas Greer."

"You mean Undersecretary Greer?"

"One and the same. Undersecretary for International Development. Seems to be a good guy. He's back and forth between D.C. and this part of the world pretty regular. But yesterday he stopped by to ask about the Hansen killing. This green-on-blue stuff's made everybody jumpy."

"Everybody thinks they're going to be next. Is that it?"

"Just about." Suddenly very serious, Stan said, "And I take it, that's why you're here. Because of Pete." When I nodded, Stan said, "I remember Pete one time mentioning you guys were together at Fort Bragg."

I nodded, recalling that long-ago time in my life. "We were providing some training for a bunch of Rangers. I was young then, didn't mind the physical stuff. Around that time Wanda arrived."

"Wanda Nyland, right?"

"*Captain* Wanda Nyland?"

Stan nodded. "Wanda and Pete hit it off right away. Pete told me they got married in the Fort Bragg chapel. Were you best man?"

I shook my head. "I probably would have been, but I'd already left for Bosnia. That's when you and I ran into one another."

"I remember. I was filing daily reports back to D.C. on how the drone program was shaping up. We'd outfitted them with cameras. After 9/11, someone got the idea they'd be good as attack aircraft. I was out on the tarmac at Eagle Base every day after that. You know the rest."

Seated again behind his desk, Stan ran his hand through what was left of his hair. His expression changed suddenly. "It was tragic, Alex, Pete dying like that." He shook his head. "These characters are brazen."

"They seem to be getting more brazen all the time."

"Everybody's got the jitters."

I took a sip of coffee. "I can understand why."

"The thing is, they're people you're working with, day in and day out. One minute the guy's your best buddy. Then, a second later, he turns on you and shoots you. I mean, we give them the weapons and ammo, show them how to shoot. How can you explain shit like that?" Stan began talking more rapidly, obviously carried away by the subject. Understandably. It was a subject that for us was hard to understand. "Something else. How can we prevent this stuff from happening?"

"There's only one way. Don't give them weapons."

"Yeah, that's not working either. I mean, that's why we're here. To help the Afghans establish a modern country, and that means a police force to keep order."

"They need an army, too."

"Right. To protect themselves from invasions, in case the Russkis want to come back." Stan flashed a malicious smirk. We knew that was an unlikely development.

"Anyway, Alex, they need guns. So we're between a rock and a hard place. If we provide training and weapons, they turn around and shoot us. And if we don't, there's no sense in us being here." Stan paused. "So how come you're here?"

"Jerry Shenlee sent me." When Stan only shrugged, I said, "Jerry's an NSC staffer."

"Don't know him. But why send you here? What's up?"

"I knew Pete. I guess you could say it's partly personal."

Stan grimaced, making no effort to conceal his skepticism. He knew no one would care about Pete being a friend of mine. "Don't they have other priorities in the National Security Council? C'mon, Alex. You can't expect me to believe that."

The truth was, I was still trying to puzzle out why Jerry had sent me over. In this business, when you can't figure things out real quick, you might end up paying for your ignorance with your life. The post-9/11 world is a dangerous place. And in Afghanistan it's doubly dangerous.

Stan fixed me with a cool stare. "I hope you're not going to get us into hot water. If you're only here to look over our shoulders, you won't be popular. I guarantee that."

Ignoring Stan's veiled warning, I said, "Do you need help with the investigation?"

"We can always use as much help as we can get. I don't think you know Todd Hammond. He's the only agent I have now. He's been working night and day." Stan shrugged. "The White House wants everyone gone out of Afghanistan by the end of next year. We're so shorthanded, it's ridiculous."

"What else can you tell me?"

"Pete worked over in the ISAF Headquarters building, in the 'Oversight and Accountability' section. Exactly what he was working on I don't know, but there's someone you can ask."

"Who?"

"Eric Page. Captain Eric Page. He worked for Pete, in the same office." Stan paused. "I talked with Page, but maybe you can get more out of him than I could." After a brief pause, Stan said, "You know how Pete was. He didn't always communicate well—and he could be tetchy at times."

"Aren't we all tetchy at times?"

Stan smiled. "I guess. It's hard to see yourself the way others see you. Anyway, yeah, at times he was difficult. Whatever Pete was doing, the job had a lot of pressure. You'll see that after you've been around for a while. We all feel it. We've got more people back in D.C. looking over our shoulders than you can shake a stick at."

"How did it happen?"

Stan took a sip of cold coffee, gazed for a long moment at the cup, which was imprinted with the letters OEF and an American flag. "It was one of the Afghans, one of those who've been cleared to handle files and to work in Headquarters. I guess he knew some English. There aren't that many." When I only nodded, he continued to talk. "Somehow this character managed to carry a weapon into the building, an M9. He wasn't supposed to have one, not on him anyway. One of Pete's jobs was to keep track of financial stuff, whatever wasn't right."

"Who were his sources? Who was Pete talking to?"

"He spent a lot of time at the Embassy, I can tell you that."

"Doing what?"

"Talking to people investigating the bank fraud," Stan said. "You know about the Kabul Bank?"

"I know it went bankrupt. Who's doing the investigating?"

Stan seemed reluctant to talk all of a sudden. When he spoke again, he lowered his voice. "It's very hush-hush. They're people from the States trying to find out what happened. They're called the

Finance Cell. They won't talk to anyone, not even to the diplomats at the Embassy."

"But they talked to Pete?"

"I guess. For a time, he was at the Embassy every day. Sometimes he'd go into Kabul in the evenings." Stan paused, then added, "He also spent time outside the country, flying here and there."

"Who was he dealing with?"

"I'm not really sure. Didn't the NSC guy fill you in on this sort of thing? On what Pete was doing?" When I shook my head, Stan's face clouded over. He looked tired, as if he hadn't had a good night's sleep in a long time. Tours in Afghanistan can take a lot out of you, emotionally as well as physically. "I know what you're thinking, Alex—that I should know more about what Pete was working on." Stan pointed to his cluttered desk. "Right now I'm working on fifteen green-on-blues. Six took place right here in Kabul. Maybe you can cut us a little slack."

"No problem, Stan."

"Since they were alone in the room, we don't know exactly how it was."

"But you're sure it was Nolda."

"It must've been him. Everyone else in the building was accounted for. I can take you over, show you the office. Probably Pete was staring into his computer, and the Askar came up behind him, held the weapon against his head, and fired. We figure it must have been like that."

"No one heard the shot?"

Stan shook his head. "Door was closed. Most people were on their lunch break. Scary, when you think about it. It was maybe ten or fifteen minutes before anyone realized Pete was dead. Before anyone could stop him, the guy was out of the building. Where he is now is anybody's guess."

"How did he get out of the area?"

"Like I say, some time went by before they found Pete's body. The killer could have been anywhere in the city by then. We tightened up the checkpoints leaving the city, went over every vehicle leaving Kabul for the next three, four days with a fine-tooth comb. Searched every nook and cranny in the city."

"Any pictures?"

"Yes and no. A lot aren't that clear. The security camera wasn't working that well. Don't ask me why. Todd can fill you in on that better than me."

"What can you tell me about this guy?"

"Name's Baram Nolda. Born in Helmand Province, down south. Volunteered for the Army, got some training at Kandahar. Came up here, was in the 7th Guards. Ended up in Black Horse for more training. He could read a little, knew some English. Like I say, that's what got him assigned to the Headquarters job."

"Off the record, Stan. Any reason for this guy shooting Pete?"

"I can't sleep at night, Alex, thinking about that. We've been trying to figure that out. Some of these characters are thin-skinned. Maybe Pete yelled at him. Told him to move his butt. Who knows? Pete could be difficult at times."

I said, "What else do I need to know?"

"Well, Colonel Hansen, Pete's wife, arrived. She came in on a flight from Ramstein two nights ago."

"How's she doing?"

"Okay, I guess. She's mad as a nest of hornets. Says this never should have happened. She wants to find people to blame. She wants action. She wants us to nail her husband's murderer ASAP."

"Understandable," I said.

"Pete was on his third deployment. He extended once. He had another five months before he'd be heading back to the States."

When Stan asked if I had wheels, I told him I'd picked up a Toyota van at the motor pool.

He grinned. "I'd rather drive in Rome than Kabul. There used to be just one traffic light in the city. I think there are two now. There are cops at the big intersections, but they don't help much. Leave yourself plenty of time wherever you're going."

"In other words, things haven't changed much since the last time I was here." I got to my feet. "You say Nolda was a member of 7th Guards."

Stan nodded. "Lived in a barracks over at Black Horse."

"Is there anything you'd like me to do, Stan?"

"Like I say, we're really shorthanded. You could check on the military side of things. Todd has been trying to find out about Nolda, the kind of guy he was. He made a trip back to the village to speak with Nolda's wife, but they couldn't locate her. Helmand's chaotic."

"I could go over to the barracks, check around, try talking to his superiors."

"That would be helpful. I'll call Captain Bashiri. He was Nolda's commanding officer. Try to find out how he spent his spare time. Who he hung out with, that sort of thing." Stan shook his head. "But don't expect too much help. These people are wary of Americans."

After telling Stan good-bye, I drove back to my room where I still had some unpacking to do. As I reread the clippings Jerry had given me, I continued to wonder whether I'd been wise in letting myself get talked into this expedition, which was beginning to seem more and more complicated than it had at the start. I could already sense Stan's wariness. Even more puzzling was how Pete's death connected to the trial of bank officials, which was now going on in Kabul. One of the stories estimated the money missing from the Kabul Bank at over 900 million dollars.

Another story said it was the largest bank fraud in history.

And Pete was investigating it. That could have been the reason he was killed. Had Jerry Shenlee made that connection, and was that the reason he'd given me the bank clippings?

Stan told me that Wanda Hansen had arrived two days ago and was now at the Green Village, the Kabul housing facility built for contractors. I'd interviewed some people over there on my last assignment in this part of the world. That Wanda was angry was easy enough to understand. She'd want to know right away who killed her husband. Seeing her again under these circumstances wasn't going to be pleasant.

Late in the afternoon, I found a text message on my smartphone that Colonel Hansen wanted to see me in her room in the second floor of the D Building at the Green Village.

The last time I'd seen Wanda, she was Wanda Nyland, before she married Pete. I remember Wanda as attractive, with a great sense of humor. I also remember telling her one time that it was a good thing she met Pete first. As I recall, she hadn't laughed.

CHAPTER 4

When I knocked on the room's half-open door at 1730 hours that evening, a woman's voice said, "Come in." Seconds later, Wanda Hansen was standing in front of me. "Alex, it's really you."

Except that she looked a shade more mature, Wanda was very much as I remembered her. She appeared slightly pale, perhaps because she wasn't sleeping well.

"Hello, Wanda." After clicking the door behind me, I put my arms around her, gave her the kind of hug brothers give their sisters. "I'm very sorry."

She nodded, inhaled, pointed toward a chair. "The Headquarters billets were all filled, so they found rooms over here for me. What do you think?"

I nodded my approval. "Looks comfortable." One of the two rooms was furnished as an office, with a desk and a computer. Along with the computer there was a printer and a telephone.

"This is where the contractors stay. I have everything I need. There's even a bar downstairs. I don't think I could stand being alone in one of the guest houses." She shuddered.

"I'm on administrative leave." She pointed at the telephone. "If I have to call the States, no problem."

"Secure?"

"Probably not." She smiled, then pointed at a TV on a shelf next to the desk. "That's so I don't miss *Wheel of Fortune*." She did her best to smile. "Thank you for coming. To be honest, I'm surprised you're here."

"Jerry Shenlee sent me." When she frowned, I said, "Jerry's an NSC staffer. I'm looking into Pete's murder." I recalled Jerry's suggestion that I become familiar with financial stuff. "But there may be more to it than that. I'm not really sure."

"It's so nice having someone here I know. How long do you intend to stay?"

"I'm not sure about that either. However long Jerry wants me here."

Wanda hadn't changed much in the fifteen years since I'd last seen her. She had a frank, open expression, dark blond hair that covered her ears, and wide blue eyes. She was wearing a white blouse and dark blue slacks and tiny earrings that could have been diamonds. I still remembered Wanda's smile, and how it could light up a room. Somehow, I had the feeling she wouldn't be doing much smiling during this visit.

"I'm in one of the media relations offices at the Pentagon. They gave me time off. Now that I'm here, I'm not sure that coming over was the right thing."

"Why not?"

"I thought maybe I could help in the investigation." She smiled wryly. "Maybe I only came because I wanted to see . . . whoever did it close up."

"They still don't know much about him."

"They know his name. I don't know how much else." She pointed toward a small refrigerator in the room's far corner. "Can I get you something?" When I shook my head, she checked her watch. "I'm expecting Todd Hammond. Todd's CID. I met him yesterday. How far along the investigation is I'm not sure. Anyway, he should know. They know who the killer is. 'Baram Someone.'"

"Baram Nolda. From what I understand, he and Pete worked in the same office."

"Don't get me started on that. The way these people will turn on you . . . I mean, I just can't understand it. How can you kill a colleague? Someone you work with?"

I didn't try to answer that question. After a brief silence, I said, "Is it true Pete had five more months on this tour?"

"Yes. I was looking forward to him getting back. I'll be at the Pentagon for another year. I had a two-bedroom picked out in Alexandria . . . We were planning to . . ." Wanda shook her head, took a deep breath, and again tried to smile.

I was about to comment when someone knocked. Wanda leaped to her feet. "That's Todd." After pulling open the door, Wanda said hello to a tall, broad-shouldered guy dressed in a green jacket, blue jeans, and combat boots. Hammond was African-American, clean-shaven, and had an alert, intelligent expression.

"I'm not interrupting anything, I hope."

"No, Todd. Come in. This is Alex Klear, the person I mentioned yesterday. He was a friend of Pete's. He's come over on short notice"—she looked at me—"to lend a hand in the investigation. Alex, this is Todd Hammond."

After we'd shaken hands, Hammond said, "I only knew Colonel Hansen to say hello to, but I've heard only good things." He nodded at Wanda.

"There's one thing we all have in common," Wanda said, rearranging papers on the desk and getting to her feet. "We're all here for the same reason: to find the person who killed Pete. If I may, let me say I don't intend to rest until we find him."

There was a steely determination in her voice—and I had the feeling I was seeing a side of her that I'd never seen before. For some reason, I found it mildly unsettling.

Wanda led the way out of the apartment, then locked the door. "We're only going over to the café, Alex," she said. "You're free to join us."

"I may not be the best company. I'm still feeling some jet lag."

"No excuses," Wanda said. "The buffet is fairly good."

On the walk over to the Green Village's café, I asked Hammond where the investigation stood.

"So far as we can determine, this guy was nothing special. He doesn't seem to have been a Taliban member, although with these people it's hard to know sometimes."

"Not a fanatic?" I said.

Hammond shrugged. "Not so far as anyone can tell. I flew down to Helmand right after it happened. Me and Haji. He's a terp. We tried to find his wife, but she was off somewhere. We only had a day. We found a couple of people in the village who knew him. He had a couple of kids, and that's why he joined the Army, so he could support them. Making a living in this country is not all that easy."

"From what I understand," Wanda said, "these killings are often purely personal. An American gets an Afghan mad. The individual holds a grudge, doesn't say anything, but the next thing you know, he shoots the American."

The café was in a building on the far side of the compound, and after we'd staked out a table, I got a sandwich and salad at the buffet table. The truth was, I really was feeling major jet lag.

"Oh, one more thing, Alex," Wanda said. "I'll be stopping by Major Jones' office tomorrow, 0900 hours."

Hammond said, "Major Jones wants us all there. We'll have a chance to meet Undersecretary Greer." When I nodded, he said, "Captain Corley should also be there."

"Who's Captain Corley?" Wanda asked as she sprinkled pepper on her salad.

"I only met her yesterday," Hammond said. "She wants to be involved in the investigation. She's stationed down in Khost somewhere." He explained to Wanda that Khost was a province in the southeast, bordering on Pakistan.

"All I care about," Wanda said, "is how the investigation is proceeding."

"Slowly, ma'am, slowly. Like everything else in this country, it's taking longer than it should."

"Dammit, that's not good enough."

When he only shrugged, Wanda said, "Maybe that's why you're here, Alex. To get things moving."

I wondered how I was supposed to do that.

Fortunately, I didn't have to comment. At that moment my phone went off. It was Stan.

"Alex, can you get over here? I've got a couple of MPs here in my office." When I asked what the problem was, Stan said, "It has something to do with a fruit stand. And a little boy?" He broke off to speak with someone in his office. "It happened yesterday. Out on Airport Road."

"Oh, that."

"Yeah, they have some questions. I'm not sure what—"

"Okay, Stan. Give me ten minutes."

Grabbing my tray, I said, "Stan needs me."

"Good luck with Bashiri tomorrow," Hammond said, referring to Nolda's CO. "I couldn't get much out of him."

When I said I'd see everyone in the morning, Hammond nodded and took a bite of his sandwich. Although he had been more than friendly, I sensed that, like Stan, he wasn't happy about my sudden arrival. I couldn't blame him.

How do I get into these situations?

* * *

"What the hell happened out there, anyway?" Stan Jones said, unable to keep the exasperation out of his voice.

It was fifteen minutes later, and I was back in Stan's office. Also there were two military policemen, Sergeant Deming and Sergeant McCabe, and a serious-looking, slightly built Afghan, who'd introduced himself as Haji Longel.

We were all standing in front of Stan's desk, and Deming was holding a clipboard.

Stan said, "They say you wrecked some guy's fruit stand. And what's this about a kid?"

I said, "Yesterday on the way in—"

Deming interrupted. "What it is, sir, Haji was called to the main gate last night." He nodded at the Afghan. "According to Force Protection, there was quite a flap. Some people were complaining . . . about an American." Deming pointed at me. "Are you Mr. Klear?" When I said I was, Deming turned to Haji. "This here gentleman is the terp—"

"The interpreter," Stan said.

"Right, sir, the interpreter. The story he told us is that—"

Raising his hand, Stan said, "Why don't we let Haji tell the story, Sergeant?"

When Deming said, "Yes, sir, very good, sir," Haji said, "I was called to the gate by Force Protection at 1900 hours. There were many Afghan people there—"

"How many?" Stan asked. "About."

"Ten, maybe. They were all very excited, one man particularly. His name is Jalal Nandash." Haji said to me, "He says you owe him one thousand dollars—"

"Why does he say that?" I asked. I remembered the fruit dealer, a short, square-faced guy with a graying beard, a real loudmouth. I'd had all I could do to keep from decking him.

"His fruit stand," Deming said. "You broke up his fruit stand." He consulted a report on his clipboard. "Broke the legs, right, Haji?"

Haji nodded. "Yes, he had many people with him who agreed that is what happened. And then the other man said this American man—"

"Mr. Klear," Deming said. "How do you spell your name, sir?" After he'd written down my name, Deming said to Haji, "Who else was there?"

"Other people said Mr. Klear hurt a young boy. It was all very confusing."

"Someone said a woman complained because Mr. Klear struck her boy. They had pictures of the boy where he was hurt. Red marks. All this happened yesterday afternoon on Airport Road." Haji paused. "They want a thousand dollars."

"Was the woman there?" Stan asked. "Did you talk with her?"

"She was not there. Just the people with the fruit dealer—"

"All right, all right." Stan raised his hand, a signal for everyone to stop talking. "We have Mr. Klear right here. Alex, why don't you tell us? What the hell happened yesterday on the way in from the airport?"

I said, "I was in a Humvee on the way in from KIA, when a truck from the opposite direction came over the center line, forcing us over toward the sewer trench. Our driver did one helluva job of getting us back on the road, and that's where an IED was. But we didn't hit it straight on. We landed in the other direction upside down—"

"You went over an IED?" Stan couldn't keep the surprise out of his voice.

"We didn't hit it squarely."

"Still, you were lucky. You okay?"

"I'm fine. Our gunner was shaken up."

"Then what?"

"The next thing we knew, a couple of guys were shooting at us. We were firing back with a couple of AR-10s, which we had in the vehicle. Then, I saw a kid, eight or nine years old, wandering toward me—"

"Into the line of fire?"

When I nodded, Stan shook his head.

"He had no idea what was going on, thought it was some kind of game. I took off after the kid, grabbed him. We hit the deck next to a bunch of fruit on a stand."

"Where was his mother?"

I shrugged. "Inside a building somewhere? I don't know. Anyway, when it was over, she came running out, grabbed the boy, started shouting at me—"

To the MPs, Stan said, "It sounds to me like Klear here maybe saved the kid's life."

"One more thing," Haji said. "Someone said the father of the boy is a very influential elder, a member of an important tribe, the Korengalis . . . they are from Kunar Province. The man who owns the fruit stand says—"

Stan interrupted again. "We're not too interested in what he says. Mr. Nandash sounds like an opportunist."

Deming asked a few more questions, which I answered. Then he said, "Thank you, Mr. Klear. Thank you, sir."

Haji gave each of us a small bow before leaving the office.

With the MPs and the interpreter gone, Stan said, "These things are happening all the time. Nobody knows what anyone else is saying. The woman was upset. The fruit vendor's obviously an opportunist, wanting to hit up Uncle Sugar for damages."

I said, "Hopefully, it'll blow over."

"You met Haji. He's the best of our interpreters. I use him when I can." Stan seated himself again behind his desk and pointed to some folders. "I have to get through this stuff by tomorrow."

An hour later, back in my hooch, I put in a call to Irmie.

"How are things in Munich, honey? I miss you."

"Difficult, Alex, if you really want to know."

When I foolishly asked why, Irmie sounded irritable, as though it was a dumb question. "I was on the telephone for half the morning canceling the arrangements I'd made. Since you were supposed to arrive in two weeks, I'd made appointments for us to talk with the caterer and a wedding planner. Actually, I have to say, they were very understanding."

From just the tone of her voice I could tell that Irmie was under stress. Before I could comment, she was talking again. "But it's not just the wedding. Today I had to travel out to the prison to interrogate a suspected terrorist, a very disagreeable individual. Even when I told him he might not have to face jail time if he cooperated, he began cursing and threatening me with all kinds of . . . Oh, you don't want to hear all this."

"I wish I was with you, Irmie. I know how unpleasant—"

"That was the plan, Alex. For you to be here with me and for us to decide everything together."

"I've tried to explain. This was an extraordinary situation—"

"I still can't see why you had to go to Afghanistan. Of all the places—"

"I've already said why."

"Your friend." She paused. "I'm just getting ready to go to bed, Alex. I'm too tired to talk." When I asked if she'd received my e-mail, she said, "Yes, thank you for sending it."

"I just wanted to let you know I arrived safely over here. I can't wait to see you again, Irmie."

"I appreciate the e-mail, Alex." She paused. "But when you say you're looking forward . . . to seeing me . . ."

I knew what Irmie was thinking. If I was *looking forward to seeing her*, I wouldn't be in Afghanistan. Time-wise, Munich is three and a half hours behind Kabul, which meant it was seven p.m. there. I wondered whether she was really going to bed.

"I have to hang up now."

"Good night, Irmie." My fiancée certainly wasn't concealing the fact that she was unhappy about my accepting this assignment. I knew what she must be thinking. She was wondering whether she shouldn't return the engagement ring.

I had to admit that when I saw Pete Hansen's name, I hardly considered how difficult it would be for Irmie to cancel the plans she'd been making. When I signed on for this assignment, I was thinking more about myself than anyone else. How dumb can I get?

CHAPTER 5

"Gentlemen, there is one thing I want to make clear. I do not intend to rest until the slimy coward who shot my husband is in captivity. Or better, until he is dead." Wanda emphasized "dead."

Neither Undersecretary Greer, Major Jones, Agent Hammond, Captain Leslie Corley, nor I felt there was anything we could add, and we remained silent. We were in Jones' office in Camp Phoenix. Having drunk three coffees in the chow hall, I was now sucking on a bottle of water.

"Speaking for myself," she continued, "I find these attacks on coalition forces, these so-called green-on-blue murders, reprehensible beyond belief. What kind of people can suddenly turn on a person they work with from day to day and then shoot him? Why can't we identify them in advance? Why are we giving these people weapons? How fucking goddamn dumb are we? Tell me that."

"It's a different world over here, Wanda," Stan said, obviously trying to mollify Wanda's feelings. I didn't envy his position. The investigation hadn't gone all that far. "Afghans live by a different set of values."

"I'm not buying that. I'm not buying that as a reason for not already having this individual in custody."

Stan gazed toward me, an expression of exasperation on his face.

"We understand your feelings, Wanda," I said, "but—"

"You understand my feelings!" Wanda repeated my words, her tone dripping with sarcasm. "Sure you do, Alex."

I went on, undeterred. "But they know we'll be out of here in two years. The ANA will—"

"I know, I know. The Afghan National Army will have to defend the country without American help. And it figures to have its hands full trying to do so."

"You're correct, Wanda. The Taliban have been regrouping and getting a lot of help from Pakistan," Stan said. "What we don't want is the Taliban reestablishing training camps. They had a sanctuary here. That's what made 9/11 possible." He paused. "That's why we're here, to prevent that from reoccurring."

"Please, Stan, please. I know all that. I don't live in a cave on a mountain somewhere. I'm stationed at the Pentagon." She paused. "Anyway, I also wonder what our trainers are actually doing. Can't they tell when one of these characters is unreliable?"

"Our people do what they can," Hammond said, not doing much better in penetrating Wanda's hostility than I had. "I talk to trainers constantly. They do their best to vet the recruits, but some of them switch sides after we take them on."

"What do you mean?"

"For whatever reason, they decide they want to ingratiate themselves with the Taliban. One way to do that is to shoot an American. Others are coerced into doing it."

"Permit me to get in on this," Doug Greer said. "Part of the problem, Wanda, is, as we draw down, the Taliban increase their efforts to infiltrate the Afghan security forces. Like Alex said, they know the day will come when we'll be gone."

I said, "From what I've been told, we've discharged dozens of people who might be Taliban sympathizers."

I focused my attention on Captain Corley, who was seated away from the table at the end of the row of file cabinets. She was a brunette, with very dark eyes and pale skin. Her expression was noncommittal, and she seemed more of an observer of the meeting than a participant. Until now, she was the only one who hadn't commented. Her fatigue uniform couldn't completely conceal her curves. I guessed her age at around thirty, maybe a year or two older.

"Any recruit suspected of having contact with the Taliban," Hammond said, "is gone. It's an ISAF rule. We've gotten rid of over a hundred so far."

"We know how you feel," Undersecretary Greer said. "I think we all feel like you. Frustrated."

I noticed Captain Corley carried her M9 in a shoulder holster. When I directed my gaze in her direction, she tilted her head and quickly glanced away. For some reason, I had a feeling she'd been observing me.

"We wish we could turn back the clock," Stan said. "But there's no way of knowing in advance who's going to commit a green-on-blue."

"All right, all right." Wanda shook her head, took a sip from her cup of coffee. "I still say Pete's death could have been prevented." She paused, nodded at me and at Hammond. "Two of the people in this room are investigating Pete's death. I'd like to know—"

"I'd also like to know," Undersecretary Greer said. "What's actually happening with the investigation?"

"Why haven't we been able to locate this Nolda person?" Wanda considered everyone at the table. "It's been ten days since he killed Pete."

"By now, he could be anywhere," Stan said, "but there's a good chance he's back in Helmand."

"We have people down there, ma'am," Hammond added. "They're asking around. We'll find him—"

"Investigating a murder over here is nothing like investigating a murder in the States," Stan interrupted. And for a lot of different reasons."

"Like what?" Wanda couldn't keep the sarcasm out of her voice.

"Like the language barrier, and the cultural barrier, and all the other barriers. We can investigate within the military community as effectively here as anywhere else, but when it comes to going out to the city, we have to depend on our interpreters."

"And don't forget the personal agendas," Hammond said. "The Afghans all have them."

Shaking her head, Wanda got to her feet. "I'm not buying all the excuses, gentlemen. In fact, that's all I've heard in the last three days, in the time I've been here. Excuses." Standing at the door, she said, "Reasons why you can't do things. You people are good at that."

A minute later Colonel Wanda Hansen was gone. Very likely, each of us breathed a sigh of relief. I know I did. I got to my feet, headed across the office to Stan's wastebasket, and dropped in my empty bottle.

Stan poured out a cup of java for himself and Greer.

"I could use something stronger than coffee at this moment," Greer said, "but I'll take it."

"She wants results," Stan said. "You can't blame her."

"I'm not blaming her."

Hammond passed me a green folder, which he'd had on his lap. "Here's the file on Nolda. Where he was born, when he enlisted. You may want to check out some of the stuff. There's the name of the captain in the outfit where he served. Bashiri. I set up an appointment for 1500."

"How about other soldiers, the people he served with?"

Hammond said, "We talked with a bunch. Most didn't have all that much to say. You can come around and see the transcripts of the interviews. I've got them all written out and translated. Basically, what we found out was zilch."

I flipped through the file, which contained lots of paper. I'd go through this stuff tonight. Briefly, I wondered what Irmie was doing at this moment. Since it was close to 1000 hours here, it would be 0630 hours in Munich. Irmie would be in her car and on the way to work, perhaps already halfway there.

Standing at the office door, Captain Corley pushed back her hair and put on her fatigue cap. She then waved a silent good-bye.

Doug Greer arched an eyebrow. "Who is she?"

Stan said, "She's got an interest in the investigation, wants to stay informed about how it's going."

"What kind of interest?" When Stan shrugged, Greer said, "She reminds me of someone, a movie actress."

Hammond grinned. "Audrey Hepburn, maybe. Except she's taller."

"If you want to see her, you'll have to take a ride down to Khost, Doug," Stan said. "She's stationed at Chapman."

"She's CIA?" We all knew that Camp Chapman was the agency station closest to Pakistan. "I don't suppose she's with the Khost Protection Force." When Stan said he thought she was, Greer seemed impressed. Or maybe just puzzled.

The Khost Protection Force is a paramilitary operation, made up largely of native Pashtuns, which effectively uses surprise to conduct across-the-border raids on the Haqqani network in North Waziristan.

Standing with his hands on his hips, Greer continued to frown. "How would she fit in with a bunch of Pashtuns?"

Nobody had an answer.

Following the short silence, I said, "I'll say this much for the KPF. They move fast. On one of the ops I was on, we went all the way to Quetta."

Greer only continued to shake his head, seemingly puzzled.

I asked Hammond, "How does someone qualify to become a soldier in the Afghan Army?"

"The truth is," he replied, "almost any male can become a soldier. The bar in this country isn't high."

"There must be some qualifications you have to meet."

Stan said, "Basically only negative. For instance, you're not supposed to be a drug addict, but there are a lot of addicts in the Army. There's not anyone around who cares enough to enforce the rules."

"You're not supposed to have a criminal record," Undersecretary Greer said. "That's critical." Pulling on his jacket, he smiled. "Even I know that." He waved and headed for the door. "See you, guys."

Stan shook his head. "But who keeps records in this country? That's one reason it's so hard to investigate over here."

Hammond said, "I can answer a lot of your questions, Alex. I have the files, and my office is right across the way."

Standing up, Hammond and I told Stan good-bye. Stan didn't appear unhappy to see us leaving. It wasn't even 1000 hours, but I had an idea he might be helping himself to one of the bottles of Weihenstephan beer that I noticed in his office refrigerator. Or maybe even to a shot from the bottle of vodka I figured he had stashed in a desk drawer.

CHAPTER 6

"HERE'S THE ENTIRE file, Alex. Everything we could gather." Hammond and I were in his office in a wooden building two minutes away from Stan's CID office. After turning on an electric heater, Hammond bustled around, opening his file cabinet and desk drawers and rummaging through papers stacked on a table beneath the window.

He dropped folders on the desk one after the other. "Let's start with Nolda's basic records, his 201 file, you might say." He reached for a sheet of paper, ran his hand across it to smooth it out. "Here is what he started with, the volunteer form. This indicates his desire to become a soldier. Also a couple of his reasons. He says he wants to defend his village. The usual baloney. As you can see, all this stuff's been translated. Haji helped with that."

The volunteer form was creased and ink blots were all over, a real mess. I shook my head at the sloppiness. The Afghan military ain't the American military, where the emphasis is very much on spit and polish, and the assumption is, if you're a squared-away soldier, you'll be a good soldier. Just another reminder that the differences between the countries begin with the fundamentals.

At that moment there was a gentle tap at the door. When Hammond opened it, I saw Captain Leslie Corley. Behind her, I could see falling snow. She said, "Bad weather. There won't be any helicopters flying to Bagram for the next couple of hours." When Hammond motioned her inside, she stamped her feet and said, "I hope I'm not interrupting. Major Jones said—"

I stood up. "Hammond's filling me in on Nolda's background."

"You're welcome to join us, ma'am," Hammond said, pulling up a chair and pointing to the coat rack.

With Captain Corley alongside me, I picked up three photographs. "Are these him?" I took a long look, trying to read the countenance of Pete's killer.

"Yeah, every recruit has to submit pictures of himself."

Nolda had a typical Afghan expression, maybe a bit resigned, but many Afghans come across that way. He had dark curly hair, heavy eyebrows, a mustache over his thin lips. He didn't appear angry, but he didn't seem happy either. All in all, he was hard to read.

As Corley and I listened, Hammond explained. "You can see the Army wanted basic information—who his parents were, where he was born. There are no records to back up what he says. Mosques don't keep track of births and marriages the way our churches do back home. These stamps indicate someone checked out what he claimed and found it to be accurate."

"How carefully do they check out these statements?" Corley asked.

Sitting next to her, I saw she had dark liquid eyes and angular features that reminded me of a long-ago girlfriend named Madeleine. If Captain Corley was anything like Madeleine, she had substantial breasts, a slim and attractive figure. As Hammond said, she did resemble Audrey Hepburn, except for her expression, which was totally businesslike. As I made an effort to refocus on what Hammond was saying, I couldn't help recalling how Madeleine enjoyed moving around in her bedroom while scantily dressed.

"I think I know the answer to that question," I said. "Not too carefully."

Hammond shook his head and shrugged. "I would say it varies. Naturally, in this country everyone can be bribed. But when no one offers them money, they'll often do their jobs right. Here are his fingerprints. Here's another form. Some elders from his village commenting on his character. He didn't seem to have any problem getting people to put in a good word for him." Hammond paused. "That, I would say, is in his favor. When I was in his village, I got the impression most people liked him."

"How about these other forms?" Corley pointed at some official-looking documents.

"These describe his military service, ma'am. He was out in the west, and he seems to have been a good soldier. There's even a report in here from one of our trainers attesting that he carried out orders, never caused problems. He was involved in a couple of firefights, did a good job of shooting up the Talibs. All in all, not a bad guy, it would seem."

"No reason to suspect him, in other words." I was thinking of Wanda's point that we should be able to figure out in advance who the green-on-blue killers would be.

"None at all," Hammond said.

I opened a manila folder filled with paper. On the cover was a label: "For Official Use Only." Beneath the label was a stamp: "Law Enforcement Sensitive."

"This is all our investigation," Hammond explained. "That's Fred Markham's Investigation Report. Fred was the agent who handled the investigation and did most of the local interviewing. But he's gone, left earlier this week for the States." When I went through the stack, I found a sketch of the murder scene and photographs of Pete lying on the floor in a pool of blood. It wasn't necessary to comment. I pushed the pile to Corley, who began going through it.

Hammond continued, "This packet here are the interviews. Fred did some, and I did some." When I asked which might be worth following up on, Hammond said, "I talked with Captain Page. They worked together in the Oversight and Accountability office. When we spoke, it was right after it happened, like the next day. To be honest, I don't think he was telling me everything." I nodded, recalling Stan saying he hadn't gotten much out of Page either.

Hammond said, "You can talk with him. His office is in ISAF Headquarters."

There were eight or nine other statements from NATO people who worked in the Headquarters building, none of them particularly helpful. After passing them to Corley, I couldn't keep from again glancing at her smooth pale skin. Recalling Audrey Hepburn, I remembered how her eyes twinkled. Captain Corley's eyes were cold.

"We talked with people," Hammond said, "but got pretty much the same answer from everyone. We figure Pete was killed shortly after noon. Most people were on their lunch breaks. What I should also mention, the murder took place on a Wednesday. Nolda had been on leave for the week before, and this was his first day back."

Corley said, "What time did he come into work on that day?"

"The Headquarters guards signed him in at . . . let's see . . . at 0950 hours. He was late."

I checked the sign-in log. "That means he was in the office for much of the morning." When Hammond nodded, I said, "And we assume he killed Pete and then walked out of the building."

"That's the way it must have happened," Hammond said. "At that time Colonel Hansen was alone in his office. Nolda had the desk on the far side of the room." Hammond pointed to one of the photos, which showed how Pete's office was laid out. "After committing the murder, he left the building. It was a while before anyone knew Pete was dead."

As I flipped through the interviews, one comment caught my eye. It was from Captain Page. I remembered Stan saying Page and Pete worked in the same office and used to talk from time to time. "Here's a guy who says Pete seemed to be growing more despondent by the day. What would cause him to be despondent?"

"Did he have personal problems?" Corley asked.

"Who knows?" Hammond said. "He had a tough job with a lot of pressure, that much I know."

I made a note to interview Page.

"You also spoke to this Afghan officer? Nolda's company commander?"

Hammond shrugged. "Over at Black Horse. I didn't get much out of him."

"Okay." I knew Black Horse was one of the ANA training installations in Kabul. "Does he speak English?"

"Indeed," Corley said. Again I couldn't help noticing how clipped her comments were—and how little she seemed to reveal of herself. I briefly wondered if it was intentional, then decided it was.

"Yeah, Bashiri speaks English," Hammond said. "But you might want to bring Haji or one of the other interpreters just in case."

Corley said, "I was at the main gate last night. Someone was asking about you. He wanted your name."

"I tipped over a guy's fruit stand," I said. "There were watermelons all over."

She got to her feet. "He had nothing to do with fruit stands."

Shoving all my notes into a large envelope, I stood up and shook hands with Hammond.

"I'm leaving, too," Corley said as she zipped up her field jacket.

When we were outside, I was surprised by how thick the snow had become. I said, "I could go for something warm. Tea? Coffee?"

"Some tea might be nice."

I pointed the way toward the Green Bean, the coffee shop located just off Camp Phoenix's main drag.

When we'd gotten our tea and found places at one of the long wooden tables, I said, "What makes someone like Nolda tick?"

"Do you mean, what leads him to want to shoot someone he works with day after day?" When I nodded, "Any number of things, assuming it was Nolda who committed the murder."

"Doesn't it look that way?"

The big room was drafty and, with a couple of dozen GIs letting off steam, noisy. It seemed Captain Corley had a somewhat different take on Pete's murder than everyone else.

"We'll know more when we catch up with him . . . if we catch up with him." Before I could comment, she said, "How much do you know about what Colonel Hansen was working on?"

"So far, not a great deal. Why?"

"It could be important."

"What exactly was he working on?"

"He was investigating the failure of the Kabul Bank. I assume you know about that." She fixed me with a searing stare. "You could be approaching this from the wrong direction."

"You're suggesting that what Pete was working on is what we should be looking at." I recalled the envelope full of stories about the bank that Jerry had given me.

"I'll go even further than that, Mr. Klear. I'd go so far as to say this wasn't a green-on-blue."

"Do you have evidence to back up that statement, ma'am?"

Rather than answer the question, she said, "I understand that you knew Colonel Hansen personally."

I wondered how she knew that. "We got to know one another back in the States."

"At Fort Bragg?" When I nodded, she said, "You knew his wife, too. She had quite a bit to say at the meeting."

"She's upset." But even as I said the words, I realized I was making excuses for Wanda. This conversation had taken a turn I hadn't anticipated.

I watched as Corley punched some numbers into her phone and spent half a minute listening. Then she drank the last of her tea and began zipping up her field jacket. "The snow's letting up. A helicopter is getting ready to fly to Bagram. From there it shouldn't be a problem getting a flight down to Khost." She stuck out her hand. "It's been nice meeting you, Mr. Klear."

"Alex."

"Good luck with your interview with Nolda's company commander."

Without saying anything more, she turned and left.

*　*　*

Captain Jarheed Bashiri had a round, pleasant face and a friendly handshake. My appointment was for 1500 hours, and Haji and I had arrived a few minutes early, having driven over to Black Horse in my van. At least the snow had let up. Hammond had said Captain Bashiri had been in charge of Nolda's company when Nolda was stationed in Kabul. My first impression after entering his office, which was on the second floor of a wooden building on the Black Horse training facility, was that Captain Bashiri paid only casual attention to the clerical end of his job.

Clutter was all over, and it seemed every flat surface had piles of paper on it. The first thing Bashiri did after our arrival was order his assistant to brew tea. Although Bashiri spoke English, I had Haji with me just in case.

While we were waiting, I asked an obvious question. "What kind of soldier was Sergeant Nolda?"

Bashiri touched his hand to his mustache. "Better than most, I would say. But not . . . *bihbud*. His uniform was not always perfect. Otherwise, okay, I would say."

Bashiri's own uniform didn't look that sharp. His tunic was wrinkled, for one thing, and his brass was smudged. He assured me that he was very unhappy about Colonel Hansen's death. He said he had never met him personally, but like all officers in the Afghan Army, he was upset by the news. When he said, "Green-on-blue very bad," I agreed.

For the first five minutes, I hadn't needed Haji's help.

Bashiri said, "Corporal Nolda spoke some English, which made him . . . *shoeh*."

"Valuable," Haji said.

"Yes, valuable in office. Americans will never learn Pashto or Dari." When I nodded and said that was true enough, he smiled.

After telling him his English was also very good, I said, "What I really want to know about are his political affiliations. Was he a Taliban sympathizer?"

Bashiri shrugged. "Not that I know of."

Obviously perturbed by Bashiri's curt answers, Haji interrupted. Speaking in rapid Pashto, he asked a number of questions, then he said, "Even if he were a Taliban sympathizer, Captain Bashiri says it is unlikely that he would know that. Nolda would certainly not have advertised the fact. He would have kept it to himself."

"Ask him if Nolda had friends."

After a brief exchange, Haji said, "Yes. He had friends. Bashiri says Nolda and the other soldiers spent a lot of time watching videos on their telephones. Silly shows, people singing, making senseless comments."

"Who were his friends?"

"Bashiri says the friends were other members of his platoon. If he had friends outside the military, he would not know that."

I nodded. "The way he describes him, Nolda doesn't sound much different from a lot of other people his age." When Haji asked if I had any other questions, I said, "Ask him why he thinks Nolda joined the Army."

When they'd finished yakking, Haji said, "Captain Bashiri thinks he joined for the same reason most Afghan men join the Army. Because they can't find work anywhere else. Captain Bashiri also says Nolda was married and he needed an income." Haji paused. "He says the man from your CID already asked some of these questions."

When the cell phone on his desk went off, Bashiri stood up suddenly and announced he had to leave. As we stood uncertainly at the door, he spoke briefly with Haji.

After a second, Haji said, "Captain Bashiri has kindly arranged for us to talk with a *dost,* a friend of Nolda's. They were soldiers in the same platoon." Bashiri pointed to an Afghan soldier standing forlornly in the corridor outside the office.

With Bashiri gone, Haji did the honors, telling me the soldier's name was Gholam.

Outside the building, we walked across the muddy installation to a row of wooden buildings in front of which was a stand selling fruit and vegetables. I paid for three apples and told Haji to ask Gholam if he'd like anything else. After he shook his head, we found benches, which were located beneath a canvas tarp and which provided some protection from the wind.

According to Haji, Gholam got to know Nolda when they were teenagers. Haji said, "Nolda's first job was working for a man in a bazaar, selling vegetables, but he could not make a living. The man who owned the stand did not pay him enough. They had an argument, and Nolda quit the job. He says around this time Nolda began studying English."

I said, "Nolda sounds ambitious."

"Gholam says Nolda later found a job with a security firm and guarded buildings. He says Nolda arranged for him to also get a job with that firm. But then the firm lost its contract, and they were both again out of work. That was when they both decided to join the Army.

"Gholam says Nolda joined the Army because he knew some English and thought this would help him. He says Nolda's wife is still back in their village."

"Anything else?"

"Gholam says Nolda liked the Army."

I said, "Pete was Nolda's boss. Ask Gholam if Nolda was mad at his boss."

After a brief exchange, Haji shook his head. "Gholam says Nolda liked working for Americans. He doubts his friend was mad at his superiors."

I said to Haji, "Ask this guy the sixty-four-thousand-dollar question. Then we'll get going."

"Sixty-four-thousand-dollar question, Alex?"

"That means the important question. Ask him if his buddy Nolda was a Taliban sympathizer." After some back and forth, Haji shook his head. "Gholam says Nolda despised the Taliban."

"Did he say why?"

"Yes. He says his uncle was a farmer and grew poppies, but the Taliban kept taxing him. And they kept increasing the taxes. Finally, his uncle said he could not pay any more, and they killed him. In Nolda's village, Gholam says, the Taliban committed many atrocities and no one liked them."

"Ask him if he thinks Nolda was the kind of person to commit a green-on-blue killing."

A second later, Haji said, "Loosely translated, Alex, Gholam says Nolda is not a person who would carry out a killing like that."

"Ask him if he's sure."

"He says he knows Nolda as well as anyone, and he's sure."

"Ask him if he's only saying that because Nolda is his *dost*."

"Gholam will be offended if I ask him again."

"Ask him anyway."

When Gholam didn't get mad and only laughed, I had an idea Haji hadn't posed the question I asked him to pose, and they'd spent a couple of minutes talking about girls or sports. I knew we'd squeezed as much useful information out of Gholam as we were going to get.

After giving Gholam a ride across Black Horse to his barracks, I drove back to Camp Phoenix. We walked back to the Green Bean, where we got on the beverage line.

While we waited, Haji shook his head. "Not much progress."

When I asked Haji if he felt Gholam was being honest, Haji scratched his head. When I said, "Well?" Haji looked away toward the room's big windows, then shrugged.

I was finding it harder and harder to get a yes or no answer out of Haji. Maybe the fact that he was born thirty-one years ago into a chaotic country contributed to his skepticism where America was concerned. Like a lot of Afghans, Haji had seen them come and go. First, the warlords, then the Russians, then the Taliban, and now us.

Maybe because they've experienced so much history close-up, many Afghans tend to take things in stride. That fact wasn't going to make my job easier. Like all Afghans, Haji knew America was scheduled to leave Afghanistan at the end of 2014. That meant the official end of Operation Enduring Freedom, the military operation that had kicked off in October 2001.

Finally, Haji said, "I think Gholam was being honest, Alex. Yes."

"If you're right, that presents a small problem. Assuming Gholam is a good judge of character, Nolda is not the person who shot Colonel Hansen."

After we'd given our tea orders, Haji said, "I see what you mean, Alex. But all the other people are positive it was Nolda who killed Colonel Hansen."

"They are relying on the information they have, and it all seems to point in that direction. But they have not spoken with Gholam, as we have. Who should we believe, Haji?"

I knew Haji wouldn't answer the questions. Like most Afghans, he is innately cautious, and when dealing with foreigners, he tends to be suspicious.

With the sun still shining, we decided to brave the chill and drink our tea down on the smoking deck. We found a table near the street where we could observe the action.

Haji smiled, sighed, gazed at me with his alert dark eyes. "It is difficult, Alex. People don't like to talk. Captain Bashiri was very reticent. Even if Nolda was a Taliban sympathizer, it's not likely he would tell you."

A boisterous group of Marines from a newly arrived company of leathernecks went by on the road. In a couple of days they'd be out in the provinces mixing it up with the Talibs. I could have told them that by shooting up the countryside they wouldn't be helping much in bringing our two nations together.

"I see what you mean, Haji."

In the distance the sky was a clear blue, and the mountains were a visible reminder of Afghanistan's rugged natural beauty.

I couldn't blame the Afghans for not wanting to talk to Americans.

At least not wanting to talk honestly and openly. In their eyes, we were unpredictable.

I watched soldiers drifting around and military vehicles moving back and forth on Camp Phoenix's main street. It was already clear to me that in Afghanistan it's difficult to accomplish even the simplest tasks. I had a feeling it was going to be impossible to agree on who had killed Pete Hansen to everyone's satisfaction.

And, I had my doubts about Sergeant Nolda being the murderer.

With his hand around his cup of tea, Haji watched me, his head tilted. He, too, was an enigma, and I was finding it difficult to know what he was thinking.

I asked, "Is it possible Nolda was pressured to kill Colonel Hansen?"

Haji hesitated, then nodded. "The Taliban threaten a soldier's family to force him to do what they want. That has happened." When I said I wasn't satisfied with the way our interviews had gone, Haji said, "The people are difficult. They do not like it when I come around asking a lot of questions. This is a difficult job, Alex."

"All jobs are difficult. That's why you get paid."

"I don't get paid enough." One of the things Afghans have acquired from Americans is an interest in money.

"None of us do."

"I was out at the gate last night, Alex. Captain Corley was also there. She was talking to a messenger from the father of the boy."

"Captain Corley speaks Pashto?"

"Yes. Perfectly."

"What were they talking about?"

"I do not overhear other people's conversations."

I resisted an urge to ask Haji who he thought he was kidding.

I took a last swallow of tea and stood up. The next individual on my list was Captain Eric Page, who worked in the ISAF Headquarters building. Hammond said Page had worked closely with Pete. I decided this might be a good time to drop by. I told Haji good-bye and walked back to the van. With the sun now shining and the storm over, driving had become less hazardous.

At the entrance to the ISAF compound, I flashed my badge and explained my business to the Afghan sentries.

Holding down the fort behind a desk outside Captain Page's office was a young African-American sergeant in starched fatigues. Her name plaque said she was Sergeant Payne.

When I'd identified myself and said my visit related to Colonel Pete Hansen, she shook her head. "Captain Page is out at Herat. We expect him back either late today or early tomorrow." Herat is way out at the western end of the country, not far from the border with Iran. I thanked her and said I'd drop by the next day.

The last thing I did that evening was call Irmie, but I only got her machine. I knew I had to make amends. "It's evening here, Irmie. Whenever a day ends, I tell myself that I'm one day closer to seeing you again. I love you, honey. I love you."

CHAPTER 7

"Have you ever been in an Afghan hospital, Alex?" It was the voice of Stan Jones, and my bedside digital clock said it was 0210 hours. When I said, "Huh?" Stan said, "Meet Todd over at Phoenix, at the main gate. Ten minutes. Don't be late."

Before I had time to mumble a "yes, sir," Stan had hung up.

Less than ten minutes later, Todd Hammond and I were in a van with a female sergeant driving us through the streets of Kabul, which were lit only by an occasional market fire or the headlights of another vehicle.

"Major Jones thought you'd want to be in on this," Hammond said. "They've found Nolda. He's dead. His body washed up on the shore of one of the lakes."

"Which lake?"

"The big one, the reservoir. It's only four or five miles outside the city. I forget the name. There's a dam out there."

"Qargha Lake?"

"Yeah, that's it. Whoever found him took his body to the hospital where they treat the Afghan security forces, cops, and soldiers. Dawood Military Hospital. I was only there once. It's pretty chaotic. It's not like an American hospital. No one speaks English."

When I said, "That's where we're going?" Hammond only nodded.

We drove up the Airport Road past the Mahoud Intersection, turned off, drove down a couple of hundred yards, then pulled into a large parking area behind a six-story rectangular building. I assumed this was Dawood Military Hospital. Two American military vehicles were parked near the hospital's admitting entrance, which was lit by a pair of bright bulbs. Three or four people, all Afghans, wearing blue smocks and obviously taking a smoke break, eyed us silently as we climbed out of our vehicle.

On our way into the building, I said, "Morgue?"

Although I repeated the word a couple of times, saying it loudly and clearly, no one responded.

Inside was a large desk manned by a bearded individual in a blue smock. Behind him was a long dimly lit corridor. He didn't know the word "morgue" either. Not that I'd expected him to.

The wards were located on either side of the corridor. We peeked in, saw patients in beds. I wondered about the kind of care these people were getting. Many were in obvious pain. One guy had bloody open gashes on one leg.

When Hammond said something about "staying out of hospitals in this country," I nodded. Where were the nurses?

A sign said "OT," which I knew meant operating theater. There seemed to be half-a-dozen of them. Further on, we saw a room that was probably the pharmacy. A guy standing at a counter looked at us blankly. He didn't know the word "morgue" either. A big room turned out to be the Intensive Care Unit. After more wandering, we finally found someone to ask, a red-haired woman dressed in scrubs who told us in a German accent that there was a ward just for "*die wichtigen Leute*"—in other words, VIPs. I told her we wanted the *Leichenschauhaus*.

She pointed down a corridor and said the morgue was adjacent to the side entrance, in the hospital basement.

After finding the entrance, we saw a flight of stone steps leading downward.

We found the morgue and walked into a dismal room. The only light came from scattered small bulbs, and the air was saturated with the smell of formaldehyde. A couple of fans were blowing, keeping the air cool. Half-a-dozen bodies, each covered by a cloth, hadn't yet been placed up on the racks and lay alongside one another on pallets that were on the ground. Two uniformed military police nodded when they saw us. While we were introducing ourselves, two workers carrying a stretcher with a body beneath a piece of cloth entered the room, dropped the stretcher, and left.

Hammond only shrugged. One of the MPs winced as if to say that's the way they do things over here.

"I'm Sergeant Olin. You're here to see this Nolda guy?" When we said we were, he pointed, then walked down the row of bodies. We all pulled out our flashlights. He yanked off a sheet, exposing a bloated corpse.

"A floater," Hammond said. "Looks like he was in the water a couple of days." For good reason, Hammond stuck his handkerchief over his nose. The corpse stank.

Overcoming my aversion to bad smells, I got down on my haunches and shone my flashlight into the corpse's eyes, on his face, on his skin. I pulled back some of his clothing to see that portions of his body were totally gone. I wondered whether he wasn't in the water longer than *a couple of days*. Body parts had been eaten away, the result, I assumed, of having been dead quite a while. And the corpse was so bloated it seemed to have ballooned.

"Someone fished him out of the reservoir, sir. Because he was wearing a uniform, they called someone from ANA, and they called us."

"And then they brought him up here?" I asked, getting back to my feet.

Sergeant Olin nodded. "This is the hospital for Afghan security people, sir. Dispatcher told us to come out here. No ID, just dog tags. That's how they ID'd him."

I took another look. Despite the condition of the body, there were enough facial features to see this was definitely the guy whose picture Hammond had showed me. This was our man.

When Hammond asked what I thought, I said, "We need to autopsy the body."

"Right. Get the cause of death. He drowned, apparently."

"He'd been in the water awhile. Is there anyone around here who can perform an autopsy?"

"Probably is." Hammond took the MPs aside and told them to stay with the corpse. "Nobody touches the body. Is that clear?"

"How long, sir?"

"Not too long, hopefully. We have to autopsy the body. If we can't get a doctor over here, we fly the body to Bagram." Back upstairs, we started asking around. "They must have some Americans working here."

After ten minutes of trying to find someone who spoke English, we decided that 0400 hours probably wasn't the best time to obtain information. Hammond said he'd make an official inquiry later in the day, and we headed back outside.

"Breakfast?" I said when we were again in the van.

"Yeah, and I think we should invite someone," Hammond said. "What do you think?"

"Wanda? Why not?"

"I'll report everything to Major Jones." Then Hammond told the driver to take us to ISAF Headquarters.

*   *   *

An hour later, Hammond, Stan Jones, and I were wolfing down breakfast in the Headquarters dining facility, one of the few military chow halls where you'll find silverware and plates. I'd loaded my plate down with an omelet, sausage, and toast. Since I hadn't eaten the previous evening, I was hungry.

"You guys are sure?" Stan asked. "You're sure it was Nolda at the hospital?"

"It was him, all right." Hammond smeared a piece of toast with butter. "There was enough left of him so you could tell."

"So that pretty much wraps it up."

I said, "Not necessarily. Pete was killed eleven days ago. The body was bloated. Badly. It had ballooned. Lots of body parts had been eaten away."

"That's for sure," Hammond said. "It really stank."

"That body could have been in the water for two weeks," I said. "We need a pathologist to examine him."

Stan grabbed his coffee cup. "What are you, Alex, some kind of expert? Why bother with a pathologist?"

"Pete was killed eleven days ago, on January 23. Right? If he was in the water for two weeks, that means Nolda didn't kill Pete. That's all. We want to be sure."

Stan rolled his eyes. "Is this why you're here, Alex? To cause problems?"

"You're causing the problems, Stan."

"What's that supposed to mean?"

"It means there won't be any problems if you do your job right. I say we try to pinpoint the time of Nolda's death." If I was being insistent on this topic, it was because I was already having second thoughts about Nolda being Pete's killer.

Hammond continued to eat, pretending not to hear.

A couple of minutes later we were joined by Wanda, who was

carrying a tray. She slid in opposite me. Before she could comment, Stan said, "Baram Nolda has turned up. He's dead."

Hammond went on to describe our visit to the hospital.

"You say he was in one of the lakes?" Wanda's frown turned to disgust. She let the piece of toast in her hand fall back down on her plate.

"I think he'd been there awhile," I said.

Stan said, "What makes you so goddamn sure?"

"I'm not sure. But that's a mountain lake. The water's cold. The body wouldn't decompose as fast in cold water."

Stan glared. "How the fuck do you know how cold the water out there is?"

"There's a resort at Qargha. Two years ago a bunch of us drove out there. The water was cold. I didn't stay in longer than five minutes."

Stan tossed down his fork but didn't say anything more.

"It was definitely badly decomposed," Hammond said. "Who would've killed him?" Hammond seemed to be asking himself the question more than he was asking us.

"And why?" Wanda said.

"If we can get one of the local docs for an autopsy, we do it," Hammond said. "I'll call the dispensary."

I shook my head. "There won't be a pathologist at the dispensary."

"Then we send him over to Bagram," Hammond said, "to the hospital there. Let them do it."

Stan frowned. "That might be the best option in any case. The medical people there are okay, and they have a pathologist."

"You want a ride out to the hospital?" Hammond asked Wanda.

"I want to see the son of a bitch," Wanda said abruptly.

Both Stan and I were surprised by the sudden harshness of Wanda's tone, although I don't suppose we should have been.

Indifferent to our reaction, she glared at us. "The son of a bitch killed my husband. I definitely want to see him." She stood up, slurped some coffee. To Hammond, she said, "Are you ready to drive me out?"

* * *

At shortly after 1000 hours I arrived at Captain Eric Page's Headquarters building office, where I was told that Captain Page had gotten back from Herat roughly an hour before and was now in a meeting. Sitting in a chair in the anteroom outside his office, I killed time with a four-day-old copy of *Stars and Stripes*. After twenty minutes, I watched as a pair of young officers came trooping out. Five minutes later, a thin, sandy-haired guy in fatigues with two bars on his shoulders stepped out of the office. We shook hands, and Captain Page pointed me inside.

"I got your message. You want to know about Pete?" He paused, scratched his cheek. "You're investigating the case?" When I nodded, he said, "CID?" When I shook my head, he frowned. "Can I ask for some ID?"

I couldn't blame Page for being mildly puzzled. Although I still wasn't completely sure what it was Jerry Shenlee wanted me to do, I'd begun to sense that things weren't adding up. And according to Captain Corley, I should be trying to find out what it was Pete had been working on.

I said, "If you give Major Jones a call, he'll verify who I am. Someone in D.C. asked me to come over."

He hesitated when I said that. Just the mention of Stan Jones seemed to be enough to put Page at ease, at least a little bit at ease, but he'd frowned at the mention of D.C. After nervously pushing some papers back and forth on his desk, he said, "Anything in particular I can help you with?"

"Anything you can tell me could be helpful."

"In what way?"

"I've heard you and Pete were colleagues but also friends."

Page frowned. "Yeah, you could say that. We were. It was really tragic that happening. Have they got him yet?"

"We think so." I went on to explain how Hammond and I had seen Nolda's body the previous evening.

Page's face took on a blank expression. "Nolda worked in our office. Seemed like an okay guy. But I guess you never know. Not until it's too late."

I asked Page what he could tell me about Pete.

"Pete changed over the time I knew him, which was eight, close to nine months. I'm not sure exactly what the cause was, but as time went on he became despondent."

"What do you mean? 'Despondent'?"

"Pete and I worked here in adjacent offices. When I first got to know him he was an upbeat guy. Didn't let things bother him. He could give almost anything that happened a humorous twist."

"I know what you mean. I knew him personally."

Page relaxed when I said that. He leaned forward, lowered his voice. "But then he started to change. Little things began to get to him. It's hard to explain. One obvious thing. When I first got to know him, he was looking forward to going home, used to talk about it. But then, he stopped talking about it."

"Nothing more than that?"

"He began talking about extending again. He said to me one day, 'Even with all the red tape and military chickenshit, I have fewer headaches over here.'"

I nodded, recalling that Stan had said something similar. "Most people like the idea of returning to the States."

"Sure. I'm going back in a couple of months, and I'm already counting days. But Pete had things on his mind." Page hesitated, as though he was about to say something but then thought better of it.

"Whatever was bothering him, do you think it was personal or job related?"

"The job was definitely bothering him. He told me once he was finding out things he wished he wasn't finding out. I got the impression he was maybe finding out stuff that was gonna get him in trouble." Page paused. "If you know what I mean."

I shook my head and he continued, "Pete one time said he couldn't believe the scope of the stuff he was dealing with. He used that word 'scope.'"

"What was he working on?"

Page's expression clouded. "The Kabul Bank. Where the money went." He paused. "I can't say much more than that."

Under normal circumstances, the military wouldn't involve itself with the Kabul Bank and its missing money. Had Pete stumbled onto something? Page eyed me silently, perhaps wondering if I'd picked up on that. I sensed that Page knew more than he wanted to tell. "Did Pete ever mention names?"

"No. What he was doing was highly hush-hush."

"What did he do all day?"

"He used to spend a lot of time going over printouts, numbers, that sort of thing. Because he said so little about what he was doing, I never asked. You know what I mean, I'm sure. But half the stuff going on in this department here is hush-hush." He flashed a grim smile.

"Nothing too unusual there."

"No. We can't talk with reporters without getting permission."

"And if you ask for permission, they tell you 'no.'"

"I don't suppose you know anything about the Threat Finance Cell." When I said Major Jones had mentioned some people investigating the bank, Page said, "They're trying to find out what happened. Top secret stuff. They're from Treasury, the FBI, the Pentagon, you name it. Pete said when our government asked Karzai who we should appoint to run the bank, he gave them names, all his buddies. Sherkan Farnood and Khalil Ferozi ended up being the top bank officials. Ferozi never had anything to do with finance."

"Pete knew all this?"

"Another guy Pete was investigating was Omar Zakhilwal, the finance minister. According to Pete, Zakhilwal collected nearly a hundred million in bribes from the bank. It's amazing how much Pete knew. The bank officials bribed any number of Afghan government people."

Page paused, shook his head.

"A couple of times Pete spoke about the amount of money our government is spending over here. That led me to believe he knew something about how we were financing the war. He used the word 'unbelievable.'"

"What was unbelievable? The amount of money the war was costing?"

"No, we all know the war's costing a helluva lot of money. Something else." He shook his head again. "But like I said before, Mr. Klear—"

"Alex."

"—Pete was pretty depressed for the last couple of months. But exactly what was bothering him, I don't know. I'm sorry I can't be more precise."

"Don't be sorry, Captain." I stood up. I sensed that Page knew a lot more than he wanted to tell me. I said, "Pete wasn't the kind of guy to bother other people with his problems."

"That's for sure."

After we shook hands, I scrawled my telephone number on a card with my name on it. I told Captain Page to give me a shout if he recalled anything about Pete that struck him as unusual.

* * *

"It really is nice to see you again, Alex. Even under these circumstances." Wanda smiled, and we touched glasses, both of which contained Sprite.

I'd invited Wanda for a late lunch, and we were in a cozy corner of Sufi Restaurant, opposite a wall with a lot of pictures of turbaned elders. Although we had chosen a table, people in the adjacent dining room were seated on cushions on the floor. We'd each had kabob, and now we were dawdling over dessert.

"It's pleasant here. I'm kind of surprised there are places like this in Kabul."

"There's a garden outside, which is great in the nice weather if you don't mind sharing your food with lots of flies."

"But what really makes lunch here so nice is it helps me forget seeing the murderer of my husband." Wanda shuddered. "His body was horrible to look at."

I decided that this might not be the best moment to comment. I was convinced that the corpse Wanda had seen at the hospital wasn't that of Pete's murderer.

"Thanks for the tour. Kabul is different from what I expected."

I'd taken Wanda on a brief tour of downtown. "Kabul gets a lot of bad publicity, but it's a big city with all kinds of things going on. Right now, we're not far from ISAF Headquarters."

"The big yellow building? The one with all the flags in front?"

I pointed toward the window. "This is Butcher Street. You drive down a little further, you see our Embassy. Further down is the Afghan Parliament. A few years back, a suicide bomber tried to drive a car filled with explosives into the entrance of Parliament. He got close, caused a lot of damage."

"I remember reading about it. That's the reason for all the checkpoints, I assume." When I nodded, she said, "I'm beginning to go bonkers alone in my room." She shook her head. "I miss Pete."

Wanda picked up her glass, gazed into it, then took a small sip. Her dark blond hair hung to her shoulders. She was wearing a long-sleeved jacket and white blouse, which wasn't her sexiest outfit, but in Kabul, the less skin a woman shows the better. Out in the villages, women are expected to wear burqas, and you seldom see them on the street.

"I was really surprised to see you here. I mean, after all these years . . ."

"I thought you'd forgotten about me, and I couldn't blame you if you had. First, you married Pete, then you needed to pay attention to your career. I thought I'd receded into the black hole of total forgetfulness."

"Let me tell you something, Alex. You may have come in second to Pete, but it was a close second, a very close second. I liked you. I liked you very much. Anyway, you didn't propose to me. Pete did. I mean, what's a girl to do?"

At that moment a waiter arrived to refill our glasses. Wanda was right about the Sufi Restaurant. It was a nice place. With the waiter gone, she smiled at me, sighed. "Who would have thought we'd ever meet again? And under these circumstances." She paused, gazing over my shoulder toward the window. "I wasn't sure . . . if it would be the right thing to do."

"You mean to come over?"

"Yes. But somehow I just felt I had to do it. Do you understand?"

"I think I do, although in your place I wouldn't make things unnecessarily hard on myself."

"I wasn't sure if people would understand. And do you understand why I just had to go out to that hospital today and see that person?" When I nodded, she said, "Anyway, as I was saying, Alex. If you'd only paid me a little more attention way back when instead of lavishing all your attentions on Katherine. It was really too much the way you two, I mean . . ."

"Do I detect a tiny spark of jealousy?"

"Of course you do. Is there anything wrong with that? Katherine used to tell me all kinds of things about you."

"Like what?"

"I know that . . . well, that you're a sound sleeper." When I frowned, Wanda laughed. "You'd be surprised the things women talk about. But she also said you're . . . well, energetic? That's not exactly the right word, but you may know what I mean." She paused, her blue eyes twinkling. "You know, Alex, I'm just a little surprised to hear you're finally settling down."

"Why's that?"

"Oh, there's something about you, a kind of restlessness, maybe, that makes you different. I hope you'll be happy—"

At that moment my phone began to vibrate. It was Stan, and he sounded excited. "You're not gonna believe this, Alex. The body's gone, disappeared."

"Nolda's body?" When Stan grunted a yes, I said, "How the heck—"

"Don't ask me. There was some delay in the medical people coming over from Bagram. I guess that's what it was. I'm not sure. That's what we arranged. A doctor at the Bagram hospital was set to handle the autopsy."

"An autopsy would have been good. We could have figured out how long he was in the water. At least we'd get some idea."

"Well, I suppose it's not the end of the world. I'm busy, but come around later. I'll try to have the individuals in here who were supposed to be guarding the corpse. We can find out what happened."

After hanging up, I asked Wanda, "When did you see Nolda's body? At about what time?"

"I guess about 0730 hours. I rode over with Hammond. Why? You sound excited."

I told Wanda what Stan had just told me. I said, "Who was there in the morgue when you were there?"

"There was a morgue attendant, and yes, one of our people, a sergeant. Why?"

"We gave orders to a couple of MPs to guard the body. Evidently, they screwed up."

Wanda poked at the remains of her dessert. I took a long swallow of water. "The simplest kind of job, and they couldn't handle it." I may have groaned.

"I'm glad I at least saw the individual who shot my husband. But why are you so upset?"

Before I could answer, my telephone began vibrating. It was Stan again. Still mad, I answered with an angry "What now?"

"I got hold of the MPs, 1500 hours. It's one thing after another here."

"That was Stan again. He's not happy." But I had to wonder if he was really as unhappy as he sounded. I was the only one insisting on an autopsy.

Wanda said, "You don't seem happy either."

"I suppose I'm not." I didn't want to reveal the reason at that moment to Wanda, but Nolda's body suddenly disappearing was one of those things that never should have happened. This figured to make it more difficult for me to prove that someone else, not Nolda, had killed Pete. I did my best to smile. "You're right. What am I getting excited about?"

"You're also excited because Nolda's body isn't around. Same question: Is *that* a problem?"

"It could be. His body appeared to have been in the water for a while." I paused. "When was Pete shot? Eleven days ago, right?" When she nodded, I said, "If his body was in the water for longer than eleven days that would suggest he—"

"Suggest what?"

"Suggest he didn't kill Pete. That someone else did."

Wanda frowned. "I see what you're getting at, Alex. But if Nolda's body isn't available, we can't be sure. What can we do?"

"Maybe we'll find it." But I wasn't too optimistic about that happening. It was probably back in the drink somewhere, this time with weights to hold it down.

Wanda gazed downward, began toying with the stem of her glass. "Can we talk about other things?"

"Like what?"

"Anything except the disappearance of Nolda's body. It's a difficult subject for me. I feel sick when I think about . . . that person."

I said, "You want to find Pete's murderer, don't you?"

When she only nodded, I said, "I realize this is all very depressing, but it's necessary. We have to talk about it. I have to ask you questions. There's no way around it."

Wanda's eyes flashed a grim smile, and she reached across the table and touched my hand. "Thank you, Alex."

"For what?"

"For being so patient. I realize I have been letting things get to me."

A moment of silence followed. Finally, Wanda said, "Things were so different the last time we saw one another. My God! Was it really fifteen years ago?"

"We were young then."

Wanda said, "I didn't realize it, but we were, weren't we? You know I was crazy about you back then."

"If you liked me so much, why didn't you show it a little more?"

"I did, but you weren't picking up my signals."

"Too much interference?"

"I guess. I admit some of it was provided by Pete, if not all of it."

I said, "You two really made a nice pair. Even I have to concede that."

"That's nice, Alex. Nice that you should say that. Getting married to Pete there in the Fort Bragg chapel"—she touched a tissue to her eyes—"with my parents there, all the way in from Minnesota . . ." She sighed. "It was the happiest day of my life. I can't tell you how much I miss him."

For the next couple of minutes, we did our best to stay away from any subject that might touch on Pete.

I shouldn't have said it, but I did. "You still have a nice smile, Wanda."

"Thank you, but I don't smile much anymore." She hesitated. "Not as much as I used to anyway."

The melancholy thought occurred to me that none of us do.

"How is Kabul for shopping?"

"Good for rugs and shawls. Do you like to haggle?"

She laughed. "I love to haggle."

"Then you'll like Chicken Street. I'll drive you over."

When I caught the waiter's attention, I made a scribbling motion with my hands, letting him know we wanted to pay. Later, as I drove back to Phoenix, I was surprised to see that it was already 1420 hours. Time had flown by.

CHAPTER 8

"At ease, Sergeant. All right, start from the beginning."

From behind his cluttered steel desk Major Stanley Jones glared at Staff Sergeant Henry Olin, the MP we'd met at the Dawood Hospital morgue. I was seated on a straight-backed chair to Olin's right, my legs crossed and a cardboard cup of java balanced precariously on my right knee.

"We did just as we were told, sir. We waited around for someone to arrive to haul away the body. The place was a madhouse. People coming, people going. Nobody was speaking English."

"Wasn't anybody there in charge?"

"A guy in the corner behind the desk. He came in at six. He did a lot of talking. Then this Afghan guy came in, talked with the guy at the desk. He spoke English. Colonel Hansen came in and we showed her the body. After a while, the Afghan guy said I could take a break, have a smoke. I was anxious to get out of there for a while. I don't like formaldehyde. The place really stank. Anyway, I went outside. When I came back, the body was gone and so was the guy."

"Which guy? The one who spoke English?" When Olin nodded, Jones said, "How long were you gone?"

"About ten minutes."

I said, "No longer than ten minutes?"

"Maybe a little longer. Fifteen maybe."

Stan glanced at me, shrugged.

I said, "When you got back, Sergeant, did you see right away that the body was gone?"

"No, sir, I saw it wasn't where it was when I left. I thought maybe someone had moved it. I looked around for it, then I asked the guy at the desk, but he didn't speak English. I checked out all the corpses. When I didn't see it, I knew it had disappeared."

Stan nodded at Olin. "That'll be all, Sergeant." With Olin gone, Stan said sarcastically, "The place was drenched with formaldehyde." He grimaced. "Anyway, that pretty much resolves the problem of Nolda being dead when Pete was killed."

"We should have given the job to a guy who likes formaldehyde." I paused. "What I'm thinking, could it be someone wanted to get rid of the body?"

"Why would anyone give a goddamn about Nolda's body?" Stan shook his head. "I think you're making too much out of that, Alex."

I said, "Let me think about it." I didn't want to say it again to Stan, but if the pathologist determined the body was already in the water on the day Pete was shot, Stan would have no choice but to drop the green-on-blue theory—and start searching elsewhere for Pete's killer.

"Doug Greer's going to be here in fifteen, twenty minutes, Alex. Do you want to stay around?" When I said I would, Stan nodded, stood up, and crossed the room to his coffee machine.

I said, "What does Greer do when he's over here?"

"From what I understand, he's a real hands-on guy. People in D.C. like that. He even speaks a little Pashto. He determines how the infrastructure should be built up. Before the government spends money, he makes sure it's going to the right places."

As Stan stood gazing out the small window through which we could see a circling helicopter, I thought I knew what he was thinking—that considering all the stress, headaches, and danger involved in the work, it was amazing that he and I were both still doing this stuff.

"How long has it been, Alex? How long since you and I last worked together?"

"Bosnia, I arrived in Tuzla just after 9/11." Tuzla is a city in central Bosnia, the location of one of the agency's smaller stations. It was my first stop in the Balkans, the place where I got my first briefings and some sense of what I'd be doing. One of the jobs turned out to be helping escort Slobodan Milosevic out of Belgrade and over to the Hague, where he would stand trial for genocide.

"Right. And I'd been involved in Amber Star just around that time." Handing me a cup, he said, "Before that, let's see. A Christmas party in D.C.? In somebody's apartment in Georgetown?"

"Sounds right. You have a good memory."

After sitting back down, Stan said, "I'm starting to overdose on nostalgia. Not a good sign. I used to like this job. There was something new happening every day, but Afghanistan ain't much fun, not anymore . . ."

"Don't let the green-on-blues get you down, Stan."

"It's more than just that. It's the whole situation. We'll all be gone by the end of next year. I'm hoping this war hasn't been in vain, that's all." Stan paused. "Tell me, Alex, what are your reasons for thinking that Nolda didn't kill Pete?"

"First off, I spoke with his company commander—"

"Captain Bashiri."

"He didn't seem to recall Nolda that well, and in a sense, that was a plus. Nolda had never caused problems, never done anything that would have made him stick in anybody's memory. According to his records, the stuff Hammond showed me, he acquitted himself well in a couple of encounters with insurgent forces."

"I remember. For a while they were out in Herat."

"I have the idea that to commit a green-on-blue you have to be something of a fanatic. If Nolda had been a fanatic, his CO would have remembered him more clearly. If he'd been a Taliban sympathizer, he wouldn't have fought against them. That would have been noticed."

"Go on."

"I also spoke with one of Nolda's buddies, a guy from the same village."

"Nolda came from somewhere down in Helmand."

"It turned out to be a village where the Taliban wreaked a lot of havoc. Because of the stuff he saw when he was young, Nolda didn't like the Taliban. His friend said he wasn't the type to commit a green-on-blue."

"For my money, too circumstantial."

"His friend said he was a straight-ahead kind of guy."

"These people don't know the meaning of straight-ahead."

"He also said he wasn't the type to nurse hidden agendas. Also not the type to let people push him around."

"You're the only one who sees things that way. Who made you an expert on how Afghans think?" Stan got up from his desk and stared out the window. "Maybe some warlord hired Nolda to kill Pete."

"Nolda's not the guy he would have hired."

"You sound awfully sure of yourself."

"I'm wondering about his body disappearing. It disappeared because someone had a reason to get rid of it." I checked my watch, got to my feet. "I have an appointment to talk with Hammond about the pictures."

"I know. He mentioned it. We got something in from the FBI yesterday. Personally, I don't think it's significant." Stan paused. "You maybe will."

"What came in?"

Stan nodded toward the door. With his phone to his ear, he said, "I'll let Hammond show you. He's good with the PowerPoint stuff."

Five minutes later, Stan, Hammond, and I were in a classroom-like room in a neighboring building. Standing next to a screen at the front and holding a remote, Hammond said, "What I've got are photos taken by the closed-circuit security cameras at the entrance to the Headquarters building. But you're going to see there's a bit of a problem, partly because of the low quality of the images. Some of the pictures aren't bad. Like this one for instance."

On the screen in front of the room was a grainy picture of a guy with a mustache, wearing a uniform.

I said, "Maybe I know him. It's hard to tell."

"I know him," Stan said.

Hammond looked at Stan and nodded. "That's one of the Askars at the Embassy. He was in Headquarters on the day Colonel Hansen was killed."

Stan shrugged. "One of the guards probably stole the good camera. He sold it and replaced it with a cheesy one. It's happened before." Hammond put up another picture, a grainy likeness of an Afghan soldier.

I said, "Not clear. Not enough pixels."

"You're right, Alex," Hammond said. "They should be better quality. Good facial recognition requires at least sixty, seventy pixels. Most of these have from twelve to twenty."

As Hammond worked the computer, picture after picture appeared on the screen. The pictures varied in quality. "Unfortunately, there were quite a few like this."

Stan said, "The problem was, we could ID most of the people entering and leaving, but not all. We couldn't say for sure whether Nolda had entered in the morning or whether he'd left at noon."

When I asked how many pictures there were, Stan responded, "Hundreds."

"Even with the camera problems and some people facing the wrong direction," Hammond said, "we did fairly well. We ended up with eighteen photos of people we couldn't ID. I figured maybe some were visitors. Even when the quality ain't that good, it's good enough. Look at this picture."

Hammond clicked the remote, and we got another picture, this one of an American soldier. "That's someone else we know didn't fire the shot. Facial recognition ID'd him. Here's another. We ain't sure who this is."

On the screen was a guy in an ANP uniform who had turned his head at the moment the picture was taken. "Could be the guy, we're not sure. There were others like this one."

"That's part of the problem," Stan said. "We don't have a picture of Nolda, not a clear one."

Hammond said, "We have like twenty pictures so grainy we're not sure who the people are."

I said, "So we're not sure he even came to work that day." I recalled that there was no ID on Nolda's body. Using his ID, someone could have signed in as him.

"Right, as it now stands, we're not sure. He could be any one of this bunch." Hammond clicked on picture after picture, none of which was very clear. After a pause, he showed a few more. "We recognize all of these people. They worked in the building in different offices. All had alibis for the time Pete was shot. Almost all anyway."

"What do you mean *almost* all?"

"I'll show you." Hammond put up a picture of an Afghan soldier. Although he was looking toward his right, it was a good enough three-quarter likeness to be able to recognize him. Hammond adjusted the lighting and the zoom.

"Better," I said.

"Good, because this individual doesn't work in the building."

"Why was he there then?" I asked. "Was he a visitor?"

"We're not sure," Stan said.

"But I can tell you who he is." After a second, Hammond put up another picture on the screen. "When I sent it back to the States, the FBI ran it through their facial recognition database. Even though it wasn't too clear, they got a hit right away."

When Hammond again punched the keyboard, another picture appeared. "This is what came up." It was a shot of the same man, but this picture was an official photo. The name beneath the picture was Abdul Sakhi. His birthplace was given as Kunar Province. His birth date made him thirty-four years old.

Stan said, "We received a communication telling us who he is. He's one of our assets. The government has used him on three separate occasions."

"Black ops?"

"What else?" Stan shrugged. "A couple of people know how to reach him. He gets paid, that's the end of it. He's reliable."

I said, "Nevertheless, we should talk with him."

Stan said, "We would if we could. He's hard to locate."

I said, "First thing, we try to find someone in Headquarters who spoke with him."

"We already have," Hammond said. "Colonel Campbell in Special Operations knows him and has had contact with him. But he didn't speak with him the day Pete was killed."

As Hammond switched off the computer and turned on the lights, I stood up. "In other words, the investigation isn't complete." I could see Stan wasn't at all happy when I said that.

I didn't say it, but I wasn't happy either. The word to describe this investigation was "botched," but I didn't want to say it out loud.

Back in the CID office, Stan checked his watch. "Doug should be here anytime. You'd never met Greer before this week, have you?"

I shook my head. "The other day was the first time."

"I thought maybe you might have run into him the other times you'd been here. He's back and forth between D.C. and Kabul on a regular basis. He's been in Bagram the last couple of days, but he's flying over here this afternoon. Pretty influential, from all reports." When I interrupted to say I'd seen his name in the papers often enough, Stan nodded. "He's definitely high profile." Stan took a sip of coffee, gazed at me over the cup. "Being out here you kind of lose track of what's going on back home. From what I hear he's behind a lot of decisions. Right now, he's responsible for figuring out what we should be doing with heavy equipment when the big drawdown begins."

Stan was referring to the fact that the United States military was scheduled to be out of Afghanistan by the end of 2014, in other words, in another twenty-one months. That would mean the end of Operation Enduring Freedom, which had officially kicked off in Afghanistan just one month after 9/11.

A couple of minutes later, Stan got a call from one of the security people. When he got to his feet and nodded, I figured Douglas Greer had arrived. A minute later Stan returned, accompanied by the Undersecretary himself.

As we shook hands, Greer said, "That was a difficult meeting yesterday."

"I think we should all cut the lady some slack," Stan said.

Greer said to me, "Major Jones says someone from the NSC's responsible for you being over here. Who would that be?"

"Jerry Shenlee," I said.

"Don't know him personally, know the name."

"Alex and I were in Bosnia," Stan said, "helping out with the drone program."

Greer grinned at the mention of drones. "You guys got the Predators flying?"

I said, "We helped."

"I'm not sure I'd admit to that. Drones aren't all that popular in these parts."

"Especially not in Waziristan," Stan said. We all knew that Waziristan, a barren area of Pakistan that shelters al-Qaeda leaders, was the target of most drone attacks.

"A lot of drones are taking off these days from Camp Chapman," Greer said.

At the mention of Camp Chapman, I recalled that was where the unsmiling Captain Corley was stationed.

Greer gazed at me as though he might be sizing me up for something. He was a gangly six-three, had thick brown hair, a high forehead, a long face, and mildly flushed complexion, not a bad-looking guy. He was wearing a green windbreaker over a flannel shirt, tan cargo pants, and combat boots, and seemed very much at home out here. Stan had said for the last few years Greer was one of the government's most frequent visitors to Afghanistan.

As he watched Stan pulling off the caps on three bottles of Weihenstephan beer, Greer said, "How's the Hansen investigation coming?"

"It's coming," Stan said. "We found Nolda's body."

"The assassin's dead?"

"Seems to have drowned. They found his body in the water. Early this morning."

"Where'd they find him? The river?"

I said, "The river doesn't have that much water in it at this time of year. He was out in one of the lakes, but now the body's disappeared."

Stan flashed an angry look in my direction, obviously unhappy that my comment didn't reflect well on him.

"Disappeared? How the hell did that happen?" Greer seemed angry, as though I might have an answer for how Nolda's body had vanished.

Stan explained how Hammond and I had driven out to the hospital where they'd brought the body and how we'd assigned a couple of MPs to stand guard.

I said, "Now we're not even sure he's the killer. At least I'm not."

When Greer arched his eyebrows, Stan explained that none of the photos clearly showed Nolda entering the building.

"None?"

"There were some 'possibles,' but none were very clear." Stan added, "One had a low pixel count. Plus the guy had his head turned. But it could have been him."

"So we're not sure about the facial recognition?" Greer groaned. "Man, if it's not one thing, it's another."

After a pause, Stan said, "Anyway, now we're investigating the possibility that someone was in the Headquarters building who normally wouldn't be there. Someone named . . . let's see, Abdul Sakhi."

"So what was he doing there?" Greer asked.

"Right now, we're trying to get a line on him. Where he comes from. Where he might be."

"In other words, this investigation is still unfinished." He paused to take a long swallow. "What else? What's with Hansen's wife?"

Stan said, "She's doing okay. Alex may be able tell you more. They had lunch today."

"I took her into Kabul, showed her the city. We had lunch at Sufi. Wanda's tough. After we ate, she said she wanted to do some shopping. I drove her over to Chicken Street."

"If she's thinking about shopping, that's probably a good sign," Greer said, grinning.

"Give her some time and she'll be all right. Pete was headed back to the States. Wanda had already picked out a new apartment and was fixing it up. The bad news came as a real shock."

Greer stood up, walked over to the window. "Should she even be over here? I mean, what the hell can she do? Except maybe get in the way."

Stan said, "She says she wanted to see the face of the guy who turned around and in cold blood shot her husband."

Greer made a sour face. "Sounds a little . . . well, self-indulgent. What do you guys think?"

"I agree," Stan said. "As far as I'm concerned, she should have stayed home. But she got a look at the guy just before the body disappeared."

I nodded. "She said it made her feel better."

Greer, who was still standing, shook his head. "I have some people I need to talk to at the Embassy. I'll be here in Kabul for the next few days, then I fly back to Bagram. And then back to the States. When I'm not in Bagram, I'm at ISAF. I like the new officers' barracks they built. They've given me a temporary office over there. It's on the small side, but it's okay."

I said, "They finished off the new barracks just in time to give them to the Afghans."

"Alex is in Eggers." Stan grinned. "The low-rent neighborhood."

"Not only that, I'm close to Gator Alley. It's noisy."

"How about lunch tomorrow?" Greer asked me. "The Headquarters dining room okay?" When I said lunch would be fine, Greer said, "You like steak? Or are you against cholesterol?"

"There's good cholesterol and there's bad cholesterol."

Greer grinned, finished his beer with a long swallow, dropped the bottle in the wastebasket. "I'll talk to the mess sergeant. He should know the difference." As he headed toward the door, he addressed

Stan, "You should be doing more on the Hansen case. Anything happens, let me know. There are people in D.C. who care about this."

Stan left the office with Greer, and I took another swallow. When he got back, Stan said, "Greer wants action. I feel the hot breath of important people on our necks. In fact, I've been feeling it ever since you arrived, Alex." He fixed me with a hard stare. "Anyway, you're coming up in the world. Lunch with Doug Greer. He's a player back in D.C."

"I'll make sure I use the right fork."

"I'm still wondering why you're here. You're supposed to be getting married. Why did you come over?"

"My marriage wasn't too high on anybody's list of priorities."

"Except yours." When Stan smiled, it seemed to cost him some effort. "Our superiors can be hard to read at times." Looking out the window, he said, "Storm's brewing out there. Be careful driving."

I knew Stan was boiling mad at me, and I knew why. I'd been clearly skeptical of how he was running the investigation.

Although it was only 1930 hours, it had been a long day, and the wind was whipping things up. As I walked back to my van, I saw that I had a voice mail message from Captain Eric Page. "Would you be able to stop by my office at 1000 tomorrow?"

I texted a *yes*.

My telephone conversation with Irmie two days ago was still on my mind. I called because I was hoping to smooth things over. Although her "hello" wasn't all that friendly, I decided to plunge ahead.

"Irmie, I've had a thought about where we could get married. Last year, I attended a wedding at Nymphenburg Castle. The chapel had a beautiful atmosphere. I thought we might want to—"

"You're not serious, I hope. My salary for the next six months wouldn't cover the cost of a wedding there."

"The reception and wedding were beautiful. I think maybe we—"

"Let me remind you, Alex. You should be here with me. That was how we wanted to make plans. The two of us together. Instead, you go to Afghanistan. And then you call to tell me where it is *you* want to get married. And then you select the most expensive place imaginable."

"Irmie, listen. I only—"

"Don't you realize how ridiculous that is?" When I didn't immediately answer, she said, "Well?"

"It depends how you look at it."

"Let me tell you how I *look* at it," she said. "You left me here to handle everything myself while you went off on . . . some kind of jaunt." She paused. "And you seem to think I should be happy . . . about that. And happy to hear from you."

"I don't think that."

"Good. I have to run. I have things to do here."

It now seemed that whatever I did was wrong. When I called Irmie, I reminded her of my sudden departure. When I didn't call, she felt more and more abandoned.

I tossed and turned for most of the night, unable to sleep and thinking about Irmie and of the seemingly hopeless situation I'd created for myself.

CHAPTER 9

The update briefings are a daily morning ritual at ISAF Headquarters.

I attended this one because Stan was scheduled to provide the latest information pertaining to the state of the green-on-blue attacks on military personnel. Maybe because people were fearful they might be next, the auditorium was filled, with men and women on hand from just about every NATO nation.

I didn't envy Stan his job, which entailed enormous responsibility and was the focus of widespread attention within the ISAF command. Pete had been a close friend, and I wanted to be sure that the right person was identified as his killer.

The way I saw things, Baram Nolda hadn't killed Pete.

Nor did I like the way Stan had been tending to play down the importance of getting the right guy.

I felt we should at least be trying to find Abdul Sakhi in order to ask him why he had been in ISAF Headquarters the day Pete was killed.

After Stan had given his talk describing the measures being taken to guard against green-on-blue attacks, hands went up.

"Sir," one of the British officers asked, "have we been able to identify the shooter who murdered Colonel Hansen here in Headquarters?"

Stan began nodding his head before the officer had finished speaking. "I can confidently say we have, and that there's no doubt that the shooter worked right here in the Oversight and Accountability Section with Colonel Hansen."

"Was that the sergeant in the office?" someone asked.

"Yes, it was," Stan said. "Sergeant Baram Nolda."

"I understand he's dead. How, exactly, did he die?"

Stan said. "He drowned. We assume he was thrown into the reservoir."

"Is it true his body has disappeared, sir?" someone asked. When I turned, I saw Captain Corley.

When Stan nodded, she said, "Who do you think caused it to disappear?"

"We have no idea, ma'am. None at all."

"What was the state of the body when it was recovered?" she persisted. "How long had it been in the water?"

"As I say, ma'am. We don't know. With the body gone, we're unable to determine that."

"Thank you, sir."

If there had been another question, it would have been to ask why someone might want to get rid of the corpse.

And the follow-up to that would be to ask if Sergeant Nolda wasn't the victim of a frame.

I would have answered that question with an emphatic yes.

I didn't ask because I thought I knew the answers. I'd already decided that the individual who got rid of Sergeant Baram Nolda's body was Pete's killer. And the reason that individual needed to dispose of the body was that Sergeant Nolda was already dead on the day Pete was killed. And a pathologist would have been able to determine that.

Even after just a cursory examination I could see the body had been in the drink for more than a couple of days, perhaps for as long as two weeks. Large portions of the corpse had been eaten away, larger portions than you would expect to lose in the cold waters of a mountain lake.

I supposed Jerry Shenlee wanted me over here because he suspected that Pete's murder wasn't a green-on-blue. But Jerry also indicated that he wasn't running the op. I still didn't know who I was reporting to, but I now had a suspicion.

Captain Corley seemed to have her own ideas regarding the murder, and I now figured she had persuaded Jerry to launch an independent investigation of Pete's murder.

The remaining questions at the briefing mostly involved precautions being undertaken to prevent future green-on-blue incidents from occurring.

With the update over, people gathered in groups in the corridor or else returned to their offices. Although I checked around for Captain Corley, I didn't see her. I assumed she'd slipped out early.

* * *

"How well did you know Colonel Hansen?" Captain Eric Page asked. It was a half hour later, and I was still in ISAF Headquarters. After the briefing, I'd gone down to the Coffee Garden and shot the breeze with some Italian officers regarding their country's chances in the World Cup, which was coming up in another year.

Now I was in Captain Page's office in the Oversight and Accountability section, the same section in which Pete had worked. On one of the walls was a familiar picture of President Truman, just the hint of a twinkle in his eyes. I had an idea he already knew something back then that we're still struggling to learn. In the far corner stood three flags, the American, the Afghan, and the NATO.

"Pete and I were good friends, but it was a while ago, about fifteen years."

"I understand his wife is over here." When Page asked if I'd like some coffee, I shook my head. "Talking to you yesterday got me thinking a little more about Colonel Hansen. The truth is there are a number of things I didn't mention yesterday. Mainly, about the kind of work he was doing."

I said, "Everything, no matter how small, is helpful."

"I guess you know about the Kabul Bank. You know the situation." When I said I knew the Kabul Bank had gone bankrupt, Page said, "Pete spent a good amount of time there."

"Doing what?"

"Trying to find out what was going on. He talked a lot with bank officials. They're all on trial now. Twenty-two of them. The trial's been running for three months. One time he said the bank was the 'Ponzi scheme to end all Ponzi schemes.'" Page paused. "Then he said, 'They're not only crooks, they're clever crooks. It's that combination that makes them dangerous.' When I asked who he'd been talking about, Page said, 'The bank officials.'"

"Interesting."

"Then he said he was surprised that they were so sophisticated. And he wondered how they'd gotten so damned smart. Neither Farnood nor Ferozi had ever had any experience in finance."

"Are you saying somebody showed them?"

"Maybe."

I asked Page what else he remembered.

"One time he said they ran things with two sets of books. One set they showed the auditors. That's why the first audit said everything was fine. In the other set, they kept track of where all the money was going. I got the idea that it was real complicated. Pete said the money was going in every direction. He said there was only one direction in which it wasn't going. And that was back to America."

I said, "Which is where it mostly all came from."

"He said this was happening in one of the world's poorest countries, the country that could least afford it. He said the fraud was going to turn out to be much greater than anybody realized. When he said that, I asked him what he meant. He said the bank failure would equal about five or six percent of Afghanistan's gross domestic product."

"That much?" When Page nodded, I said, "That would be billions of dollars." I paused. "Just one bank?"

"Afghanistan isn't a big country. I suppose that's one reason Pete was so upset. One time he said what bothered him was he felt powerless to do much. He felt frustrated. I think that's one reason he talked with me."

"He needed someone."

"I guess, and when he heard I'd majored in accounting in college, he figured I could follow what he was talking about. And he knew I cared. He once mentioned he'd been poking around in the bank when no one was around. Once, when he opened a drawer, he found a hundred stamps with the logos of corporations. The bank officials would emboss correspondence with stamps to provide an appearance of authenticity."

Page shook his head, grimaced. "Something else you should know. Pete spent a certain amount of time on the road, traveling around."

"To where?"

"One place was Dubai." When I asked, "Why Dubai?" he said, "I'm not really sure, but I have an idea that was where some of these bank officials landed. One of the insiders, he said, was the brother of Karzai."

"You mean President Karzai?"

"Yeah, his brother. It seemed he owned property down there. According to Pete, he was making things real difficult for the auditors."

"Did he say how?"

"Not really. But one time he said that over two hundred people got insider loans from the bank. That really surprised me. I got the impression some of the most important people in Afghanistan were part of the swindle."

"What kind of property?"

"He said villas and office buildings, mostly. Real expensive stuff."

I said, "From what I understand, the American government established the bank with the thought of using it to pay for whatever goods and services it required here in Afghanistan."

Page smiled grimly. "That's something else I remember Pete saying. Something about our government being naïve. He said that we accepted referrals without properly vetting the top officials. He once said we were so naïve that we almost deserved to get swindled."

"It sounds like we were getting referrals from the wrong people."

"People in Washington were buddy-buddy with Karzai around then."

Captain Page continued to talk, but by this time I knew what had been on Pete Hansen's mind. Pete had been correct about our government being incredibly naïve. It sounded like a situation that could have been avoided by exercising only minimal caution.

Before leaving, I told Captain Page to give me another call if he remembered anything new. As I drove back to Eggers, I thought I at last knew why I was over here.

Colonel Pete Hansen is murdered by someone who wants to divert suspicion and make the murder look like a green-on-blue killing. The individual engages an unlikely killer. The motive for Pete's murder relates directly to Pete's investigation of the Kabul Bank, which has been cleaned out of over 900 million dollars deposited there by the American government.

An interesting question might be: How did Jerry Shenlee know something was amiss in the investigation of Pete's murder?

Another question: Why did Jerry remove himself from the op and tell me someone would contact me?

I had an idea Captain Corley knew the answers to both questions. I figured she was running the op. I also figured she'd soon be contacting me. What I couldn't figure was why she hadn't gotten in touch already.

*　*　*

"I grew up in Akron," Doug Greer said. "My parents divorced when I was six. My mother had a problem with alcohol. I enlisted in the Marines when I was seventeen," Doug Greer continued as he sawed away on his steak. "Spent six years as a jarhead. Crazy, now that I think about it, but I figured almost anything would be better than putting in thirty years at a tire factory." We were seated at a corner table in the ISAF Headquarters dining facility, a high-ceilinged room with a picture of the president on the far wall. An array of flags stood against an adjacent wall. Close to half the diners wore the uniforms of a variety of different countries. The rest were civilians.

"Looking back," Doug said, "I have to say I was lucky. Spent some time with an intel detachment in the Mid-East. Was in Lebanon for a while. Back in the States, I was at Quantico, then was a DI at Parris Island. Great duty." He grinned. "I probably shouldn't admit it, but I liked the military. Even considered OCS for a while. Went to Ohio State on a football scholarship; Woody's still a legend there, by the way."

"Woody?"

"Woody Hayes, the coach. I can see you're not a football fan."

"I can take it or leave it."

"But you mostly leave it." He grinned. "Whenever I'd turn on a game, my wife would find me something to do. She's my ex-wife now." He took a quick swallow of Coke, smiled again. "No, football wasn't the reason. I'm not that superficial."

"If you were really superficial, you wouldn't—"

"I wouldn't admit it. You're on to me, Alex."

"And you wouldn't be the Undersecretary." When Doug put his finger to his lips, we both laughed. "Anyway, after Ohio State?"

"I applied to Georgetown. And amazingly, got accepted. More false modesty, sorry. How's the steak, by the way?"

"A little chewy, otherwise okay." After Doug said he'd mention that to the mess sergeant, I told him that I'd been talking to one of Pete Hansen's colleagues at ISAF Headquarters. "I may be wrong, but I think there could be a connection between Pete getting killed and the fraud at the Kabul Bank."

"The Kabul Bank is a disaster."

"What can you tell me about it? I assume you've spent time over there."

"Most government people over here spent time there. It wasn't easy getting things going, establishing procedures and so forth."

"I don't suppose it was easy showing the Afghans double-entry bookkeeping."

"No, it wasn't, but the officials I dealt with had financial experience and for the most part were very sharp. I frankly couldn't believe it when I heard it went bankrupt. How the hell could something like that happen anyway?" Doug popped an onion ring in his mouth. Smiling, he said, "I love these things."

"There must have been some indication that things weren't right."

"There were, but the first audit gave the bank a clean bill of health."

"I was thinking of going to the courthouse for the trial."

"Don't bother. You won't understand a word. And the translation setup isn't that good. The translator's accent was so thick I had trouble understanding him."

I said, "They loaned a lot of money to a small group of people. All insiders."

"Interest-free." Greer shook his head. "Unbelievable. In any case, the hanky-panky shouldn't be hard to prove."

"They were smart, but there's always a paper trail. The bank was a Ponzi scheme from the get-go. For the entire time, they kept two sets of books."

"Only two? Not three or four?" Shaking his head, Greer said, "You know, Alex, this is the kind of thing that upsets me—and a lot of other Americans as well. It's the way the government spends but doesn't get its money's worth in return." Pushing away his tray, he said, "What I do, I'm an adviser. We're spending money here nation-building—roads, schools, homes for the people, you name it. I make recommendations, then the government acts on them."

"Stan said you've been doing it for a while. And that you're good at it."

"I like to think I am. Anyway, has Stan given you the latest on Abdul Sakhi?" When I said he hadn't, Doug said, "We think we've located him, or at least someone who knows where he is."

"So we can find out why he was in the Headquarters building."

Greer took another swallow of Coke. "He comes from a village out in Kunar Province, the Korengal Valley."

"We've lost people out there."

"That I know. The Korengalis ain't the world's friendliest tribe. Anyway, check with Stan. Right now we're waiting on some intel, and hopefully we'll be hearing things, maybe as early as this afternoon." He shrugged. "The FBI has him in their database, and they say he's okay."

I said, "Getting back to the bank fraud. If they're convicted, these guys will be going away for a while."

"I wouldn't count on it. The Afghan courts don't look at corruption the way we do back home. The way some judges will see things, these are only guys who got caught with their hands in the cookie jar." Greer reached again for his Coke glass, shook his head.

"Something else, Doug. Those are American dollars we're talking about. A judge over here isn't paying taxes like we are. Some of them will think if we're not exercising better control and paying attention to our money, we deserve to lose it."

"A judge shouldn't be thinking that way." Greer smirked, then sighed. "But I know what you mean."

When Greer continued to shake his head, I said, "I guess you know that one of the guys involved is President Karzai's brother."

"I heard that. So Afghanistan's president may influence how the judges rule." When I didn't respond, Greer sighed. "Yeah, Alex, I guess I know all this, but it's frustrating. It's one of the things that makes my job difficult. That's why I try not to think about it." He took a quick look at his watch, then began getting slowly to his feet. "I have to do some shopping. I told a neighbor I was going to bring back some shawls from Afghanistan."

In the parking area, we shook hands and headed for our vehicles.

Lunch with the Undersecretary. I was definitely moving up in the world.

Back in my billet, I decided to write Irmie another e-mail. "Dear Irmie, I hope you're having better weather than we're having in Afghanistan. Today it's gray and cloudy, and there's slush on the ground from yesterday's snowfall. I hope everything is fine. Did you get the e-mail I sent yesterday? Anyway, I want you to know how much I love you and miss you. Yours, Alex."

Talking about the weather to the woman you love isn't very satisfactory. I hated to have to think about it, but I had the depressing feeling we were beginning to drift apart, moving on two different wavelengths. Making me more depressed was the knowledge that it was all my fault.

Irmie had been busy making arrangements for our pending marriage. Although I hadn't expected her to be happy about me

postponing my trip to Munich, I hadn't much considered the extent
to which I was upsetting her life. She had asked for time off work,
and during my stay, we intended to finalize the details—guest list,
ceremony, reception, food, flowers. We intended to spend as much
time as possible together, including a month-long honeymoon.

And we needed to make our plans for the future. Whether we
intended to live in Europe or America was still up in the air. To be
honest, I didn't care where we lived, just as long as we were together.

An hour later, while I was drinking beer and conducting an on-
line search of the Kabul Bank, my cell phone rang.

"I don't know about you, Alex," Wanda Hansen said, "but
I'm thinking this isn't the most exciting way to spend a Monday
evening."

Taking a long swallow from my bottle of Weihenstephan, I said,
"Where are you?"

"I'm in my room in the Green Village. Where else would I be?"
Before I could comment, she said, "Would you like to come over
and keep a lonely girl company?" When I said, "Why not?" she
said, "If you can bring a couple of sandwiches, I'll go downstairs
and bring up some beer."

As I slipped on my jacket, I tried not to think how Irmie would
react to me accepting Wanda's invitation.

* * *

"The rooms here aren't bad," I said. It was an hour later, and I was in
Wanda's Green Village quarters. I'd just taken the last bite of a roast
beef sandwich I brought over from the Camp Eggers chow hall.

Ignoring my attempt to keep the conversation impersonal,
Wanda said, "You know, Alex, I almost fell over when I saw you
here on Friday. I still can't get over it."

"You're not the only one who's surprised I'm here."

Wanda crossed one leg over the other, a move that exposed quite a bit of smooth thigh. "I mean, I thought you were retired."

"I thought I was, too, but I got unretired." Because of Irmie, I was still having second thoughts about having allowed Jerry Shenlee to send me over here. I was already fearing an e-mail from Irmie saying our engagement was over. If it had been anyone else but Pete who'd been murdered, I would have told Jerry no—N-O!

Holding my beer bottle, I readjusted myself on the chair. Wanda was sitting opposite me. On the cabinet to my left was a large clock. The remains from our sandwiches were on two plates, which were alongside the TV. Thinking of Irmie, I said, "This is my absolute last assignment." I took a quick swallow. "I mean it this time."

Wanda smiled. "Famous last words."

I also tried to smile but didn't quite succeed. Pete's unnecessary death continued to haunt me, and I wondered whether I'd ever be able to find his killer. Weighing on my mind was my relationship with Irmie. I wondered why she hadn't taken the time to call or at least send an e-mail. I wondered what she might be doing at this moment. It was late afternoon back in Munich, and I assumed she was at work. By this time of day it would be dark, and the lights in her office would be on.

I said, "They keep calling."

"Who keeps calling?"

"Good question. Sometimes I'm not sure myself." On my last assignment, one year before, I was attached to one of our government's smaller intelligence outfits, an outfit so small and secret I doubt more than a couple dozen people are aware of its existence. "This time Jerry showed up on my doorstep. I had no choice but to let him in."

Wanda grinned. "Why no choice? Did he have a platoon of soldiers with him? Was he holding a weapon on you?"

Recalling my conversation with Captain Page, I made an effort to steer the conversation in a serious direction. "Getting back to what you said before, I think I may know why Jerry Shenlee asked me to come over here. I think there may be a connection between Pete's killer and the work Pete was doing." When Wanda's expression clouded over, I said, "Pete was working on the failure of the Kabul Bank." When she appeared even more puzzled, I said, "Did you know that?"

"No, not really. What's the Kabul Bank? I suppose I should know." Her expression became distant. "We saw one another so seldom in the past few years. Pete was home for two weeks, but that was close to a year ago." She paused. "Alex, are you saying Pete's murder wasn't a green-on-blue?"

"I'm beginning to wonder. And that's putting it mildly."

"What do you mean?"

"It may have been carried out by someone hired to do the job. I'm beginning to think that."

"In other words, not by this . . . Nolda person." When I nodded, she said, "In some ways, that makes it even worse. You're saying someone murdered my husband . . . intentionally."

"From what I can see, Nolda wasn't the type to do something like that."

"Can you be sure?"

"It's the way I read the guy."

"And you now feel Pete was murdered because of what he was working on." Wanda took a small sip of beer, carefully replaced the glass on the desk. "It's interesting, but if you'll pardon me for saying so, Alex, that sounds slightly . . . well, over the top."

"Didn't Pete ever mention the Kabul Bank?"

Wanda shook her head, gazed at the bottle as she emptied the beer into a glass. "He'd occasionally mention what he was doing, and I suppose he mentioned the bank, but I didn't always pay that much attention." After a pause, she said, "I admit that I was sometimes bored by what he'd tell me . . ."

"And you'd tune out."

She nodded and said, "I suppose."

"The bank went bankrupt," I said. "The money that was in it disappeared. Hundreds of millions of dollars."

"That much? A bank here in Afghanistan? You're sure you're not exaggerating, Alex?"

"It was a massive fraud. The bank officials have been charged. The trial is going on right now. Right here in Kabul."

"And Pete helped convict them? Is that it? That's what you're saying?"

"I don't know. It's possible that he provided some evidence. I can't figure Pete's involvement."

"Pete was a soldier. Why would the military be involved in a financial matter?"

"The money these people stole belonged to the American government." I paused. "You're right, Wanda. It's normally not the job of the military to audit banks. But sometimes the military are in the best position to do something like that."

"So you think Pete's job was maybe to find out what happened."

I stood up, went to the fridge. "Care for another beer?" When she nodded, I took out two. "One of the advantages of staying here is you can get alcohol. I hear they're cracking down at Headquarters."

Wanda smiled and nodded as she watched me pour two glasses. We both raised our glasses. "Cheers!"

Wanting to change the subject, I said, "How do you like Kabul?"

"I feel isolated here, cut off. The city seems okay, once you get used to all the checkpoints."

"You should try to get around more."

"It doesn't seem all that dangerous, but I know things can happen . . . from one minute to the next." Suddenly, Wanda stood up, reached out, took my hand. Then she drew me to my feet and placed her hands around my waist. "I'd like it better if you were around, and if you would take me out and show me things."

Then, standing on tiptoes, she placed her lips over mine and pulled me to her. I could feel the softness of her breasts, and they were sending a message. Quite simply, the message was, "I'm available."

By quickly drawing away, I sent back a message of my own. I said, "This is so sudden."

"Is it?" Still holding my waist, she smiled. "It shouldn't be."

By stepping backwards, I managed to untangle myself.

"What are you afraid of?" When I said, "Three guesses," Wanda gave me a sudden shove. I wasn't ready for that either, and I landed on the bed. Then, laughing, she fell on top of me. "My God, what do I have to do to get a response, Alex?"

"What kind of response?"

"Can't you give me a hug?"

And so, as we lay on the bed, I dutifully gave Wanda a hug. And then she wanted a kiss. I gave her a quick one, then untangled myself and rolled away. A second later, I was back on my feet.

Wanda threw her legs over the side of the bed, looked up at me. "Since when are you such a . . . colossal bore?"

"Since always, it's just that you never noticed it."

In a serious tone, she said, "Well, I am bored in this place. There's a swimming pool downstairs, and I've been swimming every morning. But I don't have a car, which means I have to depend on taxis."

"Maybe it's time for you to go home. You were Pete's wife. I was a close friend."

"Oh, come on, Alex, I know all that. Please don't remind me that I'm a widow now . . ."

As she sat on the side of the bed, she removed a tissue from a pocket and touched it to her eyes. For maybe two minutes she sniffled. "I'm sorry, Alex. Now I'm the one who's being a . . . bore."

I didn't comment. Still standing, I emptied my beer glass with a long swallow. When I said, "I have to leave now," Wanda nodded, then said in a quiet voice, "Good night, Alex."

CHAPTER 10

STAN ASKED IF I could make a Tuesday evening meeting that was to be held at ISAF Headquarters. I said I could.

After arriving, I became quickly aware that I was in the company of five grim-faced individuals.

It was early evening, and we were seated at a long table in one of the ISAF Headquarters briefing rooms—Stan, Doug, Hammond, Captain Bud Withers, and Captain Leslie Corley. Stan was standing alongside a map at the head of the table, running the show. Except for Withers and Corley, we were all stationed in Kabul, at either ISAF, Camp Eggers, or Camp Phoenix.

According to Stan, Withers had helicoptered up from a COP, a combat outpost, in the Pech River Valley at which he was stationed. Captain Corley had arrived on a puddle jumper flight from Camp Salerno, and as we sat there, I again wondered about her interest in Pete's murder.

Stan began the meeting by saying, "For my money, Nolda's our guy, but we've got some additional information people should hear.

"When we got word from the FBI," Stan said, "that added a detail to the investigation. I'm hoping it will be a small one. The facial recognition program told us that, somehow, an Afghan had been at Headquarters on the day Colonel Hansen was shot. His name is Abdul Sakhi, and he may or may not have had a reason for being in the building. Could he have been the person who shot Colonel Hansen?

We'd like to talk with him." Stan paused, glancing at some papers in an open manila folder on the desk. "Thanks to the FBI, we know a certain amount about Abdul Sakhi, and some of it's quite interesting."

"I'd like to hear just what it is we know," Doug Greer said.

Pointing to the map, Stan said, "Abdul Sakhi comes from a village in the Korengal Valley."

"Except maybe for Helmand, we've had more problems there than anywhere," Greer said. "I've spoken with some of our people who've been out there. The Korengali tribe absolutely refuses to cooperate in any way."

Stan nodded his agreement. "The Undersecretary is absolutely correct on that score. The Korengalis have been a big problem going back seven or eight years."

Captain Withers raised his hand, then said, "Saying they're unwilling to cooperate in any way is putting it mildly." Withers was big, had a shaved head, deep voice, and what sounded like a Minnesota accent. "We've lost people in Kunar, more than in any other province."

"Captain Withers knows what he's talking about," Stan said. "He's the commander of Franklin, one of our last COPs out there."

"What can you tell us, sir?" Greer said.

"There are a couple of small Safir villages right in the area where we're at, less than two miles from the COP. We patrol through them all the time. We know the people." He hesitated. "Probably . . . only probably . . . we can find Abdul Sakhi, or at least get some information on his whereabouts."

"What do you think, guys? Are we interested?" Stan asked.

"Why not?" Hammond said.

Captain Corley's expression was attentive, but she remained noncommittal.

"What's the situation?" Greer said. "We can decide when we've heard more."

"Abdul Sakhi's a Korengali." Withers took a swallow of water. "But we might learn something from the other tribe in the vicinity, the Safirs."

"The Safirs don't like the Korengalis," Greer said. "Is that it?"

Withers nodded. "They're rivals, fighting for the land. Like I say, we're friendly with the Safirs, and we know some of the elders. They invite us to their *shuras*. Some of these people know everything that's going on."

Stan said, "So if we go talk with them, we can maybe get a line on Abdul Sakhi."

"What would it involve?" Greer asked. "If it's too dangerous . . ."

"I'd say rustle up some money for the elders." When Jones asked how much, Withers shrugged. "Can you come up with five grand? That should keep them happy. Whoever you send out, I'll provide an escort, take him into the village."

Stan shook his head. "This is beginning to sound like more trouble than it's worth."

I said, "Danger? IEDs?"

"My people are going back and forth all the time," Withers said. "But it's gotta be someone who can speak Pashto."

There were maybe twenty seconds of silence before Stan said, "Haji? Whoever goes, he'll need the terp."

"I might be able to swing it," I said. I was the only person here who thought Sakhi had killed Pete and would be worth finding.

Withers shook his head. "Like I say, military would be better than civilian."

When Greer looked in his direction, Hammond slowly shook his head.

Stan said, "I agree, no way. I need Hammond. Too much to do." He paused. "I say we forget it."

Frowning, Greer said, "How come, Stan?"

"Like I've already said, I think Nolda did it. Sakhi maybe had a reason for being at Headquarters. I've spoken with Colonel Campbell. He knows Abdul Sakhi."

Doug Greer said, "I'd go, if I could. But I'm not sure—"

"You know Kunar Province, Alex?" Stan asked.

"I know where it is. Making the loop the last time we put down in A-Bad. I know the Korengal's reputation. It's not exactly a friendly place."

Greer said, "It would be good to get someone to talk with the Safirs, make friends, take along some cash. We can always use sources out there."

"It's only two days," Withers said.

On his feet, Withers stepped up to the front of the room. "Listen up, guys, and you can get a good idea of what we're talking about. It ain't that complicated." With the pointer, he touched the map, which showed Kunar Province, which is adjacent to Pakistan. "This here is Asadabad, pretty much the last village if you're driving in from Jalalabad. The Pech River runs through the Pech Valley, which is where COP Franklin is. It's Safir country. The Korengalis are southwest, in their valley. They don't like Americans; most support the Taliban. In order to reach the Korengal, you drive along the Pech, but believe me, you don't want to go to the Korengal." He grimaced. "Up here is Tora Bora. We know what happened there."

Greer said, "That's how bin Laden made it out of Afghanistan. Through Tora Bora."

I said, "Sir, I didn't know we still had any bases in that area."

Withers' face took on a rueful expression. "Our COP is one of the last two. And there's been talk of closing it."

"It looks pretty dangerous from here," Greer said. "This job might be more paramilitary than military."

Stan nodded his agreement. "I don't see a company commander approving this mission, not as it stands."

Withers shrugged, handed Stan the pointer. "It's doable but—"

"Whether it's worth doing," Stan said, "I'm not sure. If we only want to talk with this guy, it may not be that important. I say we sleep on it. Right here tomorrow, bright and early—0800."

At the door, I spoke with Captain Corley. "What brings you back up to Kabul, ma'am?"

"I like to keep up. Have you made any further progress regarding the murder?"

"I think I have."

"What have you found out?"

"I may have an idea about the motive."

"Do you know who killed Colonel Hansen?" When I shook my head, she pushed by me and out the door. I already had an idea that I'd be reporting to Captain Corley. I wasn't looking forward to it.

Since it was still early, I decided to give Wanda a call. Sitting on the side of my bed in my hooch, I punched in her number. When she answered, I asked where she was.

"I'm in my room."

"Doing what, if I may ask?"

"I hate to admit that I'm watching the tube, some kind of cop show. I'm surprised they show this stuff over here. You called at a good time. I was about to pour myself a stiff drink. Do you want to join me?" When I said, "Not at the moment," she asked, "Why not?"

I proceeded to tell her about the meeting with Doug, Stan, and Captain Withers.

"That's Kunar Province, right?" When I said it was she said, "That's crazy! Korengal is a dangerous place."

"Withers says he can get someone in and out within a couple of days."

"IEDs are all over the place up there. Who's going?"

"No one seemed too anxious. They're still looking for volunteers. Maybe Doug will go. He's still not sure if he can make it."

"Just as long as you don't go. Don't volunteer."

"Why not? Don't you want to catch Pete's killer?" When she hesitated, I said, "Well?"

"Yes, I want to catch Pete's killer. But I also want someone to drive me around Kabul. As long as I'm here, I want to see the city."

"Is that your only reason?" When she asked if I was fishing for compliments, I said, "Of course."

"All right, you big lug. I'm going to say it. I like you, Alex. I like you very much. Well, more than very much. Much more." Just as I was about to interrupt, she said, "What I said the other day, I meant. If you had asked me back then to marry you, I would have said yes. Yes, yes, yes. But I could also see something else about you. You weren't the marrying kind. Pete was. It was clear to me he needed someone. You didn't. And let's face it, I wanted to get married."

"I suppose I shouldn't have said what I just said."

Wanda laughed. "I forgive you. Go to bed. You have to get a full night's sleep."

"When will you let me buy you dinner?"

"Let me think it over. Good night, Alex."

I thought about putting in a call to Irmie, but for some reason decided against it. Irmie's lack of responsiveness to my calls was getting me down. At the same time, I wasn't happy about the way I'd been flirting with Wanda at a time when I should only be thinking of Irmie.

CHAPTER 11

DOUG GREER TOOK a sip of coffee, gazed at me over the rim of his cup. "You met your boss back in Berlin, is that right?" Doug was referring to Jerry Shenlee.

It was Wednesday morning, and we were back sitting at the table in the briefing room, this time minus Captain Corley, who was on her way back to Camp Chapman, and Bud Withers, who was on his way back to Combat Outpost Franklin.

"Alex goes back to the Cold War, Doug," Stan said.

"You were with SE Division?" When I nodded, Doug said, "Internal ops?"

"I was mostly external ops. I went back and forth."

"Back and forth through the Wall? Recruiting?" When I again nodded, Doug shook his head. "Risky, to say the least."

"I also spent some time with the 766th MI. Things were less tense over there."

Stan shrugged, his way of saying I was foolhardy or just plain crazy. They were referring to my four years as a case officer in Germany. With my partner, I made more trips behind the Iron Curtain than I could count—or now even want to think about. I regard those years as a closed chapter in my life.

All I really wanted to do now was marry Irmie and retire. I didn't even need to go back to my ice business. Whether we lived in Germany or the States didn't make any difference, just as long as we were together. And just as long as I could stay retired.

I said, "I've heard there's no rest for the wicked, but I know for a fact there's no retirement for case officers."

Greer nodded. "I've come around to your way of thinking." Looking at me, he said, "Maybe we should have a little talk with Abdul Sakhi."

Nodding at Stan, I said, "The investigation won't be complete otherwise."

"We don't have anyone to send," Stan said. "Unless you're willing, Alex."

Hammond said, "And whoever goes has to get along with Haji."

"I've only known Haji for a few days, but we get along. I think it's worth trying to get a line on Abdul Sakhi, but I'm not sure . . ."

Doug said, "You were a friend of Pete's."

"Very definitely."

When Stan nodded at Hammond, Hammond punched some numbers into his cell phone, then said, "Can you get over to HQ? On the double?" Five minutes later, Haji pushed open the door, and Stan pointed to a place at the table.

Stan said, "Haji, are you willing to make a trip out to the Pech Valley? You know Mr. Klear. He's willing to go, but he'll need someone along who can talk to the Safirs."

"What we want, Haji, is to make a trade. Captain Withers can put us in contact with an elder. Like all of these people over here, he's greedy."

Haji shrugged. "What do we have to trade?"

"Money," Stan said.

Haji frowned, and I said, "I'm still not sure I'm the right person."

"Uh-uh, Alex. You're perfect. Besides, you two guys get along. Compared to the stuff you did with external ops, I can tell you this is a piece of cake."

"Here, Haji." Stan got to his feet, pointed at the map. "You fly out to the COP where Captain Withers is, Franklin." He stuck his finger at a point on the map. "From here you guys hoof it along the river into this little village."

"We walk?" Haji said, suddenly going pale.

Greer laughed. "Our people use this road all the time. It'll be safe. No IEDs."

Stan put down the pointer. "We can make this financially worth your while, Haji. I'll see to that."

Haji's expression was pensive. When I still didn't say anything, he nodded.

I said, "When do we leave?"

"Today. I'll check the transportation shack for a chopper." Stan slid a manila envelope across the table. Evidently, he'd been counting on someone giving a yes answer.

In my van ten minutes later, I said to Haji, "You know what you'll need. Winter gear, body armor, NVGs, a couple of flashlights, a sleeping bag. Dress warm. And be happy. You're getting a raise in pay."

I dropped Haji off at the chow hall, then headed back to Camp Eggers.

In my hooch I carefully went over the stuff Stan had given me. It wasn't all that complicated. The tribal elder was named Shergaz, and if anyone knew Abdul Sakhi's whereabouts, he'd be the one. Or he could put us in contact with someone who did. At the helicopter shack, I'd be given a satchel containing five thousand dollars, which I could use to negotiate. There was also a map showing the COP and the village where I could find Shergaz. There were some directions, which indicated that we'd be taking what might be a four- or five-kilometer hike along a narrow trail that would skirt the river and which seemed to be over hilly terrain.

Captain Withers would provide us with a squad of troopers to accompany us.

If I could close the deal with the tribal elder, we could maybe have the guy I figured could be Pete's killer within a couple of days. Although it sounded like a patched-together kind of operation, it didn't seem all that complicated. And hopefully, not dangerous.

* * *

The Black Hawk chopper carrying me and Haji had just begun its descent to Combat Outpost Franklin when, above the roar of the rotors, I heard a loud "blunk," which was immediately followed by a steady pinging, the sound of rounds striking our fuselage. Seconds later, a chunk of the helicopter's metal ceiling struck Haji's shoulder before falling to the deck. He signaled across to me that he was all right.

The chopper lurched, then righted itself. None of the eight other passengers had to be told to hold tight or that we were taking fire from some Taliban sharpshooters on the ground. A round struck the chopper's rear before ricocheting back inside.

As we continued our descent, thick dust clouds rose outside, preventing us from seeing out the windows. When we hit terra firma I already had my seat belt open. With my rucksack in my left hand and an M9 automatic in the other, I scrambled down the ramp, out of the bird, and onto the hard dirt of the landing strip. Goggles down, I saw a soldier through the dust pointing us toward the left, in the direction of the COP. I also saw that we were surrounded by a couple of squads of American GIs, who were fanning out toward the landing strip's perimeter.

The crack-crack of automatic weapons began dying out, and I had an idea that our Taliban welcoming committee had melted away, no doubt with the thought of living to fight another day.

I saw that the soldier waving at us was none other than Captain

Withers himself, and in the direction he was pointing, I could see a ten-foot-high wall with guard towers at either end. A half-dozen soldiers, loaded with packs and carrying weapons, were scrambling on to the helicopter. Dust and dirt swirled. Even with my ear plugs in, the engines of the helicopter were deafening. Within seconds of the last GI climbing on, the pilot had the big machine off the ground and shooting up toward the wild blue yonder.

Haji and I followed Withers and two other soldiers up a small hill in the direction of the COP's gate, where a bunch of troopers were gathered.

Less than ten minutes later, Captain Bud Withers, Haji, and I were seated in a cubicle in what served as Bud Withers' office, one of three rooms at the front end of a small prefab building, one of half-a-dozen on the base. There were roughly a dozen tents, a high wall that enclosed the installation on four sides. This COP was one of hundreds in Afghanistan, small operating bases that we'd established in an effort to provide stability and a semblance of order to even the remotest corners of the country. I estimated there were between fifty and sixty soldiers stationed here.

By the time we'd gotten beyond the preliminaries—the hand-shakes, the hellos, the silent appraisals—Withers broke out three half-liter bottles of Weihenstephan beer. We parked our helmets upside down on the packed earth floor, pulled metal chairs up to the desk.

When Haji shook his head at the beer bottle, Withers smirked. "You sure?" He checked his watch. "Sixteen twenty hours. The sun's over the yardarm some damn place in the world. Cheers, guys."

After a long swallow, I said, "Beer tastes even better after someone's been shooting at you."

Withers grinned. "Which is most of the time around here."

"This happen often?" I asked.

"You mean the Taliban attacks?" When I nodded, Withers said, "Three, four times a week. Fortunately, the Talibs ain't the world's greatest marksmen. We take them pretty much in stride, but yeah, we're vulnerable to that sort of stuff, no question."

Making a show of glancing around the small room, I said, "We noticed."

"I'm glad you made it. We expected you two hours ago." When I flashed a questioning frown, Withers said, "Jones thinks it's a waste of time." To Haji, Withers said, "He had to talk you into it, right?" He grinned. "Last night, no one seemed keen to make the trip here. Can't say I blame anyone. Duty here ain't easy." When I asked Withers where the other COPs were, he said, "They been closing. Only one other COP in the Pech Valley now besides Franklin. We got the word out that you guys want to talk with some elders in the village. They agreed, so there'll be a *shura* later." He took a quick swallow from the bottle. "You ready to move out tonight?"

I said we were.

Then he pointed at a map that lay under a heavy layer of glass on top of his desk. "You wanna know where we are, this is us. Here's Nangalam. The village where you meet Shergaz is here. It's real small. And this road here runs alongside a stream for a ways. Then you head off in this direction. One of our people, Sergeant Malley, has already set up a *shura* for tonight, 2030 hours."

Withers said, "Be ready to travel at 1845. That'll give you enough time. You'll have an escort."

I said, "What was it that happened last year that got everybody so hot and bothered? I heard there was a village that was very anti-American."

"One of the firebrands in the village was shot. No one knows who shot him. It wasn't one of us. I wasn't here at the time."

I said, "From what I heard, it caused a big ruckus in the village. Was it a Talib who killed this guy?"

"Unlikely," Withers said. "The guy was very anti-American. He'd been giving speeches in the mosque, getting people riled up . . ."

I said, "The fact he was anti-American wouldn't be a reason to shoot him. Or would it?"

"It'd be a reason for one of us to shoot him, but that's not what happened. Anyway, you're not going there. Hopefully, it's pretty much blown over." Withers shrugged.

"Are our soldiers here trigger happy?" Haji asked. "Shoot-first, ask-questions-later types?"

Withers smiled. "We're all like that, trigger happy. If you're not like that when you arrive, you become like that pretty fast. Or else."

We didn't need to ask what Withers meant by "or else." I saw that Haji had turned a shade paler than usual. I could see that he sensed trouble—and was now probably wishing he hadn't signed on for this expedition.

CHAPTER 12

ANY KIND OF lights on a COP are a no-no. The Talibs are all over, and you don't want to make the installation an easier target than it already is. After getting in, we'd found a couple of spare mattresses and were able to sack out for an hour. At a few minutes after 1800 we were making our way across the installation to Captain Withers' office, both of us using green flashlights to light the way and carrying half-loaded rucksacks. My M9 was holstered. I was wearing my body armor, had two bottles of water, a pair of NVGs, some MREs, a change of underwear, and a sleeping bag in my rucksack. I also had five packs of hundred-dollar bills, ten bills in each pack.

Haji was carrying the same, minus a weapon and minus the cash.

In the office Withers pointed to a map on the wall, showing the COP and also showing the hamlet.

"It's a no-brainer. Straight ahead, no more than two miles into the village. We do it all the time. I've been in touch with the people there, and Shergaz will be expecting you. A couple of his people will meet you just outside the hamlet. There's only one road in and out. They're holding a *shura*. What you two guys want to do is talk with Shergaz privately. From what I understand, it'll be pretty much yes or no, and it depends to what extent he knows Abdul Sakhi. A couple of grand is a lot of loot to these people."

According to Withers, the path we'd take first would lead into a wider footpath, which was used by the locals to reach the river. On the far bank we'd pass a food market. Because of heavy local traffic, that stretch of the road was unlikely to have an IED anywhere along it. Up to that point, though, we had to be careful and, according to Withers, the two soldiers out in front were the best they had at detecting IEDs.

In Withers' office I shook hands with Sully and Mackey, the squad leader and assistant squad leader who would take us the whole way. Outside, I said hello to Jeremy, Danny, and Buzz, the other three troopers. Each of us had his face smeared with grease, and we wore NVGs.

The air was cold and a solid blanket of clouds blocked out the stars. We left the COP in the company of the five soldiers, two single-file maybe ten meters in front of us, three more bringing up the rear. On the donkey path, which would take us into the wider road, it was slow going, with the two guys in front having to test the ground pretty much foot by foot. Making it more difficult was the terrain, which was hilly and rocky the whole way.

It took a while, but we made it to the wider road without any problem—and without any IEDs blowing up in our faces. Until now, we'd been in heavy brush on a five-foot-wide path.

When we moved out of the heavy brush, we found ourselves on a dirt road, and one that was considerably wider than the donkey trail we had been on. Here, the going was easier.

"This is where Buzz and I leave you," Jeremy said. He pointed off into the darkness. "There shouldn't be any problem from here on in. Sully and Mack can take you the rest of the way. Danny will be behind you, just in case. It's about a mile, maybe a little more."

We thanked them for getting us this far, and the five of us set off in the direction of the little village. It was still slow going, and in the darkness you couldn't see your hand in front of you. The road, which was maybe ten feet wide, was hilly and turned one way and then the other. With dense underbrush growing close to both sides of the road, I was having difficulty getting my bearings. The only sounds were our boots grinding on the trail.

As we walked, I was aware of the silence. I reached down to touch my M9, which I had in a holster on my right hip.

After we'd gone roughly two hundred meters, me first and Haji fifteen feet behind me, I heard the sounds of a scuffle in front of me, but even with my NVGs on, I couldn't see much. Sully, who was in front of us, called out, then began cursing, and then I heard Mackey, who was with Sully and about twenty feet in front of us, also shouting. I had my M9 in my hand, and then I heard Haji start shouting.

"Alex, look out! They're trying to—" Haji was cut short in mid-sentence. I turned but saw only moving forms, definitely not clearly enough to fire my weapon. Suddenly, two dark figures plunged out of the underbrush, and one was holding my right arm. I managed to break his hold, but before I could fire someone tackled me. I still had my weapon, but I didn't want to fire into the darkness, fearful that I'd hit Mackey or Sully.

Danny and Haji were involved in a scuffle, but I couldn't see what was happening. And then a couple more guys were on top of me, keeping me on the ground. I got off two wild shots before the weapon was knocked from my hand. I heard another shot up front.

With the thick brush alongside the trail, they'd been able to get real close, and it was all over within seconds. I didn't know how many they were, but there had to be ten or more. I was on my stomach, and my face was being forced down so hard I was eating dirt. After pounding the weapon out of my hand, two of them kept me pinned while one of them pulled my head back, and someone else jammed a hood down over my head. Then my wrists were forced together, and I felt my hands being tied with some kind of tape.

There were shouted Pashto commands, and I assumed someone was telling me to get on my feet. A guy kept shoving me and saying something in an angry tone, his mouth just inches from my ear. I didn't understand the words, but it didn't require a genius to know he wanted me moving faster. The hood prevented me from seeing where I was going and who these guys were. Then I stumbled, and that brought some more angry shouts from my new friends. One of them gave me a couple of angry kicks before dragging me back to my feet.

As we went, someone behind kept pushing me, and at some point someone else grabbed hold of my belt and pulled me, trying to get me to move faster. Branches slapped against the hood. Besides the two guys moving me along, there were other people in the group, but I couldn't tell how many.

I wondered what had happened to the other soldiers, Sully, Danny, and Mack. Most of all, I wondered about Haji. I had heard half-a-dozen shots, and I was hoping no one had been killed.

I did my best to try and recall the map I'd studied before we left the COP, trying to figure where we might be headed. The road would have taken us into the hamlet where the *shura* was supposed to take place, so I figured we were now going someplace else. I hoped we weren't going to the village Withers told me about, where they hate Americans. At the same time I knew there weren't that many other villages around here.

We ploughed through brush and went up and down hills, and I figured we walked for an hour before we stopped. I thought we might be in a small clearing, but with the hood on I couldn't be sure. I assumed we were out in the middle of nowhere, some godforsaken corner of the Pech Valley, which is enormous. Since no one yet knew we were missing, no one would know where to search when they eventually found out. Although I did my best not to think in those terms, it dawned on me that our situation was pretty close to hopeless.

I felt someone patting me down. The Beretta was long gone along with my rucksack with the money. Whoever it was, he went through my pockets, emptying them of everything. Just to let me know we weren't among friends, he slugged me, once in the face and once in the solar plexus. I hit the ground hard.

"Thanks, pal. Maybe I can do something for you sometime."

I lay there for maybe ten minutes. Then I heard an automobile engine. I was yanked onto my feet, and then shoved into a vehicle, probably a van, where I ended up lying on the floor. The driver ground the gears before we lurched forward. Then the engine conked out. In Afghanistan, driver's licenses are optional.

We finally started moving. By the time the vehicle halted, I'd lost track of time. We could have been riding for twenty minutes or two hours. I only knew I ached all over.

They dragged me out of the vehicle and pushed me along until we reached a building. After being shoved through some rooms, I was on some narrow stone steps. Because I was still wearing the hood, I missed a step and tumbled down the rest of the way, headfirst. When I was back on my feet, a guy shoved me into a corner and snatched off the hood. Another guy with an AK-47 in his hands silently watched. He had a beard and was wearing a turban, and his dumb expression imprinted itself on my memory. The first guy ripped the tape off my hands and then fastened them together with a chain. There was some kind of pipe running along the wall about a foot from the ground, and he fastened the chain around that.

When I tried asking in English where we were and whether I could speak with the American Embassy in Kabul, I never completed the sentence. I got a fist square in the mouth, probably from the same guy who'd slugged me before. I took that as a less than gentle hint that I wasn't supposed to talk. To say this situation was not good was the understatement of the year.

A few minutes later I was aware of more people coming in from outside. There was a brief exchange of conversation, and I thought I recognized Haji's voice.

By this time, my eyes had become accustomed to the darkness. The guy wore a *shalwar kameez,* the standard dress around here. He might have been in his thirties but he was probably younger. People age quickly in this country.

He pointed to himself and said something I didn't understand. Haji asked him something. After a brief conversation with Haji, he left.

Whenever you're taken prisoner, you can at least be sure things can't get much worse. Chained to a pipe in the cellar of a stone hut in the boondocks of Afghanistan, I had an idea that I'd reached the absolute low point in my life. I also had an idea that the next twenty-four hours were going to be the most miserable day I'd ever experienced.

The only light came in through a small window high on the wall. Haji was about ten feet away, but I could barely see him. Like me, he was chained to the pipe running along the wall. "What was that all about?" I said.

Haji said, "He told us he is a proud member of the Taliban. He also said that they're going to behead us when the executioner gets here."

"When's that going to be?"

"He said sometime tomorrow. He didn't know exactly when."

I said, "Let's hope he runs into heavy traffic on the way over."

CHAPTER 13

Early the following morning a teenaged boy came in to tend to us. When he saw us, he shook his head. I couldn't blame him. After giving each of us a cup of water and an orange, he exchanged a few words with Haji. With my hands chained, I accidentally spilled most of the water, and I got mad because of my clumsiness. But I ate the orange, rind and all.

With the kid gone, I asked Haji what he'd learned.

"He said the elders of the tribe hate Americans because of something that happened here last year."

"Did he say a mullah was killed?"

"Yes, he did. That's why they're going to turn us over to the executioner. We're in the wrong village. The boy also said the executioner is an important person in the Taliban. And he wants to have us beheaded publicly."

I was silent after that, wondering why this situation didn't seem to make much sense. Haji was hardly talking, and I had an idea I knew what he was thinking. If it hadn't been for me, he wouldn't be in this mess. I was the one who wanted to follow up on the Abdul Sakhi lead.

The building we were in was made of stone. There was distant noise, and the sound of people moving around. I had an idea there were rooms on the first floor, and from the sound of people's voices, I assumed people slept in them at night. Our cell had a pile of useless furniture piled in one corner and all kinds of junk in the other. It had a dirt floor and one heavy door. The small window was just big enough to let in some sunlight. With the chains wound around the pipe, I assumed this place was used as a jail, a place where the locals kept their bad actors on ice.

About once every hour a guard carrying an AK-47 would enter, look things over, and leave. I assumed he was a Talib, and Haji never spoke with him.

During the late afternoon the kid came back in and gave each of us half a bottle of water. You can't drink the water in Afghanistan, so I figured we had a choice between dying from being beheaded or dying from dysentery. I took a couple of sips and hoped for the best.

When you're a prisoner you have time to think about things—and to go over what you would have done differently. Wanda had been right when she said I was making a big mistake by going on this expedition. She'd poo-pooed the idea of my being loyal to Pete. My meeting with Jerry now seemed to have taken place so long ago and so far away, it seemed to have been in another lifetime on another planet.

Being chained up here for ten hours felt like two weeks. Something else that was strange was that Haji and I had so little to say to one another. But maybe it wasn't so strange. What was there to say? I assumed that the Taliban had somehow gotten word of our little expedition and the fact I had five grand in my rucksack. Whoever the executioner was, he clearly had a grudge against Americans.

Time dragged, and I suppose from time to time I dozed.

Through the small window I could see the arrival of darkness. Whoever the guy was, he was supposed to arrive any time now. Did that mean we had just a few more hours to live? Eight? Seven? Six?

Maybe less. Maybe he'd already arrived, and was out there honing his axe.

I did my best to force all those depressing thoughts from my mind. I thought of all the things I might have accomplished in my life but didn't. Number one on the list was marrying Irmie.

The one thought I couldn't force out of my mind was the realization that none of this had to have happened. I could have told Jerry Shenlee "no" easily enough. I could have said I couldn't leave my business. I could have said I had wedding plans. I could have said my fiancée didn't want me to leave. I could have said I didn't want to go back to Afghanistan. I could have dreamed up any number of reasons for staying at home.

I could even have said that my days working "special ops" were over. Why didn't I? Strangely, I wasn't sure of the answer to that question.

Maybe the time I should have said "no" was that long-ago day at Fort Bragg when the intelligence recruiter said he saw in me something different, a quality that makes good case officers. It went beyond just an ability to keep whatever happened to myself. He described it as a different way of thinking—an ability to find my way out of impossible situations and solve tough problems in my own way.

Remembering his words, I smiled to myself. Those are qualities I could definitely use at this moment.

The truth was, though, that over the years when I hadn't been smart, I'd been lucky. I hated to have to admit it, but it was true. I'd been in any number of situations and on any number of missions that could have ended differently. All those crazy helicopter rides, clandestine meetings, face-to-face encounters with desperate individuals—not to mention the trips into Iron Curtain countries with a false passport and visa and the countless attempts to recruit agents for our side. One of the craziest took place in a Black Sea hotel room, a place from which I had no business escaping but somehow did. Another was a series of incidents that began with a visit to an East German chess club. And then there was the "hand-holding"— the constant reassurances to agents that they were doing the right thing after they'd made the irreversible fateful decision.

Eventually, your luck runs out. It happens to the best of them. Jimmy the Greek, the famous gambler, won millions but died penniless.

I suppose that's what had happened to me. My luck, like Jimmy's, had run out.

This tiny cell not only stank, it was totally dark and eerily silent, Haji's breathing and the movement of his chain being the only sound. Late afternoon arrived. With my hands chained, it was impossible to find a comfortable position and my body ached all over. I continued to doze intermittently.

Then, at some time during the night, I was aware of the cell door creaking open and people standing in the doorway.

One of them began talking, first quietly then more loudly. I didn't know what he was saying, and just lay there listening. He sounded angry.

Then I heard Haji's voice. "This man, Alex, he says he is our *dussman* . . . our enemy. He is an executioner. He says he wants to introduce himself, and he wants us to see him before we die. He intends to behead us in the morning. He says he is looking forward to it. He also says he wants you to know who he is. His name is Izat. *Izat* means 'respect.' He is a Taliban. He says he was captured by Americans who threw him into the prison at Bagram."

"Tell Izat to let us go, and then I'll respect him."

"Izat says he was tortured for no reason."

"Izat's a liar."

"He says he was deprived of food and sleep. He says he dislikes Americans and wants you to know what he experienced . . ."

And then I received a ferocious kick to my kidneys, more than one. Someone unlocked the chain holding my wrists and pulled me to my feet. My arms were pulled upward. They pushed me against the wall, then hung the chain over one of the pipes in such a way that I was hanging from my arms. My shoulders felt like they were being pulled out of their joints.

Before leaving, Izat began talking again. One of the guys swung his weapon and struck the side of my leg above the knee. The pain was excruciating.

Haji didn't bother to tell me whatever it was this piece of shit said. He knew I wouldn't be interested.

Then the door slammed shut.

In the darkness, time crawled . . .

Across the table from me, a smiling young woman in a blue dress raised her glass, said, "To us, Alex." After we both emptied our glasses, I reached for the bottle of champagne and refilled them. In the background someone was playing the fiddle, my favorite song, "Yours Is My Heart Alone." I said, "I love you, Irmie. I'll always love you . . ."

I was half hallucinating. In another dream I was back in East Germany, a country that hasn't even existed for the last twenty-five years . . .

CHAPTER 14

I KNEW THERE were people in the cell. Men with weapons slung over their shoulders, self-styled *mujahedeen*. They were talking. When someone shook the chain, I groaned. When a guy bent over and unlocked the chain, I fell to the ground, aware of nothing besides the pain, which was shooting through my entire body. I heard Haji speaking to someone. I didn't understand what they were saying.

I don't understand Pashto.

Someone kicked me in the ribs.

Someone else prodded me with the barrel of a weapon, another person dragged me to my feet. I looked at his face, into his dark eyes. He grabbed my arms and tied my wrists behind my back. Because of the stiffness and the pain in my legs, I had trouble walking, each step causing a shooting pain. Climbing the narrow steps was agonizing. I knew Haji was somewhere behind me. Behind him was a *mooj* with a gun.

We stepped out of the building. The air was cold, but the sun was bright, briefly blinding. We were in the middle of a dirt street, which ran uphill. There were mud huts on either side, and behind the huts to our right was a steep hill. We were truly in the boondocks, at the western end of the Pech Valley. More than that I didn't know. I followed two men with weapons slung over their shoulders. They were talking with each other. One of them said something, and the other laughed.

Stop laughing, you creep . . .

As we walked, my mind began to clear.

Behind me, a *mooj* prodded me with the barrel of his weapon. Then, I saw people. Both sides of the street were lined with onlookers, standing silently, watching, curious. I briefly considered making a dash, but there was no place to run. I wouldn't get far. Then I wondered whether being shot mightn't be preferable to having my head hacked off.

There were four *mooj* now. We turned, and they marched us down a dusty unpaved street to a wide clearing, where roughly fifty people were already gathered in a circle. Executions draw crowds. More people began drifting in, swelling the crowd, which was totally silent. At the center of the circle was the stump of an ancient tree, and I could feel someone shoving me forward.

When I said "Stop pushing!" he shouted something.

A number of bystanders raised their fists and yelled. I supposed they were yelling at me.

Alongside the tree stump stood an individual dressed for the occasion, in black, wearing a hood. I supposed that was Izat. He was holding a long curved sword with a carved handle. Oh, wonderful. I also supposed that was the elegant tool with which he expected to do the honors.

My only thought was that my worst nightmare was about to become reality. I was about to have my head hacked off by this imbecile. I could feel myself shaking. My breath was coming in gasps.

He said something to Haji and pointed to me.

"Alex, he wants you to know he was a prisoner in the Bagram jail."

"He told us that last night. Whatever he's saying, I don't want to hear it. He's an imbecile. Tell him I said that."

"Alex, you can't—"

"What's the word for 'imbecile'? I'll tell him myself."

When Izat continued to talk, Haji said, "He lived in a cage for six months before they released him. He says he was beaten many times. He also says he did not receive adequate food. He says he hates all Americans."

"Tell him I don't believe him."

The circle of people, which numbered at least a hundred, was now totally silent. I supposed the guy in black was giving his speech partly for their benefit. A few, I noticed, began to mumble and were nodding their heads. Nodding their approval of what was about to happen. I supposed that was what this goofball wanted.

"Goddamn you guys! To hell with all of you!"

Izat continued his rant.

I said to Haji, "Tell this imbecile I'm not interested in his problems."

"He says he was humiliated by Americans. He wants you to apologize."

I gave him my answer. "Tell him to get a goddamned therapist!"

Haji only shook his head, obviously reluctant to pass on what I'd said. "He wants to know what you just told me."

"Tell him they never should have released him. Tell him he's a piece of shit. He deserved his beatings."

Haji's eyes widened, but he didn't say anything.

"Tell him to go chase himself. Tell him—"

All at once I could feel the guy with the AK-47 shoving his weapon into my back. Now he was yelling something. Izat was pointing at me to kneel down. I was supposed to stick my head on the stump, make it easy for him to start hacking it off. Was that what they wanted me to do?

Then Izat stepped forward, pointed down.

"His feet, Alex."

"What about them?"

"He says you should kiss his feet." This situation was getting weirder by the second. When I mumbled more profanity, Haji said, "You have to do it."

"Like hell!"

"That will show the people here that you deserve to die."

As I continued to shout, someone shoved me, and one of the *mooj* grabbed me. When I tried to get off a kick, I got a rifle butt against my cheek and went down. Hard. I was flat on my back and still yelling.

Then I heard someone shouting *"Tersha! Tersha!"* Move!

"Wasla dee parmzaka kegda!" Drop the gun!

Then I heard shots . . .

What was this all about?

Bang! And then another loud bang. Who was shooting? All at once the circle of people began to break up. People were scattering in every direction.

"Zah! Korta zah!" Beat it! Go home!

What was happening? On my back with my hands tied, I was not only helpless, I was in the worst position possible to see what was going on.

"Zaman da amruno paerawi wukra!" Follow our orders! *"Korta zah!"*

When I heard the chatter of an automatic weapon, I wondered who could be firing. I could hear women shrieking, and I thought I heard a baby crying. People were running.

"Zah! Zah!" Get going! *"Ta poheegee?"* You understand? *"Zah! Zah!"*

No one was paying attention to me anymore. Placing my hands against the stump, I managed to struggle, first to my knees, then back to my feet. I saw Izat, the guy in black, lying in the dust. Blood was oozing out of his chest. He'd been shot, more than once. Alongside him was his sword.

His friend with the AK-47 had dropped his weapon. His hands were in the air. His face was contorted with fear. The two other *mooj* had disappeared.

Good riddance!

A team of three armed Afghans had stepped out of the crowd, and one of them was talking to Haji. Another stepped around behind me, cut the rope around my wrists, said something in Pashto that, needless to say, I didn't understand.

Then he said, *"Delta wadarega,"* which means "Stay here." I nodded.

A second later, a van came roaring onto the clearing, narrowly missing the last couple of stragglers, then whirled around, and screeched to a halt. The driver, obviously a frustrated NASCAR fan, shouted something, and one of the newcomers yanked back the door. No one had to tell Haji or me to climb in. With five of us inside, the driver jammed his foot down on the gas. As we shot forward, the driver honked, and people scattered.

I heard some shots. "Who are these guys?" I asked Haji.

Haji only shrugged. He didn't know who they were either.

I said it again, loudly. "Who the hell are they?"

Haji said, "Don't talk, Alex." After a second, he said quietly, "Whoever they are, be thankful they came in time."

I couldn't argue with that.

I supposed they knew where we were going. I also supposed we weren't going to drive over an IED and get ourselves blown to smithereens. As we drove, the guy in charge used his telephone twice, speaking Pashto and keeping his conversations short each time.

The roads in Afghanistan are treacherous. Many are made nearly impassable by the hilly terrain. Some of the roads we were on weren't much wider than donkey trails. Where were we going? Our driver didn't look to be more than sixteen, but he not only knew where he was heading, he also knew what he was doing, when to give gas and when to slow down. Squeezed into the corner of the rear seat, I held on for dear life. After a half hour of driving, I saw that we were passing small villages, some perched precariously on the sides of mountains.

After a brief exchange with one of the new arrivals, Haji said, "He says the village we just passed is named Kalaygal."

"I never heard of it."

A minute later, Haji whispered, "Kalaygal is in the Korengal. These people are from the Korengali tribe."

I recalled Bud Withers saying the Korengalis were the fiercest tribe in Afghanistan. They'd fought the American Army to a standstill, and in 2010 forced NATO to withdraw completely from this area of Afghanistan. Americans weren't exactly beloved around here. They were really going to love me.

Out of the frying pan and into the fire?

The drive lasted two hours, maybe longer. When we finally slowed down, I could see the outlines of stone buildings. We drove into a quiet village, surrounded by rolling hills and farms, then down an unpaved curving street, at the end of which there was a compound. A row of children, their faces filled with curiosity, stood silently, gazing at us. One of our guys hopped out and pushed open the gate, waved to the driver, and we turned in. Inside was a small complex of stone buildings. As we climbed out of the van, the driver pointed to the largest building. At least no one was pointing a weapon at me. Although my arms and shoulders hurt, my legs were okay, and I could walk well enough. We entered single file. Inside, the only light came from a couple of burning gas canisters.

We moved on to a large room; a fire burned inside. Seven men were standing in a group and speaking quietly. When we entered, they all turned. All had beards and wore traditional clothing, shawls and turbans. No one said anything. There was total silence.

I glanced nervously at Haji, but his face was a blank. Except that we knew we were somewhere in the Korengal Valley, we had no idea where we were or what was happening. I could see the men were elders, and I assumed that some kind of meeting, or *shura*, was going on. Whatever it was, their looks were curious, not unfriendly.

Then at the far end of the big room a broad-shouldered, bearded individual dressed in a flowing robe and holding a young boy by the hand stepped into the glare of the firelight. As he approached me, I stiffened, making myself ready for whatever was coming. At least he wasn't holding a big sword. Or an AK-47.

When he was a foot away, he said, *"Kha raaghlaast."* Haji whispered, "That means 'Welcome.'" Then the bearded guy pointed to himself. *"Zma nowm Shah Mahmood dai."*

This much Pashto I understood. He was saying his name.

Then he pointed at the boy, who shyly smiled. The youngster said something that sounded like *"ma-nana."* I knew the word meant "thank you."

Thank you? I hadn't done anything! I hadn't any idea what he was thanking me for.

What was all this?

All at once the elder placed his left arm on my arm and his right hand on my shoulder, and then we shook hands. After the first squeeze, he looked me in the eye and began talking. As he talked, he gave me another hug. Not knowing what else to do, I responded with a hug of my own.

What was this all about?

I knew the lives of people in this area of Afghanistan were guided by a strict code of conduct called *Pashtunwali,* which emphasizes loyalty, hospitality, and revenge. Beyond that, I knew almost nothing.

As the elders approached me, each gave me a half-hug followed by a handshake. Then they drifted off, formed a circle, and began speaking among themselves. I felt that I was part of some kind of strange ritual. In fact I began to feel as if I was the center of it.

"Alex!" Haji said suddenly. "Alex! The boy! The boy, Alex! Look at him! Don't you recognize him? Don't you remember? Alex, Alex. His father says you saved his life."

The youngster, who was maybe eight or nine years old and had tousled black hair, was gazing up at me. In the half-light I could see a shy smile on his face.

And then it struck me!

On the way in from the airport! I'd all but forgotten!

This was the youngster who'd wandered into the line of fire while I was blasting away at the Talibs. I'd tackled him and we'd ended up under the fruit stand together.

I hadn't had a chance to introduce myself back then. I stuck out my hand.

His father was standing by, nodding his head and looking very happy.

"*Zma nowm Alex dai.*"

"*Zma nowm Jawid dai.*"

"His father's name is Shah Mahmood," Haji said.

Sticking out my hand, I again said my name in Pashto.

"Shah Mahmood says he is grateful to have the chance to thank you."

I was flabbergasted. These were people who supposedly hated Americans.

We were guests of honor!

Haji and I were the ones who should be saying thank you.

We were being treated like royalty!

"Alex, they want us to join them," Haji said, pointing to the elders gathered sitting cross-legged in a circle near the fire. Shah Mahmood pointed to where we could sit. As we eased ourselves down on cushions, I became aware of how stiff I was. We sat cross-legged on the ground by the fire, not the most comfortable position for me at that moment, but I wasn't complaining. Then boys brought in cups of tea. Shah Mahmood had taken a place next to me. As he spoke, Haji translated.

"Shah Mahmood is apologizing for his wife," Haji said. "She was upset that she'd lost sight of her boy."

"Tell Shah Mahmood there is no need to apologize."

Haji continued to talk, with Shah Mahmood and with some of the other elders. After fifteen minutes, Haji said, "These people are members of the Korengali tribe. The members of the other tribe were Safirs. In the village where we were they dislike Americans because their most beloved mullah was killed last year, perhaps by an American. The Korengalis have lived in this end of the valley for many hundreds of years. The man who wanted to execute us, they say, had become a Taliban fanatic and had fought against Americans and had been imprisoned. They say after he escaped from American prison, he was seeking any opportunity to execute Americans. When Shah Mahmood heard your name mentioned as the American Izat intended to execute, he sent his men to rescue us."

After perhaps an hour, some boys rolled out a rubber mat and began bringing food, bowls of soup, plates of chicken, bread.

Shah Mahmood pointed at the food. *Wutskha!* Eat! Another word I knew.

We were given water to wash our hands. Then, using our hands, we dug in. I told Haji to tell Shah Mahmood how good the food tasted.

After we'd eaten, we drank more tea.

Then Shah Mahmood began to talk. With Haji listening, he spoke calmly and without letup. When he stopped, Haji said, "Shah

Mahmood wants you to understand the situation here in the Korengal Valley. Because it is one of Afghanistan's remotest areas, Shah Mahmood says his people were always independent and governed themselves. He says it was only after the American occupation that people here in the Korengal were forced to choose—between the Taliban and the Americans. They chose the Taliban, he says, not because of dislike for America, but because his people have a tradition of independence and do not want to be ruled by outsiders. Americans were outsiders. Shah Mahmood says for this reason he and others have fought with the Taliban. Then he tells this story, Alex. He was with a group of Taliban soldiers in Kabul on the day you arrived. They had buried an IED in Airport Road, and as your vehicle approached the IED, Shah Mahmood was waiting and ready to set it off. When your vehicle rode over the bomb, Shah Mahmood touched the two wires together, causing the IED to explode. He witnessed the entire incident—how your vehicle rode over the bomb, turned over, landed upside down, and made you helpless targets. Then he gave the orders to his soldiers to start shooting.

"A minute later he saw that because his wife had become distracted, his son had wandered out of the building, and wanted to see what was happening and walked into the line of fire. Shah Mahmood says he could not believe how, in the moment when he was shooting and trying to kill you, you jumped out of the Humvee and risked your life to save his son."

As Shah Mahmood talked with Haji, I gazed at the elders and drank more tea.

"Shah Mahmood says he felt terrible remorse for trying to kill you while you were risking your life to save his only son. Shah Mahmood says he will never forget your unselfish actions on his and his son's behalf. He says your deed changed forever his view of Americans."

In time the other guests rose, said good-bye to one another and to Shah Mahmood. Before leaving, each elder bowed toward me.

Haji said, "Shah Mahmood has arranged beds for us, Alex. We can stay here in the village."

The time was late afternoon. A boy led us across the road to another building. Inside was a room with blankets, mattresses, and cushions spread out on the floor. By this time I was beginning to feel very tired.

Haji said, "Do you understand the word *milmastia*?" When I said I didn't, Haji said, "*Milmastia* is the Pashto for hospitality. Shah Mahmood and his people here want us to feel as if we are in our own homes."

Haji's words were the last I remember. Within minutes I was fast asleep.

* * *

When I awoke, it was already dark. Haji was seated next to me. "It's seven in the evening," he said. "Don't worry, Alex. We can remain here as long as we like."

I was stiff but felt somewhat better. I got to my feet and took a walk around the room. I asked Haji the name of the village.

"We are in a small hamlet. The nearest large village is Bibiyal," Haji said. "The Korengal people are independent, and have never been ruled by outsiders. Before America came, they fought off the Russians."

Afterward, a boy brought tea and asked Haji if we were still hungry. Haji must have said yes because another boy arrived with bread and fruit.

Then a messenger came in and spoke with Haji. Haji said, "Shah Mahmood says we are welcome to stay here tonight. He says whenever we want to leave, he can provide transportation. But before we leave he wants to talk with us."

I said, "Tell Shah Mahmood we will take advantage of his hospitality and stay tonight and tomorrow. And that we are very grateful for everything."

In order to stretch my legs I did some exercises and took a fifteen-minute walk around the village. The exertion was enough to make me feel better. Shortly afterward, I fell asleep and didn't wake until the next morning.

Early the next day, we returned to Shah Mahmood's building. After we'd eaten, Shah Mahmood, Haji, and I sat on cushions in a small circle. As Shah Mahmood spoke, Haji translated.

"Shah Mahmood says he apologizes for the fruit vendor. He says the man will no longer complain. On the second evening, Shah Mahmood sent someone to say that he no longer supported the vendor's request for money. He says his messenger spoke with a woman at the gate and from her he learned your name." When I told Haji to say whatever confusion there was had been resolved, I saw Shah Mahmood nodding his head.

When Haji said to me, "Do you know who the woman was?" I said, "I assume it was Captain Corley."

After a few minutes, Haji said, "Shah Mahmood suggests we relax. Later, he will send a van and we can take a trip into Bibiyal."

After the banging around I'd gotten from the Talibs, I was happy to spend another day in the Korengal Valley, the place that supposedly was so inhospitable to Americans. Again I told Haji to say we were grateful for Shah Mahmood's *milmastia*.

That afternoon Haji and I were driven on a winding road through a narrow valley that after a mile opened onto a broad expanse of farmland. As we strolled through the ancient city of Bibiyal, Haji reminded me that I was one of very few Americans to visit the city after the withdrawal of the NATO armies three years before.

I could well understand why Shah Mahmood wanted us to see the Korengal Valley. It was lush and fertile farmland as far as the eye could see, and unbelievably beautiful. The broad valley was nestled between mountains that rose gently toward the clouds. Seeing this incomparably beautiful area of Afghanistan, I found it easy to understand why the Korengalis were such ferocious defenders of their homeland. There could hardly be a more beautiful place anywhere.

On Saturday night, I again slept very soundly.

As we were getting ready to leave the next morning, Shah Mahmood came around to say good-bye. As we sat in a circle eating, he and Haji held a long conversation.

After a few minutes, Haji turned to me. "Shah Mahmood says Abdul Sakhi grew up in Kunar Province. He belonged once to Shah Mahmood's tribe, not to the Safirs." After speaking again with Shah Mahmood, Haji said, "Abdul Sakhi left many years ago. He no longer has contact with the Korengali tribe."

I again told Haji to thank Shah Mahmood for his help and his hospitality.

"Shah Mahmood also says you are the only American he has ever known. Because he says the dead Izat may have friends, he prefers that we not reveal to anyone how the Korengalis rescued us."

Haji and Shah Mahmood spoke awhile longer. I'd begun to wonder how we'd come to land in the Safir village, the one place hostile to Americans. It was clear we'd been given all kinds of wrong information.

"Shah Mahmood says he hopes we will remain friends and stay in touch and that we will again be his guests." After a brief exchange, Haji said, "When we are ready to go, he will provide transportation."

An hour later, as we were leaving the house, Jawid, Shah Mahmood's son, appeared. As we climbed into the van, I waved good-bye.
"Da khoo-die pah aman, Jawid.*"*

"Da khoo-die pah aman, Alex.*"*

"The driver says they know the way, and they can drive us part of
the distance to the Pech River, near the COP. After that, we have to
walk." When I asked how far, Haji said, "Perhaps two miles. He also
says there won't be any problems with IEDs."

And then the driver started the engine.

CHAPTER 15

SUNDAY, FEBRUARY 10, 2013

"I DON'T GET it," Bud Withers said angrily. "Where did you guys disappear to?"

"I don't get it either," I said. "How come you gave us wrong information?"

We were back in the COP, in Withers' command post. I had just helped myself to one of the bottles of water on the dirt floor alongside Withers' desk. I was aware of Withers eyeing me as I sat back down.

"Well?" I said. "I'm waiting. You call that intel?"

Maybe I wasn't doing a good job of staying calm, but Withers and his know-it-all attitude was bothering me. At the same time, I definitely wasn't going to tell this guy that I was two minutes away from having my head hacked off.

I had an idea he wouldn't have believed me anyway.

One of the company NCOs was also in the room, a sergeant named Malley. When Withers nodded to him, he decided to stay around.

"We didn't exactly disappear. A bunch of Talibs grabbed us."

Withers rolled his eyes. He gave the impression he didn't believe me. "You didn't just go along with them?"

Before I could answer, Malley said, "We lost a man out there that night." He spoke in a matter-of-fact tone. "Sully. Sergeant Sulzberg. He was one of our best. Danny Mayo, the other guy, found some cover. When he started shooting, you guys took off."

"They hauled us out of there," I said. "We didn't go because we wanted to go."

"That's what we can't understand," Withers said. "There was supposed to be a *shura*. That was Wednesday night. Here it is Sunday. Where the hell were you?"

"We weren't where we were supposed to be. We were in the other village, that's where we were."

"Why would they just take you guys? Did they know who you were?"

"Good question." I looked at Haji, but his face remained a blank. "In this village where we were they were hostile to Americans."

Withers frowned. "You ended up in the wrong village."

"We ended up where they took us." I decided not to add that the way I now saw things this entire expedition was goofy from the get-go. It had been Withers who'd set it in motion and said we should meet with the Safirs. According to Shah Mahmood, they wouldn't have known anything about Abdul Sakhi.

"We lost a soldier out there the other night," Sergeant Malley said again. "One of my men." The way he glared at us I could see he thought we were responsible for Sully's death. "Ain't nothing like that's ever happened before."

I decided to remain silent. Haji shifted nervously in his chair. It was plain the conversation had reached its end. It was also plain that Captain Withers wanted us off his base, which was fine with me.

Sergeant Malley checked his watch. "Chopper should be here in another half hour."

Captain Withers stood up. "I have an idea you guys will want to be on it. I'll call it in. You might also want to let people in ISAF know what's going on." He looked at Malley and smirked. "You can get yourselves some chow over in Building 8. MREs are on the menu today."

Malley pointed toward the door. "Take a right when you leave. Be ready at the gate when you hear the chopper."

None of us shook hands. There were no good-byes when we left the building. But I could feel Withers' eyes focused on me as I pushed open the door. It felt like they were burning holes in my back.

Haji and I waited for the chopper seated on benches in what passed for a mess hall on the COP. Since it was rough duty out here, I couldn't much blame Withers for being unhappy. He had a lot of things to be unhappy about. I wondered whether he was right— whether I could have prevented Sully's death. One thing was sure. I didn't like the idea of being told I was responsible.

* * *

Like the people back on the combat outpost, Stan Jones and Doug Greer were skeptical of how things had worked out—or at least of my version of how they'd worked out.

The debriefing had taken place in the office of Colonel Gardner Boyd, who was attached to the commander's office.

It was late afternoon, nearly four hours after we'd left the COP. On the ride back on the Black Hawk helicopter we'd made the loop, stopping at Bagram and a number of bases before putting down at Camp Phoenix.

When we arrived, there had been a van waiting at the Phoenix helicopter pad to take me over to ISAF Headquarters.

Doug Greer only shook his head when I had completed the story. "You were gone almost four days, for God's sakes!"

"And you say you were in the Taliban prison all that time?" Colonel Boyd said, frowning.

I said, "For some reason we landed in a village that's hostile to Americans."

Stan had made the trip over from Phoenix just to hear what had happened. "So you never got to talk to Shergaz, the elder." He shook his head. "And you never found out where this Abdul Sakhi is."

"I don't get it. I mean, it's just not logical." Colonel Boyd pointed to me. "Who do you report to?" he said.

"He reports to someone on the NSC," Stan said.

I still didn't know who I was reporting to. Jerry had said someone would contact me, but so far no one had.

"I hope you can tell your boss a more believable story than what you just told us," Greer said, standing up.

People had good reasons to be skeptical. I hadn't said how Shah Mahmood's people had rescued us from the individual who wanted to chop off our heads. That would remain our little secret, for a while anyway. We'd do our best to tell the story without mentioning Shah Mahmood and his people.

I kind of doubted anyone would believe the story anyway.

I said, "Has there been any progress finding out who it was shot Pete?"

Stan shook his head. "Nothing you don't already know."

Although I felt someone could have said that it was nice to have us back in one piece I knew no one would. People's minds were on other things.

Colonel Boyd said, "We have a meeting scheduled tomorrow at 0900 hours. We're hoping we can wrap up the investigation."

I said I'd be there.

"We can talk again in the morning," Stan said.

When I got back to Camp Eggers, I remembered that among the things I'd lost out there was the five thousand bucks I was supposed to give the elder. I had an idea I'd be hearing about that.

Something else I'd lost was my room key, and I needed to call a female sergeant from the Room Assignment building to open my door. And that took a while. It was after 1900 hours when I finally flopped onto my cot. It wasn't the right moment to call Irmie. I was still too full of what had happened in the Korengal Valley, and I certainly didn't want Irmie to know anything about that. I knew she was already worrying too much, even though she would never admit it. I hated to think how unhappy I was making her.

Those were my last thoughts. Despite all the shouting and screaming I'd been doing, I slept soundly.

CHAPTER 16

I decided to skip chow the next morning. After climbing out of my van at the Headquarters parking area, I still felt stiff but a lot better than two days ago. I saw I had twenty minutes to spare and stretched my legs with a walk through the Destille Garden and over to the Coffee Garden for a cup of java. The Coffee Garden, in the ISAF Headquarters building, was filled with office workers grabbing tea and coffee to take back to their offices. Listening in, I caught snatches of French, Italian, and Swedish. In a sense, Kabul had changed since my first visit two years before, and was becoming one of the world's crossroads.

Kabul is a nice city—if you're willing to overlook the frequent Taliban attacks, the traffic chaos, the many military checkpoints, the occasional IED explosions, and the unpredictable green-on-blue killings.

Something else that was on my mind was the ongoing trial of the twenty-two officials of the Kabul Bank. Like everyone else, I wondered whether the Afghan judges had enough strength of character to find these individuals guilty.

As I dawdled with my coffee, I shuddered when I thought about how close Haji and I had been to losing our heads. I was still having difficulty trying to figure how the people who grabbed us would have known when we were coming. When I checked my watch, I saw the meeting, which was to take place in a second-floor conference room and was scheduled for 0900 hours, was about to begin. I took a last swallow of coffee and somewhat reluctantly headed upstairs.

After seating myself at a long table, I realized that the verdict was already a foregone conclusion. Stan hadn't made any secret out of his intention to find Baram Nolda guilty of shooting Pete. Since I was now convinced that Pete had been killed by Abdul Sakhi, I knew I was going to irritate some people when I stated my opinion.

For that reason, I only listened for the first fifteen minutes while Stan recounted the details of the investigation for Colonel Boyd's benefit—Nolda's background, the interviews, the camera problems.

Finally, he said, "According to the FBI, one of our assets, an Askar named Abdul Sakhi, was in the building the day Colonel Hansen was shot."

When Colonel Boyd frowned, Doug said, "He could have been there for any number of reasons. Only Alex thinks Sakhi killed Pete."

With all eyes upon me, including those of Colonel Boyd, I said, "I read Nolda differently right from the start. After talking to his CO and one of his buddies, I was convinced he wasn't the type to pull a green-on-blue."

Hammond shook his head. "As far as I'm concerned, the Askars are hard to read."

"I agree," Colonel Boyd said. "Too circumstantial."

I said, "There's more. Last week Nolda's body turned up in Qargha Lake. This would have been eleven days after Pete was killed. When I saw the body, I got the impression he'd been in the water for a while, maybe longer than eleven days."

Colonel Boyd said, "You were able to determine this individual had been dead for that long? Just by looking at him?" I heard the skeptical tone in his voice.

"It had the signs, sir. A floater tends to become bloated. You can tell from the color of the skin." I paused. "And the appearance of the body." When Colonel Boyd grimaced, I said, "The body had been significantly eaten away. Decomposition would have occurred more slowly in a cold-water lake like Qargha." Before Colonel Boyd could comment, I said emphatically, "But then the body disappeared."

Stan said, "That hospital's chaotic. There could be any number of reasons for—"

I said, "A pathologist was set to fly over from Bagram. He could have determined that Nolda was already dead when Pete was shot."

Greer said, "Alex, I just don't see how you could tell from a quick look—"

Colonel Boyd shook his head. "I don't either. Sorry. Let's wrap this up."

When Stan said, "How many here think it was Sergeant Nolda killed Colonel Hansen?" I was the only one who didn't raise a hand.

Colonel Boyd spent a minute writing in his pad, then stood up and nodded toward Stan.

"That's the official version?" Greer said, getting to his feet. "That's what I can tell the people back in D.C.?"

"I would say so," Colonel Boyd said briskly and headed for the door.

With the meeting adjourned, I felt mildly depressed. Outside, in the Headquarters parking area, I called Wanda.

"Do you feel like lunch?"

"I heard that you're back. I was worried."

"I'm glad someone was worried."

"Poor boy."

"I'm fishing for sympathy again."

"I can see that, but I'm not available for lunch. You won't believe what I've done." Before I could reply, she said, "I'm moving. I'm leaving the Green Village and moving into a hotel for my last week in Kabul. What do you think of that?"

"It depends on the hotel."

"I've booked a room at the best hotel in Kabul. At least everyone says the Serena is Kabul's best hotel. I move in tomorrow."

"They don't serve booze."

"No, but they serve high tea. I'm inviting you."

"I can't wait." In the background, I could hear people talking. "Where are you now?"

"On Flower Street, shopping. Looking for stuff I can bring back to the States. I'm beginning to like Kabul, at least a little bit. There are some great bazaars here."

"Another time then."

And then I had another thought. I knew I needed to let off some steam. That meant I'd need to find a place serving alcohol. I recalled the Gandamack Lodge being an occasional hangout during my two earlier visits. I wondered what Captain Page might be doing. He answered with his name.

"How are you doing?"

"Do you want my real answer or my diplomatic answer?"

"Neither. I'm going to be at the Gandamack this evening. In the basement bar. I thought you might want to drop by."

"Sounds good," he said.

Although it still wasn't noon, I needed some time to think. And with my shoulders still aching, I also needed some rest. But I also felt a little groggy, which meant I needed more coffee.

I called Haji and told him to meet me in the Green Bean coffee shop at 1230 hours.

Camp Phoenix's Green Bean is in a crumbling stone building that is one story above a haphazard bunch of offices and meeting rooms. The building, which was originally built by the Russians during their ill-fated occupation of Afghanistan, was definitely showing its age.

After finding myself a place at one of the rear tables, I gazed around at the GIs waiting in line for coffee, at two attractive women in scrubs, no doubt medical personnel at the dispensary, chatting at the next table. I was about to get on the coffee line again when Haji arrived.

"You don't look good," Haji said, shaking his head and placing a large cardboard cup of cappuccino down on the wooden table. As I watched him slowly gnawing on one of the Green Bean's chocolate chip cookies, I had the impression Haji's mind was elsewhere, perhaps still on our close call in Kunar Province.

"Our little adventure took more out of me than I want to admit, Haji. Maybe I'm not as young as I used to be." I didn't say it, but thanks to Izat, my left shoulder still ached. Izat was gone, but not completely forgotten. At least not by me.

Haji smiled but didn't say anything. Like many Afghans, he's learned to be diplomatic.

"What we have to do, Haji, is find out more about this Abdul Sakhi individual. I'm going to tell you what I think. But I don't want you to repeat any of this to anyone." When Haji nodded, I said, "I don't believe Sergeant Nolda killed Colonel Hansen."

"But why not?"

"Reason number one: He was already dead on the day Colonel Hansen was shot. Reason number two: It's my gut feeling."

"I respect your gut feeling, Alex. I assume you think Abdul Sakhi killed Colonel Hansen." When I nodded, Haji said, "I must remind you that what we know about this man is he is an enemy of the Taliban and—"

"And American soldiers, like Colonel Hansen, also are enemies of the Taliban."

"Yes. It does not seem logical that such a person would want to kill Colonel Hansen."

"It's a confusing situation. I agree. Nevertheless, I do not think Baram Nolda killed Colonel Hansen."

"And you believe the murderer might be Abdul Sakhi. I have another question. Why is it so important?"

"You're beginning to sound like the military people here. They do not think it's important either. They believe because American forces will be leaving Afghanistan at the end of next year, there are other more important matters for them to handle."

"How do you know they think this way?"

"I have just returned from a meeting at which such sentiments were expressed, not directly but indirectly."

"I agree with your colleagues, Alex. I, too, do not feel that in this case the identity of the murderer is of the highest importance." Haji smiled. "That is *my* gut feeling."

I took a sip of my tea. "As you know, Haji, I also respect your gut feelings. However, in this instance I have to be blunt. I think you are wrong." When Haji frowned, I said, "What is important is to determine the motive behind Colonel Hansen's murder."

Haji gazed at me over the rim of his cappuccino cup with his dark eyes, obviously waiting for me to explain myself.

I said, "If Nolda was the murderer, it would then be a green-on-blue, and that would mean we know the motive. However, if the murder was the work of someone who was only trying to make it appear to be a green-on-blue, it would then be something quite different. In that case, I would like to know what the motive was for committing the murder."

"Even if that is true, Alex, I do not see it as such an important reason. I think you will agree that we have many other important matters to occupy us at the present time."

Haji was becoming difficult. I took a sip of tea, carefully placed my cup back down on the wooden table, felt myself becoming impatient. Although Haji's point was a reasonable one, I recalled my conversation with Jerry Shenlee. Jerry said his reason for sending me here had to do with my being a friend of Pete Hansen's, but I knew Jerry well enough to know he wouldn't let friendships and personal feelings interfere with his job.

Jerry's reason for wanting me here had to do with the Kabul Bank. I also recalled Captain Corley saying that was the direction from which we should investigate the murder.

"I feel it is important for us to know why someone might want to kill Colonel Hansen. And because I feel the killer might have been Abdul Sakhi, I think we should try and learn more about him."

"Officially, the case is closed."

"For me, the case is not closed. Colonel Hansen knew something that we still do not know." I paused. "Is there someone among the Korengalis who might provide information about Abdul Sakhi?"

After a brief hesitation, Haji said quietly, "I can speak with some elders."

Because I knew he was doing it reluctantly, I said, "*Ma-nana.* Thank you."

CHAPTER 17

"Do you know about the poker games?" Eric Page said over the mumble of voices.

He took a sip of bourbon, his second. We were two deep at the Hare and Hound, the basement bar of the Gandamack Lodge on Sherpur Square. Since American service people aren't allowed to drink alcohol while serving in Afghanistan, Page was in civvies, dressed in a light tan windbreaker and jeans. He had on a Yankees cap, which he was wearing backwards, and which made him look like a mildly retarded fan.

I thought it was a good disguise. Page was anything but retarded. He was smart, an insightful observer, and I was finding him a good source on the financial skullduggery at the Kabul Bank.

When I shook my head, he flashed a grim smile. "You should know about the poker games."

Because the Hare and Hound sold booze and was located a block from the British Embassy, there were no locals in the crowd, and the conversations I could overhear were mostly in English. I took a slug of Heineken, which I was drinking out of the bottle since the Gandamack didn't have beer on tap. It didn't have a saucy young woman behind the bar either. You can't have everything.

"Pete tried to go to the poker games when he could. They played in Farnood's house, a real fancy place, expensive furniture, servants. Pete said every time he went there he felt like he was walking into the Sultan's palace." He paused. "You know who Sherkhan Farnood is."

"He was chairman of the bank. I know he likes poker."

"He likes money, too. Nine hundred million dollars is missing. Pete said once that's a conservative figure. Farnood probably siphoned off more than half. The trial's been going on since November."

"No wonder he has a nice house." I took a swallow from my beer bottle. "How was Pete able to get into that crowd? I'm assuming the guests were all insiders."

"Do you know Captain Corley?" When I nodded, he said, "She spent a lot of time in Pete's office when she was in Kabul. She knows her way around. She had the entrée. By the way, she's a knockout when she dresses up. They used to go together." Page reached into his pocket, took out a Galaxy, flicked on the camera.

"Have a look. Here's some pictures I took. I used to drive them."

Two pictures were of Pete, one of them together, three of Captain Corley alone. Her hair hung to her shoulders, and she was dressed in a tight-fitting knee-length white dress. She wasn't smiling. A green and red silk scarf was wrapped around her neck.

When I nodded my approval, Page said, "She must've driven those bank guys nuts. Nice tits, a real looker."

"Yeah, but there's something not right. American officers shouldn't be going to these card games."

Page shrugged. "I don't get it either. They shouldn't have been hanging around with that crowd, but they were." Page took a long swallow of bourbon. "She speaks Pashto, on top of it."

"Where did she learn Pashto?"

"Who knows? Monterey? She's an Army officer, but she operates outside the chain of command."

"In other words, she's her own boss."

"No question. And something else. She also knows how the locals think. She told me once the problem wasn't just that people here think different than us. The problem is, we don't understand how they're different. She said that when these guys steal our money, they don't think they've done something bad. They think they've done something good."

"And the people running the show back home don't understand that?" When Page nodded, I said, "But Pete would've had a specific reason for going there. What was it?"

Page raised his glass, looked at it as if it might contain the answer to my question. "It was hard to figure what he was going after. I suppose anyone who might be able to throw some light on where the money went."

I was silent for a moment. "The names are a matter of public knowledge. Where's the mystery? Twenty-two people have been indicted. We know who worked at the bank. We know the names of the insiders, the people who borrowed money and never paid it back."

Page said, "Pete was on to something more than that. What was it? That's the mystery." Lifting his glass, he took a sip of bourbon, licked his lips. "You're right about Pete being persistent. He even learned a little Pashto." When I asked who was giving him lessons, Page smiled knowingly. I didn't ask a follow-up to that question.

As I sucked on my beer, I thought about Pete. He was stubborn and persistent—and he wasn't the type to waste his time when there was work to be done. He wasn't the type to cheat on his wife either. There was a reason for him wanting to be at the poker games.

What could he have been looking for?

"Different people showed up every week for the poker. They were all confident nothing bad was ever going to happen." Page waved to the bartender and ordered another round.

"They're being tried. That's bad."

"NATO is outta here the end of next year. America is outta here. I don't think an Afghan government is gonna want to keep people in jail because they stole some American money." Page's face had a pained expression. He shook his head.

I said, "I suppose that's why the prosecution was stalling."

"Pete thought they might never be indicted." Page readjusted his Yankee cap. "But when the bank people realized there was an election coming up, it dawned on them Karzai wouldn't be around much longer. Next year is the election. Karzai's gone. And no one can say who his successor will be."

"Maybe someone who could be influenced by our government. Is that what you mean? A guy unlike Karzai, who maybe wouldn't go along."

"That's what Captain Corley thought, too. Maybe you should talk with her." After passing me another bottle, Page said, "The auditors have gone over all the bank's books from the day it was founded. They've been able to track down some of the loot."

"Where is it?"

"Some of it's in Dubai. The bank officials had every kind of dodge. One was they borrowed money and formed phony companies, mostly construction and transportation, in places like Dubai and Pakistan. Then they'd use borrowed bank money to provide services for Uncle Sam."

I said, "And make a profit. What that means is, the Kabul Bank swindle cost our country over a billion dollars."

"Way over. You can't fight corruption because it's the way people do business in the country. Pete said the bank had sixteen shareholders, and they all received interest-free loans. Karzai's brother got six million to buy a villa in Dubai, a real fancy place. Something else Pete said was that some of the money was ending up in accounts belonging to the Taliban."

"It looks as if our government is not only financing our war effort but that of our enemy as well."

"In Afghanistan," Page said, "anything is possible. Some of the security firms that we deal with are run by the insurgents."

"Where else might the money be going?" I asked.

"This much is clear. A lot of it's no longer in the country. Some of it was loaned to the airline."

"Pamir Airways?"

When Page nodded, I said, "They went bankrupt."

"I know. They used to carry money out of the country for some of the big shots. Concealed in the food trays. A couple of hundred million went to buy luxury villas in Dubai, in the section near that man-made island. It was when Dubai's property values started to collapse that the auditors realized the bank was having serious financial problems." Page shook his head. "It's the biggest bank failure in history, Alex."

Page downed his third bourbon with a long swallow. "People here figure if money's there to grab, you should grab it. I'm not sure the Koran says that, but that's the way some people interpret it."

"Did Captain Corley say that's the way things are?"

Page nodded. "Like I say, you should talk with her. You know where Khost is?" When I said I did, Page said, "She moves around a lot. For a time, she was at Chapman, with that paramilitary outfit. But the last I heard she moved over to Camp Salerno."

I said, "The paramilitary outfits are mostly all Pashtun. You say she speaks Pashto. She's probably a liaison between us and them."

"And CIA. They tune in on the Haqqani network and decide which targets to hit." Page glanced at his watch. "Tomorrow's Tuesday. I have an early day."

I said I'd drive him back to ISAF Headquarters.

After dropping Page off at the gate, I drove slowly back to the billets. I had so much I wanted to say to Irmie. Although I realized there was no way to communicate over the telephone what had happened, I knew I had to talk with her and tell her how much I loved her and missed her.

When I made the call, she answered in a distant tone, "It would be nice to let me hear from you from time to time, Alex."

I almost had the feeling she had someone with her in the apartment. Then it occurred to me that might be something else to worry about. "I've had a busy four days."

Irmie sighed, waiting for an explanation.

Finally, I said, "It's not something I want to talk about on the telephone." Since I didn't want her to worry, I said, "Everything's fine, Irmie. It really is. I'll tell you everything when I see you."

"When is that going to be?"

"I'm not sure." I knew Irmie felt she was playing second fiddle to my military assignments. I didn't want to admit it, even to myself, that she might have been correct.

"Things just aren't working out for us, Alex. You have to admit that. Be honest." Before I could respond, she said, "I never imagined that you'd cancel our time together at the last minute. This has been a difficult time for me. Do you realize that?"

"Of course I do." I hesitated. "But what happened was . . . unavoidable."

"That's a strange thing to say. I don't see how going to Afghanistan was unavoidable. No one else I know is going to Afghanistan." When I didn't respond, Irmie continued, "I don't think you realize how disappointing this has been for me."

"I do realize that." I again thought of how close I'd come to losing my head only a few days before. "I'll be there as soon as I can, Irmie. We can get right back on track with our plans."

"I'm all alone here. This isn't a relationship. Talking to you when you feel like calling, hearing about your assignment—isn't what I want. We were supposed to be together right now. We have so much to . . . discuss. Have you forgotten all that? Or doesn't it even matter to you?"

"Of course I haven't—yes, it matters, very much . . ."

"Something else, Alex. You could at least tell me when you expect to be back. Why can't you do that?"

I couldn't give a date because I didn't know myself when this op figured to be over.

"When I know, Irmie, I'll let you know. At the moment I just can't say . . ." I left the sentence unfinished.

"I have to be honest. I'm tired of your excuses—or reasons—or whatever they are. I just don't feel I can depend on you." Before I could answer, Irmie said, "Oh, wait one second. I have a pot on the stove. It's boiling over." Then, after a brief pause, she said, "I have to hang up."

I sat unmoving in the hooch's one chair for twenty minutes. As I looked around at the sparsely furnished room—bed, a tiny fridge, some shelves, a closet—I knew I was going to spend another sleepless night.

CHAPTER 18

"So what's the news, Haji?"

It was shortly after noon the next day, and I'd found Haji in the chow hall wolfing down what appeared to be a fricasseed chicken. I put down my own tray, also loaded down with chicken, and slid in opposite him. Although I'd been eating in Army mess halls ever since I was nineteen years old, I was now finding the constant clang-clang of dishes and trays annoying. Even the dining facility over at Headquarters was loud.

Before speaking, Haji wiped his mouth with his napkin. "There is news, Alex. I have been in touch with Shah Mahmood's people."

"What have you found out?"

"People remember Abdul Sakhi. He is not a person you want as a friend." Haji flashed a thin smile, then went back to his chicken.

Between forkfuls of salad, I said, "Did I indicate that I wanted Sakhi as a friend?" I tossed a stern look in Haji's direction. "I'm waiting, Haji."

"There are a few Korengali people who are still sympathetic to the Taliban. They might know where Abdul Sakhi is." When I nodded, Haji gazed directly at me and reached for a piece of bread. "I am told that there is a Taliban leader who may have some information about Abdul Sakhi. This person became interested when he heard we were looking for him."

Just as I was about to ask how I could get in touch with the Taliban leader, my cell phone went off. On the other end was Stan Jones. "Fourteen thirty, Alex. In Doug Greer's office at ISAF." Stan sounded tense.

"Can I ask what it's about?"

"It's about the money. Bud Withers and Doug Greer will be there. I can tell you that much."

"I've already spoken with Doug about what happened in the Korengal."

"I know, I know. Just be there."

"I also spoke with Withers—" Stan punched off before I could finish the sentence.

I turned my attention back to Haji.

Before saying anything, I thought things over for a minute as I disposed of my salad and moved on to my chicken. I was aware of Haji silently watching me. Finally, I said, "My next question, Haji. Can I get in touch with this Taliban individual?"

"My understanding is that he is highly placed. His time is valuable."

Pushing away my chicken, I thought about that for a while. As I sipped coffee and watched two female officers in their blue Class A's carrying their trays to the exit, I said, "Pass the word that I want to speak with him. Also pass the word that I can be trusted."

"It will be difficult, but I will try my best." Haji paused. "Abdul Sakhi is rumored to have been the one to have killed Mullah Anbar. The Taliban leader you will be speaking with is Mullah Anbar's brother. Are you sure—"

"Yes, Haji. I'm sure."

* * *

"Simmer down, Bud. Okay? Simmer the hell down!" Doug Greer stared at me from behind his desk in his office, grimaced, then shrugged. He was having a hard time keeping Captain Bud Withers under control.

"Why the hell should I simmer down?"

When I'd entered Greer's office a second before, Withers sprang to his feet, with the result we were now standing ten feet from one another. He was eyeing me like he might eye an insubordinate recruit, one who was headed for two weeks extra duty and then some.

"C'mon, Bud," Stan said.

"I lost a good man out there." Withers waved an arm excitedly. "Sergeant Sulzberg was one of the best. He was headed back to the States in a couple of weeks. And Sergeant Mayo has a knife gash in his arm this long. It still hasn't healed."

"It wasn't Klear who gashed Sergeant Mayo's arm," Greer said. Then he turned to me. "Maybe you should go over it again, Alex. What was it happened out there?"

I said, "I can't add much to what I've already reported."

"Captain Withers wasn't here at that time," Stan said quietly. "Just give it to us again, in a nutshell."

"Captain Withers and I spoke out at Franklin. He knows what happened."

When Greer said, "Tell us again, for God's sakes," I shrugged, then went over the events. How we'd gone out with Sergeant Sulzberg's squad, how he'd sent two guys back when we'd reached the stream. "Then we proceeded forward on a donkey path. It was pitch dark, with Haji and me in the middle, and Sergeant Mayo bringing up the rear . . ."

"Then what?" Doug asked.

"Oh, come on," Withers said. "Don't tell me you believe this bullshit. This guy's blowin' smoke."

"Suddenly, they were all over us. We'd just left the donkey path and were on the road. They had me pinned. Someone got off a couple of rounds, Sully probably. It was over in less than a minute. They grabbed Haji and me before we could do much. We went further along on the road. Someone had a gun barrel in my back the whole way. Later on, they piled us into a vehicle."

"This is what I don't get," Withers said. "You were armed but didn't resist."

"I was ready to fire but couldn't see anything. I could have hit one of our guys."

"I could've hit one of our guys." Withers made my statement sound like the stupidest thing he'd ever heard.

Withers said, "You know what I think?"

"No," I said. "And I don't particularly care what you think." To Greer, I said, "Is this what you got me over here for?"

Withers moved forward, so that his sneering face was directly in front of mine. "We got you here because of the money. Where is it?" To Stan, he said, "I think bright boy here has the five grand."

"That's why we asked you over," Stan said. "Doug has to fill out a report for the finance office. Disposition of funds."

"I had the money in my rucksack. Those guys grabbed it real quick." To Greer, I said, "Write that the Safir tribe stole it."

"You don't have it." Greer began typing on the computer. "Money stolen."

"What bullshit!"

"All right!" Greer said. "All right!"

I said, "I can't say who stole it."

"I know who stole it!" Withers' face was beet red.

Swinging his chair around to face Withers, Greer said, "We can understand that you're pissed, Bud."

"Pissed ain't the word. How'd these Talibs get that close? And something else. Him and his buddy—"

"Haji, you mean?"

"The terp, yeah. Another con artist. They probably split it."

I said quietly, "What are you talking about?"

"I'll tell you what I'm talking about. You just don't let them get that close to you, that's all. I don't care how dark it was out there. And something else—"

"What's that?"

"You're back here in one piece. We're supposed to believe this story?" Withers said. "They were in a jail cell the whole night? They go out on Wednesday and come back on Sunday. Who got them out, the Lone Fucking Ranger? I mean, c'mon."

"He's right," Stan said to me. "We're still not real clear on how you made it out of there."

"I'm still not buyin' any of it," Withers shouted. "I'll tell you what happened. He never took the money out there with him. He left it back in his hooch."

When Stan looked at me, I shook my head.

Stan said, "We can search his billet."

"He stashed it." Turning to me Withers said, "You fuckin' stashed it, right?" Then he reached out and gave me a shove. "You're a god-damn liar."

To Greer, I said, "Do I have to put up with this?"

"Yeah," Withers said, "you do—"

Because I wasn't looking at him, Withers wasn't ready for the punch I threw, which caught him solidly on the side of his head. He recovered quickly, threw a haymaker at me. I ducked, but he caught me on the side of the face with his left, causing me to see stars for one second. I slugged him back, and when he temporarily lost his balance, I shoved him backwards, hard. He staggered, grabbing the two flags standing at the side of the room. He went down, pulling the Afghan flag and staff down with him.

I was aware of Stan and Doug shouting at us to stop it.

Back on his feet and cursing, Withers charged, and we both went down in a heap.

As we rolled around on the floor, I was aware of the office door flying open and a number of guys in fatigues charging into the room. One of the newcomers grabbed me by the arm and dragged me to my feet. Withers was still raging, and it took Stan and one of the newcomers to quiet him down.

A minute later Colonel Boyd was standing in the doorway, shaking his head. "You guys think you're back in the goddamned schoolyard? You'll have to write this up. Get it to me tomorrow."

One of the soldiers in fatigues escorted me into the corridor. He stood silently by as I checked my clothing and tucked in some loose ends.

From inside the office I heard Colonel Boyd say, "You're dismissed, Captain Withers!"

While I waited, another soldier walked Withers down to the stairwell. Five minutes later, I left.

Sitting in my van in the ISAF parking area, I checked my face in the rearview mirror. An abrasion, a cut on my right cheek. I decided it could be worse. I wondered about possible disciplinary action. If the military wanted me gone, they now had a good reason, and I could be ordered out of my quarters within twenty-four hours. My badge would be rescinded, and I would be denied entrance to ISAF Headquarters and all military facilities. Understandably, military authorities are sensitive to even the smallest breaches of discipline, but soldiers by nature are fighters, and a few fisticuffs are not necessarily anything to get overly excited about.

I decided to take this incident in stride. For my money, Withers was just another hothead, a guy who'd been stationed on a lonely COP for too long. Considered in another way, this was a reminder that some people didn't want me around, doing what I was doing.

I felt I was being pulled in all kinds of directions. I'd spoken with Irmie the previous evening, and she'd made it plain she was running out of patience. Stan felt I was looking over his shoulder and wanted me gone because he knew I thought he'd botched the murder investigation. Withers and I had been wary of one another from the minute we'd met.

But I still wanted to find out who it was that had murdered Pete.

And I knew Jerry Shenlee had stuck his neck out to get me over here. Wonderful! This op was so "black" I still didn't know who was running it.

*　*　*

When my phone started ringing, I was sound asleep on the cot in my room. After the second ring, I struggled into a sitting position on the side of the bed. My bedside clock said 0045 hours. With the telephone at my ear I grunted a hello. It was Haji.

"What's up, Haji? Something good, I hope."

"Whether it is good or not, Alex, I do not know. But I have received a message from an elder, who thinks he can be of help in finding Abdul Sakhi. He is a Taliban leader." Haji paused. "Is that good or not good?"

"It may be good. I'm not sure. What else did the elder say?"

"He said he knows someone who . . . has had some experience with Abdul Sakhi and may know something about him." Haji paused. "He says he can arrange a meeting with this person."

"Who is this person?"

"As I told you, he is the brother of the slain mullah."

Rubbing sleep out of my eyes, I asked Haji to run it by me again. He said, "The person who can tell us more about Abdul Sakhi is able to meet this evening."

"But you say he is a member of the Taliban?"

"Yes, Alex. A condition is that you cannot say anything about this meeting to any of your American military colleagues. You understand that, I hope. Shah Mahmood told Niaz you are . . . *emandara* . . . a man of honor."

"I'm assuming Niaz is also *emandara*. The reputation the Taliban have back in America is not all that good."

"America is not Afghanistan. Maybe you've noticed—"

"Don't be saucy, Haji. Just say when and where."

"Do you know where the Massoud Monument is, Alex?"

"Everybody knows the monument."

"Good. We will meet the person at the monument. From there we will drive to the meeting place, which is on the outskirts of Kabul."

I was silent for a moment. "I'm not sure if I like this arrangement. If I can't tell anyone about it, we could be walking into a trap." No question I'd become gun-shy. I was thinking of our recent expedition to COP Franklin.

"I'm not sure I like it either."

"Could you possibly make the meeting for another evening?"

"No, Alex. It is tonight or never."

I gave it some more thought. Finally, I said, "I'll pick you up in Phoenix, across from the motor pool."

* * *

Kabul is a city without street lights and can be scary after dark. Haji and I were in our van and parked on the broad street in between the American Embassy and the monument at Massoud Circle. We were waiting to make contact with whoever it was who was supposed to show us the way to our meeting with the Taliban leader.

We'd been waiting for less than ten minutes when a beat-up pickup truck pulled alongside us. There were two people in front, the driver, who kept his eyes straight ahead, and the passenger, who spent two minutes looking us over. After a minute, he gave a wave, which I assumed was a signal to us to follow them. I turned over the engine.

After two minutes of driving, I said, "They're heading out toward the road to the west. Where will that take us?"

"To Kandahar if we drive long enough. But probably only as far as Wardak Province." I didn't say anything, but I had an idea we wouldn't be going even that far. Beyond the city, the Taliban were well entrenched.

After another five minutes of driving we reached the first checkpoint, which was manned by half-a-dozen Askars. One of the soldiers stuck his head in the van's window, said something to Haji, then waved us through. The road west winds and is lined with junked vehicles, some rusted-out tanks, and old buildings on either side. Fifteen minutes beyond the checkpoint, we arrived in what might be described as a small village, but which was nothing more than a collection of haphazardly situated wood and stone buildings. I couldn't imagine people living in these crumbling structures, but in Afghanistan you never know. At the end of a dirt street, the truck halted alongside a small walled-in compound.

When Haji asked what we'd do, I said, "We wait."

After a minute, both Talibs climbed out of their vehicle and entered the compound. After another minute, one of them reappeared and waved. We climbed out and followed him through an iron gate that hung on one hinge. I was aware of the sound of our boots crunching the gravel.

Inside the compound, two more individuals, both on the young side and carrying automatic weapons, pointed us into a one-story stone building. We were directed to sit, which we did, and a couple of minutes later we saw an elderly man with a cane emerge from one of the back rooms. He had a gray beard and was dressed in a white blouse over which was wound a checkered shawl. He wore a *chitrali* hat. After easing himself down on a cushion, he said, *Assalamu alaykom,* and we returned the greeting. One of the guards brought two glasses of tea.

Haji spoke briefly, giving our names and saying who we were.

Then the old man started talking to Haji, who would listen to a couple of sentences and then tell me what had been said.

"Alex, this man's name is Niaz. He says he comes from Ganez—that's a city in the Korengal Valley."

"Can we believe him?"

"He says he understands you to be an honorable person, someone with good reasons for wanting to know the whereabouts of Abdul Sakhi."

Sitting cross-legged in this dark building, I wondered what this guy could tell us. Of course, if his brother had been killed by Abdul Sakhi, he maybe had a reason for talking with me. "Tell him thank you for the compliment. Say something nice about the Taliban. Then ask him about Abdul Sakhi."

Haji and his opposite number spoke for another couple of minutes before Haji turned back to me. "Niaz says the Taliban have good reasons for wanting to kill Abdul Sakhi."

"We know that. He's killed some of their people."

"He says Abdul Sakhi has a *ghla*—"

"What's a *ghla*?"

"A female partner, but not a nice person. They have killed a number of Taliban by trickery. Among them was Mullah Mendos. Do you know him, Alex?"

"I know the name. I know he was a leader down in Helmand Province."

"According to Niaz, Abdul Sakhi assassinated other Taliban leaders besides Mendos."

"Ask Niaz why he did that."

After Haji and Niaz had spoken for another five minutes, Haji turned back to me. "You are not going to believe this, Alex. Niaz says Abdul Sakhi has also killed many Americans."

I was silent, trying to grasp the significance of this. If this was true, it became easy to believe Abdul Sakhi had killed Pete.

"Niaz says Abdul Sakhi works for whoever pays him money."

Although the FBI had Abdul Sakhi listed as a "friendly," as someone Americans could work with, maybe this was only half the story. There's a well-known saying that, while you can't buy an Afghan, you can always rent one. That seemed to explain Sakhi.

When I didn't comment, Niaz seemed to understand what I was thinking because he all at once began nodding his head, as if to emphasize the truth of what he'd said. When I glanced back at Haji, Niaz continued to nod his head.

Haji said, "Although Abdul Sakhi grew up in the Korengali tribe and they supported the Taliban, he left ten years ago. When he is paid, he works for either side. Niaz says Abdul Sakhi cares only about money and himself. He has no allegiance to any group. Niaz says he will work for whoever it is that offers him the most money."

"Ask Niaz where we can find Abdul Sakhi."

"Niaz wants to know why you would want to locate Abdul Sakhi. He wonders whether you want to give him an assignment to kill more Taliban."

"Say I think Abdul Sakhi killed my friend."

Haji shrugged, then turned again to Niaz. After they'd talked for a few more minutes, Haji said, "Niaz says Abdul Sakhi is difficult to contact. He says if he knew where Abdul Sakhi was, he would send people to have him killed."

I thought that over for a second. Finally, I said, "Tell Niaz thanks. This place is giving me the creeps. Tell him we're leaving."

"Niaz says to give the money to the guards."

"Money? Whoever said anything about money?"

At that moment Niaz got to his feet, nodded to us, and left the room. Suddenly, we were surrounded by three guys pointing their weapons in our direction. Outside, I could hear one of the truck engines turning over.

At the entrance, the guard with the automatic weapon barred the way.

"Do you have any money with you, Alex?"

"A couple of hundred euros." Reaching into my pocket, I found 300 euros. After I'd counted out six fifties, Haji spoke briefly with the guards.

"They said we should be relieved that it was enough and that we should wait ten minutes. They also said we were wise to pay the money. Otherwise, on our way back into Kabul we would have run over an IED. They say they are now on their way to deactivate the explosive."

Outside, when I heard another truck engine turning over, I figured the three guards were taking off with my 300 euros. I couldn't exactly say the money was going for a good cause. On the drive back, Haji asked, "Was the information worth 300 euros, Alex?"

After a brief hesitation, I said quietly, "Yes, Haji. I think maybe it was."

As we drove, I took another look at the message I'd received on my smartphone a couple of hours earlier.

"Report to me at Camp Salerno ASAP. Leslie Corley. Captain, U.S. Army."

The message confirmed what I already suspected—that the person I'd be reporting to was Captain Corley. Since we hadn't exactly hit it off in our two brief encounters, I can't say I was overjoyed by the news.

CHAPTER 19

SINCE FOB SALERNO'S short dirt runway makes it off limits for larger aircraft, getting down to the province of Khost in the winter is pretty much a crapshoot. And for me it took longer than I'd hoped it would, which turned out to be much of the next day. After helicoptering over to Bagram, I hung around for over two hours before I was able to hitch a ride on a small prop plane to Salerno.

Like I say, simple things in Afghanistan become complex, and everything takes more time than it should.

Because Salerno lies just four or five kilometers inside the Durand Line, it's an easy target for the Haqqani network, which operates across the border out of North Waziristan and hardly lets a night go by without launching a rocket attack. Although the border exists on the map, it doesn't exist in real life. When I was on patrol in the area with Askar training units, I was often unsure which country we were in.

As far as the rocket attacks go, personnel on the base have at least a minute to find a bunker before the rockets come screaming in, a situation that has led to Salerno acquiring the nickname of "Rocket City."

After arriving, I was assigned to a bed in the transients' barracks. I found Captain Leslie Corley behind a desk in the wooden frame building that houses military headquarters on the base.

When Corley stood up to shake my hand, I saw she was easily five-ten, maybe a half-inch more. Seeing her, I recalled the pictures of her taken by Eric Page—elegantly dressed and on her way to a Kabul poker party. Again, I couldn't help noticing her figure. At the same time, I got the feeling she didn't like the movement of my eyes. She was the kind of woman who could express approval and disapproval with only the slightest change of expression.

"Actually, I expected you yesterday," she said.

"I know, ma'am. I was delayed in getting down here." I was already on the defensive.

After checking her watch, she said, "This evening's my night at the gym. I prefer not to miss." When I said, "Would you mind company?" she said, "If you wish."

An hour later, while I was running on the treadmill, Captain Corley dressed in a sweat suit and sneakers entered and immediately headed for a set of dumbbells. After pressing what could have been a hundred pounds, she spent a few minutes pounding the big bag. For a while, we ran side by side on the treadmill. When she headed for the basketball court, I followed.

I fed her a couple of passes, watched as she dropped in a pair of twenty-footers, and said, "Impressive."

She shrugged. "I played varsity at college."

"I skipped college. I'm a self-made man."

"You've got a nice hook shot. Too bad it never goes in."

I resisted an urge to say "Ha ha."

For the next twenty minutes, we silently shot baskets. Finally, she said, "Let's take foul shots. Five and five. You first."

I shot five, made three. She shot five, made four. Although I made four of my last five, Captain Corley sank all five. It didn't take a genius to see the point she wanted to make.

Forty-five minutes later, after we'd showered and changed, we walked over to her hooch in the officers' billets. After pointing me to a chair, she opened her small fridge.

I said, "Would you have a beer?"

She handed me a bottle of water. "No alcohol allowed on the base." She fixed me with a disapproving stare. "I would have thought you knew that." She paused. "You're working for me. I only want people who follow the rules and who I can trust."

I nodded, pulled the cap off the water, took a swallow.

After sitting down in the desk chair, she said, "I wasn't impressed by the way you let Colonel Hansen shoot her mouth off at the meeting in the CID office."

"Ma'am, I didn't exactly let—"

"The fact that Colonel Hansen lost her husband doesn't give her the authority to say what she did. You could have pointed out where she was wrong. You failed to do that." Before I could respond, she said, "You impressed me as a wimp. I was told you could handle this assignment. Now I'm beginning to wonder."

"Who told you? Jerry Shenlee?" I was already wondering what Jerry's connection with this bossy female could be. On top of that, she was a captain, not a colonel. Jerry was a GS-16 or 17, and had much more authority if he chose to exercise it.

I said, "I'd like to know just what you're trying to accomplish." When she flashed an impatient look, I said, "Until now, I've assumed it only involved finding Pete's . . . Colonel Hansen's killer." I took a swallow of water, but couldn't help thinking that a beer would have gone down better. When she still didn't comment, I said, "Although Pete was a friend, I couldn't see what was so special about this murder, at least not at the beginning."

"It's more than just another green-on-blue killing. You've become aware of that, I hope."

"From what I can see, ma'am, Sergeant Nolda is being framed. The murder occurred on the day he supposedly returned from leave. When I saw his body, I could see he'd been in the water awhile.

When I spoke with Nolda's army buddy, I didn't get the impression he was the type to pull a green-on-blue."

"A bit circumstantial, Mr. Klear, but okay. Do you have anything solid?"

"The FBI threw an interesting monkey wrench into the situation by saying one of the people in the Headquarters building could have been Abdul Sakhi, a shadowy figure who seems to be some kind of opportunist."

"You should have followed up on that. Why didn't you?"

"It may surprise you to learn that I did. The FBI described Abdul Sakhi as a 'friendly,' someone who had murdered a number of Taliban leaders. That didn't exactly jibe with him killing an American officer." When she said, "Go on," I said, "So that's only half the story. Abdul Sakhi's also murdered a number of Americans, some of them prominent officials. Both sides have used him. He keeps a low profile. Maybe he's in Waziristan."

She nodded. "He's a killer for hire. We're finding out that some of these people have no conscience. Or sense of loyalty. They have no problem switching sides. For Americans, such a thing is inconceivable. In other words, it's possible someone could have paid him to murder Colonel Hansen." She lifted her bottle to her lips, then said, "That's why you're over here."

"I see."

After a minute, she said, "Someone wants to short-circuit the investigation. Obviously, it's not a green-on-blue. If it were, it ends there. Colonel Hansen died for no reason. America goes home next year. It's over."

Captain Corley got to her feet, crossed the room to the closet, hauled out a duffel bag. I watched as she reached into the bag and searched. After a minute she pulled out a sweater, which she unrolled to reveal two plastic folders, both jammed with paper. She laid the stuff out on the bed. I noticed that in one of the folders was a glassine envelope containing a computer disc.

She said, "These are Colonel Hansen's papers. You know what Colonel Hansen was working on."

"The Kabul Bank. I've been reading about it."

"Would you care for some more water?" After she'd given me another bottle, she remained standing. "There hasn't been that much in the news. The United States government has been embarrassed by what happened at the Kabul Bank. Understandably, very little information about the failure of the bank has reached the newspapers . . ."

"About 900 million dollars has disappeared."

"The thieves didn't stop at 900. The number is over a billion. For obvious reasons, the government doesn't want to have to admit how much money was involved. American taxpayers would be out on the barricades, and who could blame them? What else do you know?"

"Only that Pete Hansen was involved with the bank almost to the point where it had become an obsession." When she asked how I knew that, I said, "I spoke a few times with Captain Page." I paused. "Captain Page rotates back to the States in a couple of weeks. He said his involvement with the Kabul Bank is over."

"I'm surprised he told you anything. Captain Page feels that by pursuing the bank matter and revealing what he knows, he'll be jeopardizing his career." When I said, "Won't you be jeopardizing your career, ma'am?" she flashed me an angry look. "Please be so kind as to not interfere in my personal or professional life."

I could have told her I didn't give a damn about either her personal or professional life.

"I'm going to explain some things to you. Please refrain from making any dumb remarks."

"I'll do my best."

"The Kabul Bank was founded by the United States government largely as a conduit to finance operations here in Afghanistan—in order to make it possible to pay the bills for rebuilding the country's infrastructure and financing the war. No country in history has been as generous to another country as America has been to Afghanistan."

"What about the Marshall Plan?"

"Not even the Marshall Plan. As you know, the bank is now bankrupt. You have to ask yourself how such a thing is possible."

I said, "It's not the first time a bank went belly-up. Quite a few back home have—"

"Please don't interrupt. When a bank or business in the United States fails, financial people know why it happened and where the money went. In this case, the money disappeared. Into thin air. Over a billion dollars."

"A billion is the number one with nine zeros."

"You keep making dumb comments, and you're trying my patience."

"I know it's a dumb comment, but I'm trying to grasp how enormous that amount of money is."

"I hope you're not doing it on purpose."

"Doing what on purpose, ma'am?"

"Trying my patience." As Captain Corley lifted her water bottle to her lips, I couldn't keep from admiring her hooded eyes and mildly upturned nose. With a brief movement, she touched her hand to an unruly strand of hair. How is it that women always know when a man finds them interesting to look at?

She said, "Colonel Hansen had learned something that was making him nervous."

"Pete was a pretty cool type. He didn't let—"

"He didn't let things bother him. I know that."

"From what I understand, he was constantly going back and forth into Kabul." I paused. "Often in your company."

She colored, obviously irritated that I knew of her relationship with Pete.

Thinking of the poker games, I said, "I know he had access to quite a few prominent people. Did that include Karzai?"

She said, "He had access to everyone for a time. But after people learned that Karzai's brother was a stockholder in Kabul Bank, he never again visited the presidential palace." When I asked how she knew that, she pointed to Pete's notes. "Colonel Hansen kept a calendar. It's possible to trace how he spent his days."

Pointing at the folders on the bed, I asked how she'd obtained them.

"I had access to Colonel Hansen's office within hours of the shooting. I removed them. His computer could be read by people at ISAF. There's only one disc of any interest. Everything we want to know is handwritten. But his notes are hard to read." She glanced at her watch, got to her feet. "Take his notes with you. See what you come up with."

As I scooped up Pete's papers, she said, "Quite a few of the documents are in Arabic. Others are in French and German. Much is just lists of numbers. I wondered if they weren't bank account numbers. And there's lots of other stuff. Oh yes, there's a transcript in a foreign language of a court proceeding. I think it's a preliminary hearing for the trial."

"Anything else, ma'am?"

"Yes, you'll see. There are news stories, some in English. Also some letters he wrote, some to a person in Dubai. Take them to your room. Read them. Bring them back tomorrow."

"When can I catch up with you?"

"I run in the morning. I skip breakfast. I'm on the job at eight. I'm hungry by lunchtime."

Gathering up the papers, I said, "In the chow hall at noon." Seconds later, she closed the door behind me.

* * *

Captain Corley hadn't been exaggerating when she said it wasn't easy to decipher Pete Hansen's notes. After nearly three hours I didn't come away with much more than she had. There were numbers that could have been for bank accounts, and there was an entire collection of hard-to-figure-out phrases that could have been passwords. I also concluded that the collection of photocopied documents in Arabic comprised deeds for property in Dubai. Other deeds were for property in Switzerland. Someone seemed to be buying up land in some of the world's most expensive cities.

In any event, I could now see why Jerry had said I should brush up on finances and banking procedures.

Another thing that struck me was the name of a businessman that was mentioned in a number of newspaper stories and to whom Pete had written a letter inquiring about property. Since Pete had made two trips to Dubai, I was assuming he'd wanted to speak with him personally. The businessman's address was for a company in Dubai.

His name was Taraki Hamed.

My reading was interrupted by a blaring loudspeaker: "Attention on the FOB! Incoming . . . !" A minute later there was an explosion that caused the barracks to shake and the lights to go out. Then another. The "all clear" sounded forty minutes later.

It was the kind of distraction you get used to in "Rocket City."

Although I continued to read with my flashlight, I decided to pack it in at around 0300 hours.

* * *

"So CID in Kabul has identified Colonel Hansen's murderer," Corley said. It was shortly after noon of the following day and she was speaking over the chow hall din. "They think the killer was the ANA soldier. What's his name?"

"Nolda. Baram Nolda."

"In other words, they're saying it's a green-on-blue killing, and that's what the people back in America will be told." When I nodded, she said, "But your take on the situation is that—"

"Is that Abdul Sakhi killed Colonel Hansen."

Corley was silent for a minute. "The way you see things, it sounds like you're suggesting there's a cover-up."

I cut up a piece of chicken, shook my head. "I didn't say that." Of course I thought that.

"But CID disagrees with your take on the situation."

"Ma'am, it's differences of opinion that make horses run."

She threw down her knife and fork, loud enough to cause people further down the table to glance in our direction. "Dammit! Will you kindly stop making these irrelevant remarks? We're not talking about goddamned horse races."

"Okay."

"Christ, I hate talking to people who keep making dumb remarks. Let's get back to the subject."

I said, "Who's covering up and what's being covered up?"

"What's being covered up is the identity of the person who committed the murder. That's what's being covered up. And some details regarding the bank fraud are being covered up." After a brief pause, she said quietly, "How far did you get with Colonel Hansen's notes?"

"I'd like to talk with some of the people he mentions. Maybe start with this Dubai businessman."

"The one in the news stories?" When I nodded, she said, "He caught my attention, too."

"As soon as I can set something up, I'll fly down." When she said she'd accompany me, I said I could handle things alone. "I'm going back to Kabul for a couple of days, but I'll be around tonight. I'll bring back Pete's . . . Colonel Hansen's papers before I leave."

Although I spent the rest of the afternoon drinking coffee and reading Pete's notes, I didn't feel I'd learned all that much. In the course of the afternoon I sent an e-mail to Taraki Hamed, saying who I was and that I wanted to see him in connection with Kabul Bank. He replied within an hour.

I stopped by Captain Corley's room at a few minutes after 1900.

After pointing me to the chair, she said, "I'm taking some leave time, but I'm not sure when I can fly. I think we should fly down together."

What she was saying was, she didn't trust me to handle it alone.

"Hamed sent an e-mail, ma'am, and said he'll be available all week." I paused. "I'm going to fly down to Dubai in two or three days. There's a direct flight from Kabul."

"I'd appreciate it if you'd wait for me. This is the kind of thing I'd like to—"

"I can handle it alone."

"You think you can!"

She pushed a stray lock of brunette hair away from her left eye. "Why are you looking at me like that?"

"I'm not looking at you. I'm thinking."

"If you're thinking what I think you're thinking, it's time for you to leave."

I got to my feet and slipped on my jacket. "Gladly, ma'am."

"What's that supposed to mean?"

"It means that I'm tired, and I'll be glad to return to my room, ma'am—and go to bed."

Needless to say, she slammed the door. And needless to say, I was not happy having to report to Captain Corley.

CHAPTER 20

The following morning I caught a chopper back to Kabul and landed at Camp Phoenix shortly before noon. Stan Jones was talking to a group of officers from Headquarters when I arrived. Twenty minutes later, with his visitors gone, Stan waved me into his office.

When I asked about his visitors, Stan rolled his eyes. "A couple of senators have scheduled a visit, but that won't be until the spring. We have to make sure everything's secure, just in case. I doubt they'll make it to Kabul. They'll probably spend most of their time at Bagram."

Seated on a metal chair with my left elbow resting on his desk and seeing Stan up close, I couldn't help noticing how frazzled he seemed, different from the way he looked when I arrived two weeks before.

"What did you do down there, Alex?"

"Talked to some people. Dodged some rockets." Stan knew that I was keeping the details regarding what Pete was doing to myself, and it was obvious that my vague answers were making him unhappy. Just my presence seemed to make people nervous. "Not a great deal. Anything new up here?"

"Doug Greer has gone back to D.C., left yesterday early," Stan said. "He said to say good-bye when you got in." As an afterthought, he said, "I hope you're not unhappy about the Nolda business."

"Who said I was unhappy?"

"You're not good at concealing your feelings, Alex. It was written all over your face."

"I just don't think it was Nolda, that's all."

"Well, I signed off on the official verdict: Sergeant Baram Nolda of the ANA killed Colonel Peter Hansen. It was a green-on-blue. End of story." Stan shrugged, gazed down at some paper on his desk. "If anything comes up that causes us to change our minds, we'll definitely look at it."

"Baloney, Stan."

Stan's eyes flashed. "You're out of line, Alex, way out of line." He grabbed his cup, took a sip of cold coffee, put down the cup with a bang. "I'm tired of your attitude."

"You've already got plenty of reason not to believe Nolda killed Pete. Save the bureaucratic stuff for the rubber-stamp guys at Headquarters—or for the suits in D.C. I know better."

"We're gonna be out of this country in less than two years! We've got more important things to think about."

"Like what?"

Stan banged his hand down on the desk. "You've been going way over the line with your smart-alecky talk, Alex. People here wonder how you think you can get away with stuff like this. Doug wonders, too. I remember back in Bosnia, the colonel calling you 'a loose cannon to end all loose cannons.'"

Stan was right, of course, that I had my way of doing things. Strangely, I had a feeling that was the reason Jerry wanted me over here. He knew this wasn't a cushy assignment, and definitely not a job for a career-oriented, by-the-book type. But what I saw as independence and self-reliance could, within a military environment, be regarded as insubordination.

"Bud Withers thinks we've cut you way too much slack." I already knew what Bud Withers thought of me and what Stan was about to say. "What really happened out there in the Pech Valley? There are four days totally unaccounted for. Okay, some Talibs grabbed you. And like you say, they chained you up. And I could see you and the terp got banged around. But what happened then? How long were you there? How come they let you go? Bud lost a man there, and he says—"

"He says it was because of me, but he's wrong. It was an ambush. They knew we were coming."

"How would they?"

"Ask Withers. He's in charge of the COP."

"Withers has been out there for nearly three months. You're suggesting he's been out there too long?"

"I'm not suggesting anything. Maybe he needed to let off steam, get it out of his system. As far as I'm concerned, no harm done."

"Maybe the military may not see it that way. The legal adviser at HQ called the States. He's still looking at the report. You may have your orders rescinded. You'll lose access to ISAF."

"Because I threw a few punches? What the hell happened to the Army I knew?"

"You're not a buck private anymore." Stan grimaced. "Not just that. One thing that went in the report was the missing money. Five thousand dollars. You were the last person to have it in your possession."

"Did you have to put that in a report about two guys punching each other? What were you thinking?"

Stan gazed straight at me, his expression revealing nothing.

I resisted the urge to say he wasn't a buck private anymore, either. Instead, I told him I'd catch up with him later.

When I went back to my hooch, I put in a call to Wanda and left a message. She called a half hour later.

I said, "Where are you?"

"In my room in Kabul's best hotel, the Serena. I told you I was moving out of that place with all the contractors."

"How is it?"

"I should have moved over here sooner. There are real people around, not all those military types. I love it."

"Like some company?"

"Three thirty, Alex, for tea in the lounge." She hung up before I could say another word.

* * *

"Well, at least I saw Pete's killer," Wanda said. "Since he was already dead, I could have saved myself the trouble of coming over."

"You had to come."

"I suppose."

"Look at the bright side."

"What bright side?"

"You've gotten to know Afghanistan, at least a little bit." I caught the attention of our waiter and told him to bring us another pot of tea.

"I've learned to drink tea." Wanda gazed at me across the table. Her expression was grim. "One nice thing, Alex. Even under these circumstances, we've been able to renew our friendship. I mean, who would have ever thought we'd run into each other here?"

It was true. Despite everything that was going on around us and the fact that we hadn't seen one another in fifteen years, we were still comfortable in each other's company.

Wanda was silent for a moment. "Let's be serious for a second. Seeing you again, Alex . . . even under these circumstances . . . has meant a great deal to me. I'm not sure I would have gotten through these two weeks without you here. Like I said, and I meant it, I've always had a soft spot in my heart for you." She paused. "Maybe you have one for me?"

Before I could answer, the waiter arrived with the stainless silver pot of tea, and we watched as he deftly carried out the pouring ritual. After filling our cups, he left, and I offered a toast. "How do you say 'cheers' in Pashto?" When Wanda smiled, I said, "Cheer up, Wanda."

"I think I'll put in for leave, maybe go somewhere. Pete and I bought a country place in Loudon County, in Virginia. It's beautiful. Out in the woods."

"Maybe it's better to just keep working."

As she forked up the last piece of gooey cake, Wanda said, "What are your plans?"

"I don't call the shots. I may have to go back to D.C."

"So you're not going to Germany to get married, then? At least not right away?"

"My life isn't my own. I go where I'm told to go."

"It would be great if we could see one another in the States. Will you call me?" Wanda passed over a card. "Promise."

The Serena was Kabul's only five-star hotel and the atmosphere was relaxed and pleasant. Although there was a high wall surrounding the expansive grounds and guards checked people passing through the front gate, here in the hotel it couldn't have been quieter. But just beyond the outskirts of the city, we knew battles were being fought and people were dying.

To me, it seemed everyone in the Serena was doing their best to ignore reality.

"You know, I was really concerned when you went off on that . . .

that wild goose chase." Wanda paused to take a sip of tea. "I still can't see why you said yes. I mean, it was obvious from the beginning that something there wasn't right."

"You knew?"

"I sensed something. That's all. From what Todd Hammond said, you were lucky to come back alive."

Wanda had argued against my going, and I didn't need to be reminded what a close call Haji and I had.

"What happened down in Khost? You didn't go down there to see that Captain Corley person?"

Did Wanda suspect that Leslie Corley had been having an affair with her husband? Women have a sixth sense in some things. But was it true? Or was there another reason she disliked Corley?

"Yes, among other things."

"What other things?" She took a sip of tea, then said, "People don't like Captain Corley. They can't figure her out. What's she like to work with?"

"She's a hard-charger, as the saying goes. Everything by the book. A stickler for detail."

"What's her take on Pete's killer?"

"She's like me. She doesn't think it was Nolda. Pete kept her up to speed on what he was working on."

"Which was?"

"You were Pete's wife, Wanda. Are you saying you had no idea what Pete was working on?"

"Financial stuff. I know that much. Oversight? He said that on a couple of occasions."

"What did he say about the Kabul Bank?" When Wanda only shrugged, I said, "Try and remember."

She closed her eyes and put a hand to her forehead. After a few seconds, she said, "We spoke on the phone, but you know how that is.

You always have the feeling someone's listening in." When I nodded, Wanda said, "Pete wasn't keen on e-mail. He knew how many people can access an account, especially from a military address. So the answer to your question is, I didn't know very much at all about what he was working on. Why do you ask?"

I didn't immediately respond, took a sip of my tea, and waited.

"Are you suggesting there might be a connection between what Pete was working on and his murder?" Reaching for the silver pot, Wanda said, "That doesn't really make sense. I mean, this Nolda individual . . . What would he know about the Kabul Bank? He was from out in the boondocks somewhere."

"You're assuming it was Nolda who killed Pete."

"You think it might have been someone else?"

I could have said I didn't think it was someone else, I *knew* it was someone else.

While I stayed silent, Wanda said, "Okay, you think you know better than everyone else, even the people whose job it is to investigate these killings. At times, Alex, you come across as downright arrogant."

I decided to ignore Wanda's irritation. "Did you intend to stay married to Pete, Wanda?"

"I find that question impertinent."

"You shouldn't mind answering it."

"I don't mind answering it. But I feel like you're giving me the third degree."

Even if Wanda had reasons not to answer the question, I thought she was being overly touchy. Finally, I said, "I apologize."

When Wanda lifted her teacup, I lifted mine. She smiled. "You're forgiven."

After the waiter had removed the plates, I said, "The tea was nice, but to be honest, I could go for something stronger."

I was about to suggest we go to dinner when Wanda said, "I have a better idea." She pushed back her chair. "Follow me." Before I could say "Where to?" she said, "I have brandy in my room. My one criticism of the Serena is they don't serve alcohol."

"I think it's better if we go somewhere for dinner." Recalling my earlier visit to Wanda's room at the Green Village, I said, "I'm not sure..."

"I promise I'll be on my best behavior."

We walked from the lounge into the lobby, then across to the elevator. On the third floor, she removed a plastic card from her purse and opened a door.

"What do you think of my place? The best hotel in Kabul. I just couldn't stand living in the Green Village any longer."

We walked into a nicely appointed suite, beyond which was a door leading into a bedroom. "How long have you been here?"

"Since Tuesday. I feel more relaxed here. Being so close to where Pete died—not knowing who killed him—the frustration was getting to me." Wanda pointed to an easy chair in front of the room's big window. "Make yourself comfortable, Alex." She opened the door of a sideboard, situated along the wall, and held up a bottle of Courvoisier. "As I recall, you used to like brandy. I'm assuming you still do."

"Yes, but I'm curious. Where did you get it?"

Wanda laughed. "You won't believe what this cost me. I marched into one of the restaurants downtown and asked the manager what kind of brandy they had. After a lot of hemming and hawing, he agreed to sell me an unopened bottle."

I watched as Wanda poured out two glasses of brandy. I knew what she meant about frustration. I felt the same way. After replacing the bottle, Wanda sat down on the edge of the sofa, facing me. She raised her glass. "I have to ask again, Alex. Do you think we'll find Pete's killer? What's your gut feeling?"

"There's a lot of confusion."

"What do you mean? What kind of confusion?"

"In the investigation. Stan's one of the best, but he's having trouble getting a handle on things. He still thinks the killer is Nolda, the guy who worked with Pete in the office. At least that's what he says."

"But it seems logical. You can't figure these people." When I shrugged, Wanda said, "You think it's someone else? You think it wasn't Nolda?"

"I saw Sergeant Nolda's body. Except for you and Todd Hammond, no one else did. He'd been dead for a while."

"I was there, but I just couldn't look . . . at that person, knowing what he'd done." Wanda removed a tissue from the pocket of her dress, touched it to her eyes. She then reached for the brandy.

"Go easy on the brandy, Wanda."

"Are you sure you don't want another?" When I shook my head, she said, "I'm wondering if I shouldn't retire." She took a long swallow from her glass.

"Give it some time. Don't make any hasty decisions."

"You're right, Alex. That's good advice." She reached for the bottle and poured herself a half-glass. "Anyway, what's this trip to Dubai all about? You're leaving tomorrow?"

"Bright and early. Who told you?"

"Stan mentioned it."

"I'm following up on one of Pete's leads." I checked my watch and eased myself out of my seat. "Early day tomorrow."

"It's not even six o'clock." Standing up, Wanda crossed the room and put her arms around me. "When am I going to see you again? When do you get back from Dubai?"

"I'll be there for two days."

"I'll see you then before I fly home." Wanda planted a kiss on my lips. "You're being pushed and pulled in all kinds of directions, Alex. Your fiancée wants you to go back to Germany, and people want you in Dubai."

"Don't forget Kabul."

She kissed me again. "And I want you here in Kabul." She pushed herself against me. "I want you very bad."

As Wanda again tried to kiss me, I made an effort to reach across her body and grab the door handle. I didn't succeed.

Wanda smiled. "As you can see, I still haven't given up hope." We kissed again. Wanda's lips were soft and inviting—but inviting me where? And then with a sudden push, she tumbled me down on the sofa.

"Conversations like this are more interesting. Don't you agree?"

"You mean when the two people are horizontal?"

Wanda smiled, took my hand, and brought my fingers to her lips. For some reason, I felt like a bolt of electricity had shot through me. The chemistry was still there.

"These conversations are not appropriate for a guy who's engaged to another woman."

"We could fix that."

"We could, but we won't."

I finally untangled myself from Wanda's embrace and stood up. This time I made it across the room without her stopping me.

Before I could close the door, she waved and blew me a kiss.

CHAPTER 21

THE NEXT MORNING with my gear in my carry-on, I drove from Camp Eggers to Camp Phoenix and stopped by Stan's office to say good-bye. "When do you expect to be back, Alex?"

"I figure I'll be there two days."

"I won't ask what you're working on. I'm just hoping it's not something that's going to get all of us into hot water."

Hot water, an odd remark. My visit with Stan was brief, but it confirmed my earlier impression that he wasn't looking well. Even his handshake felt limp. He seemed worried.

"The report on who killed Pete is in Washington. I think that's going to be pretty much the end of it." Stan paused. "Doug Greer's back at work. He was quoted in a news story yesterday. Something about bringing better communications into Afghanistan."

I checked my watch. "I'm headed for the airport."

"Take care, Alex."

* * *

The flight left on time, and I arrived at Dubai's spacious, modern airport at 1430, four and a half hours later.

I'd booked a room at the Ritz-Carlton because it's situated on the edge of Dubai's Financial Center. At the airport I exchanged euros for dirhams, enough to pay for a taxi to the hotel. After checking in,

I took a quick look around and counted four restaurants and three bars. I wouldn't have to go hungry or thirsty during my stay.

Hamed had given me his extension, and I put in the call at a few minutes before 1700 hours. He answered on the second ring.

"Ah, Mr. Klear. You've arrived." When I said he sounded surprised, he laughed. "To tell the truth, I thought you'd decided not to come."

"I was delayed."

"I suggest we meet in my office. I'm located in the Almas Tower, on the 51st floor. Do you know Dubai?"

"A little. I'm here for the second time."

"Dubai is a very easy city in which to get around. What do you intend to do this evening?"

"I didn't get to see the fountain when I was last here." The Dubai Fountain is a prime tourist attraction and always jammed with people.

"If you go, you'll have plenty of company." I got the impression Mr. Hamed wasn't impressed by my plans for the evening. He hung up without saying good-bye.

Dubai is hot, but is otherwise a good city for walking. The streets are broad and the buildings modern. Heading out of the hotel, I walked up 4th Street toward the world's highest building, then back on Sheikh Zayed Road for a short distance. I was pushing through the Metro Station crowd going in the direction of the Emirates Towers when I noticed a man who somehow looked familiar. As I walked, I asked myself where I had seen that face before. It took me a couple of minutes to make the connection. His face was the face we'd received from the FBI's facial recognition program.

Abdul Sakhi.

In the picture I'd seen, he'd been clean shaven. Now his face was hidden behind a beard and a thick pair of glasses.

Otherwise, he was dressed as a worker, in a long jacket, jeans, and cap, and was carrying a toolbox. He had just come from the far side to this side of the road. After two minutes, I stopped to gaze into a shop window. He was waiting for me thirty yards further on, gazing into a shop window of his own. I figured his partner would very likely be a woman. Spotting her turned out to be more difficult because of the numerous women whose faces were partially concealed behind veils.

Among the crowd were a number of European females, and I definitely wouldn't have noticed her if her partner hadn't made me wary. She was blond, dressed in a nondescript pair of gray slacks and carrying a glossy handbag.

Okay, so I was the rabbit.

When I stopped walking, so did the woman. When I speeded up, so did she. As I walked, I didn't see Abdul Sakhi again until I emerged from a souk that sold jewelry. Now he was dressed in a dark suit, and looked very much like a successful business type. He'd jettisoned the beard but still wore the glasses. The one jarring note was his boots, which clashed with his suit and which he hadn't had time to change. I let him precede me up the sidewalk. When we reached the Emirates Towers, there were fewer people on the sidewalk, which made their job more difficult. Although I hadn't seen his partner for a while, I now assumed she had me in her sights. I also figured she would now be wearing a burqa, the perfect disguise for this part of the world.

I decided to give them a chance to chase the rabbit and earn their salaries. I hailed an empty taxi. I got out when I reached downtown, then walked back toward the Dubai Mall, which isn't far from the Ritz-Carlton. After a short tour of the mall, I walked to the hotel. I didn't see either of my friends, but that didn't mean they weren't watching me.

Walking around Dubai was a lot different from walking around Kabul. On my one previous stay I'd learned that in Dubai alcohol is available only in certain bars in the city. But it is available in all hotels. Since I was perspiring mildly, I felt as if I'd earned myself a beer. I also wanted to do some thinking. In the hotel's Café Belge I ordered a Stella Artois.

When I decided to do some sightseeing, it was because I had a reason. I'd become mildly paranoid after my experience in Kunar Province, and it now seemed as if someone cared enough about me to want to know how I'd be spending my time in Dubai. One thing was sure. Sakhi and the woman were an experienced team, very definitely professionals. If I hadn't seen the FBI photo, I doubt I would have tumbled to the fact I was being tailed.

Two things I'd figured out: One, that Abdul Sakhi had murdered Pete. Two, his reason had something to do with Pete's work on the Kabul Bank.

* * *

Taraki Hamed was right about the Almas Tower not being far from the hotel. When I walked over the next day, the trip was less than ten minutes. I assumed I was being tailed, but when I made a couple of detours and sudden turns in direction, I couldn't spot anyone. Recalling that watching and being watched was part and parcel of the business I was in, I decided not to let the surveillance bother me.

After giving my name to the guards, I walked across the lobby of the Almas Tower to the elevator where, after a brief wait, I was joined by a burly gentleman who had a bulge beneath his breast pocket and who rode up with me and also exited at the 51st floor. I wasn't surprised when he also entered the office with me and, in fact, even held the door. Something else to wonder about was why Mr. Hamed needed security people.

After introducing myself to the female receptionist, I saw a tall, broad-shouldered man with a friendly smile standing at the door to the firm's spacious inner office.

"I'm Taraki Hamed," he said.

I said my name, and we shook hands.

I estimated Hamed to be in his late forties. He had dark, wavy hair, a swarthy complexion, and a thin mustache. I stepped inside the elegant space. His firm, S&A, was described on the downstairs directory as dealing in personal services, which was a description so broad I couldn't help being curious as to what it meant.

A minute later, the receptionist came in with a tray filled with pastries and a pot of green tea. We adjourned to a corner of the office, which was furnished with a sofa, two chairs, a large coffee table, and some green plants. Across the room the sun shone through a large window from which, beyond the roofs of a number of buildings, I could see a sliver of blue, the waters of the Arabian Gulf.

When Hamed asked how I was finding Dubai, I said, "Different from Kabul."

"Yes, it's quite different. I agree." He smiled.

Some of the news stories I'd found among Pete's papers mentioned that Hamed had been an official of the Kabul Bank. I asked how long he'd been in Dubai.

"Less than a year. Dubai is warm, to be sure, but otherwise a nice place to live." As he poured tea, he said suddenly, "Can I ask what is it you wanted to speak to me about?"

I decided to be blunt. "About the Kabul Bank. I was hoping you could help me."

"How?"

"By providing me with some information."

He flashed a condescending smile. "The Kabul Bank is bankrupt. The founder of the bank and other officials are on trial for fraud."

"You are a former official of the bank. Twenty-two of your

colleagues . . . former colleagues . . . are being tried. But you have escaped prosecution."

"I am not being prosecuted for a very simple reason. I haven't done anything wrong." He smiled, shrugged to emphasize the point, then took a cookie from the tray. "Let me ask, Mr. Klear. What is your interest in the Kabul Bank?"

"In my e-mail I said that I was following up on the work of Colonel Hansen. You might say I am Colonel Hansen's successor. As I'm sure you know, Colonel Hansen is dead, the victim of an assassin's bullet." When he nodded, I said, "Is it possible that someone who was involved in the fraud is not being prosecuted?"

"Mr. Klear, forgive me, but the way you talk makes you sound naïve, as if you are hardly aware of the realities. I would have expected more from a man who describes himself as Colonel Hansen's successor."

"I'm listening, Mr. Hamed."

"So far as I know, all the people who were involved with the Kabul Bank fraud are on trial."

"All except you."

He smiled again. "As I said before, I have not committed any crime."

Aware that I wasn't getting anywhere, I took a sip of tea. I decided to try a different tack. "How often did Colonel Hansen visit you here in Dubai?" When Hamed said, "Half-a-dozen times," I knew this guy was important. I couldn't let him get away. At the same time I didn't really know why Hamed was important.

Why had Pete come down here?

I said, "People estimate that 900 million dollars has disappeared. The money belonged to the American government."

"The American government has been very generous to the people of Afghanistan." He touched his finger to his face. "And to the people of Dubai. Here in Dubai some of the prosperity has been underwritten by the American people, but perhaps unwittingly." When I asked him to be more specific, he said, "Many of the luxury villas have been financed by money from America."

"The money from the Kabul Bank was meant to be spent in other ways. Not on luxury villas in Dubai."

"Of course. To help the people of Afghanistan to recover from the damage inflicted by the war in their country."

"According to an audit by an American firm, twenty-two individuals benefitted from the bankruptcy of the Kabul Bank. The number of firms is doubtless in the hundreds."

"That could be a conservative number." Hamed watched as I took a sip of tea, replaced the cup, and reached for a cookie.

"Mr. Klear, we've been beating around the bush for too long. And I am a busy man. You say you are a successor to Colonel Hansen."

I nodded.

"Colonel Hansen was a military man, an employee, you might say, of the American government." Hamed took a tiny sip of tea, replaced the cup. "As a result, he was unable to raise the money to pay for what it was he wanted from me. In the course of his visits here, he was never able to persuade me to just give him what he wanted. He made numerous appeals—to my patriotism, to my country's indebtedness to America, and so on."

"Your country?"

"I'm still an Afghan, from a remote province. But as I say"— Hamed smiled—"all his appeals were in vain. Mr. Klear, I don't know who your principals are. I don't know if you are ready to pay the money I am asking."

At the risk of sounding dumb, I asked the question. "What will I be buying?"

Hamed hesitated, looked at me thoughtfully. "You know, Mr.

Klear, that is precisely the question Colonel Hansen asked me on his first visit to Dubai."

"And how did you answer?"

"I said that I was a good observer. I said he would be buying the results of my hard work. Does that make sense to you?"

"Can you be more specific?"

"He would be buying information that the bank auditors have not discovered, and never will discover. Detailed information of how money was removed from the bank, where the money is now, and who controls it. But he would also have been buying something perhaps equally important."

"What would that be?"

"More than that I'd prefer not to say."

"How much are you asking?"

"Twenty-five million euros."

I realized why Pete hadn't been able to obtain what he wanted.

"The information is contained on a USB drive. You would need to buy it. There is one copy, and one copy only. No more will be made. The hard drive on which the drive was composed has been destroyed. I have to tell you, there may be other bidders for this information."

"Which means?"

"Which means you will have to act quickly. Whoever acts first and is willing to pay what I am asking will receive the one copy." Hamed got to his feet. "As I say, no other copies will exist."

Now I knew why Hamed needed security.

I stood up, and at the door we shook hands.

"I wish you a pleasant stay in Dubai, Mr. Klear."

I nodded and headed out of the office and down to the elevator.

Corley's plane was due to arrive at a few minutes after two. It was now just eleven, which meant I had time to take a walk and get to know Dubai a little better. In the course of my walk I didn't see Abdul Sakhi or his female companion.

* * *

While seated on a sofa in the crowded Ritz-Carlton lobby, I saw Captain Corley, her carry-on slung over her shoulder, push her way through the big revolving door and take a quick look around. She was wearing a light blue jacket over a white blouse and a matching skirt. From thirty feet away, I could see an impatient frown on her face. She appeared angry. I had an idea she'd be angrier after she'd heard what I had to say.

"My plane was late," she said. "Did you—"

"I arrived yesterday afternoon."

"I know that. I don't suppose that means—"

"Yes, I've already been to see Hamed." I shrugged. "I'll save you the trouble of asking, ma'am. The meeting was less than satisfactory."

After a brief pause during which she seemed to be trying to keep her irritation under control, she mumbled something under her breath. It sounded like choice profanity. Finally, she said, "I remember telling you to wait—"

A couple standing a few feet from us turned to look, their faces filled with curiosity.

She pushed me to a point where we couldn't be overheard. "If you'd listen to me, we—"

"I thought I handled things quite well, at least as well as can be expected."

"It certainly doesn't sound like it."

Abruptly, she turned and marched across the Ritz-Carlton lobby to the reception. After she'd checked in, she returned to where I was standing.

"I'm perspiring. The receptionist says there's a nice pool on the roof."

We rode together on the elevator, Corley to the fourth floor, me to the sixth.

She was right. The Ritz-Carlton's pool was very nice, and she was already there, doing laps, when I arrived fifteen minutes later. I took the plunge and caught up with her at the far end, where she was taking a short breather.

I said, "Wanna race, ma'am?"

"Four laps, loser buys dinner." And off we went.

"You're pretty good," I said five minutes later between gasps.

"Better than you." She pushed off in the direction of the ladder. When I said, "I let you win," she flashed a look of disgust. "Has anyone ever called you a male chauvinist?"

"Of course not!" As I watched Corley climb the ladder, I found myself again admiring her trim figure, her arms, her tits, her thighs. The thought occurred to me that it was too bad her personality was such a disaster.

Something else I wondered about: How could Pete have put up with this woman?

"Tell me about Mr. Hamed," she commanded. We were seated in adjacent reclining chairs, wrapped in bathrobes, holding bottles of water and watching two women doing backstrokes.

After describing Hamed and his sumptuous office, I said, "Pete had been down here half-a-dozen times. Hamed has something Pete wanted very badly." After a sip of water, I said, "Hamed's been here in Dubai for close to a year."

"In other words, not that long. He comes from Afghanistan, am I correct?"

"He said he's from one of the remote provinces. He didn't say which one. I'm assuming he moved down here after the Kabul Bank collapsed."

"That was in 2012, a year ago."

"Here he's a partner in a firm dealing in personal services, what-ever that may mean. He was a highly placed official in the bank."

"I know that." When I didn't comment, she said, "I have a question."

I knew what the question was going to be.

"Why didn't they charge Hamed with fraud?"

"According to Hamed, he hasn't been charged because he didn't commit fraud."

"Do you believe him?"

"At first, I was skeptical. After thinking it over, I do believe him. In the course of our conversation this morning, he said he learned to be a good observer."

"Why is that important?"

"I think what must have happened is that, right at the begin-ning, Hamed decided he didn't want to have anything to do with the fraud because he saw the danger of antagonizing the American government. He didn't like running the risk of going to jail. But that didn't mean he didn't like money as much as all the other bank officials. He merely decided he was going to get rich another way."

"How?"

"By closely observing what was happening. I think what he did was write down everything—names, numbers, dates."

"It must have been an enormous job to track a billion dollars."

"Last year, there were two detailed and thorough audits. Hamed got his hands on both audits."

"Pete told me that. He compared what he knew with what was in the official audits. The prosecutors are, of course, basing their cases on what the auditors found. But Hamed knows some things that the auditors and prosecutors don't know. Clever."

"More than clever. Brilliant. He says he has everything in one document."

"That's what Pete wanted: the drive that contains the complete story."

"How do you know?" When she only said, "I know," I said, "Why would it have been so important to Pete?"

Quietly, she said, "Pete was killed because of what's in Hamed's document. It's as simple as that." When I said, "Are you sure?" she said, "Take it to the bank."

I couldn't resist. "The Kabul Bank?"

"God, I hate you! Can't you ever be serious?"

Ignoring the flare-up, I said, "Hamed said the information is of critical importance."

"Important to whom?"

"He didn't say."

"Why would it be important?"

"I don't know why it's worth so much money." When she said, "How much?" I told her.

"Twenty-five million euros."

"That's ridiculous."

I paused to gaze out at the two swimmers, one blond and one brunette, who were climbing out of the pool. Both were slim and long-legged and wore revealing bikinis. The blond had an especially nice figure.

"Hamed wants twenty-five million euros for the one copy of some document?" When I only nodded, she didn't respond, clearly irritated by my ogling the women.

Finally, I said, "At least you now know the reasons why Pete never was able to get his hands on the information."

"Was there more than one reason?"

"There were twenty-five million reasons," I said.

CHAPTER 22

SUNDAY, FEBRUARY 17, 2013

"YOU LOOK UNHAPPY," I said. "Don't you like the food?" I scooped a last forkful of rice and raisins, a dish called Muhammar, which I was eating for the first time and which had tasted better than I thought it would.

"Food's all right, I guess." Captain Corley took a swallow of mineral water, then pushed aside her plate. "I'm not that hungry."

It was late Sunday evening, and we were seated at a rear table in the Sahib restaurant, a dark, quiet place located on the second floor of a three-story building in the Al Garhoud section of Dubai. The neighborhood was chock-a-block with souks, a number of which were in the same ornate building as the restaurant. Adjacent to the restaurant I noticed a small construction site.

We were among the last diners. Over her left shoulder I could see the restaurant entrance, where the headwaiter was in conversation with a newly arrived couple. For some reason the new arrivals looked familiar.

The waiter may have been telling them the place was near its closing hour.

"We need that document," Corley said. "Pete had an idea what was in it." She touched a napkin to her lips. "Pete wanted it, and now I want it."

The woman had her blond hair piled up on top of her head and was wearing a white pants suit.

"Did you hear what I said?"

As the man spoke with the headwaiter, the woman gazed around. I may have noticed her because of her unusual hairstyle. It seemed that the waiter was trying to discourage them, but they were being persistent.

The waiter finally nodded and began leading them back toward us, halting at a table roughly twenty feet from ours.

"I'm talking. Are you listening?"

"Of course I'm listening."

At that moment, our waiter arrived and began clearing our table. Corley asked to see the dessert menu.

"It's important," she said. "You're not listening?"

"Dessert's important?"

I once read somewhere that we all possess a sixth sense, an ability that evolved over millions of years that provides us an additional measure of protection in a world not always as friendly as we might like it to be.

"Yes, ma'am. Of course, ma'am."

"Stop calling me 'ma'am'! I have a name. Use it!"

That sixth sense has come to my rescue on more than one occasion, so I'm inclined to pay attention when I become aware of it.

"I think I'll order the ice cream," Corley said.

As I glanced around in search of the waiter, I noticed out of the corner of my eye that, with the waiter gone, both of the newcomers, the man and the woman, were now getting to their feet— and both were moving in our direction, their eyes locked on this table.

"Will you kindly pay attention to what I'm saying?"

The guy had his hand inside his jacket and was approaching from ten o'clock, while the woman had stepped around an adjacent table and seemed to be coming at us from six o'clock, in other words, from directly behind me.

These were the two people who'd been tailing me when I left the hotel yesterday!

When I turned, I saw Abdul Sakhi.

Now he was standing just ten feet away and, having removed his hand from his pocket, had a gun pointed directly at me. Without thinking, I picked up a glass and hurled it in his direction. It struck him in the chest at precisely the moment he squeezed off his first and second rounds. With the two bullets flying by me, I got up, charged by the adjoining table, and tackled him before he could get off another shot. His weapon fell to the floor, but he aimed a karate chop at my neck, which sent me to my knees.

This guy was good, no question.

Corley had grabbed the woman before she could fire. She retaliated by giving Corley a shove back toward our table. As Sakhi tried to shake himself free, I picked up the weapon on the floor. He pulled out a pistol, and for an instant, we both aimed weapons at each other.

We squeezed off our rounds simultaneously. The difference was my shot struck him while his missed me. He spun around, then crashed slowly down on top of a table, pulling the tablecloth and everything on the table down on top of himself.

While he was still on the floor, I became aware of the woman, who was still holding her weapon and was now pushing aside tables and chairs. She wanted a clear shot at me. But as she tried to aim her weapon, Corley, who was again on her feet, stepped forward, grabbed her wrist, and twisted. When she released the woman's arm, the woman went crashing against another table and fell to her knees.

Within seconds, Sakhi and the woman were both back on their feet, shoving aside two diners and pushing aside empty tables in an effort to reach the exit. Sakhi was clutching his arm. I assumed they weren't eager to speak with the police, who would be arriving in short order.

With both assailants gone, I signed to Corley that we also had to get out. We weren't eager to speak with the cops either. But getting out wasn't going to be easy.

By now, half-a-dozen diners were on their feet, pointing and shouting. The headwaiter raised his arms, trying to quiet them down. Kitchen staff, waiters, and diners crowded at the entrance, effectively blocking that escape route.

Corley was clutching her bag. The expression on her face said, "What do we do now?"

The place was in total chaos. People milling, chattering in multiple languages, and for a moment, not paying attention to us.

Which meant we had a chance—if we acted quickly.

The restaurant's staff circulated through the room, picking up tables and chairs as best they could. An individual in a dark suit, probably the manager, had appeared from somewhere and was at the door talking to a waiter.

I pointed toward the rear of the big room. Maybe we could get out that way.

"Let's try the kitchen." I began heading toward the rear.

When I looked back, I saw two policemen had already arrived and were immediately surrounded by people eager to tell their stories. The cop in charge had everyone's attention and was speaking with the man in the dark suit.

The more aware I was of this situation, the more desperate I was to get out of it.

The kitchen had two doors. Through one, the waitstaff entered; through the other, they left with food. When we got there and pushed our way in, I took a quick look around, saw the room was empty. No doubt the cooks had stormed out when they'd heard the shooting and screaming outside. Glancing around, I saw we were in a large space well equipped with stoves, tables, work areas, receptacles, and refrigerators. Closets and cabinets were all over. Pots, pans, knives, and equipment of all kinds hung from long metal bars attached to the ceiling. A pile of canvas covered what seemed to be boxes of equipment and carpenter's tools. They were strewn along a portion of the rear wall where a bank of shelves was being torn out for a new closet.

On the far wall was a metal door, which I opened. Beyond the door was a long metal staircase, which led down to an alley.

As I was about to tell Corley to follow me down, I heard voices. People were down at the street-level entrance, talking loudly. Cops? Then as I listened, I could hear them beginning to come up the stairs. I shut the door quietly. In a minute they'd be here in the kitchen. A closet would be the logical place to hide, but I didn't see one large enough at this end of the kitchen to hold both of us. There was a door that led into a large refrigerator, but I didn't want to go in there.

I grabbed a large piece of canvas from out of the workmen's pile. As I unfolded it, I pointed and Corley nodded. She lay down flat beneath a table, stretching out her arms. I spread the canvas out over her, then grabbed a cutting board and a frying pan. I crawled under the canvas myself and tossed the objects on top. Hopefully, whatever bumps showed, they didn't look like a couple of human beings spread out on the floor.

Seconds later, I heard the door banging open and people entering the room. I was curious but didn't dare peek. In fact, I was hardly breathing. I heard a couple of doors being thrown open and figured they were conducting a quick search. From the voices, I assumed there were four people, all men, all yakking in Arabic. One guy, no doubt the person in charge, did most of the talking. As they moved out, I lifted the canvas, took a quick look. They wore blue uniforms. Definitely police.

After pulling off the canvas, we got to our feet and headed again for the door leading to the back steps.

It was locked. The cops were sealing up all the exits. Good police work, guys.

"Over there, a window," Corley announced. She was back in the role of giving orders.

At the window, I looked out. Below was a courtyard with a high fence topped with barbed wire on all sides. Even if we made it down, we'd never make it out of the courtyard. Twenty feet from the building was the trunk of a very thick, very old palm tree. I couldn't see that as much help. Farther down, at the construction site, was a small tower, alongside which stood a crane. The tower was too far away to reach. I pushed open the window, looked up. We were on the second floor. Twenty feet above us was the roof. But to get up there we'd need to scale the building's sheer brick wall.

Impossible!

We had to get out of here fast.

I shook my head. "We need a good strong rope."

Corley nodded, then began ransacking the carpenter's equipment. When she found a medium-thick coil of rope and held it up, I shook my head. "Not thick enough. Keep looking." She continued to pull out all kinds of stuff from the carpenter's pile. After rummaging through two large wooden boxes, she removed a neatly rolled length of thick rope.

"What are you thinking of?" she said.

"I'm still not sure."

After handing me the rope, she pushed up the window, leaned out, and peered upward. "There's nothing up there," she said.

I leaned out. "There may be."

I was considering a stone statue, a kind of gargoyle about four feet in height, sitting on the edge of the roof. One of the statue's arms was extended. Although the statue looked solid, was it stable?

I figured it for about eighteen feet above us.

Pointing upward, I said, "I need to get the rope around the arm."

"It doesn't look that strong. I don't think it will hold us."

"There's one way to find out."

It was a good length of rope. I began with an overhand knot, then slipped the tail of the rope back through it. As a Boy Scout I learned to tie a honda knot many years ago, but now I had to do some experimenting and reach back into my memory, first trying this, then trying that.

"Why are you taking so long?"

It did take a while, probably over five minutes, but I finally got the knot the way I wanted it. I pulled the knot so that the loop was large enough to go around the statue.

I leaned out and began tossing the lasso upward, trying to get it around the gargoyle's arm. At first, I didn't come close, but by the fifth or sixth try I was just missing. On the next try, I nearly fell out the window.

Corley grabbed me by the belt, which made it possible for me to lean out further. On maybe my fifteenth try, I got the loop around the gargoyle's arm. I pulled down hard. The statue didn't budge, and the arm didn't break. So far, so good.

She frowned. "I'm not sure we should try this."

"You won't be helping your military career by spending a couple of years in an Arab jail." When she grimaced, I said, "I'm going to swing out and up the wall. I should be able to make it." I didn't add "as long as the statue holds."

I was wearing sneakers, but Corley was wearing low-heeled dress shoes. She removed them, stuck them in her handbag, and gave me the handbag, which I fastened to the back of my belt.

"There's a wall running along the side of the roof. Can we get over it?"

I said, "I'll know when I get up there."

"I'll go first," she said. "I'm the better athlete."

"No, you're not. You just think you are."

No sense in arguing. I shoved her aside and hopped onto the windowsill, grasped the rope, then gave myself a mighty push. The rope didn't snap and the gargoyle continued to sit up there with his arm extended. With my feet against the wall, I began pulling myself hand-over-hand up the rope. As I pulled, I was reminded of a wall-climbing exercise in basic training. I also remembered that I hadn't been very good at it.

As I climbed, the pain in my arms increased with every pull. It probably wasn't more than five minutes, but it seemed like five years.

When I reached the statue, I was able to get my arms around the gargoyle's head. Up close, I could see it was grinning ear to ear.

With my arms around the gargoyle, I was able to scramble over the wall. Then I dropped the rope back down. Corley grabbed it. As I peered over the wall, I could see her looking down. When she hesitated, I wondered if she was afraid of heights. I waved, calling down some words of encouragement.

She continued to hesitate. Again, I called, this time mentioning something about her athletic ability.

Finally, she jumped. The gargoyle remained unmoving—and continued to smile.

"That's a good fella." I patted his head.

With her bare feet against the wall, she pulled herself upwards, one hand after the other. The truth was, she was a good athlete. If she hadn't been, she wouldn't have made it. When she was even with the statue's arm, I was able to reach out, grab her arms, and lift her over the wall.

"Never a doubt," I said, gasping.

"You're an idiot," she said as she began putting on her shoes. "If you knew how close you came to breaking your neck, you wouldn't make dumb remarks."

The thought occurred to me that maybe I should have let her fall.

Pointing across the roof, I said, "That way."

After clambering over a couple of small walls, we were on the roof of an adjacent building. I pointed to a trap door. "I think that's how we get inside."

I yanked at the trap door. When it wouldn't budge, I thought it might only be stuck from disuse. After a minute tugging and yanking, I assumed it was locked from inside. I flashed a look of disgust.

Then I said, "Let's both pull."

It was some kind of tin, and with the two of us pulling and yanking, the door began slowly to bend. Finally, the metal gave. The lock held, but we had an opening. Doing my best not to cut my hands, I bent it back until it was large enough to slip through.

"You go first," she said.

"Yes, ma'am."

After climbing down a short ladder, we were on the building's upper landing. We descended two flights of steps to the ground floor. Outside, there was a crowd of people and vehicles with flashing lights but no one paying any attention to the door of the building from which we were about to emerge.

Crowds were gathered around the restaurant's entrance.

When I said, "We go out slowly," she nodded.

More people, attracted by the excitement, were coming up the street. We mixed in while moving away from the hubbub. The street was wide and curving, and parked at the curb, I saw a police vehicle. The cops were eyeing people, and there were no convenient corners we could duck around.

Moving straight ahead, we continued to walk, and the police didn't stop us. After another fifty yards, there were a couple of souks, one selling lights and fixtures, the other selling clothing.

We entered the souk selling lighting fixtures.

She said, "I'm a mess."

While standing in front of some reflecting glass, she fixed herself up. I checked out my jacket and did my best to get my hair under control. When we left the souk, there were only a few strollers on the sidewalk. More important, we looked civilized again.

A little further on, we approached an expensive-looking restaurant, with some people standing in front and waiting for a taxi. We joined them. When a cab arrived, the driver would assume we'd just left the restaurant. I didn't want anyone in this part of the city to remember us.

I gave him the address of the Warwick Hotel, which I knew wasn't far from the Ritz-Carlton. After I'd paid the driver, we walked the last couple of hundred yards and entered the lobby as though we were returning from an evening stroll. As we waited for the elevator, Corley said, "Would you care for a nightcap?"

"Why not?" I said.

Ten minutes later we were in her hotel room, and I was seated in the room's most comfortable arm chair, ogling my dinner companion's legs, which were spread in front of her and resting on an ottoman.

I said, "That's the first time I ever left a restaurant without paying."

"It sounds as if your conscience is bothering you." We were both clutching glasses filled with scotch, water, and ice and doing our best to pretend that nothing had happened. The TV was turned to the English-language news station with the volume off.

Corley took a sip, then gazed into the glass as though it were a crystal ball. "What do you think?" she said finally.

"I think you must have had experience swinging on ropes. Where did you get it?"

Suddenly her expression became serious. "Would you kindly stop making irrelevant comments?"

"What I think is, someone may want one or both of us dead."

"Hamed?

"Possibly, but why?"

"Maybe he doesn't like Americans."

"Around these parts, there are quite a few people who don't like Americans. They only pretend to like us. But that doesn't mean they want to go to the trouble of killing us."

"You mentioned that you thought someone had been tailing you around. Were these the same people?"

"Yes, and I think these were the people who killed Pete."

"Abdul Sakhi?"

I nodded. "They're professionals."

"Wet work specialists, that's what they are."

I was surprised to hear her use that phrase, which had its origin with the KGB. I didn't comment. I explained in detail how they'd been able to change clothes within brief periods of time. "Only professionals can work like that."

"Someone hired Sakhi to kill Pete."

"And to make it look like a green-on-blue."

Corley pointed at the TV, turned up the volume. Under "breaking news" an announcer wearing a striped shirt, a bow tie, and speaking with a British accent was describing "a terrorist attack in a quiet Dubai restaurant." After briefly describing the assailants, he said, "Both are believed to be associated with a radical anti-government group. They began firing wildly into the crowd of diners. According to police, they got away when—"

She turned off the sound. "Not quite an accurate report of what happened." She sipped some scotch, took a deep breath.

Trying to change the subject, I said, "What time is your flight tomorrow?"

"At 1320."

"Mine's at 1520. We can ride out to the airport together, have lunch."

"Suppose they caught up with us, what would they do?"

"I hate to think about it, but I have an idea we'd be looking at a long stay here in the Emirates. Even worse, we'd be sitting ducks for whoever wants us out of the way." I finished off my drink with a long swallow and got to my feet.

She stood up and put her arms around me. "You're not going to leave me here alone, I hope." Her voice had become soft. She held up her left hand. "I'm still shaking."

"Maybe you should call a doctor. Or better yet, have another drink."

In a still softer voice she said, "I don't drink."

"Just sometimes?"

All of a sudden, she seemed irresistibly feminine. Then she put her hand around my neck, pulled me down to her. She silently kissed me. At the same time I could feel her hand on my thigh. Was this real?

I said, "I hadn't planned for the evening to end like this."

"I'd appreciate it if you didn't go back to your room. Not right away. I want you to stay here with me tonight. All night. Is that all right?" Before I could respond, she said, "I'm shaking. I'm not used to being shot at."

Neither was I, but I didn't say it.

"Come into the bedroom with me."

I was about to say "Yes, ma'am," but then thought better of it.

I watched her enter the bedroom. Before closing the door, she turned and smiled.

I wondered what that was all about.

Was it a honey trap? If so, who was she working for? And what would she have to gain?

With the volume off, the TV was now showing two Arab guys in business suits carrying on an intense conversation. I had no idea what they were talking about. The scotch went down smoothly, and I poured myself a third. Or was it a fourth?

After an hour, I assumed Corley was fast asleep. I switched off the TV, washed up, and quietly let myself out of the room.

Irmie, I hope I'm getting credit for dodging all these bullets.

* * *

"You've been awfully quiet," Corley said. "I don't like that."

We were seated opposite one another at a small table in Paul's Café, a sandwich and salad joint at the airport. We'd checked out of the hotel a half hour before. Her flight was scheduled to leave in an hour. She was right. I wasn't doing much talking, but I was doing a lot of thinking, puzzling over who wanted us out of their lives so badly that they'd risk sending their goons to a crowded restaurant to shoot us.

Who was Abdul Sakhi's employer?

"On the ride over here, you hardly said anything. Something's bothering you. I can tell." When I only nodded, she glared. "I want to know."

"Those people were sent by someone, and I'm wondering who. That's all." I smeared butter on a roll, took a small bite. "And why."

"You spotted them quickly. You're observant."

I tried to smile. "You could say that." I thought again of how Sakhi had fired at me and missed. I'd fired back and hit him in the shoulder. Maybe I was observant, but the fact I'd noticed them tailing me on the street had made the difference. If I hadn't noticed them, we'd both be dead now. I said, "By the way, how are you going to get back down to Khost?"

"I'm not going to Khost tonight. I requested billets at Headquarters. I want to be at the update briefing. You and I have things to talk about." She stood up. "I expect to see you there, 0900 hours." She was obviously recovered from yesterday evening's so-called attack of nerves and was again on her high horse—issuing orders and expecting me to follow them.

"Yes, ma'am. Very good, ma'am." I resisted an urge to salute.

CHAPTER 23

The morning briefing at ISAF Headquarters began with a British colonel using PowerPoint to report on two Taliban attacks on Camp Bastion, the U.K. installation in Helmand Province.

After that, an American officer was scheduled to speak on the Kabul Bank situation and the trial of the twenty-two bank officials—the reason Corley was there.

The British colonel was bombarded with a number of questions, most of them having to do with trends in Taliban activity in Helmand.

The American officer followed. After describing the crimes of the bank officials in some detail and the bank situation generally, he asked for questions.

"Sir," Corley said, raising her hand. "I have a question. Have the auditors been able to account for all the missing money?"

"Most of it, ma'am, I would say."

"How much, sir, would you say remains unaccounted for?"

Shaking his head, the captain said, "Ma'am, I'd have to get back to you on that."

"Would it be in the hundreds of millions?"

"Again, ma'am, I'm not sure—"

"If I may, sir, one more question? Is it possible that there were people involved in the fraud who, as yet, have not been identified?"

"None that we know of, ma'am. The auditors have identified everyone involved."

"Sir, have there been any Americans involved in the Kabul Bank fraud?"

"Ma'am, I can guarantee that no Americans were involved—"

"But, sir, how can we be sure when the auditors' reports don't appear to be complete?"

"I have to take issue with you there, ma'am. The auditors' reports—"

"How many reports have there been?"

"I'm not really sure. Again, I'd have to get back to you on that."

"Sir, there have been three to date. The first one gave the bank a clean bill of health."

"Thank you, ma'am."

"Thank you, sir."

There were two additional briefings, both from officers belonging to European NATO nations, each speaking fluent but accented English.

Stan came next. He spoke briefly, giving an update on measures being used to prevent any further green-on-blue attacks.

When I saw Corley leaving, I followed her into the corridor. She tilted her head in the direction of the Coffee Garden, which was at the far end of the Headquarters building.

"This is as good a place to talk as any," she said. We'd found ourselves a corner table. She had a notebook on the table, and had pushed her cup off to the side. Her uniform cap lay on one of the chairs. In uniform, she looked very sharp—and, if I'm allowed to say it, attractive.

I thought about the previous evening and her obvious attempt to drag me into her bedroom. That was very definitely "conduct unbecoming an officer." It had truly surprised me. Somehow, it was inconsistent with Captain Corley's otherwise by-the-book behavior, and it bothered me.

I said, "You obviously don't believe all the money has been accounted for."

She said, "You heard the update."

"Why did you ask if everyone involved in the fraud has been charged?"

"Why do you think?"

"Because you believe there are guilty people who have not been charged."

"Colonel Hansen knew enough to blow the lid off the biggest bank fraud in the history of the world. It's clear that what he had uncovered has been lost. When he was murdered, there was no one there to pick up where he left off." She paused. "The embezzlers had two sets of books. The first audit, as you know, gave the bank a clean bill of health even though by then hundreds of millions were missing."

I said, "It's not the job of the military to handle matters like this."

"True. But over here the military are the only people to conduct an investigation on behalf of the American people."

I shook my head. "There would have to be more to it than that."

Corley was about to answer, but at that moment, Stan and three other officers entered the coffee bar and found a table on the far side of the big room. I supposed Stan was explaining more about the green-on-blue killings he was investigating.

"Pete made a number of trips to Dubai," Corley said. "He was after the information that Hamed possessed that the auditors missed. Maybe someone fears that we may be able to get the document from Hamed."

"If so, that would mean Hamed's USB drive contains information about the fraud that the auditors have missed. But that would also mean—"

"That the USB drive would tell us who the people are who

ordered Abdul Sakhi to kill Colonel Hansen."

I paused to take another bite of toast. "There's a question I have to ask you, ma'am."

She closed her notebook, then looked at me over the rim of her coffee cup.

Stan had spotted us. With the officers gone, he came walking across the room, coffee cup in hand.

"You can ask, but you won't get an answer."

I decided to ask anyway. "What is your involvement in this situation? What are you trying to accomplish?"

Her dark eyes took on a distant look. When I said, "Well?" she responded, "I told you I wouldn't answer that question."

At that moment Stan arrived. "Do you mind if I join you?" After grabbing an empty chair, he said, "How was Dubai?"

"Hot."

"You're both looking good. Hot weather must agree with you." He took a small sip of java.

"Congratulations," Corley said to Stan. "I saw your name on the promotion list."

I stuck my hand out to congratulate him. His promotion would lead to light colonel. If things went well, one day general. Career-wise, he'd made it over a big hurdle.

"I just got new orders," he said. "In April I leave for Fort Stewart." To Corley, Stan said, "You've also been here for a while, ma'am, if I'm not mistaken." Stan was also curious about her. Hard not to be.

She nodded, her expression remaining serious. "I'll be here for a while."

A minute later, Wanda arrived, carrying a tray. "My breakfast," she said, smiling.

"Time to go." Stan climbed to his feet.

"Me, too," added Corley.

Wanda turned to me. "You're not going to leave me here alone, I hope."

"Perish the thought." I silently watched as she settled her tray on the table.

With everyone gone, Wanda blurted, "My God! I hate that woman! What a harridan. How can you stand her?"

"She's not so—"

"Don't tell me she's not so bad! She's awful! Are you working with her?"

"We were together in Dubai."

"Dubai. Right. I hear it's a great place to visit. They have ski slopes, but it's always ninety degrees."

"It may be a great place in some ways, but I didn't get very much accomplished."

"Well, it couldn't have been as bad as the trip you made . . . to that outpost. Was it?"

"No, not quite."

She drank the last of her orange juice and pushed back her tray.

I carried it to the rack, and we headed down the corridor to the main exit. Outside, I pointed to my van and asked if I could drop her somewhere. "I don't suppose you'd want to take me to Chicken Street. On second thought, I'll walk over. It's not that far."

"I've gotten some people mad at me over here," I said.

"I know you have. It's your own fault. You always have to be the odd man out, don't you? I don't blame Stan for being irritated. He's got to show a coherent report to ISAF Headquarters."

I stuck the key into the car door. "Was Stan irritated?"

"Don't act so . . . so goddamned dumb. You know he was."

"What are you doing this evening?"

"Are you suggesting an evening out on the town? Let's go somewhere where people won't start shooting at us, okay?"

"We're in Afghanistan. You never know when people will start shooting at us."

Wanda smiled. "The Serena is safe. Let's have dinner there."

"How does 1900 sound? I'll make a reservation."

"Okay." Wanda waved, turned, and with a purposeful stride, headed off toward the gate.

I knew that the two shooters in the restaurant would still be gunning for me, a thought I couldn't get out of my mind. I'd seen them tailing me on my first evening in the city. And when they were at the entrance of the restaurant, they told the waiter they wanted a table near ours. They would try again. It was no wonder I was looking forward to leaving Afghanistan.

But I wasn't looking forward to spending more time with Corley. She'd already indicated that she wanted me to fly back to D.C. Again I kicked myself for saying yes to Jerry Shenlee—and for signing on to an op before I knew who was running it.

An hour later, while I was walking up the main drag in Camp Eggers, my phone rang.

"You won't believe what I just did, Alex." Wanda didn't waste time with pleasantries.

"Bought a thousand bucks worth of shawls on Chicken Street?"

"I booked my flight back home. I leave late tomorrow. You said tonight 1900 hours, right? That's good. I'll be packed by then. I have a flight out of Bagram, leaving tomorrow at 2200."

"It sounds like you can't wait to leave."

"In some ways yes, in others no. But mostly yes." When I said, "Afghanistan grows on you," Wanda said, "Speak for yourself!"

That afternoon I spent a couple of hours at the Afghan military barracks, where I shot the breeze with a couple of our military trainers. I couldn't find anyone who had known Nolda.

I told the trainers they had the country's most important job. The transition was to begin in four months and would be complete by the end of next year. Without a dependable, professionally trained Afghan Army, Afghanistan couldn't hope to prevent the Talibs from again seizing power. It was as simple as that.

Of course, even with a dependable, professionally trained Afghan Army, the Taliban might seize power again anyway.

At 1600 I met Haji at the Green Bean coffee shop in Camp Phoenix.

The sun was still strong, so we took our tea outside to the smoking deck. Wherever you are in Afghanistan, the mountains are never far away, and on this day they seemed especially close—and as always, beautiful.

But I had other things on my mind.

After swearing Haji to secrecy, I told him of my trip to Dubai, and how Captain Corley and I became the targets of a pair of gun-wielding assassins.

"You're sure they were trying to kill you, Alex? You're sure they weren't terrorists?"

"I'm positive." As I sipped my tea, I said, "There's a good chance I'll be leaving before long. I'm not sure exactly when. While I'm gone, I want you to keep your eyes and ears open. I also want you to stay in touch with Shah Mahmood. You can do that, I hope."

"Yes, it's not difficult, Alex. In Shah Mahmood you have a life-long friend."

"I hope you're not exaggerating."

"I'm not." Haji fixed me with his dark eyes. When he again spoke, his voice was low.

"One of the elders told me this story. Shah Mahmood had two sons. The other was the oldest. The first American force arrived in the Korengal in 2008. When they came to Shah Mahmood's village, Shah Mahmood's oldest boy got up early every day and waited outside to greet the soldiers as they passed by on the road. He even learned some words of English. But when the Americans were driven out of the Korengal, the Taliban returned. When some of the Taliban learned of the boy's friendliness toward American soldiers, the Taliban ordered Shah Mahmood's boy to be executed."

"How?" I spoke quietly, almost fearing what Haji would tell me.

"He was beheaded. Shah Mahmood says only you prevented him from losing his second son."

I shook my head, thinking of what a violent, unpredictable place we were in. I took a sip of tea but didn't say anything. All our lives seemed to be hanging by nothing more than a thread. Who lived and who died nothing more than a matter of chance. On the road a company of soldiers passed, marching by in formation, a female sergeant counting cadence. "Your left, and a one two . . ." Her chant was lost in the sound of two passing truck engines.

"At one time Shah Mahmood was sympathetic to the Taliban, Alex. He has confided to his friends he now hopes that his son might one day visit the United States."

As I stood up, told Haji good-bye, I was struck by a sudden pang of guilt. I realized it was now early afternoon in Munich, and Irmie would have just returned from lunch at the canteen—or maybe she'd eaten at her desk. In another hour, I was planning to meet Wanda for dinner at the Serena, Kabul's most fashionable hotel.

CHAPTER 24

"How are you going to spend your time, Alex, once I'm gone?"

"I'll be lonely, no question."

Wanda and I were in the crowded main dining room of the Serena Hotel, a colorful room decorated with silks and flowers and with a platoon of white-jacketed waiters rushing back and forth. We'd both had lamb and were now considering dessert. We'd also finished off a bottle of very dry mineral water. I would have liked a very dry Riesling, but in the Serena alcohol is a no-no. All in all, it had been a nice dinner.

"Expensive evening," I commented. I knew that rooms in this hotel could run up to a thousand dollars a night and with this lavish meal . . .

"You have to know how to live. Do you know what my mother used to tell me when I was just a child?" Before I could answer, Wanda said, "Always marry for money."

"Your mother sounds like a very practical person."

"She was more than practical. She was insightful. She understood what life was all about." Wanda paused to take a sip of water. "I'm not saying that life is only about money. There are other things—"

"Name ten."

"I'm serious. In order to live life—"

"Did you follow your mother's advice?"

"I married Pete. No, I didn't obviously. I married . . . for love."

She tried to smile, but didn't quite succeed. "I'm not sure I'll marry again, but if I do—"

"You'll follow your mother's advice."

"My mother emigrated from Norway when she was a girl. Her younger brother, my uncle, did very well. He's president of a Norwegian bank." She shrugged. "You're making a joke out of it. But yes, if I marry again, I will follow my mother's advice. But Pete was . . . well, Pete. We always had enough to live on, but an Army colonel's salary just isn't that much."

I said, "It's my understanding that you and Pete were planning to divorce. Is that true?"

Before she could answer, the waiter arrived. Wanda said she wanted the watermelon. I ordered a cup of fruit. After placing our order, I took another swallow of water.

"Well?"

Wanda touched a napkin to her lips, then said, "Where did you hear that latrine rumor?"

"One of Pete's colleagues told me. I'm wondering if it's true. You never mentioned it."

"Over the years Pete and I had our disagreements, sure. What married couple hasn't?" Wanda sounded irritated. "Maybe the word 'divorce' came up occasionally, I don't remember to be honest." She paused. "But to answer your question. No, I had no intention of divorcing Pete." When I only shrugged, Wanda said, "But maybe Pete wanted to divorce me. Maybe he'd found some chippie—"

At that moment the waiter arrived with dessert. After he'd refilled our water glasses and left, Wanda said, "I'm thinking about what happened down in Dubai. I'm glad you told me. My God! It sounds horrible. People shooting at you."

"It was a shade unpleasant."

"I should think so. Were they terrorists, or what?"

"I don't think so."

"What do the police down there think?" When I said I didn't know, Wanda said, "Didn't you talk to them?"

"To answer your first question. I think these individuals had me in their sights. I was in the restaurant with a female companion."

Wanda grinned. "I should have known. You're never without female company. I've never known anyone like you. It was Corley, wasn't it? God, I hate that woman." I thought I knew why Wanda didn't like Leslie Corley, and I supposed her dislike was natural enough. According to Captain Page, she may have had a romantic relationship with Pete, who, of course, was Wanda's husband.

"Captain Leslie Corley. She's stationed down in Salerno."

"She's working with you?"

I nodded, offering no further comment.

"What in the world were you doing in Dubai? I mean, what are you doing over here, anyway? You're so secretive."

"Ask Jerry Shenlee."

"Who's Jerry Shenlee?"

"The guy who sent me over here."

"Todd says you're here to investigate Pete's death. I guess I can understand that." Wanda paused to scoop up some watermelon. "But then you're traveling to Dubai for some reason." She shook her head. "I mean, what's the connection?"

"One thing always leads to another."

"Does it have anything to do with the Kabul Bank?"

"I can't go into detail, Wanda."

"Okay, I know I shouldn't be asking questions like that. Still, we've known each other a long time." She smiled. "It's not like I'm working for the Taliban."

"This much I can tell you. I was unable to do what I wanted to do in Dubai."

"Which was?"

"Find out what really happened at the Kabul Bank." I went back to eating my dessert.

When Wanda had finished her watermelon, I said, "You have an early day tomorrow."

"Not that early. Do you know what I'm going to suggest? That we adjourn to my room and break open a bottle of champagne."

"You have champagne?"

"The proprietor of that restaurant has gotten to know me. That's where I bought the brandy. Half a bottle of brandy is still in my room."

I said, "We can't let it go to waste." Our meal had been good, but the truth was, I would have enjoyed a bottle of wine.

Before I could say anything, Wanda said, "My last night in Afghanistan. Who knows if I'll ever come back? We're celebrating. Get the check, Alex."

* * *

"Cheers." Wanda lifted her glass and flashed a look of irritation. "We're drinking champagne out of water glasses." It was a half hour later, and she'd seated herself alongside me on the love seat in her hotel room.

"No champagne flutes?"

"Since the Serena doesn't serve alcohol, there's no need for them." Wanda smiled. "I spent a half hour at one of the bazaars looking through glassware. I couldn't even find wine glasses." Still smiling, she said, "Cheers anyway."

"These really are nice rooms," I said, checking out the furniture, the neat little kitchen on one side, a desk on the other. The bed was inside the small bedroom.

"At eight-hundred dollars a night they should be nice."

"When I was in the Army I never could have afforded—"

"When you were in the Army—that was a while ago. Didn't you once say you made corporal before the agency recruited you?"

"Now you're pulling rank on me."

"Kiss me, Alex." When I didn't respond, Wanda smiled. "Remember RHIP. Rank has its privileges." When I wavered, she said, "I know. You're engaged to be married." Wanda picked up her glass and leaned into me. As she sipped, she gazed at me over the rim. Her eyes, round and deep blue, were slightly red-rimmed. She placed her hand on my thigh. "Your fiancée is in Germany. She'll never know."

"Of course she will. Women can read men's minds, as you well know."

"I'm certainly having a hard time reading yours." As she put down her glass, Wanda said, "I think I'll open another bottle."

"You'll have to drink it alone. I've had enough for one night."

"You're such a spoilsport. Were you always like this?"

"Like how?" When she placed the softness of her lips against mine, I felt myself beginning to weaken. Not good. Wanda seemed eager to move us from the sofa to the bedroom.

"When did you become such a fuddy-duddy, Alex?"

"It's probably in my DNA."

"No, it isn't. You never used to be like this. I have the feeling I'm kissing . . . a stone statue."

As I raised my hands defensively, she sighed and readjusted her seat on the sofa. "Okay, Alex, I know." Then she smiled. "You're engaged. But you're still not married, you know."

"What's that supposed to mean?"

Wanda continued to smile. "What it means is, you're still fair game."

"Why can't we just be friends?"

Folding her arms across her chest as though she was shivering, she said, "I'm cold, and I can see you're not going to warm me up. Would you mind adjusting the air conditioner?" She pointed toward a small switch on the wall. I got to my feet, crossed the room, and gave the dial a tiny push downwards.

As I returned to the sofa, I said something about leaving. Wanda pointed again to the nearly empty champagne bottle. She poured out the last of the bottle into our glasses.

I said, "Don't forget. You have to be up early. You still need to shop."

"You're right."

"Have you ordered a taxi to take you downtown?" What a dumb question. There are plenty of taxis.

"That's nice, Alex."

"What's nice?" I suddenly felt kind of strange.

"That you're concerned about my welfare." Wanda's voice seemed to be coming from far away, out of an echo chamber.

It hit me hard, a wave of light-headedness sweeping downwards through my body, from my head through my legs and into my feet. Although the sensation wasn't exactly unpleasant, my alarm bells began ringing. I didn't like what I thought might be happening.

Without hesitating, and summoning all my willpower, I got to my feet. I found I could stand. When Wanda said, "Alex!" I didn't answer, only focused my eyes on the door on the far side of the room. Unsure of whether I could reach it, I stumbled in that direction. As I went, I thought the floor seemed to be tilting. Wanda was alongside me now, calling my name. When she tried to grab my arm, I shook her off. She continued calling my name. Feeling around for the door lever, but unable to focus my eyes, I finally got my hand around it. I yanked the door open. Where was the elevator? To my right. Holding the wall, I felt my way along.

Two women were standing, waiting. Waiting for what? The elevator. When it arrived, I pushed by the women. Seconds later, the elevator door opened, and I saw the hotel lobby, the registration desk at the far end, heard the sound of voices. People were coming and going, everyone too busy to take any notice of me. Outside the elevator, I negotiated the last twenty feet to a large armchair and fell into it. In a daze, I sat there silently for probably thirty minutes, long enough for my head to clear and the dizzy feeling to finally pass.

I waited another ten minutes to make sure. The dose, whatever it was, probably hadn't been that strong, not strong enough to knock me for a loop. Or I just hadn't swallowed that much of my drink. Either way, I was lucky, very lucky. Finally, I got up, tested my legs. I was fine, my old self again. Outside, there was a line of waiting taxis. I decided the safe thing was not to drive. Twenty minutes later I was back at Camp Eggers, strolling up Gator Alley toward my billet, and taking deep breaths as I went.

The van, in which I'd driven to the Serena, was in the hotel parking lot. I'd pick it up the next day.

As I lay on my bed, I couldn't keep from smiling, but I didn't feel I am that wonderful—or desirable. I supposed that Wanda, on her last evening, wanted to rekindle feelings we might have had for one another way back when. Whatever she'd given me, I recognized the sensation immediately when it hit me. A long, long time ago, someone had fed me what is commonly called a "Mickey Finn" but what is actually chloral hydrate, which, when combined with alcohol, packs a punch. From what I'd heard, there were all kinds of drugs easily available to do what the Russian woman in East Berlin wanted to do.

Wanda must have dropped something in my glass when I'd gotten up to adjust the air-conditioning. Thankfully, I'd not drunk enough to render me totally immobile and I'd reacted immediately. As it was, I'd had just enough presence to be able to make it out of the room, onto the elevator, and down to the lobby.

I decided to take the incident in stride and not let it bother me. In fact, I should be flattered that a woman thought enough of me to go to such extreme lengths to get me into bed.

CHAPTER 25

The e-mail message arrived during the night. "Attention Alex Klear: Report to my office at ISAF Headquarters, Room 216, 20 February 2013 at 1500 hours. Gardner Boyd, Colonel, U.S. Army, ISAF Mission Command."

I had an idea I knew what that was about. It wouldn't be good.

The following morning, I was able to hitch a ride halfway to the Serena with a couple of GIs on their way to the airport. It was a cool, pleasant day, and I walked the final quarter mile through the broad Kabul streets. At the hotel gate I spoke briefly with the three guards, passing the time of day and giving them an opportunity to practice their English. I then made a short tour of the Serena's garden on the way to the parking area. If I'd approached the parking lot, which was chock-a-block with guests' cars, from the hotel side, the two people climbing out of a blue Mercedes sedan would almost certainly have seen me before I saw them.

I dropped into a low crouch behind an SUV.

They stood talking quietly before heading off through the maze of cars in the direction of the hotel.

The man was Abdul Sakhi, and his left arm was in a sling.

Three days ago he and his female companion had tried to kill Corley and me in the Dubai restaurant.

Now, they were back in Kabul in the hotel parking lot waiting for me to retrieve my van.

Why? Then I thought I might have the answer to that question.

I slid under my vehicle and saw it immediately. It was, in fact, easy to spot, and I vividly recalled the heads-up and the advice we received during our readiness training: Always check out your vehicle before climbing in. The military calls them VBIEDs— vehicle-borne improvised explosive devices. This one was attached to the underside of the van's chassis with a magnet. Fastened horizontally next to the manifold was a small tube half-filled with what could have been mercury. Two wires ran from the explosive to opposite ends of the tube. A small bump while driving would have been enough to close the circuit and set off the explosive.

Using my Leatherman, I unscrewed one of the wires at the explosive end, then unscrewed the fasteners holding the tube. Holding the tube with my left hand, I lifted off the IED itself. Once on my feet, I checked the mercury in the tube. It wouldn't require much of a bump to detonate the explosive.

The operation had required five minutes. I'd need another five. I assumed that Sakhi and the woman were having breakfast. Whatever they were doing, I didn't have much time. Underneath the Mercedes, I attached the explosive to the chassis, found a place to fasten the tube, then tightened the two screws. Working carefully, I screwed on the connecting wire.

When I was again on my feet, I didn't see Sakhi or the blond woman.

I got the engine of the van started and drove slowly out to the road leading to the hotel gate.

For people in Kabul, a car exploding was like another day at the office.

As I drove, another question occurred to me: How would these characters have known which vehicle was mine?

I needed some time to think, and since I didn't have anything pressing to do, I decided a ride around the city might help to calm me down. Unfortunately, Kabul's chaotic traffic only served to make me jumpier. I finally stopped at the zoo. After touring the animal cages, I sat down on a bench. My phone went off.

Corley said, "I just learned you have an appointment at Headquarters this afternoon."

"Roger that."

"Not good. This could mess things up badly."

"Why, ma'am?"

"We'll be going to the States, but right now I need you over here. I can't handle everything alone." Before I could respond, she said, "We'll talk tonight."

* * *

Colonel Boyd waited for the printer on the table adjacent to his desk to discharge three pieces of paper.

"What this is," he said, "is a Breach of Discipline Report." He seated himself behind his desk. In front of the wall to my right stood three flags, NATO's, Afghanistan's, and the Stars and Stripes. On the wall behind his desk was a picture of the president. As Colonel Boyd reread the document, he shook his head, then cleared his throat. "I asked for this, Mr. Klear, after you and Captain Withers began fighting."

"I'll admit, sir, that it was my fault." When he nodded, I said, "I threw the first punch."

"Boys will be boys, Mr. Klear, and I understand that." He paused. "All our tempers become frayed from time to time."

"Thank you, sir."

"But it's not the brawling that disturbs me. It's everything else I'm reading here." Again he paused. "According to Captain Withers, you made a trip to COP Franklin, and then were responsible for one of his troopers being killed."

I then explained the information that had led me to the COP.

"You lost your weapon out there."

"My weapon was taken forcibly. I've explained that in a report. I've also explained the loss of the money. It was an ambush. They were all over us within a matter of seconds."

Colonel Boyd shook his head. "How would they have known you were coming? An ambush seems unlikely. Captain Withers thinks you stole the money and made up the ambush story."

"I can only say—"

"All right, all right. But there's also this account of being— captured? And then you mysteriously make it back to the COP four days later? Everyone is skeptical of that. The Taliban don't let Americans go, not without paying a ransom. Or else they kill you. You didn't say what happened. According to your account, you and the interpreter were captured by a bunch of Talibs."

"That's what happened."

"How did you get away? You've clammed up there. No, Mr. Klear, if you were in the military, you couldn't get by with a story like that. How dumb are we supposed to be?"

Colonel Boyd was right, of course. I hadn't said anything about how Shah Mahmood and his people shot our way out. I knew I wouldn't be helping Shah Mahmood by saying he'd managed our escape. We needed to keep that part of our story to ourselves.

"According to Major Jones and Undersecretary Greer, you've said you were sent here . . . by Gerald R. Shenlee, who is on the staff of the NSC. Is that correct?"

I nodded. I had an idea what was coming. Jerry wouldn't want his name connected to whatever I was doing.

"Mr. Klear, we've been in touch with Mr. Shenlee. Although he says he knows you personally, he hasn't had any contact with you in . . . let's see, over a year. He says he last saw you at a reunion of former officers in November 2011."

At that point, I knew there was no sense trying to explain anything. I was on my own, really on my own now.

Colonel Boyd got to his feet. "You have twenty-four hours to clear the post. After this time tomorrow, you will be denied access to all ISAF facilities. Should you be anywhere within ISAF jurisdiction after 1600 hours tomorrow, you will be forcibly escorted off-post. You're not subject to the UCMJ, but if you persist, you'll be turned over to the local authorities, the Afghan police. I assume that won't be necessary. Do I make myself clear, mister?"

"Perfectly, sir."

Colonel Boyd held the door, and I exited his office.

From Headquarters I drove over to Camp Phoenix, where I turned in the van at the motor pool, did some shopping at the PX, and grabbed a bite at the chow hall.

I stopped by Stan's office to say good-bye. Stan's manner was that of a guy brimming with self-confidence. With the promotion to light colonel, his future looked bright. Barring an unforeseen disaster, he'd very likely make it all the way to two-star or even to three-star.

After a couple of minutes shooting the breeze, Stan got up, came out from behind his desk, stuck out his hand. "Have a good flight, Alex. I don't suppose you'll be back."

"Never say 'never again,' Stan. You know better than that."

"Yeah, I suppose I do."

I knew my departure meant one less headache for Stan and that he was happy to see me go.

When I reached my billet at Eggers, Corley was waiting for me. After I'd finished telling her what had happened in the Serena

Hotel parking lot, she said, "Someone wants you dead." She said the words matter-of-factly, without feeling. As I'd already noticed, she wasn't a person to express emotion, no less sympathy.

"I think Abdul Sakhi and the woman were only waiting there to make sure."

"And you say that you attached the IED they had put under your car to their car."

"Were there any news reports of exploding vehicles today?"

"None that I know of." She paused. "Someone is very afraid of you."

"If we knew why, we might know who killed Pete."

"It could have something to do with your trip to Dubai."

"My trip to Dubai wasn't any more successful than Pete's had been."

"Colonel Hansen is dead."

"A helicopter leaves for Bagram tomorrow at 0800 hours. I have to be on it. Otherwise, they'll throw me off the post."

"You should be on it only if you're going back to the States." When I frowned, she said, "I've decided you should remain over here. I need backup."

Again, I had an urge to ask Corley all kinds of questions, beginning with "Who are you?" and "What kind of op are you running?"

"You've lived in Kabul before, haven't you?" When I nodded, she pointed toward the door of the hooch. I picked up my carry-on and, outside, tossed it into the rear of her van. We climbed in and drove slowly up Gator Alley toward Camp Eggers' main gate. I can't say I was all that sorry to be leaving. As the sentries passed us through, I gave a small wave.

When I asked, "Where are we headed?" she didn't respond.

As we drove, I eyed the shops and bazaars along the road. I knew Corley had something in mind, but I had no idea what it was. As she drove, I realized I'd never seen her this nervous. I also recalled her comment on the telephone two nights ago that she needed me. It was unusual for her to admit something like that. As she drove, she spent a lot of time eyeing the rearview mirror. We headed toward the center of the city and then toward the eastern end of Kabul. The streets out here were narrower and filled with people. She did a good job of maneuvering around the carts and slow-moving pedestrians.

"Char Qala," she said. "Do you know it?"

"Unfortunately, yes." Char Qala is one of Kabul's less desirable neighborhoods, a place where I'd had a run-in with a couple of opium smugglers on an earlier visit. One of them was dead, and I hoped I wouldn't run into his buddy.

"We'll be staying at a safe house belonging to people I know." When I asked where Haji was, she said, "He'll come tonight. I hope you're ready to travel."

I wondered where I'd be traveling to. I also wondered why we needed to be in a safe house when we could have booked a room in one of Kabul's many guesthouses. I decided not to ask.

As we drove, Corley made two brief telephone calls. I could see that we were in Kabul's eastern outskirts. We turned on to a street full of tired, destitute-looking people and shabby buildings and continued for five minutes. We stopped in front of a compound shielded only by a crumbling wall. At the gate, an old beggar, who appeared blind, shouted, "*Assalamu alaykom! Salam!*" I lowered my window and dropped money into his cup. After Corley had driven inside, I closed the rusted gate, removed my carry-on from the back seat, and stared at the building. Even by Kabul standards, this place was decrepit.

"Two widows live downstairs here with their children," Corley said. "They won't bother us. There are rooms upstairs where we will stay." The building was made of mud and stone and had one small window on the front wall. Covering the doorway was a large, heavy blanket that moved in the breeze. The kitchen window was covered with a piece of cardboard.

The flight of steps was dark. Upstairs there were three rooms opening off an unlit corridor. Corley said the widows sometimes rented them out. I couldn't help wondering who would want to stay in a place like this. In one of the rooms I tossed my carry-on on top of an ancient bed covered by a ripped, stained spread.

Before I could object, Corley said, "I have errands to run. Grab some shut-eye."

"Yes, ma'am, will do."

Corley's expression turned grim, but she didn't comment. At the door, she said, "Haji should be here by 2000 hours. Then we'll move out."

"Where are we going?" I was being kept totally in the dark.

"Haji will tell you." Then she stepped outside and pulled the creaky, ill-fitting door closed.

After a few minutes I fell into a sound sleep for perhaps an hour, until I was awakened by the sound of someone moving around in the corridor outside. As I lay listening, I heard the sound of voices. I assumed they belonged to the women who lived downstairs.

I was wrong.

As I saw the door creaking its way open, I leaped off the bed. But by that time it was too late. A man holding an automatic weapon pushed his way into the room. Behind him, a blond woman entered and shut the door.

The man was medium height and wearing the *shalwar kameez*. Although he'd been dressed differently in Dubai, I recognized him. Abdul Sakhi. His arm was no longer in a sling. And he was certainly not dead. Needless to say, I was sorry he wasn't. At least I no longer had a guilty conscience about attaching a bomb to his car.

The blond woman said, "I know what you're thinking. We're not dead. We're very much alive. We hate to disappoint you." She spoke with a British accent. When Sakhi said something more, she said, "You thought you were so clever, Mr. Klear."

Hatred burned in Abdul Sakhi's eyes. With an AK-47 pointed directly at me and the safety off, he only had to squeeze the trigger. This was the guy who'd killed Pete. Now he intended to kill me. He spoke again to the woman, who spoke fluent Pashto.

"He wants you to know how we tricked you. Abdul wants you to know that we were watching you the entire time from inside the hotel."

I knew immediately she was talking about my attempt to turn the tables in the Serena Hotel parking lot. Probably they'd seen me enter the parking area and had only pretended to leave their vehicle and go inside the hotel building. They no doubt were watching as I removed the IED from my own vehicle and placed it beneath theirs.

Now I knew why there had been no news report that day of a car exploding in Kabul. Their car hadn't exploded.

"I'm Fiona, by the way." Although her blond hair was stringy, I found Fiona mildly attractive, sexy even. She had a round face and thin lips. Beneath her jeans she had on a pair of combat boots. She was trim and looked to be very much at home in this part of the world.

I said, "People will catch on sooner or later, Fiona. You can't do this sort of thing forever."

"What sort of thing, love? You mean taking money from both sides?" Before I could answer, she said, "Why not?" She placed a hand on Sakhi's shoulder, and he flashed a small grin. "My man here figured it all out. I do the deals with you Yanks, and he does the deals with the Talibs."

It was at that moment I noticed the door opening very, very slowly.

"My man delivers. Once he turns you into a corpse, we'll have another payday." Fiona said something more in Pashto, causing Sakhi to again smile.

The door moved another half-inch.

"Someone—"

"Yes, love. Someone wants to send you bye-bye. Why, I don't know. Perhaps you've stuck your nose somewhere where it doesn't belong."

Not allowing my glance to go to the door, I said, "You were in Dubai—"

"You were lucky down there, you know. You should already be dead now." She said something to Sakhi, who nodded.

Without taking his eyes off me and with the muzzle of his AK-47 pointed directly at my stomach, he mumbled something back.

She could be telling him anything, like "Shoot the bastard!"

The door, which was again moving, was about to creak. When he heard the creak, I knew what would happen. The safety was off. Abdul Sakhi would pull the trigger. I would have, at best, a hundredth of a second.

Two seconds later, when the door creaked, I was ready. I dove behind the bed. Sakhi fired a burst—and standing at the door, Corley fired a burst of her own. Sakhi sagged, dropped the weapon, went down beside the bed.

With Corley's gun pointed at her, Fiona quickly raised a hand. "Don't shoot!"

As the two women glared at each other, Corley kept her weapon up, remaining silent. That proved the right move. Reaching behind her, Fiona suddenly grabbed for the automatic on her belt. I was in position to jerk her wrist just as she fired.

Again, Corley fired a brief burst, this one sending Fiona down in a heap.

"I was waiting for them," she said calmly, stepping into the room. "But they found you before I found them. Are you all right?"

"Thanks." I touched my forehead, which was damp with perspiration. I did my best to act as if nothing had happened.

With the barrel of the M4, she moved Abdul Sakhi's head so the sightless eyes stared upwards, directly at us. Corley's eyes showed no emotion.

"You were right. He murdered Colonel Hansen. It wasn't Sergeant Nolda."

We stared at the bodies, each of which oozed blood. I tried not to think what might have happened if I'd been half a second slower. Bullet holes riddled the wall behind where I'd stood.

"Let's go downstairs," Corley said after a half-minute. "We'll have the women clean up." Then she led the way out of the room, down the flight of dark steps. After talking with one of the women, we went out to the gate. The blind beggar was now smoking a cigarette and he smiled at me.

Corley said, "Khan sent the word that they'd come." She said something to Khan, who from beneath his shirt produced a telephone. He said, "*Allahu Akbar!*" then smiled as he held it up for my benefit.

She said, "They've been following me on and off for two days. They've been waiting to get the two of us together. When I picked you up at Eggers, I knew they'd try something—and this was the perfect place. As we were driving, I called Khan."

I nodded, recalling her telephoning as she drove.

She said, "There's a back entrance through the wall. I came in through there." She looked at her watch. "When Haji arrives, you'll leave with him. I'll remain here."

I knew if I asked where Haji and I would be going, she wouldn't say.

Later that evening, Corley and I went downstairs. We sat at a rickety table in a battered room next to the kitchen. The two women brought us in a meal of lamb smothered under rice and carrots.

Corley said, "In some ways, I'm glad you were kicked off the post." She hesitated, frowned. When I didn't comment, she grabbed a piece of *naan* and held it up. "Do you like Afghan bread?" When I said I did, she pointed at the food. "Because that's what you'll be eating now that you're not allowed in the chow hall anymore." After a second, she angrily threw down the piece of bread. "Something has happened."

"What happened, ma'am?" Whatever it was, I could see she was upset.

"Something happened that shouldn't have happened. Right now we're awaiting word of what we need to do."

I felt like saying, "Yes, dear." I ate the lamb, using my hands and my own piece of *naan*. It tasted delicious.

* * *

By the time I awoke from a nightmare-filled sleep the following morning, Corley was gone. To where, I had no idea.

When I entered the downstairs room next to the kitchen, I surprised one of the women. It was the only room in the house with a table. She retreated into the kitchen and returned a few minutes later wearing a burqa and carrying a glass of tea, two pieces of bread, a cantaloupe, and an apple. I ate it all, using my Leatherman to carve up the melon.

When she returned, I said, "*ma-nana*," and she bowed. I knew she wouldn't accept money for her *milmastia*, but I'd place a few hundred euros under my pillow before leaving.

Sometime after 1500 hours Corley drove her van through the gate and into the open space in front of the house. As she climbed out, she pointed toward the house, letting me know we needed to talk.

After we'd seated ourselves at the big table, one of the women brought in tea, then headed back to the kitchen. Corley said, "You're going to have to do some traveling."

"Where are we going?"

"You and Haji are going somewhere. I can't leave." She paused. "Something happened."

When the woman returned a few minutes later with a plate full of fruit, Corley thanked her. As we ate, I said, "What happened?"

"It happened while you and I were in Dubai. Haji will fill you in when he gets here. He should arrive in a couple of hours." Before I could comment, Corley checked her watch, then said, "Better that Haji tells you."

Whatever it was, it wouldn't be good news.

CHAPTER 26

HAJI ONLY NODDED when I greeted him three hours later. I couldn't help noticing his worried expression. Standing in the darkened compound, he placed his hand on my shoulder and gave me a silent half-hug, a common greeting among friends in Afghanistan. Then he pointed to the driver of the van in which he'd arrived, a young Afghan.

"You remember Najib, Alex. He drove us to Shah Mahmood the last time. He drives for Shah Mahmood. He'll be our *badrah,* our guide. American soldiers have been gone from the Korengal for three years, but on the way there we will encounter ANA soldiers. They have many checkpoints along the Pech River. Najib knows the soldiers, having driven through many times. We will be stopped, but he will get us through."

I gave Najib a wave. He smiled and waved back.

Strangely, I was becoming more comfortable with the Afghans I knew than with the Americans over here.

Finally, Haji said, "It's good you're here, Alex. I do not think there's much time." He spoke quietly. When I asked, "Time for what?" he only shook his head.

I tossed my rucksack in the van, looked around. I couldn't help wondering how this trip to Kunar Province was going to turn out—better, I hoped, than my last one.

Corley emerged from the house and spoke briefly with Haji in Pashto.

As Najib turned over the engine, we climbed in, Haji in front, me in back. We drove out through the compound gate and hung a left on the road outside. Seconds later, we were riding past a row of small shops and shabby bazaars in a part of the city I seldom visited. After three minutes we were on a wide thoroughfare leading to Kabul's eastern outskirts.

Kabul sits on an arid plain, and with the sun having set, the mountains in the distance were transformed into looming dark silhouettes. Traffic on city streets was light. Alongside the highway were all kinds of heavy equipment, everything from tractors to ancient Russian tanks, all of it rusted, vandalized and abandoned, and now useless eyesores, reminders of the violence that, beginning with the Russian invasion in 1979, had gripped this country.

Haji passed me a battered map. "We're taking the highway to Jalalabad."

I nodded. On my way to our airbase up there, I'd driven the highway to Jalalabad a number of times. The trip could be three to four hours, depending on traffic.

"And then into Kunar Province, first to Asadabad. From there we drive out through the Pech Valley." He was silent for a second. "Shah Mahmood wants to see you. We are going all the way to the Korengal by car. To Shah Mahmood's village."

I nodded. I'd gathered as much. Haji was telling me as little as possible, and I wondered why.

We encountered the first checkpoint just before reaching the outskirts of the city. Haji got out and conducted a brief conversation with some ANA soldiers.

I couldn't say this to Haji, but this was a trip I would rather have made by helicopter, or better yet, not have made at all. The risk of driving over an IED in Afghanistan is ever present. Haji had said our driver was familiar with the road and how to drive it.

We reached Jalalabad in good time, then turned west on a well-maintained two-lane highway.

Asadabad is a nice city, situated on the side of a mountain, and was completely dark as we drove past. After a couple of miles, we stopped at a deserted roadside gas station. Najib got out and went behind a building. Haji and I got out to stretch our legs.

Najib returned a few minutes later and said something to Haji.

"We need gas," Haji said, "but the owner says we have to wait."

A half hour later, two turbaned workers arrived. One of the workers got the gas pump going. A few minutes later, we were on the road again. Streaks of light in the dark sky were the first signs of the new day.

We were well into the Pech Valley when we encountered another checkpoint. According to Najib, the military facility here was an abandoned American firebase. Although I knew that the Army and Marines had abandoned a number of outposts in this area, I didn't know which this one was. After a brief discussion with the soldiers, Najib got us going again. At times I was able to see the Pech River from the road. From time to time Najib spoke into his telephone, perhaps reporting our whereabouts to someone on the other end.

Further on, we were again stopped. As an ANA officer checked our passports, Haji got out to speak with the soldiers. He seemed a shade paler when he climbed back in the van.

I thought I knew why. They'd told him of occasional Taliban activity at night and warned him of the real possibility of driving over an IED on this stretch of road. Haji had been right about our driver. I don't believe the soldiers would have let an American through if they hadn't known Najib.

Finally, the officer shrugged and gave us the go-ahead, and we started off again.

We drove through a number of small villages, then over a bridge with a broken railing and onto a narrow road, which twisted and turned.

After a time the landscape became more hilly and the road more treacherous. Every time we hit a pothole I felt myself tense up, probably a result of going over the IED on the way in from the airport.

We entered a small village, which seemed familiar. We drove down the dirt road, our car engine the only sound in the morning silence.

When we halted in front of a walled compound, Haji said, "We're at Shah Mahmood's home."

I recognized the main road and the haphazard collection of buildings. This was such a sparse settlement, I wondered if it even had a name. I knew I'd never forget having been brought here with Haji after our close call with the executioner's axe.

"Prepare yourself," Haji said. "Shah Mahmood is waiting for us."

The driver opened the van door and pointed us toward the gate, which had a half-opened door. Inside, we crossed the compound and entered the building. We were in a dark corridor, and two young women stepped aside to allow Haji and me to pass. And then we were in a room without furniture and lit only by some candles and a kerosene lamp. Shah Mahmood was lying on a mattress, which was on a kind of raised pallet, and standing off to the side were Shah Mahmood's wife and their son, Jawid. Another woman was kneeling alongside Shah Mahmood's bed. Holding a wet compress, she was gently bathing Shah Mahmood's face.

A white bandage covered his entire scalp, and there was a patch over his left eye. His right eye was closed, and he was breathing deeply. Beneath the blanket I saw his left arm was swathed in bandages.

"The Taliban did it," Haji said. "When they heard that Shah Mahmood was the person who carried out our rescue, they wanted revenge for Izat. Two men cornered Shah Mahmood in front of the bazaar, emptied their weapons at him. He's been seriously wounded. He won't last long."

"When did this happen, Haji?"

"Three days ago. They will wake him now." The kneeling woman touched Shah Mahmood on the face, then on the shoulder. She silently watched us. I wondered if Shah Mahmood was still breathing. We waited. After two minutes, he opened his one eye. It took maybe ten seconds for him to recognize me. Shah Mahmood's wife glanced at the other woman, and they withdrew. I crouched alongside Shah Mahmood.

When he put out his hand, I glanced at Haji, who nodded. Shah Mahmood took hold of my wrist and began haltingly to speak. Haji translated.

"Shah Mahmood thanks you for coming. He can't believe you traveled all the way to the Korengal because of an old man dying. He says he will never forget your thoughtfulness and thinks of you as his son, and hopes you will look out for little Jawid. Shah Mahmood says maybe in the future you can provide in some way for your little brother, who now only has his mother."

I told Haji to say I was honored that Shah Mahmood thought of me as his son. "Whatever he wishes, Haji."

With his eyes closed, Shah Mahmood listened and nodded. Maybe he smiled, I couldn't be sure. Then he waved a hand, moving it with great effort, telling Haji to come closer.

"Shah Mahmood is too weak to speak any more. He says to call his wife. She will give you something."

With her head bowed, Shah Mahmood's wife handed me a large envelope. I said "*Ma-nana*." Again, she withdrew.

Shah Mahmood's eyes were closed and it seemed he was now

sleeping again. After speaking with the women, Haji pointed me toward the doorway. In the outer room, we sat down and a boy brought us glasses of tea. A minute later he reappeared with a plate of cheese and fruit. Then he brought more tea and some crackers.

Afterwards, Haji spoke with Shah Mahmood's wife, and I was shown into a room with blankets spread on the ground. "Shah Mahmood wants to offer us his hospitality for as long as we wish to stay." Before he left the room, Haji said, "Later, Alex, I will tell you what is in the envelope."

I lay down but was too wound up to sleep. An hour later Haji returned. "The driver has to leave now. If we don't go with him, it will be difficult to return to Kabul."

In the other room, I took one last look at Shah Mahmood. His wife was kneeling silently next to her sleeping husband, sobbing softly. She only nodded when I said good-bye.

* * *

It was already early evening of the next day when we arrived at the Kabul house that we'd left thirty hours earlier. Corley was standing in the compound as I climbed out of the van.

After Haji and I said good-bye to Najib, Haji said, "We need to talk." I had an idea Corley already knew what we needed to talk about. I suggested going upstairs.

In my room we gathered around the small table. I opened the envelope and removed its contents—a letter written in Arabic on thick gray paper.

Corley picked up the letter, and after reading it, placed it back down.

Haji said quietly, "I must first explain the background to you. And how this letter came to be written."

The only light in the little room was from a lamp with a weak bulb. I'd brought bottles of water up from downstairs, broke one open, and poured water into three paper cups. Corley and I watched as Haji took a sip before speaking.

"For Americans," Haji said, still speaking softly, "Afghanistan can be a difficult country to understand. Loyalties, alliances, and enmities often go back hundreds of years. Shah Mahmood is an influential man, the leader of his tribe. Hamed"—Haji fixed me with a stern look—"is also a member of the Korengali tribe, the tribe to which he owes his loyalty. The fact that he is a wealthy businessman in Dubai does not alter that. A century ago Hamed's family farmed a fertile area in a northern province. It was Shah Mahmood's people who saved Hamed's people from losing their land."

Corley said, "Hamed in a sense owes his existence to Shah Mahmood's people."

"As one of the elders of his tribe," Haji said, "Shah Mahmood is in a position to ask favors of Hamed. Under normal circumstances he would not make a demand of Hamed. But this situation is extraordinary." Haji pointed at the letter. "This first line identifies you, Alex, as the honored bearer of this greeting from Shah Mahmood's people to Hamed, Hamed's family, and his people. Shah Mahmood addresses the letter personally to Hamed."

"Then what?"

"Then it says that Shah Mahmood is in your debt. He also comments on your courage and your integrity. Then he goes on to request that Hamed grant any favor to you that you may ask of him."

"I only want from Hamed what Colonel Hansen wanted from Hamed—the information he has concerning the looting of the Kabul Bank. Pete, in a sense, sacrificed his life for it. It's the information that the auditors couldn't find and was not in their report."

Haji frowned. "And you say this information is in Hamed's

possession." When I nodded, Haji said quietly, "You need only present this letter to Hamed and make your request."

Corley nodded. She, too, seemed amazed by the letter. Finally, she said, "Shah Mahmood also gave up his life. He did this for you."

Haji said, "I indicated to Zubair, one of Shah Mahmood's advisers, that Alex had made a trip to Dubai to see Hamed. After Shah Mahmood heard this, he dictated the letter." Haji pointed. "At the bottom, you see Shah Mahmood's signature, which is all he could write." Haji said quietly, "This is an unbelievable document. Truly."

Corley shook her head. "He did this after he'd been shot?"

"Yes, after he'd been shot. With his last ounce of strength."

We sat in silence for a long moment, aware of the character of Shah Mahmood and the kind of man who did what he had done. In his character and actions he exhibited a concern for other people that no longer seems to have a place in the world. It could be seen in Shah Mahmood's generosity, his hospitality, his loyalty. His way of living seemed somehow out of place in our century, but had rather a medieval quality.

In the silent room, I knew that I was experiencing a moment beyond what most people could ever imagine—and again I recalled *Pashtunwali,* the thousand-year-old code of values that guides the lives of so many Afghans.

Speaking quietly, Haji said, "The driver received a telephone call during the ride back. Shah Mahmood has died. He heard the women wailing in the background. They would be taking Shah Mahmood to the mosque. He was . . . a very special person."

"We know," Corley said.

Then Haji got to his feet. "I must be getting back." Standing at the door, he asked, "Will I see you before your return to the United States?"

Corley shook her head, and Haji came forward and gave me a

silent hug, saying softly, *"Da Khoday pa amaan."* After I nodded, and said my own good-bye, Haji turned and opened the door. A second later he was gone.

Corley said, "You said Hamed was asking twenty-five million euros for the document. Who could pay that kind of money?"

I shrugged. "I don't know. But over a billion was looted from the bank. Maybe a twenty-five-million-euro price tag isn't that unreasonable."

"I have to wonder to whom it would be worth so much."

"I have an idea that it has another kind of value. I think it may help in leading us to the individual who hired someone to kill Pete Hansen. That's the reason I care about it."

I wasn't sure why Corley cared about this information, but it was clear that she did.

What had been her relationship with my old buddy? I still wasn't clear about that. I knew her reasons for obtaining this information were different from mine.

Why had she made such a blatant attempt to seduce me in Dubai?

There was still much more to this woman than I had been able to puzzle out. Again, I wondered about the circumstances under which she'd come to know Pete.

"I'll book the flight to Dubai," she said.

I reached for my carry-on and opened the cover of my laptop. "Let me. Window or an aisle seat?"

CHAPTER 27

My second interview with Taraki Hamed went down differently from my first one. One difference was that this time Corley, who was wearing a blue business suit for the occasion, was with me. I had a feeling she'd cheated on the length of the skirt, which showed her legs to excellent advantage. Not surprisingly, Hamed was having difficulty keeping his eyes off her. It was Monday, midafternoon, two days after our return to Kabul from the Korengal Valley, and we were in Hamed's lavish air-conditioned 51st-floor office.

When I telephoned, I'd asked if I could bring someone with me.

"I must confess that I was most surprised to receive your telephone call." Hamed put down his coffee cup.

"Pleasantly surprised, I hope."

He shook his head. "Neither pleasantly nor unpleasantly. Only curious, Mr. Klear. Only curious." He looked at his watch. "But I'm also busy. We're in the middle of consummating what you Americans call a very big deal."

"What kind of deal, Mr. Hamed?" Corley's tone was innocent.

"A merger, Ms. Corley. Two firms coming together can be quite a complex arrangement." He touched a finger to his wavy hair, permitted himself a thin smile. "Nearly as complex, one might say, as two people coming together."

Corley couldn't let that go by without commenting. "It would depend on the people, wouldn't it, sir?"

Hamed's eyes twinkled. "Isn't it women who bring the complexity to a relationship, Ms. Corley?"

"Is complexity a bad thing, Mr. Hamed?"

"Not at all. I would go so far as to say that it is complexity that makes life . . . interesting." Hamed's expression all at once became deadly serious. Looking at me, he said, "I can't for the life of me imagine why you wanted another meeting."

I sipped some coffee, let some time go by, put down my cup. "Quite simply, I'm hoping you'll be able to provide me with the information I asked for last time." I flashed a pained smile. "I know you're busy."

"If we're again talking about the same document—"

"We are."

"I think I was very precise in stating what it is I expect in return—the sum of twenty-five million euros." He paused, letting the enormity of what he wanted to sink in. "In that respect, nothing has changed. You understand that, I hope you do. Last time, you were clear in stating there was no possibility of your being able to raise that amount of money." When I fidgeted with impatience, he said, "I am correct, am I not?" He looked from me to Corley, smiled, then back to me. He didn't seem quite as sure of himself as he had a second ago.

"Your memory of my last visit, Mr. Hamed, is impeccable."

Corley nodded. "That's precisely the way Mr. Klear described things to me, Mr. Hamed." She was really laying it on. I wondered why.

"Am I to assume there's been a new development?" Hamed arched his eyebrows, perhaps wondering if he could anticipate a big payday.

Corley nodded her head.

"What is it then?" As I slowly withdrew the envelope containing Shah Mahmood's letter from my breast pocket, his expression changed, going from one of ill-concealed impatience to bafflement. "This is for me?" When I nodded, he stared at the still folded letter. Finally, he picked it up. Before reading, he looked first at me, then at Corley, whose expression remained noncommittal.

After he'd read it, I broke the silence. "You know Shah Mahmood, I'm sure. As you can see, Mr. Hamed, it's addressed to you. Shah Mahmood dictated and had it written on my behalf. At the conclusion, you can see his signature."

"I concede I am surprised that you, Mr. Klear, are in possession of such an . . . extraordinary document." Frowning, he said, "Nevertheless, I am curious as to how—"

"As to how Mr. Klear came into possession of this letter." When he nodded, Corley said, "We are not here to indulge your curiosity, Mr. Hamed." She paused, switching from impeccable English to Pashto. I didn't know what it was she said. She could have been criticizing him or flattering him.

Hamed answered in Pashto. I got the impression from his somewhat halting tone that he was defending himself. Which, I supposed, was her intention. There was no doubt that he was astonished by her command of his native language.

I said, "The important thing is that you're ready to act on Shah Mahmood's request. What my principals want is the complete account of how the money was taken from the bank. I emphasize the word 'complete.'"

"Twenty-two people have been charged. Whether they are guilty..."

"Only time will tell."

Hamed gazed at the cups and the uneaten cookies on the coffee table before us.

I could understand his initial reluctance to want to turn over his document. I was prepared to be patient.

Frowning, he said to me, "You say you are acting on behalf of the American government."

"I'm not sure Mr. Klear needs to reveal that kind of information."

Although I remained silent, I found Corley's interjection interesting.

I said, "Colonel Hansen was acting on behalf of the American government. That doesn't mean I am." The fact is, I was no longer completely sure on whose behalf I was acting. At one time I would have assumed that Corley, an officer in the U.S. Army, would be representing the American government.

I no longer assumed that.

"You described yourself as Colonel Hansen's successor."

"Only in certain respects."

He scrutinized me further. "I see."

A half-minute of silence, then Corley said, "In the Korengal the families all know one another. Am I correct?" When he nodded, Corley said, "In your actions you are guided by the traditions of your people and your tribe." And then she again began speaking Pashto. I heard a reference to *Pashtunwali*.

When she paused, Hamed answered, going on at length. When she responded, he smiled. The conversation went on in this manner for a couple of minutes.

For all I knew, they could have been making a dinner date for this evening. I found it interesting that at the end of their little exchange, neither one made any attempt to tell me what they'd said to each other.

Then Hamed said, "Tomorrow evening I can provide you with the information you seek." He pointed to Shah Mahmood's letter on his desk. "But I will first have to verify the authenticity of Shah Mahmood's wishes."

"Of course," Corley said.

He paused. "I'm afraid your government will find this information of only minimal value. The stolen money is largely unrecoverable."

"Why?" I asked.

"What you will find are transactions, legitimate business transactions, made by scores of people. In many cases people acquiring or selling property and shares in stock markets around the world. Some transactions are currency exchanges."

I said, "None of these transactions and business arrangements are in the auditors' reports. Is that true?"

Hamed said, "You will be the only person with complete knowledge of the Kabul Bank fraud. The crucial point is, I was not indicted or charged. The trial is going on without me. I was an official of the bank, a highly placed official, someone in a position to know precisely what was happening during the time it was happening."

"And you wrote it all down."

"Something I must concede. You have done a surprising job of picking up where Colonel Hansen left off. This letter is extraordinary. You know, Mr. Klear, when you first asked me for information about the collapse of the Kabul Bank, I knew you were following the trail Colonel Hansen had been following. I was of the opinion you would not be successful."

Finally and without a word, Hamed got to his feet, an obvious signal that he'd made up his mind and that the meeting was over.

Standing at the door of his office, he put out his hand, first to Corley, then to me. "Tomorrow, in the lobby of the hotel. Shall we say five p.m.?" He hesitated. "I assume that will be satisfactory. You won't have to return here. You can spend the day sightseeing. There's much to see here in Dubai."

"What's the name of the big mall?" Corley asked, trying to show only a superficial understanding of what had been discussed in the previous half hour. "I like to shop." I noticed her putting the card

Hamed had given her in her bag.

"My favorite is the Wafi Mall. I wish you a pleasant day."

The beefy gentleman whom I'd met on my first visit to Hamed accompanied us on our elevator trip down to the lobby. He gallantly held the elevator door, a gesture for which I naturally thanked him.

Back out on the street, we walked for a couple of minutes in silence, both of us thinking over the meeting with Hamed.

I said finally, "I'm wondering..."

"Whether he will deliver his document?" When I nodded, Corley said, "You don't know the tribe's mind-set. For a man in Hamed's position to violate the traditions of the Korengalis is ... inconceivable. He follows the code of *Pashtunwali*." She paused. "Like Shah Mahmood."

"Hamed is different from Shah Mahmood."

"It would be fatal for him to violate the values of his people."

"Fatal in what way?"

"In every way. Professionally, socially ... and in perhaps other ways. Believe me, he'll deliver his document." She paused at a shop window, then said, "He has no choice."

"Before we went, I never thought he'd change his mind."

"That's because you don't understand the Afghan culture."

"I'm still skeptical," I said. I didn't add that I may not understand Afghan culture, but I understand human nature. And no matter how you slice it, twenty-five million euros is a lot of loot.

When I said that, Corley pretended to smile.

CHAPTER 28

AT FOUR THIRTY on Tuesday evening, after Corley and I found places on a sofa in the lobby of the Ritz-Carlton Hotel, she placed her laptop between us. On my lap I had a copy of *The Financial Times* but had only given the front page a quick glance. We sat silently for forty minutes, neither of us saying what we were both thinking.

When was Hamed's guy going to arrive?

"Should I call him?" Corley asked finally. The time was five twenty. When I said, "Do you think it will do any good?" she shook her head and answered her own question.

"I counsel patience," I said, trying to sound authoritative but not knowing what else to say.

After another twenty minutes, I said, "Do people believe in punctuality in this part of the world?" I knew they didn't.

She shook her head.

I looked longingly in the direction of the Café Belge, which was now well filled, most of the customers obviously European, all jabbering in their own languages.

Then, at a few minutes after six, a beefy individual with a familiar face pushed his way through the revolving door. I recognized the individual with whom I'd ridden up and down in the elevator in Hamed's building. Today he was wearing a brown sports jacket over a white and blue shirt and was carrying a slim leather case. He gazed quickly around. When I stood up, we made eye contact. He approached, said, "Your name?"

I nodded. "I'm Alex Klear."

He was carrying a slim attaché case. After sitting down next to Corley, he placed the case on his lap, opened it, and removed a small box. "I've been told to give you this."

Corley took the box, snapped it open. Inside was a USB drive. She placed the drive in her laptop, hit some keys. We waited for close to five minutes as she went over the document.

She shrugged, frowned. Finally, after another five minutes, she nodded.

He gave us a paper to sign. It described the contents of the document in a general way. The time, date, and place. When I looked at Corley, she nodded approval, and we signed.

After closing the attaché case, he stood up and said, "Good evening." Seconds later, he was pushing his way through the revolving door.

"Let's go upstairs," I said, anxious to examine the contents of Hamed's document.

Corley shook her head and stood up. "I'll go upstairs." Again, it was obvious who was running this little show. Although I was irritated, I didn't see any sense in showing it. She pointed toward the Café Belge at the end of the lobby. "You go relax."

I drank a Stella Artois, then a second. After an hour, still at the bar, I was gazing out at the lobby when I saw Corley emerge from the elevator and cross the lobby. Page had said she was a knockout when she got dressed up. He hadn't exaggerated.

A raincoat was draped over her arm. She wore a royal blue sheath dress, which highlighted the contours of her frame. The dress, adorned with beads and sequins, barely made it to her knees. Her long hair was styled with a dramatic sweep. A string of what appeared to be diamonds circled her neck and more dangled from her ears. A pair of stiletto heels accented the curves of her ankles and long legs.

Before she left the lobby, she slipped on the raincoat. I could see why.

I had an idea where she was going, and I didn't like it. She was decked out like an expensive whore. I leaped off the barstool and ran across the lobby. I caught up with her in front of the hotel, where she was about to climb into a taxi.

"What do you think you're doing?" I said, grabbing her arm.

"Leave me alone. I know what I'm doing. Get away!" She shook off my hand.

"I'll go with you. You'll need backup."

The driver held the door of the cab open for her. "I don't need backup. I can handle this." When she climbed into the taxi, the driver stepped in front of me and shut the door. I pulled the door handle, thinking I could drag her back out. It was locked. I banged on the window, but she continued to ignore me. The car pulled away from the curb; I stood watching it disappear into traffic.

"Damn!" I said and stormed back inside.

When I got to my room, I saw that Irmie had called. Emotionally, for me, this may not have been the best moment, but I called her anyway.

"Hello, Alex. I'm glad you called. I've been thinking about you—" Before I could interrupt, she said, "About us, actually."

"I've been thinking about us, too—"

"Please let me finish. About the future. I don't feel I'm making you happy. I know things are difficult for you where you are. I feel I'm only . . . well, being a nuisance or whatever."

"Irmie! That's not true. You are everything to me."

"Living like this isn't right, Alex. It really isn't. Married people should be together. They have to be. There's no other way. We've already talked about that, and I don't want to say anything more. I don't like to have to say it, but I've come to the conclusion—"

"What conclusion?"

"I don't think things would be that different if we were married. The way you left leaves me with no other choice but to believe that. I just think you'd always be going off somewhere."

"Irmie, if you'd let me say a word—"

"I can't escape the feeling that I'd be alone most of the time." After a brief hesitation, she said, "I may be wrong, but I've thought about it for a long time, and I can't escape that feeling."

"Irmie, this was—"

"I realize you have your work, but I don't think I can fit into your life. I want you to know that. I'm ending our engagement. You can forget any feelings you ever had for me."

"Can't we wait and talk . . . before we decide to make this decision?"

"No, it's over, Alex."

"Honey, I understand how you feel, but this is not the right thing."

"Alex, we're no longer engaged. You're free to do whatever . . . you want to do." Irmie paused and I thought I could hear a sob. "I'm sorry, but I have to go now. Good-bye, Alex."

I stood for a long time in the middle of my Ritz-Carlton hotel room holding the telephone in my hand. I supposed I could have stormed around, kicked a table, or reached for a whiskey bottle. I remained calm. I have to admit I'd sensed what was coming. I understood Irmie's feelings. I had promised that I wouldn't be taking any more assignments from the United States government. If it had been anyone else besides Pete who'd been killed, I wouldn't have accepted this assignment.

We'd talked about our future. If she wanted, I'd move to Germany. With my knowledge of English, I wouldn't have any difficulty landing a job with a European firm. There was also the possibility of starting my own business. With Irmie continuing to work, our future together looked bright.

And now I faced living the rest of my life without the woman I loved. After an hour of doing my best to put my broken engagement—my broken life—out of my mind, I decided to see if Corley was back. I walked down the hall to her room and knocked. No answer.

There was no answer when I knocked an hour after that. And none an hour after that.

I tried again at a few minutes after midnight with the same result.

Two hours later, at 0210 hours, there was a gentle tap at my door. At first, I didn't recognize the woman in the corridor: Leslie Corley. No longer decked out in the provocative dress. She had on a black burqa, which revealed only her eyes. Once inside the room, she drew the face veil aside so I could see the abrasion on her cheek. Shabby sandals replaced the stilettos on her feet, making her ankles look chubby.

Her first words: "Why did I listen to you? I hate you!"

"What did I say?"

"You said the document he'd given us wasn't complete. I believed you. You said he would never sacrifice the twenty-five million euros just because of a letter. You recall he gave me his card when we left his office?" When I nodded, she said, "The card contained the address of a villa in the Jumeirah Lake District. It also had a time, 7:30 p.m., written on it."

"So you accepted his invitation and went out there. You shouldn't have."

"A guard admitted me at the gate. Hamed was waiting for me at the front door, smiling, very friendly. We talked for a while, then he gave me a tour of his villa. It's luxurious, beautiful, the furniture alone is breathtaking, worth millions. The villa has everything, even a swimming pool."

"I assume the tour ended in his bedroom."

"Of course. I was ready for that. I had a switchblade. When I knew he was defenseless, I snapped it open, showed it to him. I told him if he didn't give me the complete document I was going to cut off his ears. I told him he could guess what else I would cut off."

"Were you serious?"

"Yes. Yes, I was serious."

"That was crazy, stupid."

"He had a bodyguard in the closet. Before I knew it, this big man grabbed my knife, lifted me off the bed, and threw me on the floor." She shook her head. "Naked, humiliated."

"What happened then?"

"They watched as I crawled to my clothes and dressed."

"Nice guys."

"For men like Hamed, women have no rights, they're subservient, and I understand that. I also realized that I'd insulted him. Then, Hamed and I went into a dinette off the kitchen. One of his people had prepared a meal, a delicious meal. Truly." She paused. "First falafel. Then a servant brought *esh asarya.*"

"Cheesecake?"

"Yes. He reached out and touched me. He said he wanted to see me on my next trip to the Emirates."

"Confusing. I don't get it."

"He was treating me kindly now. He wanted to be nice, but as we ate, he lectured me, saying I had been a fool to listen to you. He said the people of the modern world are materialistic and not to be trusted. He spoke of *Pashtunwali* and of the importance of keeping this belief alive in the modern world." She paused. "And then he said something else. He said he knew my reason for coming was to force him to hand over the real document. He said he knew that I would listen to you rather than give him *izat*, the respect he was entitled to."

"You're saying we already had the complete document?"

"Yes, he'd given us the complete document. He'd done what he said he would do. By questioning him in that way, I'd insulted him. He told me I deserved the humiliation."

"But how were you supposed to know that we had the real document?"

"That's what I said, trying to defend myself. I should never have said that. He became very angry. He said if I'd properly understood my place, I would never have doubted him. He yanked off my jewelry, told me to undress, and made me watch as he ripped my dress to small shreds with a pair of scissors. All this to further humiliate me. Then he gave me this, a burqa. A lesson, he said, to make me understand how proper beliefs are more potent than the false beliefs of the modern world—and that I could only understand it if dressed appropriately."

"I see."

"You were very wrong about him, horribly wrong. I should have known. By this time, all his servants had left, even his bodyguard. When he showed me to the door, I turned on him. I'd been able to steal a knife from the kitchen. I forced him to the floor. Again I threatened him physically."

"Why?"

"I wanted to humiliate him the way he humiliated me."

"Was that smart?" I already knew one of Corley's failings was an uncontrollable desire to indulge her emotions. Standing in the middle of the room, she stared sullenly at the floor, her head bowed.

I said, "What did Hamed do?"

"When he got to his feet, he only said I was *ajex*, pathetic. Then he took me to the door."

"So you're now convinced we already had the complete document?"

"Yes. He'd given us the complete document."

"So I was wrong. Is that it?"

"You were horribly wrong." As I watched, she emptied her glass of scotch with a trembling hand.

I was becoming more and more uncomfortable with this woman. Still wearing the burqa while pouring out another scotch, she seemed like a totally different person.

Trying to change the subject, I said, "But you know for sure this USB drive contains the complete story of the fraud, and you know also that it's accurate."

"Yes, I'm satisfied."

I'd given up the hope she might ever reveal who she was and what she was attempting to accomplish. She had the rank of captain in the U.S. Army, but she was obviously no ordinary military officer. Whoever she was, I was now more eager than ever to break off our relationship and disassociate myself from whatever new schemes she might have in mind. I just wasn't completely sure how to go about it.

Alone in my room, I ran over all that in my mind for a good hour while drinking more scotch. I did my best not to think about Irmie, but I thought about her anyway. A great deal of time elapsed before I was finally able to fall into a troubled sleep.

* * *

After a quick breakfast the following morning, Corley, her expression still empty, silently pointed the way upstairs. At least she wasn't wearing the burqa. She had on a tan blouse and today her skirt reached her knees. In her room, we seated ourselves opposite each other, neither of us saying anything. Finally, room service arrived with a silver pot of coffee and a platter of cookies and cake.

As I poured coffee, I said, "Hamed's document has the answer, doesn't it? It contains what Pete was looking for."

As I handed her the cup, she stared at me with her dark eyes. "Yes."

"That means my job is over. For me at least, this op is history. I can book a flight for this afternoon to JFK. I'm looking forward to returning home and getting back to work." I took a sip. "Good coffee, maybe a little weak."

"Yes, you may book a flight—but not to New York, to Dulles. I expect you to remain in D.C. until you hear from me. And you'll not be communicating with friends or business partners—"

"I have a business to run."

"The op is not over." She began nibbling on a cookie.

"You haven't figured it all out yet, have you?"

"The answer is in Hamed's document. I will figure it out. It shouldn't take all that long."

I didn't reply immediately. Right from the beginning, I sensed there was more to this op than appeared on the surface. Pete was like a bulldog. Once he got his teeth into something, he didn't let go. What information did Hamed's document hold that was so important?

I decided not to let go. In some ways, Pete and I were two of a kind.

Why did she still need me? Backup? Maybe more than backup.

"Good cookies," she said quietly. "Have one."

"They are good," I said after a couple of bites.

So she wanted me in D.C. I decided I'd go along, but now I'd be doing things for my own reasons.

After another minute, I said, "I'll book that flight to Dulles." When I got to my feet, she pointed me back into the chair.

"There's more." She was giving orders again. "Have you been in touch with Wanda Hansen?"

Recalling my last visit to Wanda's hotel room, I said, "She was irritated with me when I last saw her."

"She's a widow. Don't you have any sympathy for a woman who lost her husband?"

"Of course I do."

"I would think you'd want to mention how you were following up on her husband's attempts to find out just how the bank fraud was carried out. The three of you were friends at one time." She reached for another cookie.

"Anything else?"

"You'll be staying in an apartment just outside D.C. After you arrive, take a look under the living room rug. Look for some loose floorboards. You'll find a small compartment. Remove whatever you find in there. It may be useful."

"Is that all?"

"At 1520 my flight leaves for Kabul. I'll be there for two or three days. Then I'll fly to D.C. I'll be staying in the same building you're in. We'll be able to work together."

Work together doing what?

What would we be trying to accomplish?

I said, "I look forward to seeing you in D.C."

I hoped my words sounded as if I meant them.

CHAPTER 29

THERE WERE ANY number of things I didn't intend to tell Leslie Corley. The first was, I intended to make a stop in Munich on my way back to D.C. Less than a day had elapsed since Irmie had officially called off our engagement. I wanted her to know how I felt. I booked an afternoon flight on Emirates, which got me into Munich's Franz Josef Strauss Airport at 7:40 p.m. It was already dark. At an airport flower shop I picked up a large mixed bouquet, mums, carnations, and blue irises, which I knew to be Irmie's favorite flower.

Since Irmie lives in a suburb of Munich, I rented a car. It was already a few minutes after ten when I arrived at her building in Gröbenzell. After parking in the rear, I walked around to the entrance just as two young men were leaving. Smiling at the flowers, one of the men held the door. Irmie lived in the garden apartment. I pushed the bell, and seconds later heard the peephole slide open. There was a brief pause, during which I felt my heart going into double-time, wondering if she would open. Finally, after what seemed an eternity, I heard the lock click.

Irmie has a soft heart.

"Alex." Her voice was a soft whisper. She opened the door wider, closed it, and we were together, alone in her apartment. I put my arms around her, gave her a gentle kiss. No response. I knew I would have to overcome a mountain of disappointments and frustrations.

"It's wonderful to see you, Irmie."

Her eyes did light up when she saw the flowers. Holding the irises against her cheek, she said, "Why did you come, Alex? You're only making things more difficult." Her voice was a whisper.

"I came to tell you I love you. I will always love you."

I watched as she found a vase in her kitchen. She filled it with water, arranged the flowers, and placed it on a small table in her living room.

"It's over with us, Alex," she said, turning toward me.

Irmie had a round face, wide blue eyes, blond hair. She was wearing a green nightgown. I'd obviously arrived just as she was going to bed. "I wish you hadn't come." She turned away, trying to conceal the tears dripping down her cheeks. I followed her back into the kitchen. "I'll make you some tea. Then you'll have to leave."

"We're engaged, Irmie. I want to marry you. Nothing's changed."

Irmie only shook her head. For the next five minutes, I watched silently as she boiled water and set out the places.

Then she said, "Is it finished? Your assignment, is it over?"

"I wish it was, but it's not."

Her face fell when I said that.

"I have to go back to America. I'm hoping it will soon be over."

She sighed, shook her head. "You never change." She didn't say anything more, but I knew what she was thinking.

Seated opposite me at the dinette, she took a sip of tea. "How often have you said you'll never take another assignment? My only thought is, if we were married you'd still be accepting assignments."

I tried to explain. "This was an exception. One of my oldest friends was murdered. They asked me. I had to go."

"In all America, they couldn't find someone else? No, Alex. I can't accept that." She shook her head. "I just can't."

Irmie was right. There were other people they could have sent.

I saw no sense in arguing. For nearly ten minutes Irmie and I sat silently in her dinette sipping tea. The funny thing was, I felt comfortable and relaxed in her company. Without being too obvious, I stole glances, at the smoothness of her skin, her hair, at her hands and the way she lifted her tea cup. I realized how much I'd missed her.

Strangely, I had a feeling she, too, was enjoying the moment. The fact we weren't talking didn't seem important. We communicated in other ways.

Finally, she said, "I have to be at work early tomorrow, Alex. I'm going to ask you to leave." She got to her feet.

"I know I've made you unhappy, Irmie—"

Irmie shook her head. "You said all that on the telephone."

"I'm going to come back. When this is over, I'm coming back." Then, standing at the door, I took her in my arms, and as I held her, I felt her arm around my neck. This time, the kiss wasn't completely one-sided. Her emotions were there, restrained, but they were real, tangible. Irmie couldn't completely restrain her feelings. I'd hoped for a different kind of response, a stronger response, but as I held her, I felt her relax, still finding that sense of tranquility she had when we were together. I hated the thought of leaving her.

"Good night, Irmie." I whispered the words.

I was surprised when she touched my face and gave me a gentle kiss.

I had wanted to stay with her, but as I drove back to the airport, I realized that had been too much to hope for right now.

While seated in the airport's waiting hall, I texted Corley my flight info, that I would be on the noon flight from Munich to D.C. As I waited, I continued to think about Irmie and our relationship.

Irmie had been a police detective when we'd met at a Christmas party in Munich's police headquarters. I still recall talking with her that evening and thinking, *This is the woman for me.* Although in the succeeding years, circumstances had kept us apart, I'd never forgotten that first evening. The main factor that had kept us apart was the frequent overseas assignments I kept receiving. The fact I was technically retired hadn't been important after the need for experienced case officers after 9/11.

The other factor—we were an ocean apart. But we always remained in contact, and about a year ago, we realized that we'd be happier together than apart. That's when we got engaged. Our relationship had been running smoothly until I accepted the Afghanistan assignment.

I wondered now whether I'd lost Irmie forever and what my life would amount to without her.

The flight to D.C. lasted eight hours, and it was still afternoon when I arrived in Dulles. I was greeted there by a uniformed chauffeur holding up a sign with my name on it.

I let him carry my flight bag out to the car, a comfortable limo. When I asked where we were headed, he said, "I've been told to take you to Addison Heights, sir."

Addison Heights. I'd heard of it. "Where is that?"

"It's just beyond Crystal City, sir." Crystal City I knew. It was one of our nation capital's quieter suburbs, across the Potomac, definitely out of the way.

After placing my bag in the trunk, the driver gave me an envelope, which contained an address, an apartment number, and a key. I had an idea the U.S. government wasn't paying the freight for this end of the trip, and I wondered who was. From the backseat of the limo I asked the driver if he knew who had made these arrangements.

"I have no idea, sir."

His answer didn't surprise me. I already realized that what I was involved in wasn't just a black op—it wasn't an American operation.

He let me off in front of a three-story red brick apartment building in Addison Heights, a few blocks from Virginia Highlands
Park. Behind the building were overflowing garbage cans. Someone
had stuffed tissue paper into the lock of the front door to keep it
from closing. There were four mailboxes, and I assumed four apart-
ments. The stairs were narrow and covered with frayed blue carpet.

My surmise about the apartment was confirmed when I was inside. Our government has put me up in any number of living quarters, and they all had one thing in common: They were reasonably
well maintained and as comfortable as circumstances permitted. I
even recall a low-profile safe house in East Berlin where, despite ancient furniture and a kitchen out of the 1920s, I never saw a speck
of dust and the bed linen was spanking clean.

The first thing that struck me here was the dust. In the kitchen, I
wiped the countertop with my fingers, and as I suspected, it hadn't
been cleaned recently. Although the bed was made with fresh linen,
someone had forgotten to empty a couple of wastepaper baskets.
While American government quarters are usually well stocked with
firewater, here there was no booze, not even a bottle of beer. There
was an ancient TV, which I didn't bother to turn on.

The books on the shelves were mostly in foreign languages,
Russian, Arabic, and French. The apartment appeared to have been
empty for a while.

Was Captain Corley working for the American government?

If not, who was she working for?

Pete had been investigating the looting of the Kabul Bank. What
had he been looking for?

CHAPTER 30

"WHAT WAS IT like in Dubai?" Doug Greer asked when I called the next day.

"It was hot," I said.

Doug laughed. "When I'm there, I like to go sailing if I have time. It's beautiful out on the Gulf. You've never seen such blue water. What about the bank stuff?"

"We didn't make any progress on that. We got some shopping in. That was about it." I paused. "I owe you a lunch, Doug. Would you be able to—"

"Next week is bad. Really bad. Cabinet meetings one after the other. I'll be staying late every night. We're the guys who do the behind-the-scenes work. Can we shoot for the following week?"

"Fine," I said. "I'll call."

After another cup of java, I followed Corley's direction, rolling back the living room rug and looking for the loose floorboards. With the rug gone, they were easy to spot and, using a screwdriver, easy to pry up. It was a shallow compartment, and lying at the bottom was an M9 Beretta automatic and two ammunition magazines. I wondered why Corley had made a point of mentioning a firearm. Some thoughtful person even had gone to the trouble of cleaning and oiling the weapon not that long ago.

Why would I need a weapon? Again, I had the premonition I'd be wise to disassociate myself from whatever scheme this woman had in mind. But it may be too late for that now.

I should have known better right at the start. That's why these kinds of "ops" are called "black."

I had a feeling Corley was worried. Which meant, I suppose, that I should also be worried.

After replacing the rug, I took the weapon into the bedroom, clicked the safety on and off, worked the trigger, and then laid it together with the two ammunition clips in the night table drawer.

Everything about this situation was strange, weird even. The person to ask what it was all about would be Jerry Shenlee, but Jerry had taken himself out of the picture very nicely. He'd even forgotten telling me it was crucial that I go back to Afghanistan. No doubt he'd also forgotten telling me I wouldn't be gone more than two weeks. It was now four weeks, with no end in sight. When I saw Jerry again, I'd let him know his crystal ball needs polishing.

I spent a couple of hours during the early afternoon in downtown D.C., stretching my legs and looking over my shoulder. I didn't see anyone. At one of the mobile telephone shops, I bought a couple of cell phones, using a false name and address.

In a car rental office I rented a maroon Honda Accord, a reliable vehicle but not one that would attract attention. On the way back to the apartment, I did some food shopping and picked up a six-pack of Samuel Adams beer.

In the evening, Corley called. When I asked where she was, she said, "I'm in Kabul. I can't leave at this moment."

I said, "Thank you for arranging things. I'm living in Addison Heights."

"Why did the trip take so long? You went to Munich."

"I stopped briefly in Munich, to see my fiancée. I'm planning to get married. I'm wondering when this op will ever be over."

"I'll call tomorrow evening. I'm not sure when."

A few minutes later, I fished the card Wanda had given me out of my billfold and dialed her home number.

"How's everything in Alexandria?"

"Alex! It's so nice to hear from you. Where are you?"

"I'm not that far away. In Addison Heights. If you're free tomorrow evening, I thought—"

"I'd like to get together, but we're working weekends now. I'll probably be tied up at the office into the evening. Why not come over to the Pentagon tomorrow? We could have lunch."

"I have a better idea. How about the Army Navy Club? Tomorrow night. The Eagle Grill is closed Saturdays. But the dining room stays open."

"Fine. I'll get there as soon as I can make it."

* * *

"I'm so sorry, Alex," Wanda Hansen said as she pulled back a chair and sat down. We were at a table toward the rear of the quietly elegant Army Navy Club dining room. When I said, "For what?" she sighed. "I hate being late." Pointing at my half-finished mug of beer and speaking rapidly, she said, "One of those would be great. Have you been here long?"

"This is my first. I've had two swallows."

Wanda grinned. "I wish I could believe that. Your third, probably." Wanda, who was still in uniform, shook her head, picked up a menu. "I think I'll have a steak sandwich. It's hectic at work, believe me."

After giving our order to the waitress, I said, "You don't look hassled. In fact you look great."

Wanda smiled, reached out and touched my hand. I wondered why she seemed so agitated. "Thank you, Alex. I needed that."

"What's going on at the office?"

"Do you really want to know?"

"Probably not."

"The military has become more and more bureaucratic. Pete used to complain, too. He used to talk about the Army the way it was, 'the Brown Shoe Army,' he used to call it. What happened to it? Where did it go?"

"Where are the snows of yesteryear?"

"I'm still recovering from Afghanistan. It was different over there from what I thought it would be. I'm thinking now I never should have gone." Wanda shuddered. "I was nervous the whole time." As she watched the waitress set down her mug of beer, Wanda said, "Those green-on-blue killings are just so awful."

"Agreed."

After we'd touched glasses, Wanda took a long swallow. "I mean, you never know when someone you're talking with might pull out a gun and shoot you. And the IEDs all over. You drove over one, Alex. On your trip in from the airport, right?"

"Thanks for reminding me."

"I don't know how you can remain so calm." After taking another long swallow of beer, she pointed across the room. Through the window on the far wall the lights of Farragut Square twinkled. "That's a nice sight. I've always liked the club. Pete did, too. He and I used to play tennis, then come over here. That was when he was stationed over at Meade." Wanda watched the waitress set down our sandwiches. After I'd ordered another beer for each of us, she said, "Tell me what you've been doing lately."

"I've been traveling. I went back to Dubai."

"So that's where you were! Dubai! I wondered why you didn't call." She paused to take a swallow of beer. "You were there only the previous week. Why go back?"

"Unfinished business. On the first trip I was following up on some things Pete was involved with."

"Yes, you told me that. You also said it hadn't worked out all that well. I'm assuming that this time they—"

"This time they worked out a little better."

"Which means?"

"How much do you know about what Pete was working on?"

"The bank fraud? He never said very much. You know how Pete was. He wasn't the type to broadcast what he was doing."

"Married people shouldn't have secrets from each other."

"Ha ha. Tell that to the military. The left hand's not supposed to know what the right hand is doing." Wanda caught the waitress's eye. When she said we wanted two brandies, I didn't comment. "I remember the last time we spoke you said something about the trial."

"You have a good memory."

"When's it going to be over?"

"Soon. It's been going for four months."

"I know I should know more about the bank, but I'm so busy on the job." Wanda paused as the waitress set down our brandies. "But with Pete stationed in Afghanistan and me in the Pentagon, we just didn't see each other that often. He came back on leave twice, but there was always so much going on, friends, family." She twisted her brandy glass by the stem, then picked it up. "So what did you find out this time?"

"Transactions, mostly."

"No names?"

"The information we brought back is important for one reason."

"What would that be?"

"It's information that was concealed from the auditors. The names are of cutouts, mostly. Bankers, business types, wheelers and dealers from just about every country in the world." I took a sip of brandy. "In Europe they're called straw men. They help wealthy people avoid attention and, of course, taxes. In this case, they've helped the Kabul Bank officials conceal the money they'd stolen."

"Hard to understand. I'm not good at this stuff."

"Ask your uncle in Norway, the one who's president of the bank."

Wanda smiled. "Did I mention him?"

"Once, in the Serena."

Wanda took a last long sip of brandy, then gazed at her watch and shook her head. "After ten."

"Can I give you a ride?"

"Sure," she said, "if you don't mind driving out to Alexandria."

"It will be my pleasure."

CHAPTER 31

The next day I visited Arlington Cemetery, where my father is buried, and spent a few quiet hours just walking around. I nodded at a woman with two small children, one on each hand, and hated to think of the reason for her visit.

I had no idea why Corley wanted to keep me on this job and what it was we were trying to do. Irmie was the main source of my discontent. The longer this assignment, the more damaging to our relationship, making it less and less likely that we'd be together.

I was still at Arlington when my phone went off. I was surprised to hear Doug Greer on the other end.

"Alex, I don't suppose you heard the news. About the trial." When I said I hadn't, Doug said, "It's just starting to come in. A few advance reports. It'll be in the papers tomorrow. They're all guilty, twenty-two defendants. I have to admit I'm kind of surprised."

I knew what Doug meant. The Afghan courts are unpredictable. And Afghan laws are very different from those of the United States. "That was a long trial."

"Four months. It began last November. Somehow it seems longer."

I said, "It was already in full swing when I got to Kabul. Were they found guilty on the fraud charge?"

"Yeah, that was it. They don't call it fraud, exactly. The big shots got five years, and are going to have to pay back a lot of money. Hundreds of millions."

"Five years doesn't sound like a long sentence for that kind of fraud."

"I agree. It sounds like crime pays."

"In Afghanistan, maybe."

"I know. They'll still be relatively young guys when they get out." Doug paused. "I don't know whether I should be happy or sad."

"Anyway, it sounds as if that wraps things up."

Doug laughed. "Yeah. We can start thinking about other things. Like how to solve the green-on-blue problem. I was able to speak briefly with General Dunford before he left." General Dunford was the Marine commander with the unenviable job of running ISAF in Afghanistan during the transition. "He's optimistic that we can get a handle on that problem. We'll all breathe a sigh of relief when we can hand things back to the Afghans."

"When will you be going back, Doug?"

"Not for a while. I haven't forgotten that lunch we're supposed to have. I'd suggest sometime this week except we're really busy at the moment." He paused. "How about next week?"

"Next week is fine. By the way, I think Pete knew or at least was close to finding out not only how the money was taken, but where a lot of it ended up."

Doug said, "If he knew where it ended up, that would also mean—"

"That he knew who took it? Maybe." Remembering one of Corley's comments, I added, "You could learn a lot by working backwards. If you could twist some arms."

"That's interesting, something to talk about. I'm checking my calendar here, and maybe I will have time. Let's make the lunch date for Tuesday. Day after tomorrow okay?"

I said that sounded fine.

After getting home I took a shower and was putting the finishing touches on my first beer of the evening when someone started

pounding on the apartment door. Not only wasn't I expecting visitors, I asked myself who even knew that I was in this building, or
living in Addison Heights. For that matter, who even knew that I
was back from Afghanistan?

Was it Shenlee? Definitely not.

Corley? Was she back from Afghanistan? Not yet.

Doug? We just spoke on the phone.

Wanda, no. Someone else? I could think of no one.

And who would be pounding so damned loud?

I didn't recognize the guy through the peephole, but I pulled the
door open anyway. I was confronted by a broad-shouldered individual with a shaved head wearing a leather jacket over a blue flannel shirt, cargo pants, and combat boots. I couldn't help noticing
the size of his hands and the fact that he had a good two inches
and probably twenty pounds on me. He spoke softly, with a mild
Midwestern accent

"Hello, Klear."

If the hallway had been better lit, I might have immediately recognized him. I only squinted and said, "What's up?"

"Bud Withers. Captain Bud Withers." When I said, "Oh yeah,"
he grinned. "You gonna invite me in?"

I fought against the urge to say a loud "No." Recalling all the problems this guy had caused me, I fought another urge—to slug him.
After a second's hesitation, my more civilized instincts got the better
of me. I nodded, pulled the door wider, and motioned him inside.

Standing in the middle of the living room, he unzipped his jacket.
"Nice place."

"Better maybe than COP Franklin. It's okay. It's not mine."

"The door downstairs was half-open when I got here, so I didn't
bother to ring." Eyeing the open bottle of Sam Adams on the coffee
table, he said, "I could go for one of those."

Never say that I'm not hospitable. What was this guy after? The last time I saw him we were rolling around on the floor in Doug Greer's office in the ISAF Headquarters building in Kabul. That incident led to an invitation to the ISAF commander's office and then to me getting tossed out of Afghanistan. After fetching a beer from the fridge and prying off the cap, I silently handed Withers the bottle. At least he thanked me.

"I'm on leave, Klear. On my way down to Benning." He took a swallow of beer, smacked his lips. "I heard that you left Afghanistan. I wanted to find you, but let me tell you, I had one hell of a job doing it. Would you believe, I had to get in touch with someone I know over in Fort Meade to track your phone? NSA people know everything. I mean, it's scary." When I only nodded, he said, "You mind if I sit down?"

After he'd eased his bulk into an easy chair, I found a place on the sofa opposite him, picked up my own bottle, waited. It was "his nickel," as people said in the pre-inflationary days of pay telephones.

This guy had to have a reason for wanting to talk. A good one.

He was still grinning. "You're wondering why I'm here. Why I went to the trouble to look you up."

"Something like that."

"Okay. If you're pissed, I can't say I blame you." He took another long swallow. "I heard a lot of the story of what happened out in the valley after you guys left the COP. How you were about to have your heads chopped off. Got it later, from one of the elders in the tribe. Around then I started to wonder about the whole situation."

Join the club. I've been wondering about it, too. What was on this guy's mind?

"You and the Afghan," Withers said. "The terp. What was his name?"

"Haji."

He nodded. "The story I heard, it was a miracle you and him made it out of that village alive. Man, who were those guys who showed up? Korengalis, am I correct?"

"You didn't seem so happy about that outcome the last time I saw you, Withers." I was referring to him saying I was responsible for the death of one of his troopers.

He grimaced, shrugged, as if he didn't want to be reminded of that. "I'll start at the beginning." He held up his empty bottle. "I could go for another one of these." He gazed across the room at the clock. "My flight's not until tomorrow morning."

After I'd brought back another beer, he began to speak in a low voice. "These two guys showed up at the COP from out of nowhere. One of them was civilian, American, said he was from the Ariana. He gave me a name, but I haven't been able to locate him. The other was an Askar, on the thin side. Mustache, but no beard. Anyway, they came out to Franklin, told me a story about Abdul Sakhi. They said you had it in for this guy." He leaned forward. "They said Sakhi was an asset, one of ours, and we wanted to keep him."

"I wanted to ask him some questions," I said. "Like, 'What were you doing in the Headquarters building on January 23rd?'"

"They said you wanted to terminate him."

I stood up, finished my beer. "I was just on my way out. I'm hungry. I feel like a hamburger."

On his feet, Withers said, "You mind if I join you?"

I grabbed my jacket, still not sure I wanted to spend more time with this guy and have to listen to whatever it was he wanted to tell me. On the stairs on the way out, we passed a swarthy individual, probably the building custodian, who said, "Good evening." I assumed he was the guy who was dropping into my apartment from time to time. Outside, darkness had set in and the air was chilly. I pointed the way. "There's a joint on the next block. Kevin's. They have good burgers."

It seemed like the Happy Hour crew was breaking up. Withers and I found places at the bar and ordered drafts.

"How the hell did you end up out here, Klear? You still on the agency's payroll?"

It was a good question. An honest answer would have been that I wasn't sure whose payroll I was on. We signaled to the bartender, ordered burgers. Why had Withers gone to the trouble to find me?

After a long swallow, he said, "Good beer." On the TV at the end of the bar, there were a bunch of guys gathered around a table and arguing about sports. Fortunately, the sound was off.

"You had it in for Abdul Sakhi, right?"

"I had it in for Abdul Sakhi because he killed a friend of mine. Colonel Hansen."

"You sure about that?"

"A hundred percent."

"CID said it was one of the Askars."

"They wanted to wrap it up neat and quick." I didn't add that there might have been some other motives involved as well.

"Hell, Klear, we'll be out of Afghanistan the end of next year. Why do you care so much about who did it?"

"How would you feel, Withers, if someone killed your buddy? You gonna let him live?"

When the bartender arrived and set down our hamburgers, we pushed our empty mugs forward. I watched Withers splash ketchup on his burger.

With his mouth full, he took a long swallow of beer. "What I was told, Klear, was that Abdul Sakhi was an asset. They said he offed a couple of hard-to-locate *dussmen* down in Helmand. They'd been running things in Nawzad and causing all kinds of problems. I also heard that he did an operation for us out west, in Herat, not far from Iran. He got in and out of a place none of our people could get close to."

"You make him sound like some kind of hero."

"That's one of the reasons no one would go along with your take on the situation. He was too valuable."

"You got half the story, Withers. Abdul Sakhi played both ends against the middle. He did stuff for us, but he also worked for the Talibs. He assassinated two American officers in Kandahar a while back. Who knows what else he did."

"That doesn't sound right."

"But it is right. He was for sale to the highest bidder. Like they say, 'Maybe you can't buy an Afghan, but you can always rent one.' He teamed up with a gal from the U.K., and she made it possible to work deals with us. That was his M.O." When Withers only frowned, I said, "Our people thought he was okay. The FBI even ID'd him as a 'friendly.'"

"You can see why I bought their version."

"I guess."

"We had it arranged so that when you left the COP you were on your own. We knew they had some kind of ambush set up, but I figured it would be pretty routine, you know? They were supposed to grab you and the terp. But when Sully fought back, one of those SOBs started shooting and killed him. That sure wasn't supposed to happen."

I continued to listen. This was starting to get interesting.

"I had other things on my mind, Klear. So yeah, it was only afterward that I began to think it was all pretty fishy from the start. These guys showing up with a story about you and this Sakhi character." Withers shook his head. "I made a trip to Bagram later to ask around, but no one up there would tell me anything."

Withers was quiet then and went back to his hamburger.

Finally, I said, "But still, there had to be someone running this whole thing. Who sent these people?"

Withers wiped his mouth with his napkin. "Waddaya mean?"

"Someone behind it, protecting Abdul Sakhi. Trying to make me look bad. Who was it?"

After emptying his mug with a long swallow, Withers looked thoughtful. Then he pushed the mug forward on the bar. "You remember me riding you in Doug Greer's office?" When I nodded, he said, "Greer set that up. He told me to needle you when you came in. The idea was to get us fighting. Greer spoke to the colonel, said you started it. Major Jones told me Greer wanted you out of Kabul in the worst way." Withers shrugged. "Well, I admit I figured those guys might be blowing smoke when they first told me about you. But you know how it is. Half the stuff you're doing you're not sure why you're doing it. That's the way it was over there. You're on a COP for four months, you're out of the loop, believe me."

What Withers was saying was true enough. It was tough duty in a COP, made tougher by the isolation.

"What did these people say?"

"They said you were out to get this guy, that you were pro-Talib." Withers paused. "Greer is a goddamned Undersecretary, Klear. A suit from D.C. You know how it is. They talk, we listen." After fixing me with a hard stare, he said, "And Major Jones. Pressured him, too."

I was silent, remembering Stan's promotion to light colonel.

Withers stared straight ahead, his hand clutching the handle of his beer mug like it was an M4 carbine. Although he had a lot of beer under his belt and his story was mildly incoherent, it answered all kinds of questions. He'd gotten a lot off his chest. I had a feeling he'd be feeling a lot better about himself in the morning. I hoped he would be.

"I appreciate it, Captain Withers. You and I have been asking ourselves the same questions."

"But not coming up with the right answers." He continued to stare straight ahead.

"Not yet." I tossed down a couple of fifties, slid off the barstool.

"What's that for?"

"They'll buy a lot of beer." I stuck out my hand. "Thanks for coming."

Withers flashed a grim smile. "I'm sorry about all that shouting and screaming—what happened . . ." He was still gripping his beer mug and staring straight ahead when I left.

Outside, despite a cold wind and drizzle, I decided to take a walk. I concentrate better when I'm walking. When I turned my telephone back on, I had a message from Corley.

"I'm back." When she said, "I'm here, but I'm not here," I assumed she meant she'd flown in on an "alternative" passport. "Call tomorrow. I'm one floor below you in the building."

I wasn't looking forward to seeing her. I no longer trusted her, and ever since the Dubai episode, I was finding her a little weird. She'd be giving orders, but I no longer felt obliged to follow them. From here on in, this was going to be my own little "op," and I'd run it my way.

As I walked, I thought about how Withers' story fit in with the rest of what I knew—one of the last pieces of the puzzle.

CHAPTER 32

At 1000 hours, I was in Corley's kitchen, sitting silently as she made coffee. Unlike my place, this was a two-bedroom, but, except for abstract paintings on the wall, it wasn't much different. The living room was crammed with vintage furniture, and the bookshelves half-filled with books in other languages. On the floor was an ancient Persian rug. I again wondered who owned this dingy building.

Definitely not the U.S. government.

What type of people normally stayed here? Not Americans, that much I knew. What was I involved in?

Corley was wearing a dark blue sweater, blue slacks, and sneakers. She looked sexy, but in a strange and dangerous way.

As she fussed with the machine, I decided to tell her about Captain Withers' visit the previous evening.

Sitting down opposite me, she placed two cups of coffee on the table. "At last," she said.

"What do you mean?"

"I mean that you're at last beginning to understand what you should have tumbled to a long time ago." When I frowned, she said, "Douglas Greer. You seem finally to understand how he fits into the picture."

"According to Withers, Greer wanted me out of Kabul in the worst way."

"Greer wanted you dead in the worst way, and I hope you understand why. You were the one person he couldn't control. When D.C. talks, the military listens. But you were being what you are by nature—a pest, a royal nuisance. And you were thinking independently. You turned out to be just the kind of person your superiors say you are. You wouldn't agree to the fact that Colonel Hansen was the victim of a green-on-blue killing."

I nodded. Maybe because I recalled once being a young GI myself, I read Nolda right from the start differently from everyone else. And when I saw his bloated body in the hospital, I was 80 percent positive that he hadn't killed Pete. When the body disappeared, I was 100 percent.

Corley said, "It was also clear to me from the beginning that Colonel Hansen's murder wasn't a green-on-blue. I was close enough to Colonel Hansen to see that."

She'd been close to Pete? How had she managed that?

She'd arranged for Jerry Shenlee to send someone over to take a closer look. That "someone" turned out to be me. I continued to wonder about her relationship with Pete. Something wasn't right.

I said, "Pete was investigating the Kabul Bank fraud. He was getting close to finding out something no one else knew. Why would he have told you anything?"

She ignored the question by taking a sip of coffee.

Finally, she said it. "You're right. Colonel Hansen was close to finding out what no one else knew."

She fixed me with her dark eyes. "Or even suspected."

"Which was?"

"He knew that an American had been involved in the bank fraud. In fact, that he'd orchestrated the swindle."

We were both silent for close to a minute. So that was it.

I said, "That was what Pete, but no one else, knew. And that was why he was killed."

"Do I have to spell it out for you?" When I didn't respond, she said, "The Afghans never would have come up with the idea of cleaning out the bank on their own. And if they had, they wouldn't have had the balls to carry it out."

"Someone had to give them the green light."

"Yes, and since they couldn't have figured out how to loot the bank themselves, that person had to show them how to do it." She paused to take a sip of coffee. "On their own, they almost certainly would have messed up the job. In order to do it right, they needed help. They needed a savvy American." Again she paused. "Someone from the United States government."

"The auditors never mentioned an American. The people who were charged were all Afghans."

"Greer was too smart for the auditors."

"So while staying in the background, he showed the bank officials how to do it."

"I believe so. And he remained in the background while they took the American government for every last dime it had transferred to the bank. As well as every last cent that had been deposited there by their countrymen. A billion dollars. And Greer made sure he got his cut."

"Can we prove that? If the auditors missed all that, there's no way to prove that Greer was involved."

"Greer's name never appeared anywhere in any bank transaction. The bank's shareholders were given interest-free loans. They used the money to buy property, stocks, and so forth, and to make large currency transactions. Firms headquartered in Liechtenstein and Switzerland did the buying and trading. Often they negotiated through intermediaries, straw men. These transactions were involved and complex. With the straw men working behind the scenes in different countries and unwilling to reveal anything, it would be next to impossible to pin down Greer's involvement."

I said, "But Taraki Hamed knew of the transactions that involved Greer and wrote it all down."

"Precisely. Both Colonel Hansen and Douglas Greer wanted what Hamed's document contained. Hamed, of course, knew its value—and was holding out for as much money as he could get. Once Greer realized that Pete was making trips to Dubai and talking to Hamed, he knew he had to do something."

"So he hired Abdul Sakhi to kill Pete and make it look like a green-on-blue killing."

"Yes. I hope you can see why I wanted someone—a third party— to become involved in the investigation."

I didn't comment. Why she wanted help with the messy financial situation was now clear enough.

Realizing how much I knew, I could see I was lucky to have survived.

But I still couldn't understand Corley's role. Why was she so intent on getting the goods on Doug Greer? I knew she had no intention of turning over Hamed's information to the American government.

Was it because she loved Pete and wanted revenge? For some reason, I doubted that. I didn't think she was Pete's kind of woman. Or was she? What was I missing?

There was another long silence. With her hand around the coffee mug, she stared at me. Her expression was unsmiling, in fact mildly threatening. I was feeling more and more uncomfortable in Corley's company.

Finally, I said, "As luck would have it, I have a lunch date tomorrow with Greer. At twelve thirty." When she asked, "Where?" I said, "At the Tabard. Do you know it?"

"Of course."

"Greer feels relieved that the trial is over in Kabul," I said. "He says he's happy about the guilty verdict."

"He thinks he's home free. He's still got a lot to worry about. He just doesn't know it yet."

For the next two minutes, we both sat silently. After she'd poured out more coffee, she said, "I think it will be sufficient if you only mention the second trip to Dubai. You needn't say what we've found out." She again flashed a malicious smile. "He'll figure out the rest himself."

I nodded. I certainly didn't want to have to be the one to tell Undersecretary Doug Greer that he'd eventually be facing fraud charges in an American court.

CHAPTER 33

TUESDAY, MARCH 5, 2013

"I LIKE THIS place," Greer said, as he walked into the Tabard Hotel dining room. "It's homey." We were seated at a table next to a large window overlooking a small courtyard. Pointing toward the far wall, he commented, "Nice pictures."

The waiter approached for our drink orders and Greer frowned before he decided on a martini. I told the waiter I'd stick with water.

Nodding at the paintings, he said, "I like the abstract stuff. I do some painting. I began with water colors. Lately, I've been trying oils."

"When do you find the time?"

"Weekends, Sundays," he said with a laugh. "That's about it." He continued to glance about the room. "This place definitely beats the canteen in ISAF." Picking up the large menu, he gave it a quick once-over and announced, "I'm having the steak."

When the waiter reappeared, I asked for the seared salmon.

Greer smiled a greeting to two middle-aged women in business suits who could have been government employees, then said, "My other hobby is I like to cook." He shook his head. "Military dining facilities all seem the same after a while. That's how I got involved in cooking. I like variety."

"How often have you been over there?"

"More times than I can count. Some visits I do my best to forget." When I said, "That bad?" he smiled. "Sometimes I want to kiss the tarmac on the runway as soon as we land." After smearing butter on a slice of dark bread, he said, "The Kabul Bank sure is a mess. But I have to say it's mostly our fault. I mean our country's fault." He paused. "I'm glad those bank people are finally getting what they deserve."

"We should know better."

"How can you explain the disappearance of over 900 million dollars? C'mon. Like I always say, these are people who don't have a clue where handling money is concerned. How many Afghans can balance a checkbook?" He rolled his eyes, to emphasize his point.

"I heard it was more like a billion."

Doug waved to the waiter for another martini. "You're probably right. Why quibble over a hundred million? Where'd you hear that, anyway?" Then he smirked. "I get the idea you've got your sources, Alex. This guy you visited in Dubai. Just who was he anyhow? Was he the guy who told you that?"

"His name's Taraki Hamed. Does it ring a bell?" Greer was obviously playing dumb. According to Corley, he'd been in contact with Hamed. More than once.

He shook his head. "All I know is what I read in the newspapers."

"His name was in the newspapers. He's a former official of the bank."

"Wasn't he charged? I thought we got them all. All guilty."

"The Afghan courts are unpredictable, but this time they did a pretty good job."

"I still don't see how this guy escaped prosecution. What's his name? Hamed?" Greer's expression went from a frown to a dark scowl. When I didn't answer, he said, "Well?"

"Hamed was a vice president of the Kabul Bank, Doug. I'm surprised you don't know that. He escaped prosecution because he didn't do anything wrong."

Greer's scowl turned darker when I said that.

"You're saying with all that money around he didn't try to help himself to any? What is he? A goddamned saint?"

"Just smart. He didn't want to get the American government mad at him." When Greer only shrugged, I said, "No amount of money is worth going to jail for."

"You're right," Greer said. "You can't spend money if you're behind bars." As an afterthought, he added, "No matter how much you have."

The waiter arrived at that moment, and we began moving plates to make room for our food. Greer asked for another martini. "The martinis here are great and so are the steaks. Two of my weaknesses."

After a couple of bites of steak, he returned to the subject of Afghanistan. "In some ways, I like the country, Alex, don't get me wrong. But dealing with the people hasn't always been easy." After ordering another martini, Greer continued to talk, rattling on between bites of potatoes and steak about his experience as the government Undersecretary working in Afghanistan.

At points, he began having difficulty finding the right word.

The four martinis were having an effect.

When the waiter returned, Greer announced, "The pies here are out of this world." Then, after asking for the dessert menu, he smiled and held up his empty glass. "You only live once."

We were sipping coffee when we again started talking about the Kabul Bank situation. "It's the biggest bank collapse in history. Can you believe that? And it happened right here under our noses. Yours and mine."

"And Pete's. Pete knew more about how it happened than anyone."

"A billion dollars is a lot of loot. So, okay, the money's gone. What happened to it? Where did it all go?"

"Only the bank officials know where it went. Some of it went to the Emirates. The bank would lend money to a bank official, who'd use it to buy property in Dubai. Some went to Switzerland, places like St. Moritz."

Doug again frowned. "But wouldn't that be kind of . . . well, obvious?"

"Obvious only if an individual used his own name. Not obvious if he had a cutout or, let's say, a firm headquartered in Liechtenstein, where the directors' and owners' names aren't public. They do the buying for him. They buy from another intermediary."

"A straw man. A guy who's paid to move money. Over there, the bankers and businesspeople are good at hiding money."

Greer shook his head and was silent for a long minute. Like me, he might have been doing his best to grasp how much money one billion dollars was—and how much it would buy. With his credit card out, he told the waiter he wanted to pay. On the way back out to N Street, I thanked him for the lunch.

"You're welcome. Let's go up to Dupont Circle. I can grab a taxi up there." After a brief pause, he turned and faced me. "You seem to know quite a bit about how they managed to steal the money."

"Only what I could pick up here and there."

"Like in Dubai?" Standing on the sidewalk and looking for a cab, Greer said, "What were you doing in Dubai, anyway? What were you trying to find out? I'm curious."

"I guess you could say I was playing some hunches and trying to make some educated guesses. I was only following up on what Pete . . . Colonel Hansen . . . was working on."

"Which was?"

"What the auditors missed. Some of it was critical."

"And your source was . . ."

"Taraki Hamed, the former bank official."

"You say he was never on the take."

"The United States government may, at times, seem careless, Doug, but you know better than anyone. When our government wants to, it's good at finding out things. Hamed was smart. He knew that sooner or later people were going to want to know what happened."

"So?"

"So he observed what was happening and wrote it all down. Every last transaction. Every last name. From what we can see, he didn't miss anything—or anybody."

When a taxi pulled up, Greer said, "I'd like to continue this conversation. Could you come by for dinner on Saturday evening? I'll cook." When I said fine, Greer said, "You like chicken? Strawberries?" Still holding the taxi door, he said, "Make it, say, about seven or a little after."

I gave Doug a hand as he climbed awkwardly into the cab. He threw me a quick wave as the vehicle pulled out from the curb and, seconds later, disappeared into traffic.

After an hour of walking around downtown, my curiosity got the better of me. The three-martini lunch is a beautiful American tradition. But Greer had gone it one better. I called his office.

"Mr. Greer isn't available at present," his secretary said.

"Is he in a meeting?"

"What did you say your name was?"

"Would it be better to call tomorrow?"

"That might be advisable," his secretary said.

I couldn't be sure, but I had an idea Greer hadn't made it back to the office after lunch. He definitely would have been wiser not going back.

Back in Addison Heights, I stopped by Corley's apartment.

"How was your lunch?" she asked.

"Very pleasant. I had the salmon."

"That's great. Is there anything I should know?"

I shook my head.

Although I could see that Greer had become very nervous, I decided not to mention that opinion. He wasn't just knocking down the booze; for most of the meal he'd been talking rapidly, and at times, it seemed as if his mind was somewhere else. He definitely seemed worried. Maybe he sensed the walls were closing in.

Based on what Bud Withers said, Greer was behind two attempts on my life. And he'd hired Abdul Sakhi to silence Pete.

He'd worked his way up from the bottom. Whatever he'd gotten in life, he'd earned—or taken. I knew the type well enough. But now he'd taken too much, and he was going to have to figure out how to extricate himself from this mess. Someone as smart and as slippery as Greer would try to find a solution. And I had a feeling he could stand the heat.

And that was the reason he wanted to see me again. He wanted to find out how much I knew. He wanted to start working his way out of a tight situation.

I said, "Undersecretary Greer has invited me over for supper on Saturday evening. He lives in Bethesda. He's a hobby cook and he likes having guests."

Corley looked very thoughtful. "I'm impressed. You're coming up in the world." As I stood up to leave, she said, "I have a feeling we won't be needing your services much longer."

I wondered just whom she meant by "we" but didn't ask.

Later that evening, I received a call from Wanda. When she asked what I was doing, I said I'd fallen asleep on the sofa.

"I assume you're not going back to Dubai—or Afghanistan!"

"Nothing like that. But I am preparing for Saturday."

"What's happening on Saturday?"

"Doug Greer invited me to stop by his place on Saturday evening. From what I understand, he likes to cook. We had lunch today. Talked about the situation in Afghanistan, naturally."

"That's all?"

"No, we also talked about the bank situation. Doug's interested in it. By now, I guess everybody is. The officers were running a Ponzi scheme to end all Ponzi schemes. With the trial over, they'll be doing their best to negotiate shorter sentences."

"Well, I was going to ask if you wanted to accompany me to a D.C. Summit Meeting. I get regular invitations. One of the generals will be talking. But since you've got other plans . . ."

When I asked if I could have a rain check, Wanda said, "Of course."

CHAPTER 34

At a few minutes before seven on Saturday evening I turned off the East-West Highway onto Chelton Road. I knew I was somewhere in the neighborhood of the Columbia Country Club, where once, years before, I attended a wedding party. After five minutes of driving, I turned into a cul-de-sac at the end of which was Doug Greer's place. It was a neighborhood of broad streets, well-tended lawns, and expensive homes. The rain had begun again but was now only a drizzle. A solitary street lamp provided the light on the road.

I was still fifty yards from the house, and driving slowly, when I saw a line of cars parked on the street. Two vehicles, a police van and an ambulance, had pulled onto the apron in front of Greer's house. Among the vehicles on the street were two police cars. At that moment, a TV news truck arrived, and with a squeal of brakes, halted in front of the house. A small knot of people, about ten in all, was gathered in front of Doug Greer's home.

The flashing red light from one of the police cars was reflecting off the large picture windows at the front of his house.

What was going on?

After parking, I walked up to where two policemen stood in rain gear, keeping people off the premises. Crime scene tape ran from a fence post to a tree and toward the rear of the house.

"My name is Klear, Alex Klear." I showed some ID. "What's up?"

After they'd exchanged glances, the younger policeman took

down my name and said, "Next of kin? Are you a relative of the gentleman who lives here?" When I said I was a colleague, he glanced at the older policeman, who only shook his head.

I said, "Undersecretary Douglas Greer lives here. He and I have business to discuss. That's why I'm here."

A fleeting look of uncertainty flashed across the older policeman's face. "What kind of business is that?"

"Government business."

"What kind of government business?"

"Mr. Greer is Undersecretary for International Development. We both just got back from Afghanistan." I raised my voice. "Confidential government business."

The older cop shook his head. "That doesn't mean—"

I pulled out a pad of my own. "Can I have your names? This is a government matter. We expect cooperation. I don't feel I'm getting any." I found a pen. "I'm not getting cooperation." I peered first at the older cop's face, then looked down at his name tag, began to write.

"He locked himself in his garage, turned on his car engine," the policeman said. "That's about it."

I did my best to conceal my astonishment.

I put away my pen and paper. When I asked if there was any chance of talking with someone in charge, the older cop told me that some of the waiting group were reporters and I could wait with them. Ten minutes later a detective in civvies carrying an umbrella called over the reporters. I joined them.

The detective introduced himself as Lieutenant McCormack and said he worked homicide for Montgomery County. Then, reading from a piece of paper he identified the dead man as Undersecretary Douglas Greer.

"Mr. Greer has taken his own life—check that—appears to have taken his own life. He was found in his car, which was parked in his garage, with the motor running. Mr. Greer is Undersecretary for Development." He paused. "That's International Development."

"Who found him, Lieutenant?"

"A landscaper came around to the rear of the house, where he always collects the monthly bill. No one answered the bell. While he was waiting, he thought he smelled something. Thought it might be coming from the garage. He opened the door, saw the exhaust. Then he called a neighbor. The neighbor notified the police. Let's see, that was just an hour ago. Maybe a little more."

"What kind of car was it, Lieutenant?" a reporter asked.

"An Infiniti, 2013, I believe."

"Color?"

"Green, dark green."

"Did he leave a note?"

"If he did, we haven't found it."

The reporters asked a few more questions, but the policeman said there wasn't much he could add to what he'd already said.

The group broke up and the reporters began talking into their cell phones. As Lieutenant McCormack walked back toward the rear, I caught up with him. I asked him if it would be possible to have a look inside the house.

"I can tell you now. There ain't nothing to see."

"Doug had invited me over this evening. For dinner. We had business to discuss."

"You work with him? Are you with the government, too?"

I nodded, pulled out some ID. "We were together in Afghanistan. We just got back."

"You and him were in Afghanistan?" He hesitated. "I don't think I—"

"This is starting to sound like a cover-up, Lieutenant. I just showed you my ID. If you want, call my boss." I pulled out my phone as though I was about to hand it to him. "You can—"

"We're not supposed to—"

"If there's anything in the house that's not the way it should be, I can point it out for you. A quick look should do it."

After hesitating briefly, he said, "Well, okay. That makes sense. But the forensic people are inside now. Be careful. They're gathering stuff up, not that there's anything much to find, but you never know. I went through the whole place, upstairs and down. It seems like the guy took his own life." McCormack shrugged.

At the back of the house I saw the open garage and the car still inside. Someone had killed the engine. Two paramedics, both dressed in reflective gear, were standing and talking.

We entered through the building's rear door, which led up a small stairway into the kitchen, which had a lettuce leaf and some crumbs on the linoleum. On the kitchen counter lay a knife, a bowl holding three tomatoes, three peeled potatoes. I took a quick look in the refrigerator, which was filled with food. Toward the front, I saw a package of strawberries.

We walked through the dining room into the living room, where a woman and a man were kneeling on the rug and working with small brushes. Except for some newspapers on the sofa, everything appeared in reasonably good order. Either Greer was a good housekeeper or had a cleaning lady. I suspected the latter.

Upstairs, I checked out his bedroom, which seemed to be where he watched TV. The bed was made. In another room, which was obviously an office, there was clutter, mostly papers, magazines, and books. On the desk was a computer, and next to the desk a large file cabinet. When I pulled it open, I saw lots of manila folders, all jammed together. He was the record-keeping type, but I tended to doubt he'd have anything here that would link him to the bank fraud. Then we headed back downstairs.

In the basement, I saw shelves on which were laid cans of food and some oranges. Greer had seemingly bought the ingredients for the meal that he had planned to prepare and food for the rest of the week.

"You were right," I told McCormack. "Not much to see."

"High up in the government and making a mint. And still he took his own life." McCormack's tone was heavy with disgust. He shook his head. "For whatever reason." When I only shrugged, he said, "He ain't the first. With these government guys, you never know."

Back in my car, I punched in Corley's number. Before I could say anything, she said, "I've got the TV on and just heard the news." After a brief pause during which I could hear a commentator, she said, "Can you hang around out there, see what's going on?"

"I think so. The scene's still pretty chaotic."

"Do that."

Two minutes later two black limousines arrived and disgorged a woman and four men. They all wore suits, and I had an idea they were from either the government or the FBI.

The ambulance carrying Greer's lifeless body backed off the apron a short time later, then headed back in the direction of the East-West Highway. More police arrived, some of whom fanned out to talk with neighbors. I remained in the car, watching. After another hour, I got a call from Corley.

When I said things had quieted down, she said, "Stay a little longer anyway."

Five minutes later, a team of people came out carrying the file cabinets I'd seen upstairs. One of the government guys ordered them to be put into the trunks of two limousines.

A car filled with military people in uniform arrived and headed toward the rear.

Greer was a helluva important guy!

The next time Corley called she said, "I think you can leave now. I'll talk with you tomorrow."

"Not tonight?"

"Tomorrow. Not too early. I have to send e-mails."

I wondered who she was sending them to.

CHAPTER 35

"It's a shame, a damned shame," Corley said. She shook her head. "Dammit. It's already in the papers." She pointed at a copy of the *Washington Post*. "This is really upsetting."

It was Sunday morning and we were in her apartment. When I'd arrived a few minutes before, she led me back to one of the bedrooms, which was furnished as an office. While she finished up some work on the computer, which seemed to consist of reading and sending e-mails, I sat down and watched

As she tapped the keys, I filled her in on some of the details regarding Greer's suicide.

"What did you tell him at lunch the other day?"

"About what you told me to say. I said we'd been in Dubai and talked with Hamed."

"You didn't threaten him or try to scare him."

"No, of course not. He was a trifle nervous, maybe."

"Nervous?"

"He wanted to know about the trip to Dubai. Who I had spoken with."

"He was worried about what we found out in Dubai. That makes sense."

"I mentioned that Hamed knew things that the auditors had missed. I didn't go into detail. As we ate, he ordered a couple more martinis. He invited me over on Saturday. He said he wanted to talk."

"'He wanted to find out in more detail what you picked up from Hamed.'"

Corley was wearing a man's flannel shirt, shorts, and house shoes with some kind of fur. After typing for a few minutes, she swiveled around to face me. Even if his marriage to Wanda was on the rocks, I couldn't imagine Pete falling for Corley. She was attractive, but she lacked . . . something . . . and Pete would have picked up on it.

What was it she lacked? I couldn't figure it out myself.

When she'd finished on the computer, we headed into the kitchen. She put some water on to boil and started fussing with tea tins.

"What do we know? Let's start from the beginning."

"We know Doug Greer is dead. The police think he killed himself."

As she opened a tin of cookies, she said, "Do you think he committed suicide?"

I hesitated briefly. "I don't know."

"That's not a helpful answer."

"I've been thinking about it. In fact I had trouble falling asleep running it over in my mind."

"You say he seemed nervous. Okay, he realized his role in the bank failure would eventually become public knowledge. He'd be disgraced. The future appeared so dismal he took his own life. Doesn't that sound logical?"

"Yes, but maybe too logical." When she asked what I meant, I said, "Just because someone's depressed doesn't mean they commit suicide."

"In other words, we shouldn't jump to conclusions."

I said, "You're right that he had a reason to be worried. But would that lead him to take his own life?"

"He could eventually go to prison. That's frightening."

"Yes, but Greer wasn't someone easily frightened. Or intimidated.

He joined the Marines as a kid, and he did all right. Later on, he went to college on a scholarship. He was fast on his feet. He could turn on the charm when necessary. He scrambled all the way to the top of the government bureaucracy. He did what he had to do. He was a politician, experienced, a tough, savvy guy."

"Being tough and savvy is nice, but when you're up against the United States government, you're overmatched."

"Yes, but Greer had the government backed into a corner. It would have done its best to avoid a trial. The Afghans were tried in an Afghan court, but an American official would be tried in an American court."

"A trial would reveal the government's lack of oversight in handling a billion dollars of taxpayers' money."

"Because the government didn't want to reveal the extent of the fraud, the first reports said the sum was only around 230 million. Then it jumped to 350 million. Then 535 million, then 700 million. Then the estimates went to 735 million. Then it was 800 million."

"In other words, Greer had a good negotiating position. The government didn't want to admit just how much money was involved. Plus, it wouldn't have wanted to bring charges against an American government official."

"Not when it could shove all the guilt onto a bunch of corrupt Afghans. Greer could have figured that right from the start. Which is why he was willing to take the risk."

"Okay, it could cause quite a shake-up if numbers like that were to reach the public."

"Greer could have negotiated a backroom deal. He wouldn't have given up easily—and taken his own life."

She touched a hand to her hair, the kind of gesture Audrey Hepburn made in *Breakfast at Tiffany's*. "Still, that doesn't mean that someone murdered him."

"No, it doesn't. But I noticed some things while I was in the house. He'd been preparing dinner. Greer invited me over, said to arrive between seven and seven thirty. Cooking was a hobby. When I passed through the kitchen I saw chicken breasts on the cutting board. Alongside was a box of rice. There was butter and ginger powder. Also a bottle of white wine."

"Sounds like he was preparing chicken breasts in ginger sauce with rice. I make it myself except I like curry sauce instead of ginger."

"There was broccoli on the counter as well. When I peeked in the refrigerator, I saw strawberries. He'd asked if I liked strawberries."

"Strawberries were for dessert?" When I nodded, she said, "It seems he'd already gone to a lot of trouble."

"He might have started preparing during the early afternoon. What could have happened, he was interrupted by someone." I paused. "Someone who wanted to kill him."

"And this someone wanted to make it appear like suicide."

"Everything would fit together—that is, if Greer had taken money from the Kabul Bank, the government would have the perfect scapegoat. Or if Greer's murderer was the coconspirator, that person would be home free."

"Someone might not have wanted Greer talking to you because of what he might say."

"He liked booze, obviously. He might have had a glass of wine too many—and might have revealed something that might have made me suspicious."

Corley stared at me for a long minute, putting the pieces together in her mind. "All right, let's assume he was murdered. How could it have been accomplished?"

I thought about that for a minute, then said, "The person might have made him unconscious for a short time."

"How would he do that?"

"Any number of ways. A Russian woman in East Berlin once tried to put me out with a mixture of chloral hydrate and alcohol."

"Did she succeed?"

"I don't remember." Ignoring Corley's smirk, I said, "The perpetrator would only need to get Greer into the garage, which wasn't far from the rear door of the house."

"It makes a kind of sense. It doesn't seem likely that someone as tough as Greer would kill himself. Not at this point."

"And it's not likely that someone who intended to commit suicide would bother to go food shopping and then go to the trouble of preparing a meal."

A minute went by during which neither of us said anything. Then, with the conversation at a standstill, I said something that had been on my mind for a while.

"Has anyone ever said you look a great deal like Audrey Hepburn?"

Corley took a sip of tea. "As a matter of fact, yes, a number of times. But I'm six inches taller and probably twenty-five pounds heavier." She paused. "We're different types."

"Audrey Hepburn had charm and innocence. That's why people loved her."

"But I don't have charm and innocence? Is that it?" Before I could come up with an answer, she said, "I have other qualities. One of them is, I'm logical." She paused. "I think we've reasoned our way to the conclusion that the Undersecretary didn't kill himself."

"Figuring out who killed him will be much more difficult."

"Yes, let me think how we proceed from here."

The truth was, I didn't care how she wanted to proceed from here. Until this op was over, I intended to handle things in my own way.

* * *

"It began with some forged passports," Corley said. She was seated on my sofa. I had just made her a drink, scotch over ice, which she continued to glance at but hadn't touched.

"We had someone watching the airport in Islamabad."

"Who had someone watching the airport at Islamabad?"

Ignoring my question, Corley said, "This person recognized Greer and wondered why he flew in. But when we checked with Immigration, we learned he'd flown to Pakistan on a forged American passport."

Again I would like to have asked who "we" was.

"The question was: Why would the Undersecretary use a forged passport?"

"That's easy. Because he wasn't there on government business."

"I thought that, too. Any further thoughts?" When I shook my head, she said, "He wanted to make contact with Abdul Sakhi, who at this time was in Quetta. In North Waziristan."

"I suppose you were at Camp Chapman."

"Yes, I was—and in a perfect position to observe Abdul Sakhi, who was, of course, known to us by reputation. He couldn't light a cigarette in Quetta without SOG knowing it. I wondered why the Undersecretary would want to do business with Abdul Sakhi. Two weeks later, when Colonel Hansen was killed, I thought I might have the answer. After the FBI photo showed Abdul Sakhi had been in ISAF Headquarters, I was 90 percent sure."

"But you lacked proof."

She nodded. "I flew immediately to Washington. When I spoke with your boss, I said I wanted him to send someone who could figure out what was going on. And who would be able to understand financial fraud."

I nodded, remembering that Jerry emphasized banking and fraud when we spoke in January.

Corley said, "Let's assume we're correct that someone murdered Greer and that the reason was to prevent him from speaking with you. That might mean the person was a coconspirator in the fraud."

"It would have to be someone he spoke with after having lunch with me."

I recalled Greer climbing into a taxi on Dupont Circle. An hour later, when I called his office, I got the impression he never made it back to work after his four-martini lunch.

"Can we find out who Greer spoke with after talking with you?"

"Difficult, if not impossible."

"Maybe he spoke to a colleague, a fellow worker."

"I hope you're not suggesting the American government sent someone around to kill Undersecretary Greer."

"The American government is not a bunch of angels."

"No, it's not. Although I admit such a thing is a possibility, I don't think that happened. I tend to believe it was an individual, some person close to Greer." I paused. "Was he married?"

"Divorced. His 'ex' lives on the Coast."

I nodded, recalling him saying his ex-wife was definitely not a football fan. Since Corley seemed so well informed where Greer's private life was concerned, I continued to ask. "Girlfriend? Boyfriend?"

"His one female friend that I know of was Wanda."

"Wanda?" I repeated.

"Wanda Hansen."

"I was aware they knew each other. I didn't know they were friends."

"In Kabul I ran into them one evening quite by accident. You know the Caravan restaurant?" When I nodded, Corley said, "Then you know what a dark place it is. They were carrying on an intense conversation at a rear table with nothing between them but a candle."

"Are you sure?"

"They were even holding hands."

I didn't say anything, but I recalled Wanda once saying she hardly knew Greer.

Why lie?

I also recalled Captain Page commenting on Pete being despondent because he and Wanda were headed for a breakup. Yet when I asked Wanda about that, she denied there was ever any thought of divorce. In fact, she said she'd picked out a new apartment in Alexandria.

These facts didn't fit together.

"Are you absolutely sure it was Wanda with Doug Greer in that restaurant?"

"A hundred percent." Corley stared directly at me. We both understood what the connection might signify. Pete, Wanda's husband, was tracking down the perpetrators of the bank fraud. As things now stood, it seemed one perpetrator might have been Greer.

That fact, of course, would have made Wanda wary of admitting to me she had any kind of connection to Greer.

"Doug wasn't the only gentleman who cared about the lady."

I knew what was coming.

"You used to squire her all over Kabul. Did you think people didn't notice? Lunch, sightseeing, hotels." Before I could answer, she said, "I admit I'm curious about your relationship with Colonel Hansen."

"There is no relationship. I'm not carrying on a romance with Pete's widow."

"You've known her for years. You don't deny that."

Unsure of what to say, I was silent for a long moment. "You're reading all sorts of things into . . ."

"Into an innocent friendship?" Corley smiled maliciously. "Your girlfriend wasn't shy about telling everyone about you and her—Stan, me, Doug, anyone who'd listen. And then she moved into the Serena. How many times did you visit her over there?"

"Is that important?" After a pause, I said, "A couple of times. I tried to cheer her up." After a long moment, I said, "I'm in a relationship." Or at least I had been.

"And your fiancée is where?" She shook her head. "My impression was, Wanda Hansen had you eating out of her hand."

"That's ridiculous." Corley had done a good job of putting me on the defensive. I decided not to say any more.

"Okay." Clearly, she didn't believe me.

Although I know arguing with a woman is a losing proposition, I foolishly persisted. "Wanda was visiting Kabul for the first time. She'd recently lost her husband."

"You were helping her over a rough time. Thoughtful of you."

"Actually, you have it backwards. Admittedly, a long time ago, before she married Pete, we were interested in each other. When she turned up in Kabul, she kept trying to get me into bed."

"Oh, come on. And you kept saying *no*. She's a beautiful woman. You can't expect me to believe that."

"Believe it or not. One evening she even served me a Mickey Finn. Do you know what a Mickey Finn is?"

"Yes. Of course I know."

"This really happened."

"What happened?"

"What happened was, I was lucky. I took only a small swallow. Suddenly, all I wanted to do was lie down . . ."

"Then what?"

"I knew I had to get out of the room. I had just enough strength to stagger down to the lobby. We were in the Serena."

"In her room in the Serena, no doubt. And you're saying she did this because she wanted to get you into bed. And you expect me to believe that?"

"Why not?"

"Men are all egotists, but you're worse than most."

"What do you mean?"

"You've got one-track minds. That's what I mean. Maybe she had another reason for wanting to put you under."

"Maybe but—" The funny thing was, that incident had struck me as strange as well, somehow as not characteristic of Wanda. Would Wanda have had another reason for wanting to drug me?

"Think it over, why don't you?" When I didn't respond, she said, "You were investigating her husband's death, right?"

"That wouldn't be a reason . . . to get rid of me. I think . . . you're going off in the wrong direction." But even as I said that, I was beginning to ask myself some questions. I recalled driving into the Serena Hotel parking area the next day, where Abdul Sakhi and Fiona had been waiting, observing my car. Could they have been there the previous evening, waiting to carry me away? To turn me into a corpse?

It would have been the perfect way to dispose of me. Wanda could have testified that I was fine when I left the hotel. Then, on the way back to Camp Eggers, I disappeared. People would assume the Taliban had grabbed me. In reality, I would have met the same fate as Sergeant Nolda. Fish food.

"Face the facts. There were a number of attempts on your life. It seems there were people who wanted you out of the way. Have you figured out yet who these people were?"

"I figure Greer."

"Okay, did you ever figure Greer might have had help?"

When I said I hadn't, she said in a disgusted tone, "Maybe you should try."

Those were Corley's final words. She got to her feet and headed for the door. I had long ago sensed the intensity of the dislike that existed between Wanda Hansen and Leslie Corley. I thought the reason was their involvement with Pete. But I now began to wonder if Corley didn't have an additional reason. Corley suspected that Wanda was involved in the Kabul Bank fraud.

And I'd made the suggestion that it might have been Greer's partner in the fraud who murdered him.

And Wanda would have feared Corley because she was investigating Pete's murder and suspected it was not a green-on-blue killing.

My glass was empty. I reached for Corley's untouched glass of scotch and finished it with one quick gulp.

CHAPTER 36

The more I thought about it, the more I kept coming back to the same unsettling conclusion. A conclusion I fought and one I didn't want to face. A conclusion that had to be wrong.

The truth remained that Wanda hadn't been honest regarding her and Pete's marriage. As Captain Page had indicated, Pete was despondent because Wanda had wanted a divorce.

Nor had she been honest in telling me she hardly knew Douglas Greer. Did she have plans to marry Greer after divorcing Pete?

Another thought I was unable to shake was the connection that both she and Greer had to the Kabul Bank. Wanda had been married to Pete who was investigating the fraud, and as things now stood, Greer was implicated in the scheme to defraud the bank. Although she always maintained she knew next to nothing about Pete's work investigating the bank, that had never seemed logical. Now I wondered whether Wanda hadn't known a great deal about the bank situation and the bank's vulnerability to fraud. If this were the case, it's more than likely that it was Wanda who floated the possibility of stealing the money to Greer—and not vice versa.

And as Corley said, I could have been all wrong about why Wanda wanted to drug me. I'd assumed she only wanted to drag me into bed, but now I realized it could have been a different reason entirely. It was possible that she'd arranged for Abdul Sakhi and Fiona to be waiting in the Serena parking lot to carry off my body.

And finally, Wanda knew of my Saturday evening meeting with Greer because I'd told her about it on the phone.

Could Wanda have murdered Greer because she feared what he might tell me?

Greer tended to drink too much when he was nervous or worried. Wanda would have known that—and might have worried that I'd pressure him into revealing his involvement with the bank fraud.

I kept thinking about everything that happened, and as I pieced the details together, I kept coming to the same conclusion.

The truth is, I met Wanda Hansen a long time ago, nearly sixteen years. Pete and I had been running a special ops training class at Fort Bragg when Wanda arrived. I recalled taking her for a tour of the installation on her first duty day. She was Wanda Nyland then, Captain Wanda Nyland, a newly minted O-3 and very proud of the two silver bars on her shoulders.

She was also a very good-looking O-3, and I wanted to get to know her better.

At the time I was dating Katherine Ross, an Army nurse. But after Pete began dating her, I never thought of Wanda in any way except as a friend. For the next seven or eight months the four of us spent a lot of time together, going to the O Club during the week, having dinner in Fayetteville on the weekends, and from time to time making trips to places like Williamsburg, Richmond, and D.C.

By the time Wanda and Pete married, in the Fort Bragg chapel, I was back overseas, with new problems and other things on my mind.

When I again saw Wanda in Kabul, it seemed like the old chemistry was still there. With Wanda a widow, I felt a kind of protectiveness, and I wonder what would have happened if I hadn't been engaged to Irmie. Who knows what kind of relationship might have developed between us? I shuddered to think of the culpability

I would have felt as I came to realize Wanda had been involved in the bank fraud and had murdered her husband who'd been one of my closest friends.

Truly, Irmie was always in my thoughts, and the way I now saw things, she might have saved me from a disaster that could have destroyed my life.

Of course there was the possibility that I was completely wrong about this scenario. With all my heart, I hoped I was.

In either case, I knew that I had to speak with Wanda.

Immediately after Corley left the apartment, I grabbed my throwaway cell phone and called Wanda at home—and got no answer. Then I remembered her having told me she was planning to take the week off and wanted to spend it away from the Pentagon and away from D.C., in the country place she and Pete owned in Virginia. I assumed she was there now.

She'd said their home was in one of the remote areas of Loudon County, near a body of water called Jackson Pond. It was now shortly after ten p.m. I fussed around the house, made a sandwich that I hardly touched, watched the news, went to bed.

But I couldn't get to sleep. I tossed, I turned. I got up. I went back to bed. I drank a beer. I watched the Leno show. It was no good. I knew I'd never be able to fall asleep. Finally, I decided I'd drive out to Loudon County rather than go back to bed. It also occurred to me that this might be the best moment to speak with Wanda. Letting time go by made no sense at all. Besides, I had to know.

Although I wasn't planning to shoot anyone, I considered bringing the M9 I'd found under the floorboards. Finally, I decided there was no harm in sticking it into my ankle holster.

After getting dressed, I quietly let myself out of the apartment. In the car, I programmed the GPS. Jackson Pond came up immediately. I took 287, which at midnight on a weekday had very little traffic. As I drove, I didn't bother to ask myself whether I was doing the right thing. Or the smart thing. My curiosity had gotten the better of me.

When I turned off 287, it was just after two thirty a.m. After a couple of miles, my electronic navigator indicated another turn, and then a sharp turn onto a curving right-of-way that looked like it once might have been used to drag out logs. Tall evergreens lined both sides of the narrow road.

At a fork there was a wooden sign with a number of names and some arrows. It was hard to see from inside the car and required that I get out and read it with my flashlight. I was beginning to wonder whether this expedition wasn't an exercise in futility when the name "Hansen" appeared beneath the arrow that pointed toward the right. All I could see in that direction was more dark woods, and I assumed Jackson Pond was somewhere within this densely wooded area. Two hundred yards further on, a sign with "Hansen" painted on it indicated another turn into the woods surrounding the pond.

I found a wide place in the road to park. I killed the engine, sat unmoving in the car. All I could hear were forest sounds, small creatures announcing their whereabouts to one another and a gentle breeze moving branches. I pushed the car door open, got out, began walking. I used my flashlight, which together with the half-full moon, kept me on a path toward the house, a couple of hundred feet beyond where I parked. The building was situated at the center of a clearing, beyond which was Jackson Pond. In the cleared area at the front I saw a car, which I assumed was Wanda's. Since there were no lights, I thought she'd be in bed.

I briefly reconnoitered, saw a small dock with a row boat. When I approached the house and tried the front door, it squeaked open, and I was standing on a screened-in deck. Deck furniture was all over. I decided to knock, loud.

Again I asked myself whether I was doing the right thing, arriving unannounced and uninvited. That question was immediately answered.

"Hold it right there, mister! Raise your two hands." The voice was that of a woman. "Both hands! Don't move. I'm holding a rifle!" The voice, which clearly meant business, came from out of the darkness behind me. "Don't mess with me, mister, whoever you are." I recognized the voice.

"Can I turn around? Can I say hello?"

After a second, Wanda said, "Alex! My God! My God, I almost shot you!"

"I'm sorry if I gave you a scare, Wanda. I figured you were sleeping and wanted—"

"I saw a flashlight. My God, Alex!"

Shaking her head, Wanda let the rifle drop to her side. A partly buttoned man's shirt hung loosely over her jeans. Her boots were unlaced. She approached me, stood on her tiptoes, and planted a kiss on my lips. Then she opened the front door, pointed the way inside. Seconds later, the two of us were standing at the center of a cozy living room—comfortable chairs, two lamps, a sideboard, some bookshelves, a thick rug, an animal skin on the hearth in front of a large fireplace.

"I'm just so surprised to see you." She laid the rifle on the floor next to a chair. "Why don't you get the fire going? There's kindling. Throw on a big log. How does scotch and water sound?" She shook her head. "Then you can tell me what you're doing up here."

So, while Wanda straightened things and made our drinks, I worked to get the fire going.

Less than ten minutes later we were seated opposite each other with a crackling fire warming the cozy room.

"Cheers," Wanda said. "You really are crazy, you know that? I could have shot you. I'm serious."

"I had a sudden urge to see you, Wanda. And I remembered—"

"I'm flattered. But you should have let me know you were coming."

I decided to confront the situation head-on. "I guess you heard about Doug."

"On the news. I heard it on the local channel. How awful! And to think we were all together in Kabul, not that long ago . . ."

"Were you already up here when he died?"

"I left D.C. on Thursday evening, shortly after work. I need this break badly, Alex. It's been just too much. First, Pete dying the way he did. Then Afghanistan. I never should have gone. On top of that, my job is driving me batty."

"That bad?"

"I'm putting my papers in. I'm going to retire." She smiled grimly. "Let's talk about something else." When I said, "Okay," Wanda said, "You came up here because you wanted to see me? That's nice. Do you get these uncontrollable urges often?"

"Not really, no."

"Only when you . . . think of me? Can I believe that?" When I hesitated, Wanda said quickly, "I never know what you're thinking, Alex. I'd like to believe . . . well, that you and I . . . have some kind of future together." As I watched, Wanda stood up, took our glasses to the sideboard, and refilled them. "Well, do we?" When I still didn't answer, she said, "I know I'm being blunt, but heck, we first met a long time ago."

"I left my crystal ball home this evening . . ." I noticed that Wanda had unbuttoned all but two of the buttons of her shirt. Only one drink, and we were both feeling reckless. As she handed me the glass, I could see her inviting breasts. I imagined myself ripping open her shirt and kissing her. I could imagine her response as I kissed her breasts, touched my tongue to her nipples, slipped the jeans down from her hips. It was an exciting thought, very near an overpowering one.

And would it be so awful if I did that? Briefly, I felt myself caught up in this thrilling moment, the two of us setting sail on a wild, unpredictable journey on an uncharted ocean. Did I have to care if she was responsible for Greer's death? Or that she was an accomplice in Pete's murder? Or if she'd defrauded the Kabul Bank of millions of dollars?

We'd spend the money together. And we'd have a great time doing it.

Suddenly, as though from a distance, from deep in the back of my mind, I heard a voice, Irmie's voice. It was different from Wanda's, and so faint I couldn't understand the words. And I could see Irmie's face. She wasn't smiling. I thought I saw a teardrop on her cheek . . .

I found it impossible to think of Wanda, whom I was finding so desirable, as an accomplice to murder. I just couldn't.

Why couldn't I be like everyone else and call Pete's death a green-on-blue? But then I saw Irmie's face again, and she was shaking her head.

Green-on-blue killings were still going on. There were over sixty last year, hundreds by now. One more or less hardly mattered. Give the blame to Sergeant Nolda. The government wouldn't care. The American people had other things on their minds.

Why should I care if no one else cared?

And then I was overcome by the thought that maybe I was now reading the situation wrong.

Maybe Nolda really had killed Pete. Wanda was a grieving widow. She had nothing to do with the Kabul Bank. The Afghan court had found twenty-two bank officials guilty of embezzlement and fraud. End of story.

Wanda took a quick gulp of whiskey. "In Afghanistan I told you how I feel about you, Alex. Going way back to when we first met and before I married Pete. You were the one I really wanted. I still want you. Really, I think we'd make a great team. We'd be more than a team, you and I."

"Are you sure?"

"We'd be unstoppable. Whatever we wanted . . . would be ours."

"What would we want?"

"What everyone wants . . . a beautiful life. Is that so bad?"

"What would we live on? What about my business?"

"Sell it. Give it away. Money wouldn't be a problem, believe me." When I flashed a skeptical frown, she smiled. "I'm positive about that."

Wanda's expression turned serious. She lowered her voice.

"The entire time over there . . ."

"In Afghanistan?"

"Yes." She took a sip of scotch. "I kept saying how I felt about you, and I meant it. God, how I meant it! When I saw you again that evening in the Green Village, I went weak in the knees. You must have noticed. Anyway, I realized that you and I together . . . we'd have everything." She jiggled her glass. "Is it too late now? I don't know. Tell me why you're here."

Again I thought of how easy it would be to forget my suspicion that Wanda had murdered Doug Greer and just let myself be swept along by circumstances, circumstances much bigger and more powerful than I was. As I felt the whiskey burning my throat and the alcohol relaxing me, I wondered if I shouldn't just relax and let Wanda take control.

We'd end up in her bedroom. Would that be so bad?

CHAPTER 37

"I've forgiven you, Wanda."

"For giving you a Mickey Finn? Look at it this way, Alex. That shows how badly I wanted you. How many women would do that?" She made a point of reaching down and undoing all but the last shirt button. Her shirt hung loosely, invitingly. "How badly I still want you."

"Why did you say you never should have gone to Afghanistan?"

"Stop asking annoying questions." She sighed. "You know why I shouldn't have gone. It was different from what I imagined it would be. No matter how many news stories you read or news reports, you're just not prepared for the way it is over there." She raised her glass. "I felt I was going to be blown up any minute."

After a sip of scotch, she continued to gaze at the glass. "And now Doug." She sighed audibly, her mood shifting, then grimaced. "I'm not really that great company. Not at the moment anyway. Too much on my mind." She hesitated, then asked, "Why did you drive up here in the middle of the night? You didn't answer that question. It's not like you to do something like that."

"Why not?"

"You're more . . . careful. Doug might have done it, not you."

"How well did you know Doug, Wanda?"

"Not that well, we've been at meetings together. That sort of thing . . ." She shrugged.

Recalling Corley's account of seeing Wanda and Doug together,

I said, "I mean personally." When she frowned, I wondered if I'd pushed the envelope too far.

"Personally? We nodded when we saw each other. Why? That's a strange question, Alex." Her expression seemed to harden in the flickering firelight. "And why did you ask about when it was I arrived up here?"

"Don't overreact, Wanda. It's a simple question."

"It's not important." She sipped more scotch, emptying her glass.

"It's important."

"Oh, sure. Real important. I think you're trying to trip me up, that's what I think." Her glass was empty and she stood to refill it. When she gestured to me, I shook my head. "You know, Alex, I think it's strange . . ."

"What's strange?"

"It's strange that you suddenly want to see me. You weren't too anxious to see me last week. I was throwing myself at you and—"

"When did you say you came up here? Thursday?"

"Yes, Thursday. After work." Wanda looked thoughtful, then said, "All of a sudden, I'm getting a completely different take on why you're here. It's not because you want to be with me. You have another reason. I sense it."

Wanda had laid the rifle on the floor alongside her chair. I recognized it as a BAR 30-06, a semiautomatic. A common hunting rifle. Suddenly, she reached down to pick it up, but that was the move I'd anticipated and was going to prevent.

On my feet, I crossed the room, grabbed her by the hair, but she was quicker than I'd anticipated. As I jerked her back, she'd already grabbed the rifle and swung the barrel against my temple, causing me to loosen my grip. It was enough for her to pull free. She gave me a shove with the rifle butt. Clicking off the safety, she now stood ten feet in front of me, the weapon pointed at my stomach.

"Turn around!" she shouted. "Turn around! Put your hands up."

When she motioned with the gun, I did as I was told. She moved forward, kicked my left leg. "Don't try anything." She jammed the barrel into my back, hard. "My finger's on the trigger. Okay?"

She patted me down. "Empty your pockets. Turn them inside out." When everything was lying on the floor, she told me to raise my hands. "Turn around slowly and sit down in the chair. Okay, good." Still holding the rifle, she sat back down in her own chair. "I have some questions."

She aimed the hunting rifle directly at me. "Not so bright, Alex. Asking if I knew Doug wasn't so *bright*. Right away I knew. Something else that wasn't so *bright* was coming up here in the middle of the night."

"You planned it, didn't you? You and Greer." When she only grinned, I said, "Pete's murder. You and Doug."

"Green-on-blue, Alex! Green-on-blue! The magic words, you could say. Everybody was uptight about these awful murders, how an Askar would suddenly turn around and shoot his American buddy. Pete was getting too close. Doug was getting nervous. We had to do it."

I said, "People know I'm here."

Wanda grinned. "I doubt that. I doubt you would tell anyone about this harebrained idea of driving up here in the middle of the night."

"You can't kill me without being—"

"Without being charged with murder? But I can. I will shoot you and say I am so sorry. I will say I saw you outside and thought you were an intruder. I'll call the local sheriff. I'll be bawling."

I remained silent.

"But one thing does puzzle me. How in hell did you figure that I murdered Doug?" When I hesitated before answering, she waved the rifle. "I know how to use this baby in case you're thinking of trying to get out of the mess you've created for yourself."

"To me it was obvious Greer didn't kill himself. He was fixing dinner when someone showed up. I figured whoever put him in the car would probably knock him out first. I remembered how you—"

"How I slipped you knockout drops?" Finally, she said, "You made the connection. Very good, Alex. It was ketamine I gave you. And Doug. I should have given you a bigger wallop."

"I just took a sip of the drink."

"You can buy it on the street. It's strong stuff. I know. A guy once used it to put me under. He had fun. I didn't."

"I'm sorry—"

"Don't be. He's been minus a pair of balls ever since."

I realized I was seeing a side of Wanda I'd never known existed. I wondered how well Pete had known his wife. Maybe too well. I again recalled Page's remark about Pete preferring to stay in Afghanistan to going back.

"You're right. I put Doug under. I parked my car in the country club parking lot. I walked over. I was wearing rain gear and carrying an umbrella in such a way no one can ID me. The rain gear is long gone. I had to kill Doug. He was getting cold feet."

"He left a paper trail, but it was good enough to fool the auditors."

"It would have been good enough to fool everyone. Forever. Hamed was the problem." Wanda paused. "The deciding factor was his file. You said you brought it back from Dubai. Doug knew what was in it. He told me on Friday he wanted to make a deal, talk with the auditors. I couldn't trust him to talk with you. Doug had to go."

"You can't get—"

"The funny thing, Alex, is, I really like you. If I could have gotten you to go along, you'd have been the perfect partner for me. I made every effort. I really do like you." She contorted her lips. "You're the one who spoiled it."

"Doug figured how to make himself rich. But with him gone, you won't have any access to his accounts. If you were in it fifty-fifty, you don't have anything now." I made a circle with my fingers. "*Nada*."

"Give a gal credit for having some brains, okay? I moved mine out as currency, love. Dollars and euros. By private jet, by border crossings, by car. My uncle, the bank president, told me to do it this way. Sure, I had to pay people. Eight hundred grand it cost me. I even used that airline. The pilots took it out in the food trays. They charged an arm and a leg. But even at that, I paid less than 1 percent . . ." She gestured for me to stand.

Less than 1 percent meant Wanda's share of the bank money was one hundred million dollars.

"Move! Move! Or I shoot you here."

So I moved. With Wanda behind me and now holding the rifle, I opened the door. The rifle was a semiautomatic, and the magazine held four rounds. I knew what she planned to do: She wanted me outside so she could shoot me in the back and say she thought I was an intruder. She'd let me run a couple of yards. That would make the scene more realistic. Too close would raise suspicions in an alert medical examiner. She was also right when she said this was a mess I created myself. I supposed I was as good as dead, but I wanted to stall, put it off—buy myself a few more minutes of living.

"Don't worry, lover. Don't try anything, and you'll die quick." Her voice sounded strange, unfeeling. "It's the least I can do for the man I once loved. That's the way I figure."

As I moved across the wide deck, I had a thought—and it wasn't a very good one. I'd slam the porch door. Then I'd run.

But she must have realized what I wanted to do. "I'm right behind you, lover. No funny stuff."

I opened the porch door, stepped through it. But she moved up close behind. Slamming the door on her rifle wouldn't work. Then we were outside. The area between her house and the pond was mildly overgrown. Her car was parked at the far end of the clearing, too far away to offer any help.

And because she'd moved closer, I figured I might have a chance to try something desperate. My last chance!

If I missed, I'd be dead. I reached back with my left hand and grabbed the rifle. I was lucky. I grabbed, got my hand around the barrel—and yanked.

When she pulled the trigger, the round went wide.

And then I was running. Toward a thick oak thirty yards to my left. I heard the action of the rifle, pushing the next cartridge into the chamber. I figured she was sighting it, ready to squeeze off a round. When I thought she was about to fire, I dove, hit the ground, rolled over. Bang! Her second shot. Again I heard her cock the bolt. She had another round in the chamber, the third.

She'd come forward, moved in closer.

Struggling to my feet, I saw the tree. I needed to reach it. Then I needed to get my weapon out of the holster.

Back on my feet, I began to run, not straight, dodging from left to right, hoping to give her a tougher target.

As she fired, I heard something buzz by my left ear.

If I could reach the tree, I had a chance, a small one. The M9 was in my ankle holster.

But she still had another round.

As I dove for the tree, there was a loud report. A round exploded against the tree, narrowly missing me. I hadn't heard the rifle action.

Was someone else out there?

Wanda had moved forward and was now crouched only fifteen feet behind me, so close I could hear her breathing. At this range she couldn't miss. With the barrel pointed straight at me, she cocked the rifle. It was her fourth round.

As she crouched, ready to fire, I clicked off the safety on the M9.

No sense wasting time. With the weapon in both hands, I dropped to the ground alongside the tree, rolled out in front of the tree—and squeezed the trigger.

As I fired, I heard a report, and again a round smashed against the tree, missing me by inches.

Wanda sagged. I heard a stifled groan, a gargling sound. Her rifle fell harmlessly to the ground. She never fired the last round.

I got to my feet. I moved forward cautiously. I approached Wanda's inert form; I didn't want to look . . .

But I looked anyway.

Lying there was Wanda. All I remember is I felt sick. I don't know how long I stood there.

Then I saw a person moving silently toward me, coming through the high grass across the clearing. Whoever it was had a rifle in his hand. Or her hand.

As I struggled to clear my head, I realized the person was Corley.

"I assume you're okay," she said coolly.

As we stood staring down at Wanda's lifeless body, I remembered two rounds embedding themselves in the tree.

Those rounds hadn't been fired by Wanda.

CHAPTER 38

"HOW DID YOU let her get the drop on you?"

Corley and I were back in the house, standing in the middle of the living room. In her hand, she was still holding her weapon, an M4 carbine, with a sawed-down barrel. I was aware of the smell of cordite.

The honest answer to the question would have been that Wanda had everything figured out and was way ahead of me. Instead, I said, "She was quicker than I thought she was."

"Coming up here in the middle of the night alone was stupid."

"I know."

She laid the M4 against the wall and began to take a look around.

Pushing thoughts of Wanda out of my mind, I said, "How did you know I was up here?"

"There are sensors on your apartment door. When you decided to leave at midnight, I was curious. I followed you."

"I didn't notice anyone."

"Once you got out on the highway, I knew you were headed up here, so I stayed back. I saw your parked car on the way in."

Corley's weapon was standing against the wall. I walked across the room, picked it up.

I said, "This weapon's been fired." I removed the magazine. "Twice."

"I fired it. I didn't think you had a chance. I missed her both times."

I remembered the two rounds exploding against the tree, one only inches from my left cheek.

I was going to say, "At that range? You missed?" but then thought better of it. I nodded, put the weapon back down.

"Give it to me from the beginning," she said. "What happened up here?"

"Wanda heard my car engine. She probably saw my flashlight from her bedroom window, grabbed Pete's hunting rifle. She was surprised to see the intruder was me."

"Go on."

"We talked. I didn't realize it at first, but she seemed to sense why I was here. She kept the rifle next to her chair. She figured that she could shoot me and make it seem like an accident."

"I gathered that. Your car is parked out there. She'd only have to say you were an intruder and shot you by mistake." Corley paused. "Do we call the police like good law-abiding citizens or do we remove all traces of us having been here?"

I said, "Don't ask dumb questions."

"Forensic people these days are good."

"That means we'll have to do a thorough job of cleaning up." After we'd removed our boots, I padded into the kitchen, where I found a bunch of rags. I said, "Take these and wipe anything you or I may have touched."

In a hall closet, I found a vacuum cleaner and began going over the living room rug. As I vacuumed, she washed the glasses. I found the glass I used, stuck it in my pocket. After she'd dried them, I took them and using the rags placed them back on the shelf with the other glassware. I found a brush and brushed off the bearskin on the hearth.

When the living room looked completely undisturbed, Corley went upstairs, then came back down. "Wanda's bed was slept in."

I said, "That's fine. It'll appear she got up in the middle of the night when she heard an intruder."

I removed the M9 from my ankle holster, handed it to Corley. "We don't want to forget this. You know what to do with it."

On the way out I closed the front door but didn't lock it.

Standing on the deck, I said, "Wanda walked out behind me. Footprints will be hers."

Carrying my boots, I walked carefully through the high grass toward the oak tree, which probably had saved my life. I wondered how many years it had been quietly standing there. In the dirt surrounding the tree I made sure I hadn't left any clearly marked footprints.

As I walked back, I took one quick last glance at Wanda's body. Even in death, she was beautiful. Corley stood silently, observing me. As we made our way back, she went behind. As we went, we scraped the ground and made sure we weren't leaving footprints. She said her car was parked a hundred feet beyond mine.

Before we reached my car, I saw it. Twenty-five feet above the ground and situated on the branch of a large elm tree was what looked like a two-channel security camera. One lens was pointed toward the front of the house, the other toward the road. It took me the better part of ten minutes to scramble up, unfasten the camera and the DVR, and then climb down.

I tossed the camera in the car trunk. Corley checked her watch. "I think there are a few things I would like to know."

More than a few things. This op was over. For me, it had been over when I stopped taking orders from Corley. It was definitely time to wrap it up.

I said, "I'll stop by your place." By first light, we had our vehicles on the highway, Corley in her car and me in mine. We were back in Addison Heights by six a.m. After a quick shower, I went down to Corley's apartment.

"I've been able to figure out most of it," she said, forking up the last of a plate of scrambled eggs she'd made for herself. "A few details I'm still not sure about." The events in Loudon County hadn't affected her appetite.

I said, "Wanda did quite a bit of talking. One of the difficulties of pulling off a major swindle, you can't brag about it to anyone." When Corley nodded, I said, "She knew pretty quickly why I'd come, but she was too smart to show it. We talked. I already had an idea why she killed Greer."

"She'd manipulated Greer, was that it?"

I nodded. "I imagine. After they'd become lovers, she convinced him to loot the bank, not the other way around. She'd never admit it to me, but Wanda knew the situation at the bank inside and out. I'm sure when Pete was on leave he told her everything. Wanda realized that Greer, with his constant travel to Afghanistan, was the perfect person to set the fraud in motion."

"And show the Afghans how to do it?" When I nodded, she said, "If Hamed's document reveals Greer's involvement, it will also indicate her involvement."

"Wanda was smarter than Greer. She moved her money physically, stacks of euros and dollars. From what I understand, bribing customs officials isn't that hard to do. She got some advice from an uncle in Europe. It cost her nearly a million in payoffs to move the money out of the country, but when you're talking about a hundred million that's reasonable. One conduit was Pamir Airways. She bribed the flight crews. And there were other ways."

"A hundred million dollars? That was her share?" When I nodded, she said, "Without a paper trail, there's no longer any way to connect her with the Kabul Bank—"

"Or with the missing money." Corley took a sip of coffee. "Where do you think her money ended up?"

"I don't know. She once mentioned an uncle, who was a bank president in Norway. Someone savvy about moving currency around wouldn't have any difficulty finding a safe haven for her loot." I stood up to go. "Wherever it landed, I have an idea it's not coming back. American taxpayers will take the hit."

As I was about to leave, Corley said, "A billion dollars is a great deal of money."

"Twenty-two guys are in jail. Two other people are dead. None of them is in a position to spend the billion dollars. What does that tell you?"

"I guess that honesty is the best policy."

"Very good," I said before closing the door behind me. She'd said the words, but I wondered if she believed them.

* * *

Two hours later, there was a quiet knock on my apartment door. It was Corley. She appeared to be none the worse for wear. She didn't waste words.

"It's not advisable for you to stay here any longer than necessary. Can you be packed and ready to leave by noon today?" When I said, "Yes, ma'am," she said, "I was in touch with the official from the National Security Council."

"Jerry Shenlee?"

"Yes. He e-mailed back ten minutes ago. He wants you to be in the lobby of the St. Gregory Hotel at 1030 hours tomorrow. You should be seated and reading a copy of *The Financial Times*. Do you know the St. Gregory?"

I said I did.

"We won't be seeing each other again. I'm packed, and a taxi will be taking me to the airport in twenty minutes." She stuck out her hand. "I'm grateful." She flashed a brief, artificial smile. "We all are."

Again I was curious about who "we" was. Who was she working for?

"Did things work out satisfactorily?"

She hesitated. "Maybe not with complete satisfaction, but we can live with the present situation."

For myself, I had at least been able to track down Pete Hansen's murderer. Things had certainly worked out differently than I ever thought they would. Wanda's involvement in the bank fraud and the cold-blooded murder of Doug Greer had come as terrible shocks, shocks I'd be living with for a long time—and for which I'd need a long time to get over.

And then I'd had to shoot Wanda. Although it was in self-defense, I wondered if I'd ever get beyond it.

Shortly after midday, I drove out of Addison Heights and into D.C. I booked a room for that evening at the St. Gregory. In the hotel room, I removed the DVR from the camera and plugged the DVR into the television set. The camera was infrared, motion-activated, and trained on the area directly in front of the house.

The TV picture provided an interesting record. It showed Wanda over and over, entering and leaving. Those pictures were no surprise. Others showed some workmen coming and going on two occasions. Also no surprise. There were pictures of Doug Greer visiting on several occasions. I supposed Wanda's country place was where they did a lot of talking.

Finally, I found the pictures I was most interested in. I had a feeling I was in for another surprise, and I wasn't disappointed.

I saw a video of everything that had happened, beginning with Wanda and me leaving the house—and me reaching for the rifle barrel, the weapon going off, me scrambling toward the tree, Wanda following, squeezing off one round, then another, then a third.

But in the picture there was someone else!

Corley was standing on the far side of the clearing. Then, as she watched, she raised the M4, sighted it—and as I ducked behind the tree, she fired the round that narrowly missed my left cheek.

I was moving and ducking, making myself a difficult target.

Then, she again raised her weapon, sighted, and fired. This round smashed into the oak just as I was falling to the ground.

Wanda was a relatively easy target. Yet neither round came anywhere close to hitting her.

I was left with only one conclusion: Captain Corley had been trying to shoot me!

She wanted to shoot me, and she wanted to let Wanda live. Why?

It was late afternoon, and I spent a couple of quiet hours at the National Mall trying to relax. As I walked around, I continued to think about Captain Leslie Corley. I kept asking myself the same questions: Who was she? And what was it she'd been trying to accomplish?

And why was she trying to shoot me?

I didn't come up with any answers.

That evening, I called Irmie. "It was wonderful seeing you, honey. I hope my showing up like that was a pleasant surprise."

"It was a surprise, Alex." Irmie knew I was hoping for more than that. After a pause, she said, "I'm very busy at the moment. I just don't have time to think about . . . things."

"The assignment is over, Irmie. I want you to know that."

"I'm happy for you. But I don't want to hear about the assignment. Not now, and probably never."

Before I could say anything more, she said, "Good night, Alex." To her, the news that my op was over seemed a matter of complete indifference.

CHAPTER 39

It's a reassuring feeling to be living in a country whose government fulfills its obligations to its citizens, even when it's hardly necessary, and even when those obligations, like the "black op" that took me to Afghanistan, lie deep within the grayest of gray areas.

The following day, while seated on a sofa and reading *The Financial Times* in the lobby of the St. Gregory Hotel, an attractive blond woman in a gray suit took a seat alongside me.

"Mr. Klear?"

When I said I was Alex Klear, she removed some papers from a portfolio on her lap.

She presented me with an invoice for some plumbing work done in a government building. "This is so you know what the payment's for." After reading it quickly, I nodded, and she gave me a receipt to sign. Then she handed me an envelope.

As I placed the envelope in my breast pocket, she said, "Perhaps you should count it."

When I shook my head and thanked her, she quickly zipped up her portfolio.

"Have a nice day."

Before I could say "You, too," she was on her feet and headed across the lobby to the exit. As I watched her go, I was struck by the fact that she bore, in a small way, a resemblance to the Wanda Hansen I knew sixteen years ago. I had a feeling that all kinds of things in the coming years would be reminding me of the Wanda Hansen I once knew—and of those happy-go-lucky days when four still-young people were stationed at Fort Bragg with their lives and their futures all before them.

Wanda was going to be difficult to forget. And the manner in which she died impossible to forget.

CHAPTER 40

"I still thought of you all the time." Irmie had turned to face me. "Breaking our engagement didn't help. I couldn't stop thinking of you." She extended her hand on the table and I took it.

It was Saturday evening. Irmie and I were beneath a large umbrella on the deck of her garden apartment, both of us gazing toward the west. A gentle rain was falling, making soothing pat-pat sounds on the umbrella. The rain seemed to add to the coziness of the moment. A candle was burning on the table.

I opened the wine bottle and poured each of us a glass of Chardonnay.

"I knew you were worried. That was one reason I came." I was referring to my unexpected visit to Gröbenzell, which I made only days after she broke our engagement. "I wanted you to know I was all right."

"It was a difficult time, Alex."

"Let's hope our difficult times are behind us." I felt her squeeze my hand when I said that.

I had flown into Munich five days before, arriving during the early afternoon. After booking a hotel room, I rented a car and, unannounced, drove out to Gröbenzell, the suburb in which Irmie lives. I found it hard to think of Irmie as my ex-fiancée. For Irmie, Monday was a work day, and she had been preparing dinner when I arrived.

"Alex!" she said when she'd opened the door. She seemed briefly unsure whether she should let me in. I'd had the foresight to bring a mixed bouquet and a bottle of wine.

When I saw her hesitation, I said, "At least let me give you these before I leave." She may have flashed a quick smile, I'm not sure. But she did invite me in.

As she placed the bouquet in a vase, she said, "What brings you to Munich, Alex?"

"I'll be here for a while. I just arrived this afternoon."

"How long will you be staying?"

"For a while. I'm not sure how long." I could have said, "For as long as it takes to again persuade you to marry me."

I didn't stay long on Monday evening. I hadn't been sure that arriving unannounced was the right thing. But as they say in Leadership School in the military, doing something always beats doing nothing. Even when what you're doing is totally dumb. I knew that if I called in advance, Irmie would have said, "Don't come."

On Tuesday, I again arrived unexpectedly, but at a later time. She invited me in. We drank tea and spent time discussing a homicide case she was working on. I could see she was under a lot of pressure and was glad to have someone to talk with about it. There was no mention of us and no mention of our future.

On this evening I asked about coming by on Wednesday.

"I can't make it tomorrow evening, Alex. We have a meeting scheduled." She hesitated. "What are you doing on Thursday?"

"I have an appointment with the mayor, but I'll break it." I'm sure Irmie hadn't smiled at my lame attempt at humor. "I'll bring some wine."

"You only have to bring your appetite."

At the door I gave her a brief kiss, which was all I dared. She hadn't responded, and I wondered whether Irmie inviting me to dinner wasn't her polite way of letting me down easy—and of wishing me a final good-bye. Back in my hotel in Munich, I went into the bar and ordered a double scotch. When I'd finished it, I ordered a second.

On Wednesday, I was away from the hotel for most of the day. When I returned, I received an unpleasant surprise. Irmie had left a message. "I can't make it tomorrow evening, Alex. There's just too much going on here. I'm very sorry."

Irmie hadn't said anything more than that, and I had to wonder if she wanted to see me again—ever. I headed again for the hotel bar. I can't remember how long I remained there. Irmie had sent her engagement ring back to me in America, but I'd brought it with me. I recall standing at the hotel bar and removing the ring from my jacket pocket, fingering it, gazing at the round gold band—and wondering.

I spent much of Friday still unsure of what I should do. Finally, I decided to do what I'd done on Monday. Just show up. Carrying a bouquet and a bottle of wine, I rang Irmie's doorbell at a few minutes after seven p.m.

Without any hesitation, she smiled and invited me in and told me to make myself comfortable. While she worked in the kitchen, I set the table, trying to be useful. I lit some candles, turned down the lights, doing my best to create a romantic atmosphere.

I can't remember what we talked about, but I do remember we ate Obatzda, a kind of cheese that had always been one of my favorite Bavarian dishes. Irmie had remembered.

As we chatted, I realized how much we were enjoying each other's company.

When I returned on Saturday afternoon, I brought the engagement ring with me. It was while we were sitting under the big umbrella with the rain coming down that I reached out and took Irmie's left hand in mine.

Before I slipped on the ring, I said, "Will you marry me?"

Irmie nodded, smiled, cried. "Yes, Alex, I will."

I held her. This time, I told myself, I'd be careful not to do anything dumb.

CHAPTER 41

"Well, I think I know what it is you're most interested in," Jerry Shenlee said. "You want to know who Captain Corley is. Am I correct on that?"

"You've read my mind again, Jerry."

It was a sunny, breezy Friday, a few minutes after noon, and Jerry and I were seated on a bench in Rock Creek Park. The nice weather had brought out the crowds. As I watched two laughing young women pushing baby carriages, Jerry said, "This is pretty much where it all began, Alex. Right here in the park . . ." Jerry had a handkerchief up to his face. "Aah . . . choo!"

"God bless you."

"Thanks. Damn hay fever! Every May! All this pollen in the air."

At Jerry's suggestion, I'd flown down to D.C. from Saranac for the weekend. Jerry and I hadn't laid eyes on each other since the cold January afternoon when he'd flown up to Saranac to recruit me for the Afghanistan mission. We still had things to talk about.

"I'm guessing here to some extent, Alex, but you can maybe help me fill in the blanks . . . Aah . . . choo!" After blowing his nose for about the fifth time, Jerry said, "Captain Corley was already close to Pete Hansen. She immediately suspected it wasn't a green-on-blue."

Jerry paused to watch a teenager doing all kinds of tricks with a soccer ball while never allowing it to touch the ground. "Pete being killed like that made Corley immediately suspicious. So she flew from Kabul to D.C., made some calls, got me involved. I'll tell you this much, Alex, she knew which buttons to press." As he recounted his meeting with a woman in the park, Jerry shook his head and took a quick swallow from his bottle of water. "You're still wondering who she is." Jerry pulled a large envelope from the briefcase at his feet. "So was I. For a long time."

"You're right, I'm still wondering. There's quite a bit of other stuff I'm wondering about as well." Both Jerry and I knew it's not unusual for a "black op" to end with a lot of unanswered questions. Often, they remain unanswered forever with the participants taking their secrets to the grave.

As Jerry pulled some papers out of an envelope, I said, "She told me right at the start that Nolda wasn't the guy who killed Pete. Supposedly, I was working for you, but she was calling all the shots."

"You had trouble getting used to that."

"Does that surprise you?"

"She was difficult. I could see that. Now I'm gonna tell you why." Jerry continued to fuss with his papers.

I took a long swallow from my own water bottle. I recalled that I'd spent many a pleasant evening here in Rock Creek Park when I was stationed in Fort Belvoir.

Then I couldn't help grinning. "Did you ever check out that building in Addison Heights?"

"I looked up the deed. It's owned by an Afghan, somebody Hafiz. I don't know where he lives, but he pays his taxes on time, which is all anyone cares about. The building's custodian is also an Afghan, a former intelligence agent who came down with dengue fever, so they gave him the job of taking care of their safe house for a while."

I supposed he was the guy I occasionally encountered on the stairs. I figured he was dropping by now and then when I was away. I never thanked him for the six-pack he once brought.

Shenlee had removed some newspaper and magazine clippings from the envelope. "As for the other question, I think I can give you an answer, a partial answer anyway. Captain Corley was as much a mystery to me as she was to you. At least until I saw this."

Shenlee handed me some of the clippings, which were from newspapers and magazines. A news story described some personnel changes in Afghanistan's National Directorate of Security, in other words at the highest level of Afghan Intelligence. I took a quick look. There were two other clippings with pictures, both from news magazines.

"As you know, the Afghans have a very active intelligence service. Now, look at this." Jerry pointed to an article, which was accompanied by a picture. The picture showed the intelligence director close-up. He was shaking hands with an assistant director, and standing at attention in the background were half-a-dozen people. Four of the people were men, two were women.

Shenlee then handed me a magnifying glass. "Take a close look."

It took a couple of seconds for me to realize what I was supposed to be looking at. Then I saw it.

I focused the glass on one of the two women in the background. The enlarged picture showed clearly the woman's features. She was dressed in civilian clothes and was peering, unsmiling, into the distance. Obviously, she didn't realize her picture was being taken.

I gazed at the picture for a long minute without commenting. Even from a distance, she had that Audrey Hepburn look but without the smile. The picture explained a great deal.

"That's her, right?"

I nodded. "That's her, all right. Captain Corley."

"I figured," Jerry said. "I only met her that one time, but even in this picture, I knew her."

"So she's an officer in Afghan Intelligence. Is that kosher? She's also an officer in the United States Army."

"Hell, no, it's not kosher." Shenlee smirked. "She has permission to operate outside the chain of command, and that gives her a lot of independence. Too much, maybe. The way I see things, we have a double agent on our hands. Don't worry, we know how to handle these situations."

"I'm glad to hear that."

"What do you know about the Sensitive Investigation Unit?"

When I said I knew it was appointed by the Afghan government to investigate the bank, Jerry said, "She's probably connected to them. Those people want to know in the worst way what happened at the Kabul Bank."

After pausing to again blow his nose, Jerry said, "I had to do some research, also some asking around. She's got an interesting gig, no question. Let's see, she graduated from OCS in 2004. Got her captain's bars four years later. Then she requested and got a position as liaison to the ANA."

I said, "How is it she speaks fluent Pashto?"

"She was born in Afghanistan, a village outside Kabul. Her aunt left Afghanistan shortly after the Russian invasion. The aunt persuaded her younger sister, Leslie's mother, to join her in the States. Her real name is Lailee, means 'night' in Pashto, but she uses Leslie. Her father was British—where he is who knows. Leslie was just nine years old when she arrived. That was 1991. So she already knew Pashto. After she got here, she learned English."

"How did she get tangled up with Pete?"

"Someone said she was an Audrey Hepburn look-alike. She was a honey trap, what else?"

As Jerry and I both knew, these days, allies spy on one another.

"Five years ago, Afghan Intelligence established that training compound outside Kabul, in Wardak Province. The place with the high walls. Corley spent a couple of two-week sessions there. What she was doing, we're not sure. Some of their trainers, though, are Russkis."

"What do you figure?"

"With her looks, she'd be one helluva honey trap. To us, it's inhuman the way they treat these women."

Suddenly, I realized what had bothered me about Captain Corley. She not only lacked any vestige of humor. She lacked something else. As Jerry said, the training had the likely effect of knocking the humanity out of the women. At times, Corley's devotion to her cause was so total she seemed to be more a machine than a woman.

Jerry said, "A recruitment like Hansen would have made her career. Once she focused on Hansen, he was toast."

"I knew Pete, Jerry. I'm not so sure he would've been so easy to recruit. He was too smart."

Shenlee frowned, fixed me with a questioning stare. "What do you think?"

"I have an idea Pete would've squeezed more out of her than she could've squeezed out of him. Maybe at first she was only interested in recruiting Pete as an agent, which would've been one helluva feather in her cap. But when she reported how much he knew about the bank, the Directorate of Security people would've wanted her to keep an eye on him." I didn't add that she eventually came to realize an American was involved in the fraud. Whether she found out from Pete or figured it out herself, we'd never know.

That was where I came in. When she recognized that someone set up an ambush in the Pech Valley in order to get rid of me, she figured that person was the one who had murdered Pete.

All along I'd wondered what kind of relationship had existed between Pete and Corley. Like me, Pete would have quickly sensed that with Corley something wasn't right. I could imagine a situation that was more a battle of wits than anything else—in which each was attempting to outsmart the other.

And then something else struck me!

I had the answer to the question that had haunted me for the past two months—ever since I'd seen the surveillance camera's picture of Corley firing her M4. She hadn't been firing at Wanda, as she said. She'd been firing at me.

If I hadn't shot Wanda at that moment, Corley's next round wouldn't have missed me.

Once she'd figured out Greer's involvement with the bank fraud, Corley came to the States to recruit him. I didn't realize Greer was the American involved with the fraud until the Sunday night when I spoke with Bud Withers.

Corley had already figured it out. She wanted Greer.

But then Wanda murdered Greer.

With Greer dead, she could no longer recruit the Undersecretary, but Wanda was a colonel in the U.S. Army and stationed in the Pentagon. She was, potentially, also a valuable source for the Afghan Directorate of Security. Corley knew that Wanda's involvement with the Kabul Bank made her vulnerable to blackmail. Wanda's only choice would have been to become an agent for the Afghans—or spend a lifetime behind bars.

As I knew from my own experience behind the Iron Curtain, blackmail is easily the most effective way to persuade people to come over, more effective than ideology or even money. Espionage is a dirty business.

Wanda wouldn't have been as highly placed a source as Greer, but she would have been better than nothing. Much better.

Whether I lived or died wasn't important. I wiped a drop of perspiration from my forehead.

"Something else, Alex. I didn't know you and Undersecretary Greer were friends. I'm referring to your visit to his home on the very night he died."

"He was a hobby cook. He invited me."

"What were you guys gonna talk about?" Jerry was perceptive, but Greer's involvement with the bank fraud was going to remain my little secret. Without Hamed's document, which was now in the possession of the Afghan Directorate of Security, there was no way to locate his loot or to figure out his involvement. What the Afghan Security people might do with those tidbits of information was their business—and anybody's guess.

"Doug and I got to know each other in Afghanistan. There was plenty to talk about."

"People in the government are wondering about Greer killing himself—whether he did or whether he didn't."

"What do you mean?"

"Have you ever heard of a drug called ketamine? You can buy it on the street. The autopsy of Greer's body turned up enough ketamine in his bloodstream to knock him out for a half hour. If he was in his car with the motor running . . ."

"You're suggesting he was drugged and murdered?"

"Where Greer was concerned, everyone agrees. The guy had an unblemished record and a great future. People were touting him for all kinds of things. Elective office possibly." Jerry paused to rub his eyes. "He was definitely in line for a cabinet position. What I'm saying, Alex, why would the guy kill himself?"

"No reason I can figure."

"No reason anyone can figure. He could write his own ticket. The guy was likeable, smart, and honest. And tough—he could take the heat. And everyone agrees he did a great job overseas."

"You're saying—"

"He was murdered, is what I'm saying. The question is, by whom?" After another sneeze, Jerry said quietly, "We've decided to keep it quiet. The official verdict is suicide."

Jerry was silent for a long moment, maybe waiting for me to comment. When I only took another swallow from my bottle of water, he said, "A *Post* reporter was nosing around, trying to see what she could dig up."

"That's what reporters are supposed to do, Jerry, nose around and dig things up."

"Well, she won't be doing too much nosing and digging from now on. Someone from the administration got in touch with one of the managing editors at the paper." Jerry smirked.

"So now she's covering the society page?"

"No, the women's page. She just wrote a piece on the season's new skirt lengths. You'll be happy to hear they're getting shorter." Jerry was watching me closely. "And of course the other thing . . ."

I knew what was coming.

"Wanda Hansen dying like that, just a couple of days after Greer." Jerry shook his head. "You and she . . . got along. If I'm not mistaken, you saw quite a bit of each other."

"You're not mistaken. I knew her a long time ago."

"We figure an intruder was up there. A woman alone in a house in the woods, that's not good. She'd been firing a hunting rifle, a BAR 30-06. It was lying in the grass right next to her." Jerry paused, watching my reaction. "I'll tell you what's really funny, though. Embedded in a tree not far from where she died . . . Ah . . . ah . . . choo! Damn!"

As Jerry blew his nose, I waited.

"Anyway, there was a small-caliber round embedded in a tree. A 5.56. Probably fired from a military weapon."

"Sure, the M4 carbine. We were using that round in Graf during readiness training."

"Right. And what they also found on the other side of this clearing were a couple of cartridges . . . Let's see." Jerry consulted one of his papers. "The M855A1. You're right. They would have been fired from an M4A1 weapon. I mean, what was going on out there?"

"It sounds like World War Three."

"Colonel Hansen's telephone calls are all accounted for . . . except for a couple she got that night from an untraceable phone. Fake name, naturally."

I nodded, recalling that I'd made two attempts to reach Wanda by telephone. I was glad that I'd had the presence of mind to use one of the disposable cell phones I'd picked up in D.C.

As I watched a couple of kids zooming by on their skateboards, Jerry sneezed a few more times. Finally, he began packing up his papers. "Oh, yeah, I meant to ask about your fiancée. How's everything?"

"Thanks for asking. Everything's fine. I visited for a couple of weeks, and we've pushed back the date."

"I'm surprised she didn't give you the gate. I've never known a woman to put up with the stuff you do."

"My fiancée has forgiven me. I took another assignment while I should have been with her, planning our wedding. But now I'm back safe and sound. No harm done." Not too much anyway.

Jerry shook his head. "Hardly any of our case officers stay married for very long, as you well know. It's just not the kind of job women want to put up with. Face it, Alex. Not too many women would have forgiven you for doing what you did. What the hell does she see in you anyway?"

"Irmie has a good heart, Jerry."

"It has to be more than that."

"She knows how much I love her."

"Still not enough. I hope you can make her happy."

I thought back to everything Irmie had had to put up with, having a retired intelligence officer as a fiancé.

"I hope I can, too, Jerry."

EPILOGUE

44 W Granby Street
Elkhart, IN 46514
September 2, 2013

Dear Mr. Klear,

I understand that you played a role in arranging for young Jawid to spend the summer this year with an American family. I thought you might like to know how things worked out.

We had this young Afghan boy here for the summer. He was a delightful guest and got along very well with our two boys. He was also helpful around the house. Before arriving, he'd never seen a vacuum cleaner. He was my little assistant whenever I did the housework. As he was learning English, we also picked up many words from the Pashto language. My boys would point to an object, Jawid would say the Pashto word and one of our boys the English word.

He was a marvelous person to cook for because he ate everything. He also showed me some meals that are eaten by the people in Afghanistan. One meal involves stuffing squash with tomato paste, rice, and peas and tastes delicious. He said the name but I forget it.

He also liked what he called "betsbowl." The three boys enjoyed playing catch in our backyard.

The gentleman from the exchange program asked if we'd like to have Jawid visit us again next summer, and we said yes. We were told that his father wanted him to attend an American high school. Since we've learned that his father died in Afghanistan under

difficult circumstances and was a true friend to our country's soldiers, we would like to do all we can for Jawid and for his mother.

Sincerely,

Louise Kortena

P.S. Jawid tried to tell us how he came to meet you. The way it
sounded, you ran out of a car and jumped on top of him and watermelons fell on you both. Maybe because his English is still far from
perfect, the story didn't really make much sense.

SECOND EPILOGUE

THE THREE ANA soldiers in the armored personnel carrier, a captain, a lieutenant, and a sergeant, hadn't spoken very much since leaving Kabul the previous day. The sergeant was the driver, and he had all he could do to keep his eyes on the winding, unfamiliar road. Although Helmand Province was only 400 kilometers from Kabul, they'd had to overnight on the highway to Kandahar because of the continuing danger of IEDs. At least things weren't as bad these days as they'd been when the Americans occupied the country in force.

From Kandahar, which now had far fewer Taliban sympathizers than previously, they'd proceeded on Highway 1 to Gereshk and were now bouncing along on a pothole-filled road in the Nahri Saraj District. The woman lived in a tiny village somewhere out here with her two small boys.

As the captain was told at the presidential palace, she was a widow whose husband, a sergeant in the Afghan National Army, had died nine months before under unexplained circumstances.

After a number of inquiries, they found the woman's home, which, unsurprisingly, turned out to be in a crumbling stone and mud building, which she shared with her sister-in-law. When the sergeant asked, he was told the woman was not expected back for another hour.

Sitting in the vehicle, they waited. The truth was, the captain had been puzzled by this assignment ever since receiving it late yesterday. He'd be glad to get back to Kabul. An important meeting at Headquarters was scheduled for Saturday, the day after tomorrow, and he definitely wanted to be on hand for that.

An hour later, a tired-looking woman with a shawl over her face and accompanied by two boys came slowly up the dusty lane from the street. When she pushed aside the blanket covering the entrance into the decrepit building, the captain gathered up the papers he'd been given, nodded at the lieutenant, took one last swallow of tea, and climbed out of the vehicle.

Inside the dark house, he introduced himself and, seated cross-legged on a pillow, presented the papers to the baffled woman. As she was unable to read and only shook her head, he did his very best to explain the reason for his visit.

"Effective immediately," he said, "you are to receive a monthly pension from the Afghan government." He was himself surprised by the generosity of the amount. "In addition, an apartment in one of the government's new social residences in Kabul has been set aside for you and your children. Your boys will be given the opportunity to enroll in school and pursue an education after you have moved to Kabul."

Having recovered from her surprise, the woman asked a number of halting questions, none of which the captain could answer beyond saying she would receive more detailed information in the coming weeks.

The one thing he could say was that the Afghan government was, in this instance, acting according to urgent directives from an unknown person in the American government.

That evening, after she'd told her sister-in-law of how her life would be changing, she'd dreamily recalled how her husband, who'd only joined the Army so he could support his small family, had been unjustly charged with shooting an American officer.

"But now the Americans are doing these things in his memory," she said.

"They are a hard people to understand, the Americans," her sister-in-law said, shaking her head.

"Very hard," said the widow of Baram Nolda.

AUTHOR'S NOTE

The Kabul Bank Scandal

THE KABUL BANK went bankrupt in 2010, the biggest bank failure in history. I was in Afghanistan then, and I heard there was a run on the bank. I also heard that it was necessary to station guards in front of the bank to prevent angry depositors from storming the building in Kabul.

At that time, the auditors determined that somewhere around 935 million dollars was missing and unaccounted for. It is against the background of these events that *On Edge* takes place.

During a four-month period, from November 2012 to March 2013, twenty-two bank officials were on trial in Kabul, charged with fraud. It is during this time that Alex Klear, the protagonist, is sent to Kabul to investigate the murder of a former Army buddy, a colonel who was attached to the ISAF Oversight and Accountability section. Almost immediately, Alex suspects that his friend's murder connects in some way to the bank's failure.

I'm not sure to what extent our political leaders in 2004, the year of the Kabul Bank's founding, understood that in Afghanistan people think very differently about fraud and corruption than we do in the West. I'm not sure, as we became more and more involved with Afghanistan, that they understood that what we in the West consider to be corrupt practices is the way much business is conducted in Afghanistan. And that bribery is a way of life there.

In fact, when a country as rich as America doesn't keep a close eye on its assets and its money, it seems for many Afghans that the proper approach is to help themselves. There is no question that the United States did not pay as close attention to the nearly one billion dollars it deposited in the Kabul Bank as it should have. This is one of the insights that Alex gains as he attempts to solve the murder of his old friend.

The Kabul Bank was established to provide a conduit to finance the war and to help rebuild Afghanistan's infrastructure. When the bank was established, our government naively asked President Karzai which people might be best qualified to run the bank. Unsurprisingly, he named a number of his cronies, and unsurprisingly, two of them, Khalil Ferozi and Sherkhan Farnood, ended up in charge of the bank. Except for running a hawala in Moscow, which reportedly helped drug smugglers move money, Farnood had no previous financial experience. After teaming up, the two bank officials forged documents, created nonexistent firms, and ran an elaborate Ponzi scheme to not only funnel money to Afghan government officials but also to line their own pockets. One of Farnood's early buying sprees involved spending millions of dollars on luxury villas in Palm Jumeirah, an expensive neighborhood in Dubai. So many of his colleagues did the same thing that it was the collapse of property values in Dubai in 2009 that sent the first signal that the Kabul Bank was in financial trouble.

There were sixteen shareholders in the bank, and they all received low-interest loans of millions of dollars. One of the shareholders was Mahmoud Karzai, the president's brother. Another was Haseen Fahim, a brother of one of Afghanistan's vice presidents. Mahmoud Karzai used some of the money he received to buy a six-million-dollar villa in Dubai.

In the course of the story, Alex becomes involved with some

of the attempts to
mine what happen
the bank. The Afgh
Sensitive Investigativ
their startling finding
money ended up in ac

As Alex says in the s
only financing our war e

After it was revealed th
Karzai made no effort to
tors of the fraud, and that
tween the discovery of the r   ...e trial.
According to Dexter Filkins   ...ew *Yorker*, the Kabul
Bank contributed between se...en million and fourteen million dollars to Karzai's 2009 reelection campaign. That fact may explain why Karzai failed to act. But in time, Karzai may have realized that when his term as president expired in 2014, he might be succeeded by a chief executive who would be more amenable to America's desire to punish those involved in the fraud. So he finally gave the green light for the trial of the bank officials.

Alex also has concerns about the Afghan court system. Since Afghan courts function differently from American courts and have often been susceptible to bribery, he wonders whether the judges will have the courage to find the twenty-two bank officials guilty.

In *On Edge*, the pieces in this complicated puzzle begin to fall into place, and it requires all of Alex's determination and smarts to figure out what really happened in Afghanistan and who murdered his former buddy and why.

Whether what happens in this story could really have occurred—or did really occur—will be up to the reader to decide.